A NIGHT OF WATCHING

A Night
of
WATCHING

....

by ELLIOTT ARNOLD

CHARLES SCRIBNER'S SONS · *New York*

FOR GLYNIS

"IT WAS A NIGHT OF WATCHING BY THE LORD, TO BRING THEM
OUT OF THE LAND OF EGYPT; SO THIS SAME NIGHT IS A NIGHT
OF WATCHING KEPT TO THE LORD BY ALL THE PEOPLE OF ISRAEL
THROUGHOUT THEIR GENERATIONS."

Exodus 12-42 (*Revised Standard Version*)

PART I.

1.

THERE WAS DEATH in the room, Hansen thought. They carried it with them. It came as a smell from their skins. It was in the look of their eyes and the set of their lips and the way they moved, and the smell was strongest when it came from this type, in the dark, correct, consular clothes, attaché case in hand.

Death had become part of them and when it was not right now, at this moment, it was waiting, savoring itself, death feeding upon death. It was always there, sitting at the edge of the carefully polite words. They had arrogated even that to themselves.

He stared out of the window, keeping his back to it as long as he could, knowing it was only that, a turning away of the face, and what good was it because there was so much more of it down there in the street, in the square, in the air, the blight, the stink?

Now in the fourth year of the occupation, they had made it ordinary. Only the Germans could have managed that. First to have taken it to their bosoms as a personal possession and then to make it routine, acceptable, accepted. When last was one mildly shocked to learn someone no longer lived?

From the window in his office Hansen could see Town Hall Square, now on this gentle September morning already crowded with men and women, young and old, with small children playing, babies sunning in prams, pigeons, the true owners of the square, strutting about meditating on whom to honor with their appetites.

It was a normal sight and from that same window Han-

3

sen had observed it for many years and had always found peace in it, and he tried to find some part of that peace today to pit against the death, but he could not stop his eyes from straying farther across the square until they reached the barbed-wire entanglement in front of Dagmar House, the supreme Nazi headquarters in Copenhagen.

"Well, Mr. Hansen?" The voice came from behind him.

"What is it you're afraid of?" Hansen asked without turning. "Do you people really believe anybody is going to try to force their way into the Gestapo building?"

"Mr. Hansen." The voice protested mildly.

Hansen looked at the barbed wire, now rusting and somehow obscene; at the sentry box, shoulder high so that only the heads of the SS guards could be seen, the guards rigid as rocks; at the black cars going and coming, Mercedes for the important men, Volkswagens for the others. None of it even looked new any more, hadn't for a long time. It had all become part of everything else, the days, the nights, the seasons that had passed and were to come.

That was another victory they had won, he thought, quiet but perhaps more important than others: now one was almost persuaded to forget there was a time when the Germans were not there.

"Mr. Hansen." The voice, as always, was patient, the calm patience of incontrovertible power.

Hansen's teeth tightened on the stem of the stubby pipe between his lips as he turned and looked across the office at the German. He sucked on the pipe. It was out. He groped in his pockets for matches, realized his hands might tremble, took the pipe out of his mouth and walked back to his desk.

"Have you an explanation, Mr. Hansen?" Although the question had been asked before, Georg Siebert's voice was still mild. He was big, so big the parts seemed abandoned. His eyes were set well apart; his nose was strong, mouth correct. They all were stranded in the landscape of face and bald head.

"I do the best I can," Hansen said, hoping his voice had something of Siebert's timbre. "These are not normal times."

4

Siebert shifted slightly. His body strained at every seam in the well-tailored suit. His hands, which might have been padded gloves covering his real hands, almost wholly covered the black bowler in his lap.

They all want to look British, Hansen thought; it was part of the mania. He pressed the gray ash of the imitation tobacco with his thumb, took a wooden match from a box on his desk and struck it. He held the flame over the bowl. His hands, he was relieved to see, did not shake.

"I have examined your production records for the last ten years," Siebert said in his unaccented Danish. "You now are operating at less than sixty per cent."

"These are unusual times."

"So you said."

"Then if you understand that, don't throw old figures in my face." Hansen put down the pipe, tasting bile. It would be nice if it was from what passed for tobacco; he knew it was more than that.

"I do nothing. I am a consular official and I obey orders," Siebert said.

"Yes."

The chair creaked as Siebert leaned forward slightly. "Something has always interested me, Mr. Hansen. Why do you do business with us?"

They always look for reasons, Hansen thought. They always dream that at least one time they'll discover they're liked, or at least not hated.

"Are you in sympathy?" Siebert asked.

"Let's stick to business, Mr. Siebert."

"Do you support our goals?"

"What has that got to do with anything?"

"Nothing." Siebert sat back, a small mountain settling. "Nothing, I suppose. I'm a curious man. I wonder why a Dane is so cooperative."

"Most of us are."

"More or less. But sometimes there is a difference. If there is that difference, perhaps we can move to another area." Siebert took a slim silver cigarette case out of his pocket and held it out toward Hansen.

5

Hansen hesitated for a moment and then took a cigarette and a light.

"An area," Siebert said, lighting his own cigarette, "which might alter the nature of our business."

"I'm quite content with it as it is now." Hansen stood up and walked a couple of steps away from the desk. He was a tall man in his middle thirties, with a shock of thick, unruly light hair. "Mr. Siebert, I don't know what you're trying to find out. I'm a business man. The only people I am able to do business with these days are Germans. I'm not altogether happy about that but there's nothing I can do about it. I built my company up from one small shop. If I want to hold onto what I have then I deal with you. Or else I'm kicked out and somebody else sits in this chair and makes the money that belongs to me." He dragged deeply on the cigarette. "Why am I cooperative? I have to be."

Siebert looked at him with unrelenting patience. "Nothing more?"

It was the death now that seemed to shift in its seat, its patience thinning.

"I've been connected with the consulate for a long time, Mr. Hansen," Siebert said. "From before the protectorate. From before the war."

"What does that tell me?"

"That I know of you and of what you are capable. You must strive for more efficiency."

Siebert's mild eyes looked directly at Hansen and he felt the thing in his stomach again.

"I'll do the best I can."

"Of course you will. We're really all working toward the same end."

"I'm working to make a living," Hansen said. "I'm working because I have a wife and a child and another child on the way."

"Good. Then the considerations are on the table. I would like to understand you even better."

"Why?"

"We are involved with each other."

"We do business together." Hansen sat down and stared at the German. "What are you getting at? Don't talk to me about aims and goals and ends. I'm not interested in politics. I make metal products, try to make them as good as possible, sell them for a fair price, make a profit."

"Even from the enemy?"

"That's a curious remark, coming from you."

"Most of you regard us as that, despite all these years of trying to convince you otherwise. That's what interests me in you." Siebert stood up. He moved with the peculiar grace of some heavy men. He leaned over the desk and mashed out his cigarette. He picked up his attaché case. "Then I will inform his Excellency we may expect a greater effort from the Hansen complex."

The telephone rang. Hansen picked up the receiver, listened for a moment. "Thank you."

"Other business, Mr. Hansen?"

"An associate."

"Wasn't that the voice of your secretary?"

"He called earlier. She didn't want to interrupt."

"But she did in the end interrupt."

"To remind me I have an appointment with him shortly."

Siebert nodded, bowed, walked out of the office, moving easily and with a certain style. He must, Hansen thought, have been a powerhouse before he went to lard.

When the door closed behind the German, Hansen remained motionless at his desk. He felt sweat on the palms of his hands. He wasn't gaited for this kind of thing. Kate was right, as she usually was. He was over his head, out of his element, in a game where he was just beginning to learn the rules. And yet he was there.

He got up and opened a window and the sounds from the square flowed into the room and he leaned on them. After a few moments he went back to the desk and gave his secretary a number.

He sat back and closed his eyes and ran a hand through

his hair and again felt the sweat. I'll have to go into training for this, he thought.

As Siebert departed the office building he passed a tall, rangy Danish police officer. The officer nodded civilly. Siebert returned the courtesy and then stepped off the curb and started across the square in the direction of Dagmar House. The police officer watched him for a moment and then entered the building.

2.

THE LUFTHANSA AIRCRAFT making the daily run from Berlin to Copenhagen to Stockholm rolled to a stop at Kastrup Airport outside Copenhagen as Peter Hansen and Georg Siebert were concluding their meeting.

The ramp was wheeled up immediately. The first person to emerge was a man of forty-five, slightly below middle height, hair cut so close its color was indistinguishable. His eyes were clear and blue. There were wrinkles at the edges and at the sides of the mouth, suggesting a ready amiability. He was dressed in the dark suit and bowler which was itself a kind of uniform and he carried the attaché case which was that uniform's shield.

In all he appeared a business man, senior and competent. From his positive manner and the attitude of the aircraft attendant who ran up the steps of the ramp, his business was plainly important, brisk and thriving. His name was Rudolf Buhle. His business was the Gestapo. In Denmark, with the rank of *Standartenführer*, which was the equal of colonel, he was very close to the top.

He stood on the ramp and breathed deeply. None of the other passengers in the aircraft tried to walk past him.

It was, he thought, entering a new world. Berlin was a snakepit. It smelled like a snakepit. Denmark smelled too with the lack of soap, the imitation tobacco, the wood-burning vehicles. But it didn't smell like Berlin.

He took a pigskin cigar case from inside his coat and, although smoking was forbidden in that area, the attendant instantly flicked a lighter and proffered the flame.

Even the highest had it these days, Colonel Buhle thought. Even Göring. What a reaction! First there was a laugh, as though the fat man had made a joke, and then the sudden concerted realization of what the laughter might suggest and the disappearance of the laughter and the sober agreement, judicious agreement. What the field marshal had said at the reception was, "When the Führer wishes it, two and two make five."

Colonel Buhle began an unhurried descent as the black Mercedes pulled up to the ramp. I had been away from Berlin too long, he thought.

The chauffeur was out of the car, clicking heels, shouting "Heil Hitler!" before Colonel Buhle stepped off the ramp. He entered the car, sat back. Too long, he thought, for that kind of thing.

The Mercedes waited for a Danish worker hauling an empty baggage cart to pass and then moved on.

The worker, without pausing, slipped a folded piece of paper into the hand of another worker shoving chocks under the plane wheels and then continued to the aircraft where the baggage was being offloaded.

While adjusting the chocks, the second worker inserted the piece of paper into the hollow interior of one of them. When the aircraft landed in Sweden, it would deliver the day's edition of one of the Danish underground newspapers.

The worker with the cart helped load it and then pulled it to where the debarked passengers were waiting. He went to the toilet and then to a telephone and called a Copenhagen number.

Colonel Buhle settled in the comfortable seat and puffed on his cigar and enjoyed the pleasant, unexciting Danish countryside, here, in the short distance between the airport and the city, flat and placid, not unlike the Danes who had allowed themselves to be taken over by a foreign country without firing a shot—no, not true, eight shots had been fired at the border, or was it eleven?

The chauffeur sounded his horn loudly. A Danish man riding a bicycle swerved violently to avoid being hit. He righted himself, one hand pressing against his chest to steady two metal containers dangling from his neck on a leather thong.

The black car entered Copenhagen, moved down the broad street and, without slowing, entered the square. Colonel Buhle, in a pleasant revery, the three days in Berlin a long time and a long way away, suddenly sat erect.

What had caught his eye was something that had been added to the square since his recent departure. It was a small gravestone set against the curb where the pigeons liked particularly to gather. There were two pigeons on the marker but Colonel Buhle was able to make out the inscription which was in German so not to be misunderstood by those for whom it was intended. In excellent Gothic letters it read:

Dear, Dear Little Adolf

The Mercedes crossed in front of the old Town Hall, turned right and came to a stop in front of Dagmar House. The chauffeur jumped out and opened the door. Colonel Buhle did not get out immediately. He rolled what was left of the cigar between his lips. His eyes were thoughtful. The laugh lines around them made the face appear that of a pleasant man in a mood of contemplation.

"We are here, Herr Standartenführer," the chauffeur said.

It was still another moment before Colonel Buhle left the car. He tossed aside the cigar butt and moved in his normal, moderate manner to the building entrance, accepting a rigid salute from Lance Corporal Oskar Greff, on duty at the nearest sentry station.

He went directly to his office on the third floor, ordered the SS man on duty to notify Obersturmbannführer Greiner, the SS officer in charge of the Danish police, that he had returned and would like to see him.

He was seated at his desk, his face remote, when Lieutenant Colonel Max Greiner entered. Greiner, a slender, thin-faced man with deep-set eyes, glanced at Buhle and then sat down heavily.

"So, Rudolf, it begins."

3.

LANCE CORPORAL GREFF resumed his position of monolithic attention, feeling grateful, as always, for whatever piece of luck it was that had selected him from millions of Germans and deposited him in Copenhagen.

From this particular sentry box, Corporal Greff could look across the square and see the start of the narrow, winding street that changed its name every few blocks but which was known lovingly in its entirety by every Dane as "Stroeget." This little street, hardly wider than an alley, was lined with shops such as Corporal Greff, who was nineteen and who had been brought up in a different world, had never before seen.

But it was not only the shops, nor the restaurants, nor the cafés, that stirred Corporal Greff. His dreams drew from the fact that the Stroeget was a place where the Danes walked—someone had told him the name meant "Strolling Street"—with their friends and their lovely girls. Everything that Corporal Greff wanted from Copenhagen, from life, seemed symbolized there, the warmth, the comradery, the friendliness of human beings for each other.

He wondered whether he would ever understand the Danes; more, would they ever understand him? Would they ever come to know Oskar Greff as the people in his small Bavarian village knew him? That he was a man with a good sense of humor, enjoyed laughing and drinking beer and making friends and singing songs and having a plump girl to flop around with in bed?

He had been to many beer places and cafés in Copenhagen but there was not the right feeling in any of them, not for him. The Danes were polite. But Corporal Greff was deeply in love with the Danes; he felt they were true Aryans as the Führer had said, and should happily share the Aryan world the Führer was making. They laughed and they joked and they enjoyed themselves as much as anybody in Bavaria; but this did not include Germans.

Even the Danish women. There were always women attracted to conquerors, who spread their legs for pay, for soap, for cigarettes, but this was not at all what Corporal Greff wanted. He wanted a girl whose hand he could hold while they walked slowly down the Stroeget, a girl with whom he could talk and laugh, a girl he could hug—he'd teach her German, she'd teach him Danish—a girl for whom he could buy little presents, who'd be waiting for him after duty, a girl he could tell about his house not far from Munich, about his father and mother and smaller brother and baby sister.

If the Danes only would give him a chance he would show them how he could laugh, how he could take a joke, even on himself. Like the little painted signs that somehow were left leaning against the sentry boxes. The first one he saw read TO LET. When that was translated to Corporal Greff and he understood it meant the sentry box was for rent, he had laughed, despite the grim looks of some of the other Waffen SS men.

Another time there was a different sign, a little longer. And Corporal Greff had had a good laugh out of that, although this time, discreetly, he had waited until he was alone. That sign had explained, since the parapet hid the sentry up to his neck, BECAUSE THEY HAVE NO PANTS.

4.

ON THIS SAME September morning Arne Johansen and Lili Lund were lying naked in bed in a small flat overlooking one of the harbors in the city. For quite a little while now they had contemplated each other's bodies in the morning light, remembering pleasantly how those bodies had pleasured each other, Lili remembering as though her body was separate from her, as separate and removed as was his, an instrument she put to use.

Lili Lund was a creamy-skinned Norwegian twenty-five years old, perhaps a year or two older, but no more. She was from a very good family; her father, now in a prison camp in Stavanger, had been an important Norwegian industrialist. Her mother was related to Swedish nobility. She was tall and slender, with an oval face, a cleft chin and the eyes of a Siamese cat. The eyes were always watchful, lustrous, lazy, waiting, all somehow at the same time. She had a low voice and the accents of her upbringing and education; she was an attractive woman but she possessed something more than beauty, a quality that drew men, made them turn away from more beautiful women to look at her, react to her, remember her.

There was that in her face, in those aware eyes, in the broad, rich mouth, that said she considered sex fun, not a commitment, not necessarily a romance, perhaps better not a romance, emotions could interfere, nothing but astounding, marvelous, unequalled fun, certain fun, something to be totally enjoyed; more, something she was ready to enjoy at any time, at any place, in any way, and afterward, if that was the way it was, to wiggle a hand, to smile and walk away. And the greatest charm of all about Lili Lund was that when all this invitation and promise was put to the test she demonstrated that, if anything, she had understated herself.

She felt Arne move. It was not even a movement, it was something inside.

"You're restless," she said, knowing now that the change had come over him, that what had happened had passed on; he was able to hold onto it for just so long and then his mind lashed out and the tension was there again, as though he were alone in a jungle.

He pushed himself up with one arm, reaching over her to the bedside table for a cigarette. Her body was nothing to him now, something between him and a smoke.

"It's always that way," she said, reaching for a match, striking it, holding it out for him, seeing the tight, contained face, the muscles that corrugated his belly, the twisting torso, the chest, the body that had taken her the long distance and now had left her. "When it's over, a woman wants to get closer and a man wants to get away."

"You know. You know all about that," he said.

"Only you're not like anybody else. I can feel it creeping up. I could give it a name."

The cigarette curled smoke past his gray eyes. "What would you call it?" he asked indifferently.

"Lots of things. Fear. Loneliness. The enemy. Life."

"All of those?"

"Give me time. I could turn up some more but they'd all mean the same thing."

He lay back in the bed, disinterested, and somehow it was as though he was across the room. She thought how

14

much of a stranger he was, how close he came and how far he went. That was part of it, not being able to hold.

Arne Johansen was not quite twenty-three. He was not small, five feet seven or eight, but he was built compactly, assembled with the economy of a watch, a ship, a fine gun. He moved thriftily and he seemed smaller than he was. The surprise about his face was his hair, a bright, true red. He didn't have the rest of the face to go with that. His light eyes appeared lighter under the hair; they could become so pale they seemed transparent.

"I don't know you," she said, trying to hold to something, knowing she couldn't, finding pleasure in the futile effort.

"Nothing to know."

"I don't know you at all."

"Nobody knows anybody."

"I know that, but with you it's more. Even now it's as though you're not here. I feel more alone than if you weren't."

He twisted his head and there was something about his mouth, something unexpected. "I'm sorry, Lili."

"No." She touched his lips. "I suppose when it goes so far one way, it has to go that far the other way, every way. How long do we know each other?"

"Four weeks, five."

"And I don't know you at all."

"You're the mystery."

"I? I'm as wide open as a barn door."

"A woman like you, taking up with me."

"What is a woman like me?"

"I used to read about women like you—society, the money, everything that goes with it. Sometimes when I see you somewhere, waiting for me, dressed up, I still can't believe the way it is."

She grinned. "Only when I'm dressed. The rest of the time you know."

He looked at her for a moment. "What do you want of me?"

"You'd know that better than anyone."

15

"Only that?"

"Until I can think of something better. And I've tried and I can't."

She watched him smoke the cigarette; his movements had frugality. They were controlled and nothing was wasted and they finished what they set out to do and nothing more. Maybe that's what made it so complete, to see all that management explode and break apart.

"You're worse than I am," she said.

"Worse how?"

"It goes away from me for a little while, a little while anyway. It comes back but it does go away. It goes away from you too, but not far, and then it's back, only it's something else, not us. Maybe it never really goes away at all."

"Wasn't it any good? Was it that bad?"

"You're beautiful," she said, feeling it inside her again, talking about it to him, he could bring it back faster than it had ever been brought back before and it never had taken long. "You're beautiful and it's always beautiful and when you come in me it makes me want to cry, but it doesn't stay with you, not even long enough for you to get off me sometimes; sometimes before you get off me you're back like a knot."

She looked at the red hair. It was wrong. The red hair was an after thing and he was always before.

"Why is that?" she asked, still trying to hold. "What I just said. Why doesn't it last a little longer?"

He leaned over her again, putting out the cigarette. She kissed his belly.

"I don't care," she said, pressing her cheek against his skin. "I ask questions but I don't really care. I'm always so damned frightened and those are the only times when it all doesn't seem such hell, and I'm trying to spread it a little, like now, with you next to me and we just did it and maybe we'll have time to do it again, maybe we'll have time and you'll feel like it before the world moves in again. That's all I have, Arne, that and you and here. It's what you do for me. You keep the world away."

16

After a moment he asked, "Have you heard anything about your father?"

"They tell me he's alive."

"That's something."

"I get so frightened when I go to Dagmar House. After the way it was at home I just have to look at them, the ones in the black uniforms especially, and it's all there again."

She shivered slightly. He drew her closer to him and pulled up the cover. "Fuck them," he said. "As the British say."

"I'm so afraid of them," she said in a low voice. "Every time I go there and try to find out something, and it doesn't go away until we're together and it doesn't go all the way away until we make love and then it's as though for a moment we defeated everything else."

He stroked her body. She stretched slightly and closed her eyes.

"That's the answer," she said, her body responding as the strings of a cello, giving off a rich music, the eyes half opening now and the mouth called back from wherever it had gone, everything returning, readying. "That's the whole answer. Wouldn't it be wonderful if this were really all there was, that the damned fighting would get itself over with and this would be all there was?"

"You women," he said. "All you think about. You think that's all there is."

"Isn't it? Is there anything you'd rather do now?"

"Now isn't all the time."

"No it isn't and it never could be, but it's lovely to think about it." She felt his hand go away and the protection was gone. "Do you think it will ever end, Arne, the war?"

"Has to. They always do."

"And my father. Will I see him again?"

"Probably."

She shook her head suddenly. "Oh, this damned war, this damned, damned war."

"Ah, things aren't so bad. Business is good. Germans buy anything we offer."

She looked at him and chuckled unexpectedly. "I always find it funny. You, a silk salesman."

"Why is that funny?"

"I don't know. There's nothing of a silk salesman about you."

"What do you think would suit me better?"

"I don't know. Every once in a while I seem to feel something. I don't know. Sometimes it frightens me."

"You just said I took that away."

"You do, the other kind, the world kind. But yours is something else. I'm not saying I mind it. It's exciting. When I think of you doing dangerous things, almost getting killed, I can feel it, I can feel it right here." She took his hand and placed it flat on her thighs. "Here. I can feel it start here and then move up."

"I must seem pretty sorry when you come down to earth again."

She ran her hand through his hair, pushing it back from his eyes. "There's a fire there. They ought to give the Blaze a rest and give you a try. I think you could make him look like a schoolboy."

"We're on that now."

She kissed him and pressed her body against his. "I've got a flame of my own, Arne. Please do something."

"You never get enough, do you?"

"Don't blame me for that. Whoever put the parts together, blame him. Please, Arne."

"Lili, we had all night."

"I know, but it's started again. You know how I'll be all day. I'll go crazy. Here, let me do something for you. Here. How does that feel? Oh, I can tell."

"Yes," he said.

"Then do something to me. Anywhere. Anything. Start anywhere and make a slow trip."

The telephone rang.

She seized his wrist as he reached out. "Don't answer it."

"Yes," he said into the mouthpiece. "Good. I'll be over."

There was a click on the other end and Arne cradled the

receiver. He tossed aside the cover and swung over her. She made no move to stop him, knowing he was already gone.

"Who was that?" she asked, knowing it was going to be a bad day.

"Pal of mine down the store," he said, getting dressed. "Some new stuff just came in from Sweden and he was tipping me off. I'll get down there and get some of it before the other salesmen gobble it up. Can't get enough of that material. The supermen keep sending it home to their superwomen. Maybe I can scrounge a piece for you."

"Did you ever study dancing?" she asked. "You can't make a wrong move. It's all in such order."

"Keep that to yourself." He smiled, slipping into his jacket. "Silk salesman is bad enough. But a silk salesman who moves like a dancer." He rolled his eyes.

"When will I see you?"

"Can't tell exactly."

"You don't have to go out of town today?"

"I won't know until I look at my book."

He was dressed now, moving toward the door. Taking himself, she thought, to catch up with himself, wherever that was.

"Aren't you going to kiss me good-bye?"

He returned to the bed, moving lightly, like a dancer, like a boxer coming out of his corner, silk salesman my foot, but was he, could he be, that Buhle, suspicions crawling around in his head like worms, what a world, what a miserable world, just to remain alive, just to remain alive and without pain.

She took his face between her hands and kissed him gently on the lips. "You've made up for so much."

He nodded. That expression, she thought, she rarely saw it and it was something to see, his face unlocked the way it was at the big moment and seldom any time else and look at it now. Oh God, this awful, awful world.

"Hurry back," she said. She watched him go.

She lay back on the bed touching herself. Because it's close, that close, she told him. They all of them had that, the boys in Norway, nothing about them alike except that, the closeness to the truth. And with them it was lying with it, as close as they were, almost going and not going and having it when they finally went, dying with them, each time, the supreme coming, the supreme, final, ultimate coming, and touching with their new world, briefly, fleetingly, just the fingertips reaching out and meeting and then the vision and the peace.

Arne was different, her hand moving. But they were all different. But he was the closest. It was in everything he did and with him the fingertips had touched from the beginning.

5.

ARNE JOHANSEN stepped off the tram near Central Station and walked to a restaurant not far from the entrance to Tivoli. The amusement gardens had closed for the season a couple of weeks before and looked deserted and affronted. People who passed the entrance gate looked inside sadly. It was that way each year, something went from the city when Tivoli closed and didn't return until it opened. It was that way even now, even with the Germans.

Arne entered the restaurant, glanced around, saw Niels Rider seated at a table, joined him.

"Dead eyes," Niels observed. "Gaunt face. A Grade-B?"

"A Grade-B. And if you had called ten minutes later we might have made B plus."

"She'll kill you."

"Worse ways to die." He stirred the coffee. "Everything ready?"

Niels nodded. "Odd how different my night work is from yours."

Arne lit a cigarette. "That prick. I'd've loved to have seen that German prick face when he passed the little marker." He looked at Niels. "For such a sad-looking man you have funny ideas."

Niels grunted and finished his coffee. He was taller than Arne, quite thin, and he had a long, melancholy face. He was only a year or two older than Arne but he considered Arne as some kind of son, brilliant in some respects, retarded in others, wholly irresponsible and requiring a constant eye.

"Let's get on with it," Arne said, putting down his cup.

Niels picked up a battered, dark valise and they left the restaurant. They walked to a building almost directly across the street from Dagmar House, rode on an elevator to the top floor, climbed an iron ladder to a skylight, crawled through to the roof. Niels opened the suitcase and they started to assemble the equipment inside.

6.

LIEUTENANT COLONEL MAX GREINER leaned forward, his dark eyes burning, his hands gripped. Colonel Buhle contemplated him for a moment and then moved his eyes to the ash on his cigar.

"What did I say to them, Max? What makes you think I said anything?"

"Because the whole idea is so foolish!" Greiner said harshly.

"Something ordered by the Führer? Foolish?" The question was posed in a soft voice and the laugh lines around the mouth went to work. But the words hung in the air.

"Yes, all right, Rudolf, arrest me for sedition—or is it blasphemy now? For suggesting that once in a while even Adolf Hitler can be misled."

"By whom?" Buhle inquired in the same easy way. "Who leads the Führer?"

"His emotions!" Greiner stood up and paced back and forth for a moment. "Rudolf, you know as well as I do this whole thing is stupid, idiotic."

"Emotions have nothing to do with this," Buhle said. "We are involved with State policy."

"Bullshit! We're involved with Himmler and especially with that little cunt Eichmann."

"It remains State policy."

"And you said nothing?"

"I said what could be said."

"Which was?"

"Are you interrogating me, Max?"

"What did you say?"

Buhle puffed on his cigar. He swung around in his swivel chair so that he faced a window. "I said I had only a very small business here, just getting started, you might say. I said I am now being asked to do a big job and I don't have the organization to do it with. I said I'm a sales manager with not enough salesmen to cover the territory."

"And the reply?"

Buhle's thick back shrugged. "They promised me more salesmen."

"And that was all?"

"Not quite." Buhle twisted around until he was facing Greiner again. The lines were gone from his mouth. "We've been friends for a long time, Max, good friends."

"Was that all?"

"No." Buhle swung the chair around again and looked toward the window. "I said I have been in Denmark only six months, less, and I said I don't know the Danes, I don't yet fully know the atmosphere. They said talk to Greiner,

22

he's been there more than three years, they said, and he'll tell you anything you need to know."

He swiveled round again and watched Greiner sit down heavily. "Ask Greiner," he repeated. "They said ask Obersturmbannführer Max Greiner, he's an expert on Denmark." He saw Greiner close his right hand over his left and squeeze the knuckles hard. "You are too emotional, Max," Buhle said. "But that's because you don't direct them properly, you don't direct them where they should correctly go."

"We made a pact with the Danes," Greiner said. "If I'm the expert, listen to me then. We promised them we'd leave the Jews alone."

"And so, for three and a half years, we have. That's long enough to keep a promise, almost a record."

"The Danes are still keeping theirs. To the letter. Food, clothing, even arms. How many Germans are living off Danish food? And we break our word because of a few thousand Jews?"

"The Führer has said those few thousand Jews stick in his throat."

Greiner raised haggard eyes. "Rudolf, does the word 'honor' embarrass you?"

"Not at all. But honor is like arithmetic, how the Führer defines it." He smiled. "Don't concern yourself, Max; when it's all over we will write the history book."

"Do you still believe that?"

"I will forget that question."

"But now, Rudolf, here, now. The Danes. What do you think their reaction will be?"

"Relief," Buhle said. "Everybody is anti-Semitic. It is human nature. Some people hide it, some pretend it doesn't exist, some make an adjustment. Believe me, Max, when we start our action, the Danes will discover they hate Jews the same as everybody else."

7.

A LITTLE PAST NOON on this same day a pretty girl named Ellen Oppenheim was sitting on one of the benches in the square next to a boy named Anders Jessen. This was lunch hour for Ellen, who worked in one of the department stores along the Stroeget. She had, as usual, saved some of her sandwich bread and was feeding it to the imperious pigeons waddling around as fat as though there was no rationing, no war.

A German philosopher had once observed rather wistfully that the only thing better than being a Dane was being the pet of a Dane. The pigeons were the wards of the city as were the wild birds sheltered in the artificial lakes and the storks in Randers and Odense.

Ellen turned her head slightly and rested her eyes on Anders, seeing a lad hardly out of his teens, with fine, almost delicate features, mild brown eyes surmounted by long, thick, almost girlish lashes, and, answering a question he had posed some moments before, said, "Marry you? I'd marry you if you were the last man on earth."

Anders broke into a wide, astonished grin. "You mean that." Then his face fell. "Oh, Ellen, you're always teasing me."

Her eyes, a deep violet and so large they filled her face, looked at Anders gravely. "Tell me. Why should I want to marry you?"

"Because I love you. And you love me."

"Simple as that." She nodded slowly. "And why do you love me?"

24

He looked at her in anguish. "Ellen."

"All right. Why do I love you?"

He couldn't answer.

"Just because you're young and handsome and you bake clay in an oven so people can have crazy-looking ashtrays?"

"I won a prize with one of them," he said miserably.

"You won a prize. Everybody wins a prize. It's almost impossible to go through life without winning a prize. It's true, you won yours early." She crinkled her nose. "What have you got to look forward to?"

"What prize have you ever won?" he asked.

"You." A smile danced around her lips. "Do you constitute a prize?" She looked at him more closely, at the unhappy face she loved. "I think so. A blue ribbon."

He reddened at the words which she had said very lightly, and which he didn't even dare hope she could mean. "If you feel that way and I feel that way, then why can't we get married?"

"It's too happy a time. I'll save marriage to you for a rainy day."

She turned back to the pigeons. He looked at the side of her head, at the dark hair that curled over her shoulders. All this had been gone through before and he wanted to answer it again as he had tried to answer it before, but he had failed before and he didn't have anything new to say. He turned away and looked toward Dagmar House and at the sentry box where Corporal Oskar Greff's head could be seen. He turned back to Ellen to say something to her, but he did not speak.

Anders Jessen knew very little about love and could not have defined it, if it can be defined, but at that moment he was aware he was learning something, and what he was learning was this, that there are those times in the lives of people who love each other when they catch a glimpse of something that images that love, which is perhaps unrelated to the love until that time. It was as though the experience of love is illuminated by signposts for the faithful.

It was not that Ellen Oppenheim was doing anything out

of the ordinary. What she was doing was quite the most
ordinary thing possible. She was feeding a pigeon. The bird
was perched on one of her wrists and was pecking crumbs
from the palm of the other hand. There were two birds on
one of Ellen's shoulders and another bird on the other
shoulder, all of them patiently waiting their turn.

The usually noisy birds were silent, so the moment was a
tableau, one pigeon eating, three waiting, and on the face of
the girl was an expression of such gentleness Anders felt a
shiver go through him. It was as though he was looking
upon her face for the first time.

She turned. "You were going to say something."

"Nothing."

"Tell me what you were going to say."

"Nothing. It's just that . . ." He did not now want to
intrude anything to do with a German soldier. But he could
think of nothing to substitute. He was not a quick, clever
thinker and this new sight of Ellen slowed his wits the
more.

He pointed. "That German guard . . ."

She frowned and looked and giggled. It was a happy,
tinkling giggle, as vulnerable and uncomplicated as though
from a child. "He's just a head," she laughed. "It's like a
dummy with a helmet in a hat shop."

He listened to her laughter, saw it slip into her eyes, and
he almost sighed loudly his relief. She fooled him this way
so often. Seeing something exactly as he saw it, the same
point of view, the same humor, and then at the other times
seeing things from some isolated place of her own, a place
so remote he could not conceive of it, much less attempt to
reach her there.

He watched her feed the last of the bread to the pigeons.
Those who were short-changed looked at her reproachfully
but departed, as he saw, without the normal clamorous re-
buke. She looked up at the clock in the Town Hall tower. It
showed a few minutes before one.

"I must be thinking about getting back to work," she
said. "Hasn't it been lovely?"

8.

THE TALL DANISH police officer who had nodded to Georg Siebert got off the elevator and walked down the corridor to Peter Hansen's office. Hansen's secretary looked up with a polite smile. The police officer held up his hand.

"Don't say it, Ulla. I know. I'm here again. And don't tell me Mr. Hansen isn't in. I could smell his pipe across the square."

"Captain Melchior," the girl said.

"Don't tell me he's busy. Just pick up the phone and tell him I'm here." When the secretary still hesitated, he said with pretended menace, "I'm a policeman, Ulla. I might just be here to arrest Mr. Hansen."

The girl puckered her nose, picked up the telephone. "Captain Melchior is here, sir."

Melchior took the instrument from her hand. "I'm on my way in, Peter."

Hansen was going through papers on his desk. Melchior waved away the pipe smoke. "You could hide a battleship."

"Wasn't thick enough to hide me," Hansen said.

"Ah. Warm. Friendly. Gracious. Hello, Peter." Melchior waved a greeting. "Hello, my good friend, Peter Hansen."

"What the hell do you want?"

"Civility for a start," Melchior said, sitting himself on the edge of the desk. "I have to remind you that I'm a police officer and by extension decreed by our protectors an official of the Third Reich." He rubbed his fingers lightly on his chin. "I wonder what my Führer would have to say about his Jewish policeman."

"Exactly," Hansen said. "Now get out, I'm busy."

"No, he'd say a little more than that."

"What do you want, Erik?"

"You know exactly what I want."

"I know, and the answer is no."

Melchior got off the desk and sat down in a chair and stretched his long legs. "Peter, you have to stop being such a stubborn ass. I'm a policeman. I'm better than a policeman. I'm a police captain. I see things. I hear things. I'm useful."

"You also are a Jew."

"Your mind is going, Peter," Captain Melchior said forbearingly. "I've already mentioned that."

"I'm sorry, Erik," Hansen said.

Melchior shrugged. "It wasn't my fault."

Peter Hansen looked at Melchior and, as always, shook his head. He saw a man who could have passed any Nazi standard. Not yet thirty, over six feet tall, eyes pure blue, hair so light it almost appeared bleached, skin tanned from the summer sun that had lightened the hair, Erik Melchior could have posed for one of Hitler's Aryan dreams.

"Amazing," Hansen said.

"You mean I don't look like a Jew."

Hansen waved his hand. "Sorry. I'm stupid."

"I know. I mentioned that before, too."

"Now return to your appointed rounds, as they say. I'm busy."

"Is that why you won't let me work for you?" Melchior asked. "In your secret heart you hate Jews?"

"Yes," Hansen said. "With a passion." He looked at his wrist-watch. "Siebert was just here."

"I saw him leaving the building. When he stands still he looks like a monument."

"Gave it to me in a way, I think. Tried to find out something."

"What? That in that same secret heart you're pro-Nazi?"

"Something like that." Hansen looked at Melchior's surprised face. "I'm not joking. I wonder why."

"A romance," the police officer said. "That's one of the few things we Jews don't have to suffer. The Nazis never try to make love to us."

"I remember Siebert from before the war. He wasn't quite so enormous then, come to think of it. Odd, but he always struck me as being rather decent."

"Primary Nazi characteristic. Well, Peter?"

"He gave me the chills." Hansen glanced at his watch again. "Made me feel all over again that I don't belong in this game."

"You don't. I do."

"Out of the question. You know that."

"It doesn't have to be." Melchior's mouth twisted wryly. "If one had time for the luxury, one could almost be bitter. You're stupid. Stupid and stubborn and a damned idiot. You need me. The whole damned movement could use me."

"I don't make the rules."

"You do," Melchior said. "You do now."

Hansen hit the loose ash out of his pipe. He took a small penknife from his pocket and opened a blade and pried the dottle from the bowl. "How do you know that?" he asked.

"I know a lot of things."

"Such as?" Hansen began to refill the bowl slowly.

Melchior rose to his feet. He walked to a corner of the office and picked up a putter leaning against the wall. He looked around and saw a ball on a shelf of a bookcase. He put the ball on the rug, studied the rug, tapped the ball. It came to a stop in the center of a circle in the pattern.

"Marvelous," Hansen said. "Simply marvelous. Now tell me what you think you know."

Melchior picked up the golf ball and set it down at a much greater distance from the circle in the rug. He studied the lie. "I'll tell you what I think I know, Peter," he said, setting his feet. "I know all about the little wild-eyed firebrands scattered all over the country, like Boy Scouts looking for their good deed for the day, tripping over each other's feet, sometimes colliding head on because two groups set out to commit the same obvious piece of sabotage at the same time and there was no channel of communication." He tapped the ball. He watched it roll to the edge of the circle. "You want more?"

"Yes," Hansen said.

Melchior picked up the ball again and put it back on the bookcase shelf. He sat down, still holding onto the putter. "I know that Carl Haagen had the sensible idea of trying to combine most of the hotheads into one working organization so they could all cooperate with reason and some sense and that he called on you, because if there's one thing you know in this world it's organizing. Even our friends, the protectors, are benefiting from that. Keep your shirt on, Peter," he said, balancing the putter. "I know that Haagen asked you to do that, a long time ago when you wanted to close your plants down or blow them up, so that the Germans would get to trust you a little and perhaps you'd hear things and pass them on. And you did and you have."

Melchior stopped abruptly, putting the putter on his lap. The two men studied each other.

It's already started, Hansen thought. The new world with the new values, and I must learn patience and not to press too hard and to wait and hope that it will come to me. My old friend, Erik Melchior, and I have to hurt him this way, the worst, most vicious way, the Nazi's own way, and I must not let it matter now and I must consider him in another manner because it's another life. The Nazis, what they do. Another variety of their own private covenant with death.

"I know even more than that," Melchior said, playing it out like trumps, to win with this or get out of the game. "I know the original understanding was that as soon as you picked up all the little pieces and put them together you'd get out, be able to get out. The terms you laid down. But you were sort of double-crossed. Carl Haagen managed to get in the way of a Nazi bullet and you woke up one morning to find the whole business dumped in your lap."

"How do you know about Carl Haagen?" Hansen asked.

Haagen was supposed to have been transported out of the country, alive.

Melchior began to slice the silence with the putter.

"Is that all?" Hansen asked.

"All that has anything to do with you. Not really all, at that. One has to keep a few things to one's self."

"You didn't tell me how you know all these things," Hansen said. Presently he said it again, "How do you know?"

Melchior gripped the golf club at both ends.

"How do you know?" Hansen roared.

The golf stick snapped, a crack, like a shot. "I'm a cop," Melchior said evenly.

Hansen made himself puff on the pipe, slowly, and when he could ask it quietly, he said, "Does every Danish policeman know all these things?"

"How the hell do I know? If you'd let me in I might do something about finding out." He looked disinterestedly at the broken golf club, put the two pieces down. "I'll buy you a new one. Funny, isn't it? Peter Hansen, business man, wakes up one morning and discovers he's head of the Danish underground. Job he doesn't want. Job his wife very much doesn't want." Melchior smiled. It was a hard, unamused smile. "Don't look so surprised, Peter."

"She may be right. I may not be cut out for this."

"Tell me about it," Melchior said, the hardness drifting into his voice now, something deeper than the anger.

Hansen heard the change. This was part of it as well, not only what had to come from himself, but what came from a friend and had to be ignored because nothing could be brought to a head.

"Peter Hansen, non-hero," Melchior said. "You can bet Kate is right. Maybe you ought to quit before you wreck the whole thing." He shook his head slowly. "The head man wants out. Do you know what I'd give to get in? Where would you like to start? With my life?"

"Erik . . ." Hansen began.

"This is my country as well as yours," Melchior said slowly and distinctly. "I was born here. My parents were born here. Their parents were born here. Even Hitler doesn't go back much further than that."

"Erik . . ." Hansen said again.

"What right have you to keep me out?"

"You know why."

"I know the why you always give me."

"And it's the same why. It hasn't changed."

"God damn it, Peter, now you can change it!"

Hansen put down his pipe. Then, almost unaware of what he was doing, he looked at his watch.

Melchior frowned. "What are you doing that for?"

"Erik, listen to me."

"No," Melchior said, the enemy still in his voice. "Why have you looked at your watch three times since I've been here?"

Hansen stood up, walked to the window, walked back. "Erik, I'll spell it out for you, and for the last time," he said calmly. "Erik, the Nazis have been in Denmark since April of '40."

"Tell me about that, too."

"One of the conditions the King insisted upon was that they'd leave the Jews alone. It wasn't even a condition. It was a question the King refused to even discuss. He would not even admit there was a question. He simply would not consider Danish Jews as different from any other Danes. Even the refugee Jews. the stateless Jews, were included. That was decided earlier, much earlier, long before the Germans moved into Denmark. It was something, Erik, that we were able to make stick. We may not have thrilled the world with any kind of resistance, but we came up the only German-occupied country where Jews were left unmolested. For more than three years. Still. It has to stay that way. If the Nazis caught one member of the underground who turned out to be a Jew, it would give them the provocation to take it out on every other Jew in Denmark."

Melchior was silent long enough for Hansen to sit down, pick up his pipe, begin to refill it.

"Now that you're Number One," the policeman said

mildly, "maybe you'll be able to wangle something decent for that furnace, from the RAF, when they make their drops."

Hansen looked at Melchior silently.

"Insist on it," Melchior said. "You're Number One."

Hansen struck a match.

"What are you going to do now?" Melchior asked.

"I can't tell you. We've been through all that."

"I'm not asking for secrets," Melchior said in a bleak voice. His strong hands clenched. "All I want to know is, are you quitting?"

"I don't think so," Hansen said.

"You don't know?"

"No. I don't know whether I'll be good enough."

"Nobody ever is." Melchior got up and started for the door.

"Erik, wait," Hansen said. He looked at his watch again. "Wait just a few minutes."

9.

"THE DANISH JEWS as well?" Greiner asked.

"All Jews. As far as the Führer is concerned, Jews are Jews," Buhle said. "The arrest and deportation of all Jews. Denmark must become Jew-free."

"That's quite an assignment. I don't envy you."

"Max," Buhle said quietly. "It's not my assignment alone."

"I am not part of your apparatus here."

"This is a police matter. You are supervisor of the Danish police." When Greiner did not reply, Buhle said, "Max, please don't be foolish. The Führer is not in any way a temperate man and of all things he is least temperate about Jews." When Greiner continued silent, Buhle said, "Max, as I've said, you have been here a long time. In Berlin they have a saying that six months in Denmark makes a weak Nazi. Max, as an old friend, I'm telling you you are playing with your life."

Greiner said, "What do you want me to do?"

Buhle smiled, the real smile. "You know it could be the other way round, that the Jews were determined to exterminate us."

"The Führer is convinced of that."

"So he says. And who knows, perhaps he believes it."

"What do you want me to do?"

"We'll work it out, together, as we always do," Buhle said heartily. "Max, Max, what the devil does it all matter anyway? We do our jobs. That's all. Besides, they're only Jews." He looked closely at Greiner. "Max, you agree, they are only Jews."

Greiner said slowly, in a low voice that was almost a whisper, "It is inhuman."

Buhle's face was impassive. "Max, it sounds even more melodramatic the second time around, but you are playing with your life."

Greiner stood up. "I will await your orders."

"Shit!"

The chimes in the Town Hall clock began to ring, preliminary to the striking of the hour.

"Come, Max, we'll have a good lunch," Buhle said. "The food in Berlin is worse than ever. The Führer doesn't care much about eating so everybody pretends they don't mind. I've been looking forward to a good Danish meal. Max, just one small thing else. That insulting little so-called gravestone in the square. How can you permit such a thing to remain there?"

"A safety valve," Greiner said. "It allows people to laugh."

"At the Führer?"

"Better than riots."

Buhle jutted his lower lip. "You know these people. Bones to the dogs. Perhaps you're right."

The last of the chimes floated into the office and then the clock struck the hour of one, brilliantly and clearly.

"But perhaps you'd better not allow that thing to stay out there too long," Buhle said. He walked around the desk and slapped Greiner on the back. "Now for some food."

At that moment a voice boomed into the room. "One o'clock! Hitler's time has almost run out!"

There was a sudden welling of laughter from the square. The two men walked rapidly to the window and looked down at the faces now turned up toward Dagmar House, and as though awaiting Buhle's appearance the voice announced, "Welcome back to Copenhagen, Colonel Buhle. We'll try to make your return as interesting as possible."

There was another great shout of laughter from the people in the square. Buhle looked at the mass of faces. He backed away from the window. He started to say something to Greiner but his words were drowned out by something new, music, a military brass band, coming from the same source as the voice, playing "It's a Long Way to Tipperary."

Buhle slammed the window shut, but they could still hear the music.

10.

"THE HEROES?" Melchior asked.

"None else."

"Another chapter in the epic saga of the Orange and the

Blaze?" Melchior said harshly. "Another fairy tale for school children?"

"I know," Hansen said. "Silly. Doesn't actually do very much good, does it? But it will be all over Denmark before the day is out and all over the world tomorrow. It doesn't do anything, Erik, and yet it's bloody damned wonderful."

"I suppose it is," Melchior said. "When you're part of it."

11.

CORPORAL OSKAR GREFF along with everybody else heard the announcements from the amplifier hidden on some roof, and while he did not wholly understand the Danish words he did recognize the name of the Leader and that of the Gestapo chief. And since the people were convulsed with laughter, he could understand the words made some kind of joke, against the Leader and the Gestapo. Then he heard the music, which he recognized vaguely as a British song from the last war.

It seemed to him as he stood in his sentry box that the laughter was becoming more local. By raising his head and going on his toes he could see people collecting in front of his station, looking, laughing. Corporal Greff's orders were not to leave his post except in the event of a disturbance and, while what was happening did not technically constitute a disturbance, there was a crowd collecting and despite their present good spirits the people might cause trouble, especially after what came out of the public-address amplifier. With this rationalization, Corporal Greff left his post.

The Danes parted readily, eagerly, for him, their faces saucy with laughter, and he saw that a new sign had been placed against the sentry box. Corporal Greff could see that it was not the sign about not having pants. He turned away and smiled at the Danes, a somewhat shy smile. The laughter increased and Corporal Greff hoped it meant they included him.

A middle-aged Dane walked up to him and asked in excellent German, "Do you know what that sign says?"

Corporal Greff grinned broadly. "No, friend, what does it say?"

"It says," the Dane said slowly, " 'Don't feed the animal.' "

The man walked away and the people laughed louder than before, and although Corporal Greff understood they were laughing at him he did not mind it because in some way he did not feel so alone.

He started back for his post, his automatic rifle cradled in his arms, and as he did so he saw a small Danish man pedalling a bicycle across the square. Corporal Greff continued toward the sentry box but then his eye caught something else, something bright, and he looked again and saw the sun reflecting from two metal objects hanging from the neck of the man on the bicycle. Instinctively, one of Corporal Greff's hands went to the grenades clipped onto his uniform.

The long time of efficient German military training now imposed its instantaneous and arbitrary reflexes and Corporal Greff raised his automatic rifle and squeezed the trigger and the small man tumbled from the bicycle and Corporal Greff fired another burst and now the small man's blood was mixing with something white pouring from bullet holes in the metal canisters, turning the blood into soft pink, covering the street like melted strawberry ice-cream.

The laughter of the people changed to screams. Some fled in panic. Others closed in on Corporal Greff, making other sounds, and Corporal Greff, still operating as a competent German soldier, fired at them to make them go away. He did not hear the screams of the women and children and the angry shouts of the men when the gun was operating.

37

He did not see a young dark-haired girl pick up a child shot through the head and hold the child pressed against her breast so that the child's blood spread on the shoulder where only a little while before pigeons had waited tranquilly for their food. Nor did Corporal Greff see a young man swing the girl behind him so that his body was between the girl and the German soldier.

Corporal Greff saw nothing and soon heard nothing, not even the firing of the gun, because now he was functioning as a programmed machine.

The people now were all running away in every direction to escape the aimless flow of bullets. Corporal Greff pivoted slowly and rhythmically, moving the bullets around in a half-circle as though he were spraying a lawn, and with almost the same uninvolvement.

He saw a man walking toward him, a young man wearing a cap covering vivid red hair. He lowered his rifle.

"Nobody will speak to me," Corporal Greff said.

He would have said more but the young man fired a bullet between his eyes.

12.

THE GESTAPOMAN pushed the red-head down into the tub of ice-cold water and held it there until the struggling slackened. He pulled the head out by the hair.

"So," the German said. "What have you to say now?"

The youth, gasping for breath, shook his head. The Gestapoman shoved his face below the surface again.

Watching at a long table nearby, rolling a cigar between his lips, Colonel Buhle turned to Lieutenant Colonel Greiner, saw the distaste on his face. "He is holding out well," Buhle said.

"Perhaps it's just that he has nothing to say," Greiner said.

Buhle shrugged. "Somebody will. Eventually."

"I see no reason for me to remain here," Greiner said, starting to rise.

"I do."

Greiner sat down again. He looked at the far end of the room where thirty or forty men were being held under SS guns. They were all naked and they were all red-haired.

"Do you think it helps, having them watch?"

"It may not help with the man being interviewed," Buhle said. "May even delay a confession. Pride. But it helps with them. They're all in the tub with him." Buhle turned his head and looked at Greiner. "You surprise me, Max, you know the technique as well as I do. I don't understand. You were quite professional when we worked together in the old days." He broke the ash from the cigar. "Max, we know the man who killed the guard was a red-head. I saw that myself."

"There are thousands of red-haired men in Denmark."

"So you've said. Often. But we'll test this sample. And if there's no result, we'll go on to other things."

The Gestapoman hauled the youth out of the tub again. This time he was unconscious. He was pulled back on his knees and a bottle of brandy was forced between his lips. He choked and flailed and his head was pushed into the water again.

"If it takes much longer we'll have to change the water," Buhle said. "It warms up."

"He may die before that."

"Pity." Buhle puffed unhurriedly on the cigar. "Whoever it is, that man or the others back there or somebody else entirely, it will take time. Because the man who did it was skilled. He'd done that kind of thing before. He fired that bullet precisely and then he left. That's the key, Max, the way he left. He walked. He did not run. He walked calmly and slowly, as though nothing had happened, as though there weren't other German soldiers nearby."

"The crowd closed in around him. It happened quickly."

"Not correct. It did not happen quickly at all. It was as if the man just stopped to give Greff a light or the time of day and then wandered on. No, Max, it was not the first time he killed."

"And that's why you think he may be the one they call the Blaze?"

"I don't think anything. I'm trying to find out."

The youth was pulled up from the tub unconscious again. This time the brandy did not revive him. He was dragged away. Buhle looked irritated as another red-headed youth was prodded up.

It's like a story I once read, Arne Johansen thought, standing naked among the other naked men, feeling frightened, ridiculous, curious, wary, the story about Sherlock Holmes and the company of red-headed men.

Arne had been picked up in the general roundup while seated in a café with Niels Rider. Fortunately there were others seated at the same table, so there was nothing to associate Niels with him. With the others, Niels had kept his eyes averted as the SS men took Arne away.

Now he watched as the new suspect was pushed down into a chair at the table opposite to Buhle. A new interrogator, an SS *Hauptscharführer* named Gruber, a fat, perspiring man, asked, "Do you wish to make a confession?"

"I know nothing about the shooting," the Danish youth said. "I wasn't anywhere near the square."

Warrant Officer Gruber handed Buhle the wallet and papers taken from the youth. Buhle glanced at them indifferently.

"Can you prove that?" Gruber asked.

The youth shook his head. Gruber looked at Buhle. Buhle nodded. Gruber signed to a Gestapoman who attached an electric wire to the youth's ankle while another Gestapoman bound him to the chair around his chest and at his wrists. Then the first Gestapoman began to touch parts of the youth's body with a second electric wire. At the first touch the youth jerked against his binds. He bit his lip to keep from crying out.

With a word, Arne thought, he could stop all this. But that wasn't the name of the game at all. And he still had too much to do. And if that man isn't one of us he should be.

When the Gestapoman touched the free wire to the youth's testicles he screamed and fainted. Warrant Officer Gruber slapped his face a couple of times but it was useless and the youth was untied and carried away.

Warrant Officer Gruber wiped the sweat from his face as he turned to Buhle. "I'm sorry about that, Herr Standartenführer, but he had no stamina."

"Keep going, Gruber," Buhle said.

"The Standartenführer does not consider me clumsy?"

"No. That one couldn't have done it anyway. He didn't have the balls."

The Germans laughed appreciatively. Except, Buhle noticed, Greiner.

"Ruthless toughness, Max," Buhle said almost inaudibly.

"What?" he asked Gruber.

"I asked whether the Standartenführer desires to correct me on any of my procedures," Gruber said.

"No. Just get on with it. We do not have all day."

Three or four men were given the attention of the electric wires and, when that failed to produce any results, Gruber shifted to another technique. The feet of the next suspect were cut with razors, not deeply, and just on the soles, and then he was required to walk over a flat pan of salt. He walked back and forth, sweat pouring from him, and every time he was queried he said no and then after a while he was not able to speak and he gripped his lips like a vise and in answer to the question shook his head. Half a dozen others were administered this form of inquiry.

Arne Johansen made book with himself, betting on the percentage of men who would faint or walk away under their own power. Then he felt the rifle butt in his back and he was shoved forward to the table.

He was seated in the chair and bound. Buhle looked

indifferently at his papers. Then Buhle straightened in his chair and picked up the papers and looked at them with more interest.

"Name?" Buhle asked.

"Arne Johansen."

"Business?"

"Material salesman. I work for the Magasin du Nord."

Buhle looked up from the papers. He frowned for a moment and then the connection clicked. There were so many of them being watched more or less these days that one could hardly remember them all. But this was one they had put one of the girls onto, what was her name, the Norwegian girl—well, it didn't matter. What mattered was that this one didn't look like much. Except for the hair, of course, but, as Greiner said, there were thousands of them.

"What do you know about all this?" Buhle asked.

"Nothing, sir."

"Material salesman. That's a damn stupid occupation for a healthy man these days," Buhle said. "Where were you yesterday at one o'clock?"

"I went to Elsinore in the morning, sir. If I could look at my little book there, sir. I saw Mrs. Sondergaard, I think her name was, a very good customer. I had some linen we managed to put our hands on, she always has a standing order for anything special." He looked anxiously at Gruber with the air of a man who knows he has to keep talking as long as he can. "Then I took the 12:35, I had lunch in Elsinore first, and I had an appointment in Hellerup at 1:30."

Buhle pushed the papers aside. "Enough."

"I was a little early when I got to Hellerup so I had a couple of beers," Arne said quickly, again looking at Gruber.

"I said, enough," Buhle said impatiently. This one would talk your ears off. He'd have to get the girl onto someone else. This one sounded like a warm-brother, but then he couldn't be, not with the girl—anyway, he was a pest. "What the devil is the matter with you, Gruber?"

"Of course, Herr Standartenführer," Gruber said. He

42

handed the wire to a Gestapoman and thought for a moment, rubbing his fingers nervously.

"I spoke to a friend in Hellerup, at the place where I had the beer," Arne said. "I can prove that."

"Gruber," Buhle said dangerously.

Warrant Officer Gruber snapped his fingers and then took a small wad of cotton from his pocket. He tore it into little tufts and forced the tufts between Arne Johansen's fingers. A Gestapoman had a small can of petrol ready and Warrant Officer Gruber carefully poured a small amount of petrol on each wad of cotton, being careful not to get the petrol on the hand itself because then the whole hand would go up in flames, which would be an indication of Warrant Officer Gruber's lack of skill. The wads soaked, Gruber carefully dabbed the excess alcohol from the fingers that had become slightly moistened, and then he applied a lighted match to the first wad, between the little finger and the ring finger of Arne Johansen's left hand, the left hand so to build up slowly toward the right hand.

Arne reared in his seat. He'd give them nothing, he promised himself. He had something to live up to. He braced himself against the pain and then he remembered, he wasn't who he was, he wasn't the Blaze being tortured, with the name to sustain, the things that had been done, what it would give to them, the rest of them, he wasn't that, he was Arne Johansen, silk salesman, and as that he opened his mouth and screamed. He wanted it to be a satisfactory scream and he found it wasn't hard.

It was late in the afternoon when the last of the suspects was dealt with. They had behaved in different ways, some well, some badly, but none of them had been made to admit to the slaying of Corporal Oskar Greff, and it could not be pinned on any of them. They were dismissed, except one who had died, and Colonel Buhle looked disagreeably at his cigar, his fifth that afternoon, and put it down. He was stiff and tired from the exertion of observing the interviews.

He stood up, working his shoulders. "My back. Gruber!"

The warrant officer rushed over. "Herr Standartenführer!"

"Do something about these damned chairs."

"Certainly, Herr Standartenführer! In what way?"

"Get some that are more comfortable, you idiot!"

"Yes, Herr Standartenführer!"

Buhle dug his hand into the small of his back. "I would say the Bispebjerg," he said to Greiner.

"Rudolf, I ask you to reconsider," Greiner said.

"It's the largest hospital here, isn't it?"

"Yes."

"Good. Then it will make the necessary impression. We must try to keep it to five, no more."

"There were more than five left dead in the square."

"We cannot regard them in the category of punishment." They started from the room. The SS men sprang to attention. "I need something to drink. My throat's dry as dust," Buhle said. "I must cut down on those cigars." A Gestapoman opened the door. "The Danes should consider themselves fortunate the Führer looks upon them as Aryans," Buhle said as they walked down the corridor. "In France it's fifty for one German. And do you know what it is today in Russia and Poland?"

"No," Greiner said.

"Five hundred to one. Myself, I think that's somewhat excessive, but you know what he thinks of Slavs." He ran his tongue over his dry lips. "Snaps and beer. I'm beginning to appreciate that Danish custom. What do you say to Frascati's?"

"Is it necessary to commit this action at Bispebjerg?" Greiner asked.

"You agreed it's the biggest hospital, but if you think another place more suitable I have no objections whatsoever."

"Does the action have to be committed anywhere?"

"Of course."

"There's been killing enough today, Rudolf. God in heaven, we're acting like mad dogs."

Buhle put his arm around Greiner's shoulder. "These

44

interrogations are always tedious. You'll feel better after a
few drinks. Max, don't take a stand. Morality is for children
and Americans. Or am I being redundant?" He chuckled.
Then he said in a reasonable voice, "Max, it is inadmissi-
ble that a German soldier should be shot to death in the
biggest public square in Copenhagen in front of hundreds
of people—and the crime go unpunished."

13.

WHEN THE DOCTOR in Bispebjerg Hospital finished applying
unguent to the burns and began to wrap the hand in bandage, Arne Johansen said to him, "Aren't you interested in
how it happened?"

"Shut up," Peter Hansen said.

The doctor, a young man named Stephan Moller,
glanced at Arne nervously, adjusted his thick glasses,
worked the bandage carefully around the hand.

"Why not?" Arne asked him.

"Arne, I said keep quiet," Hansen said.

"He's impossible," Niels Rider said sadly. "The only
time he's worse is when he's difficult."

Nobody said anything else until Dr. Moller finished. As
he left the little room, Arne said, "Thanks, Doctor, you're
a credit to your profession."

When the doctor was gone, Peter Hansen said, "Tell me
how it happened."

Arne put a cigarette in his mouth. Niels lit it for him.
"You know damned well how it happened," Arne said.

"Tell me why it happened."

"What did you expect me to do? Just walk away?"

"Yes." Hansen saw Arne exchange a glance with Niels.

"Are you out of your mind, Mr. Hansen?" Arne asked, in the manner of wanting to know. He nodded to Niels and, holding the bandaged hand in the palm of the other hand, he started for the door.

"I'm not through yet," Hansen said.

Arne turned, holding out the bandaged hand like a plume. "That Nazi swine shot that man and then turned his gun on everybody within range."

"I know that."

"Do you know how many he killed, wounded?"

"Yes."

Arne looked again at Niels, unable to believe what he was hearing. He turned back to Hansen. "Mr. Hansen, you're new. You just arrived on the scene, you might say. You've just inherited a seat and you've hardly warmed it. Maybe in a little while you'll find out we're fighting a war, and in a war you kill the enemy and he was the enemy. That's the way it is, Mr. Hansen."

"That's not the way it is," Hansen said. "Sit down."

Arne looked at Hansen for a moment, squinting through the cigarette smoke, again holding the bandaged hand in his other hand, and Hansen wondered what he would do if Arne told him to go to hell and walked out. What can one do with a legend who has just added to the legend?

"Sit down," Niels Rider said. "Do what the man says."

Arne whipped a swift look at Niels, whose face was mild and mournful, and perhaps he saw something Hansen did not see because he walked over to one of the couches and sat down. "Tell me how it is, Mr. Hansen," he said.

"That may have been the way it was," Hansen said. "But that's not the way it is now." He wanted to take his pipe out of his tweed jacket but he had to manage this without a prop. The room was quite silent except for hospital sounds; the smell of the anesthetic was everywhere. Arne gazed at him as though he was not very bright. "If we're going to accomplish anything, anything more than small, isolated acts of sabotage, that's not the way it can be at all."

Something came into Arne's eyes. "Small, isolated acts of sabotage?" he asked softly. "Like blowing up the Forum the day before the Nazis were going to turn it into a damned barracks? Is that what you mean, Mr. Hansen?"

The insolence was like a razor. But Arne Johansen was fighting for something, too, Hansen thought, only with better weapons.

"Order," Hansen said, knowing how ineffectual the word sounded after "Forum." "Order and orders that will be obeyed. Order and system and coordination. Otherwise we'll just go on amusing ourselves."

He saw that now even Niels Rider pulled himself up a little. Good. It was rough and it wasn't even true, but it was necessary.

"When was the last time you amused yourself that way, Mr. Hansen?" Arne asked.

"Amusing ourselves," Hansen repeated. "Indulging ourselves. Playing games. Games that even the Germans don't generally mind because they know it gives the people thrills and the illusion we're doing something, and we're really doing very little. The Forum was something. Something special. Memorable. There are other things. But taken together they're only romantic and exciting and, compared to what we can do and will do, very little. Just letting off steam for the country, and the Germans know that. It works for them. Carl Haagen knew that. That's why he wanted it all put together. That's why he asked me to do it."

"He didn't ask you to run the show," Arne said.

"No, he didn't. But I am."

"An accident."

"However." Now, because he didn't need it, he took out his pipe and pouch and began to stuff the bowl. "I'm not Carl Haagen and I don't know how he would have done it. I'm going to do it my way. And that means it's going to stop being sport for prima donnas."

"What do you know about it," Arne said harshly.

Niels' face hardened. But he murmured, "I told you, Mr. Hansen, Arne is an unpleasant man."

"I don't care what that German soldier did," Hansen said. "I don't care how many people he killed. I care, yes, but what we're talking about, it doesn't matter. We're not assassins. We don't take revenge. This is not a vendetta, not even a national vendetta. This is Denmark, involved with something quite simple, its honor." He looked silently at Arne for a moment. The boy had forgotten his bandaged hand and was staring at Hansen. "That's something you have to understand, Arne, because if we don't have that we don't have anything. We're as bad as they are. We're gangsters."

Hansen lit his pipe. Neither Arne nor Niels said anything.

"We're going to have order," Hansen said again. "Order against their order. Planning against their planning. Preciseness against theirs. And all of it coming from one source."

"You," Arne said.

"Me."

"And if I say fuck you?"

"I'll turn you in."

"To them?"

"To them." Hansen waved the match out. "I'll tell them you killed Corporal Greff."

Arne rested his bandaged hand on his knee and leaned forward a little. "They'll want to know how you knew. Even if I never gave them anything, they'd want to know that."

"Then they'd take me," Hansen said. "And if I wasn't as good as you, if I couldn't keep my mouth shut about myself, then they'd have me." He puffed on the pipe. "It's simple. You two are the best I have. But I'd rather we lost you, both of you, me too—who the hell am I?—I'd rather it went that way soon, as soon as possible, if that's the way it has to go, because in the end it would be cheap, cheap and better. In the end, otherwise the whole thing's going to peter out, like sand running through fingers. They'll get all of us, one by one, twos, threes, and then there'd be nothing except what our people would remember and the Germans would let them nourish on that. So if you want your own show the way you've been having it, I'll give you to them now, and if you want to you can give me to them and then somebody who's left will gather the pieces together again and do it right."

Hansen lit his pipe again. "Sweden," he said. "For the duration. I can ship you both there. Then you wouldn't have problems."

Arne slowly raised his burned, bandaged hand and brought it down hard on the wooden arm of the couch. Niels winced; there was not a flicker in Arne's eyes.

My God, Hansen thought.

"No," Arne said. "Thanks."

"Niels?" Hansen asked presently.

Niels Rider took a deep breath and let it out. "I like it here, too."

Arne stood up and Hansen knew he had won. Not the fight, but the round. There was one thing else. He wondered whether to risk it.

"Another thing," he said to Arne. "Lili."

There was no change in Arne, except the thing lived in his eyes again.

My God, Hansen thought again, seeing why Arne Johansen was so good. "That girl of yours. What do you know about her?"

"What business is that of yours?" Arne asked.

"She's been seen going into Dagmar House. More than once."

Arne was silent again, and this time it was as though Hansen could see him enter where he went, the place behind, where he was alone and sustained. There was nothing in the face; he was where he couldn't be touched. And if he didn't return? If he refused? If he made his stand on the girl? To have got past everything else and have it break on that.

"It's her father," Arne said. "He's in a concentration camp in Norway. She keeps trying to find out about him."

Hansen nodded. I've said my lines, now get the hell off. "I'll get in touch."

He had so much to learn, he thought as he left the room. He hoped he was learning.

14.

MORTEN TORRES, head of the Jewish community in Copenhagen, was a celebrated international lawyer and a well-known figure in the city, and when he entered the office of the acting Foreign Minister in Christiansborg Palace he was greeted by the Minister's secretary with respect. He was informed the Minister was in a meeting but would see Mr. Torres as soon as possible.

Morten Torres, in his late sixties, a descendant of a Sephardic family that had fled from Spain in the fifteenth century, was a tall, erect man with a body so spare and trim he looked more like a retired army officer than a lawyer.

For this visit to the Foreign Minister, he was dressed somewhat more formally than usual, although not much. He wore a morning coat, a dark homburg, and he carried a cane. The cane was useful now but he had carried it before it had any practical purpose.

He sat now, his hands clasped over the fine morocco handle, and as the secretary had promised it was not very long before the Minister came to the door of the ante-room himself, his arms extended in welcome.

"My dear Mr. Torres, how very good of you to come to see me," the Foreign Minister said.

"How kind of you to see me, Mr. Minister. I know how busy you are."

The Minister, a courtly man with old-fashioned manners,

gripped Torres' hand, then transferred his hand to Torres' shoulder and guided him into his office. He indicated a chair quite distant from his desk and himself picked up another chair and set it next to Torres'.

"Now, shall I order some coffee, Morten?" he asked.

"Thank you, Henrik, but no."

The Minister went to his desk, picked up a humidor, returned to Torres. "They're real," he said. "One of the perquisites of the job."

Again Torres shook his head. "Henrik, something took place last night. I don't know what it means or whether it means anything. The Jewish Community Center was broken into and all the files were taken."

The Minister, in the act of replacing the humidor, turned slowly. "What kind of files?"

"The names and addresses of the Jews in Denmark."

The Minister walked back slowly and sat down. "Could anyone identify the perpetrators?"

"We have a caretaker there, an old man. He was bound and gagged. He said there were four or five men. All in dark suits. Germans."

The Minister nodded. "I will ask Dr. Best for an audience immediately. I will call you as soon as I learn anything."

Torres stood up. "Thank you."

The Minister accompanied Torres to the door. "How are things with you, Morten?"

"As usual."

"Have you heard anything from your son?"

"No."

Torres paused at the door. He had the desire to ask the Foreign Minister whether the raid on the files might be connected with steps to be taken against Jews. He decided it was a question he could not ask. It would give thought to the unthinkable. It would violate the laws that said Danes were Danes, no matter their faith. More than that, to ask the question would in some way seem like questioning the integrity of the State.

51

"Is there anything else?" the Minister asked.

"Nothing. Good day, Henrik, and thank you."

The Minister touched his arm, stopping him. "Morten, I shall look into this matter immediately."

Torres nodded, relieved that he had not asked the question. "Yes," he said.

He walked slowly through the wide corridors of the palace—which had been twice destroyed by fire and twice restored, each time exactly as it had been. There was tradition, strength—more, endurance—to the building, which had survived its own disasters and if need be would do so again.

He stepped out of the palace into the bright sunlight. He, Morten Torres, a Jew with a Spanish name, was a Dane. So were all the other Jews in the little Scandinavian kingdom. It was an insult to think otherwise, an insult to the Jews, but, more, an insult to the country.

He stood on the broad palace steps looking at the canal on which in better days small boats carried visitors through the different parts of the harbor, at the fishmongers' stands, the women with their historic vocabulary already gone for the day but their language, a symphony of profanity, still hovering in the air.

On the other side of the canal were fish restaurants, perhaps not quite as good as in normal times, but probably still quite as good as any in the world. There were young people strolling hand in hand. There was the hum of chatter, laughter. A young man passed by, whistling a tune.

His heart was at ease as he walked down the street toward his office. A German soldier, strolling off-duty along the canal, saw the distinguished elderly gentleman approaching and stepped aside to let him pass.

Morten Torres acknowledged the courtesy with a slight inclination of his head, swung his cane and continued on, secure in himself and his land.

15.

WHEN DR. STEPHAN MOLLER finished attending Arne Johansen he walked, slightly shaken from the experience, to one of the operating theaters, where his friend, Dr. Poul Klampmann, was performing complicated abdominal surgery. Dr. Moller had not had to ask the young man how his hand had been burned. Dr. Moller had seen that type of burn before. He had seen other examples of Gestapo techniques. He had seen them and had treated them as was required of him as a doctor and a Dane but he never wanted to know anything about them beyond what he had to know to minister to them. He asked no questions and he did the best he could, and when he was finished he was always uneasy that he had even in so small a way defied the German secret police.

His inner attitude toward the Germans and the occupation was no different from that of almost all the other Danes; but Dr. Moller was no opposer. He had once been subjected to an inquiry by the Gestapo. It was a routine matter, did not involve Dr. Moller personally, and had been conducted with some courtesy and limited to words. But Dr. Moller had never quite forgotten the experience.

In the operating theater he seated himself in the front row of the gallery, took off his glasses, wiped them, and then marveled as he had marveled before at Klampmann's skill. When the surgeon finished, he saw Moller and signaled to him to wait for him. After he had washed and changed, Klampmann joined his young colleague and the two men strolled through the beautiful, landscaped hospital grounds to their quarters for lunch.

They reached the doctors' and nurses' living area and paused in front of one of the dwellings. Klampmann, a deep-voiced, imposing man, repeated to Moller, "I assure you, Gerda would be delighted to have you join us."

Moller shook his head. "Thank you, Poul, but no."

"Look, you young idiot . . ." Klampmann started.

". . . You don't have a damned thing to eat but some sardines," a woman's voice interrupted.

Both men looked up. Gerda Klampmann was leaning from a fourth-story window.

"You come along with me," she said, imitating her husband's gruff voice. "Young man like you needs something to stick to his ribs."

Moller capitulated. "All right, but let me run over to my place first. I have some cigarettes."

Klampmann put his arm around Moller's back. "We have cigarettes but we don't have all day. I've got another operation after lunch."

The two men entered the building and walked up the four flights of stairs. Klampmann slapped his wife heartily on the rump for greeting and she in her turn kissed Moller on the cheek.

The table in the dining room was set with open-faced sandwiches, sausage, herring, bread, cold beer. There were three table settings.

"You knew I would surrender," Moller said.

Klampmann surveyed the table. "Minor advantages to marriage," he said.

"Continue," Gerda said with interest. She was a tall woman with a face that was plain and quite beautiful.

"No pretty nurses, none of that," Klampmann said to Moller. "You have to give up a few things—not really give them up if you're clever about it."

"Listen to the man," Gerda said. "He can't even do his own homework."

She went into the kitchen and Klampmann and Moller opened two bottles of beer. As they were filling their glasses, they heard the sound of a motor car coming up the

54

residential street. From the sound, they recognized it as an automobile operating on gasoline, which meant it was an ambulance or the Germans. Since the latter were unlikely, they wandered over to a window to see whom among them had taken ill.

What they saw was not one but two cars, and both of them the black cars of the Gestapo.

"What's that all about?" Klampmann said.

Moller backed away from the window instinctively, thinking in sudden unreasoned terror that it had to do with the angry youth with the burned hand. He looked around, wondering where to run, and then he saw the two cars drive past the Klampmann building and stop in front of the quarters assigned to the nurses and unmarried doctors. Now Moller was certain they had come for him.

Four men jumped out of each car. They carried submachine guns.

"Oh, Christ," Klampmann said.

"What is it?" Gerda called from the kitchen.

"Stay there," Klampmann said.

"What is it?"

"Just stay there." Klampmann stared down. "A clearing murder. This time for what?"

The Gestapomen ran to two buildings, including the one in which Moller lived. With the flats of their hands, they pushed groups of buttons at the same time. They backed away and, when the doors opened, they fired. It lasted only a few seconds and then they were back in their cars and gone.

Klampmann put down his beer glass and ran out of the apartment. Moller, after a moment, followed.

"What was that?" Gerda called out. "It sounded like shooting!"

Klampmann and Moller ran into the street. Doctors, doctors' wives, nurses, interns off-duty, were looking from windows, from other doorways. Children who had been playing in another street ran over to see what had happened.

55

Klampmann and Moller, soon joined by the others, examined the victims. There were seven dead, four women and three men, and two others wounded. The dead were sprawled and uncomposed. On the faces of some of them were the smiles they had ready for the friends they assumed were calling.

"Wanton," Klampmann said. "Utterly wanton."

Moller felt the old fear of being involved in any way with the Gestapo. He looked at the dead bodies of the capriciously slain. He took off his glasses and wiped them.

16.

"THE PUNITIVE MISSION of the State Police cannot be permitted to enter into the area of discussion, Mr. Minister."

The Foreign Minister's face remained diplomatically cool as he listened to Dr. Werner Best, the Nazi civil governor of Denmark. In the year or so that he had dealt with him, the Foreign Minister had come to know the petulant voice, the sallow face, the worried, nervous mouth and the pedantic, legal phraseology. Since the Foreign Minister had frequent occasions to deal with Dr. Best, he was also particularly aware of the huge picture of the Führer which hung on the wall behind the administrator's chair.

It was the picture taken with the dog. It was, Dr. Best had told the Minister frequently, his favorite picture of the Leader, and, some said, the Leader's favorite picture as well. Both Leader and dog stared off into distant space, their faces uplifted, their eyes clear, seeing things beyond the vision of ordinary folk. The Minister had never been able to make up his mind which profile was nobler.

Seeing Dr. Best as often as he did, it had come to tickle the Minister's fancy that Dr. Best felt the Führer was listening to every word spoken in that room and conducted himself accordingly. From time to time the Minister had caught Dr. Best twisting in his chair, casting his eyes upward at the two idealized faces.

"May one ask why not?" the Minister asked now.

"The State Secret Police is a personal extension of the Führer himself," Dr. Best replied.

"Even when the Führer extends himself to shoot down some innocent people at a hospital, Dr. Best?"

The governor rested his two hands on the desk, his ten fingers arched as though the desk was a piano he was about to start playing. "I must insist, Mr. Foreign Minister, the matter may not be discussed."

The Minister nodded. " 'As long as the police carries out the will of the leadership it is acting legally.' "

"I beg your pardon?"

"Your own words, Dr. Best. Your own words when you were administrative head of the Secret Police. The philosophy you bestowed upon the Gestapo."

Best smiled, flattered. "You appear to have performed some research upon me, Mr. Minister."

"One should know at least a little about the person who is governing one's country," the Minister said.

"Only temporarily, temporarily," Best said graciously. "Until things sort themselves out again." He placed the fingertips together. "Now, Mr. Foreign Minister, I would like to assure you that I regret the so-called clearing murders at Bispebjerg Hospital. My government regrets the necessity of such acts. We are a civilized people."

The Foreign Minister wondered, as he had often wondered, why the Germans were always most insistent about the state of their civilization when they were trying to explain away an atrocity.

"But you must understand, Mr. Minister, that this action on the part of the Secret Police was provoked by the irresponsible killing of a German soldier, a soldier on duty in front of this very building, and I also must point out that the Danish police have not as yet arrested the perpetrator of the crime."

"Nor has the Gestapo, despite its own useful methods," the Minister said drily. "And as for the 'irresponsible' killing of a German soldier, Dr. Best, it's unnecessary for me to remind you, I'm sure, that this German soldier opened fire without cause on a Danish cyclist, a janitor, the father of four children, and that after that this German soldier turned his gun upon everybody in sight."

"The cyclist was engaged in a criminal act."

"Taking two canteens of milk to his children?"

"A crime, Mr. Minister. Milk has been severely rationed."

"Only because you have so decided. And in any case, even by your terms, a very minor crime."

"Minor crime begets larger crime," Dr. Best said primly. "As for the rest, the soldier was simply protecting himself against attack from an angry mob."

"I see."

"Is there any other way I can be of service, Mr. Minister?"

"Yes. The other matter I spoke to you about."

Best broke into a broad smile. "As to that, I can give you total assurance. There is nothing to it."

"Why were the files stolen?"

"Routine, Mr. Minister. We're looking for saboteurs, nothing else." His wan face exuded sincerity. "This was a very little action and I give you my word it has nothing whatsoever to do with the Jewish question."

"I must remind your Excellency there is no Jewish question."

"Of course not," Dr. Best agreed. "Mr. Minister, I can give you categoric assurance there is no action being planned against the Jews."

17.

PETER HANSEN toyed with the small glass of aquavit at the long bar of the White Hart Inn just outside of Randers in Jutland. Standing next to him, leaning against the bar, was Rolf Lange, owner of the inn and leader of the largest resistance group in Jutland. On Hansen's other side, his hands clamped around a glass of beer, sat Dr. Lars Duul, a Danish pastor and one of Lange's chief assistants.

It was after three o'clock in the morning and except for the three men and Nina Lange, Rolf's wife, the bar was empty.

"If the Germans can insure the safety of those trains by putting Danish hostages aboard, then we're checkmated," Hansen said. He had already made the point several times, but he knew that he had in no way impressed Lange.

Lange, a broad-bodied bull of a man, emptied his glass of snaps, the glass looking like a thimble in his hand, and set the glass carefully on the bar. Nina Lange refilled the glass. Lange waited until she had put down the bottle and had resumed her position on the other side of the bar, her arms folded, before he said, "That's very easy for you to say, Hansen. You're not going to have to ride those trains."

"I may," Hansen said. "All of us may. All we have to do is get caught. Not even that. Just happen to be around when they need Danes." He wet his dry mouth with snaps. "It's got to be done."

Nina Lange, a deep-breasted, earthy peasant woman, took her eyes from Hansen and turned them to her husband.

"Who's going to do it?" Lange asked softly. "If we don't, who will?"

"I will," Hansen said.

He emptied his glass and pushed it toward Nina Lange. He had known how it was going to be and, like Arne Johansen, Lange had all the things up front on his side and, like Arne Johansen, Lange was battling for something beyond the question at hand, only for Lange the stakes were higher.

When Carl Haagen had been killed, Rolf Lange loomed as his natural successor. Lange was a powerful man in all ways, he was smart and he was successful. When Haagen's authority was passed on by council to Hansen, Lange took it as a personal offense. It was to settle the problem of Lange that Hansen had come to Jutland, and the issue now hung on the trains.

Lange lifted his head and roared. He slapped his hand on the bar several times. Hansen would not have been surprised to see the stout wood shatter.

"You?" Lange jeered. "Did you ever handle a plastic bomb?"

"Nor any other kind," Hansen said. He watched Nina Lange refill his glass.

"Do you know how?"

"I'll find out."

"He'll find out. Pastor, did you hear that?" Lange asked Duul over Hansen's head.

Duul, a big, bald man whose apple-cheeks made him look like a clean-shaven Santa Claus, nodded his head. "I heard him."

Lange leaned closer to Hansen so that Hansen could smell the aquavit and beer on his breath. "How to time them so you get some of the cars as well, not just the engine, so the engine passes over some of them without exploding them?"

"I'll find out," Hansen said. "You had to find out. Nobody is born knowing how to blow up a train."

Lange roared again. "Did you hear that, Pastor? Mr.

Hansen is a comedian. Mr. Hansen, do you know you could blow yourself up before you learn this simple thing."

"I've considered that."

"He's considered that, Nina," Lange said.

"You fool," Hansen said, staring straight ahead. "You bloody, God damned fool. God damn you, Lange, do you think I like this any better than you? But it has to be done."

"You won't have to do anything, Mr. Hansen," Nina Lange said.

"Who will, then?" Lange demanded to know.

"You. And the boys. And the pastor and all the others."

"You just heard what I said, Nina. Why would I do it?"

"Because he's right."

"Right, Nina?" Lange looked at his wife in astonishment. "Killing our own people?"

"If we have to. You know he's right, Rolf." To Hansen she said in the same quiet, rich voice, "Don't be angry with him, Mr. Hansen."

Lange jerked his head. He pounded the bar with a fist like a mallet. "What the hell do I care who he's angry with? Who the hell is he?"

Nina Lange clasped her arms around her magnificent breasts and raised her head. "My husband is the one who should be giving the orders, Mr. Hansen. To you. To all of us in Denmark. We all know that. But he isn't. But he'll do as you tell him."

"Don't speak for me!" Lange said furiously. "Don't speak to him as though I'm not here. I'm here and I speak for myself!" He turned his great head to Duul. "They've joined against me, Pastor. Both of them!"

"Mr. Hansen is right," Duul said slowly. His voice, even low, had the resonance of many years in the pulpit. "And Nina is right. You'd better do what he says, Rolf. You have no choice."

"What did you say, Lars?" Lange asked.

"I said you have no choice."

"My husband should be giving the orders, Mr. Hansen,"

Nina Lange said again. "He should have taken over after Carl Haagen."

Early the next morning, Hansen lay flat on his belly in the thick copse and watched Lange, Pastor Duul and Lange's three sons fix the bombs to the tracks. The wind blew hard from north Jutland. Hansen pulled his collar tighter.

The tracks were on the main line, running from the German border to the northern tip of Jutland, connecting with the ferries to Norway. The German troops fighting across the Skagerrak were largely fed and supplied and reinforced by that line, and the resistance from the very first had made the trains a prime objective. So much so that the Germans had counter-moved by grabbing handfuls of Danes, any Danes, anywhere, and putting them on the trains.

Duul rejoined Hansen first. He lay down alongside him, breathing hard.

Presently Hansen asked, "Why did you come over to my side, Pastor?"

"I know Lange," Duul said. "He's a Number Two. A doer. The best. But no more."

"You know Lange. But you don't know me," Hansen said.

"I knew Carl Haagen," Duul said.

Hansen watched the dark figures of Lange and his sons working on the tracks five hundred yards away. "The sabotage pastor. It always surprises me."

"Hitler hates God, too, Mr. Hansen," Duul said.

Presently Lange ran back from the tracks and threw himself alongside Hansen without saying a word. One by one, as they finished, the three sons, Kai, Palle and Alfe, seventeen, eighteen and twenty, joined them. No one spoke to Hansen.

In the distance to the south they heard the train whistle lamentingly across the open land, becoming part of the driving wind. Then they could feel the earth tremble.

They raised their heads as the train rounded a curve, and

Hansen looked at Lange's profile in the gray light, thick, heavy, angry, the lips now set hard, and he smelled the acrid smoke from the engine in the wind blowing in from the sea.

The train moved closer in the beginning dawn, moving, it seemed to Hansen, with painful slowness, the windows blacked out, the clatter and thrust of the engine, and the earth now shaking as though in impending quake, and then the locomotive lifted, intact, toylike, over an explosion that seemed not that loud, and then the other explosions followed, rapidly, like the firing of an automatic gun.

It happened very quickly, the cars hurtling, falling, buckling, the tracks twisted, and then the shouts and cries of the passengers, the flames starting. Rolf Lange said something to his sons, rose and rushed away. The boys followed, vanishing immediately in the trees. After a moment Hansen and Duul got up and hurried away.

The next day, working over production charts in the office of his Randers plant, the plant that gave him a legitimate reason to go to Randers, sensing the resentment of his own employees at what they considered his excessive zeal to aid the German effort, Hansen received an urgent telephone call from Pastor Duul. He left his office immediately.

He drove to the inn and walked past the bar, glancing at Nina Lange, who was behind it as usual, a newspaper with the report of the sabotage on the front page spread out before her, through a door, downstairs, to a wine cellar.

Lange, his youngest son, Kai, and Pastor Duul turned quickly to the door.

"Who asked you to come here?" Lange asked.

"I did," Duul said.

Hansen walked over to the German officer seated in a wooden chair, manacled hands in his lap. The officer wore the rank of major and his uniform was that of the regular army. He was about thirty-five, his unshaved face evenly featured, with wide, square jaws.

"Who is he?" Hansen asked.

"Who the hell do you think he is?" Lange asked. "The Little Mermaid?"

Kai Lange grinned.

"Where does he come from?" Hansen asked.

Lange didn't answer. His face turned sullen and intransigent.

"I said, where does he come from?" Hansen asked again.

"Why don't you ask him?" Lange said. "I hear you speak German like one of them."

"I was on the train," the officer said in very good Danish. "I escaped after the little accident." He saw Hansen look at the manacles. "These came with me."

"He says he's a prisoner, was a prisoner, that the Gestapo arrested him and were taking him back to Germany," Pastor Duul said.

"That's what he says," Kai Lange said. "I think he's a damned liar." Kai, along with his two brothers, was another Rolf, as burly and as solid, more newly minted, only that. "I think it's something they're trying to do, to find out about us."

"You mean we knew that you'd blow up this particular train and that I'd get away unhurt?" the officer asked politely.

"Don't be funny," Rolf Lange said. "I don't like German humor. They knew we'd blow up one train or another. It doesn't cost that much to have somebody like you aboard, and if you did get killed they have a lot more like you."

"Reasonable," the German agreed.

"Who are you?" Hansen asked.

"Major Helmut Boldt."

"Why were you under arrest?"

"He's already told us that, if he was under arrest," Lange said.

"Tell me," Hansen said.

"For Christ sake," Kai Lange said. "We're wasting time."

"Go on, Major," Hansen said.

"I'm a career officer in the Wehrmacht," Boldt said. "A

64

coding officer. I was stationed in Stavanger. I heard some of the SS men talking about a new method they had developed to make prisoners talk."

"They don't have enough ways," Lange said.

"It was a machine," Boldt said. "A sound machine of some kind that sent impulses, sound impulses, electric, I don't know exactly. But it slowly reduces human beings to vegetables. The longer the prisoners try to hold out, the more nothing they become. The prisoners know this. The machine half accomplishes its purpose before it is used." Boldt shrugged. "And usually after having learned all they want to know, the Gestapo goes right on and finishes the job. Zombies."

"What has all that to do with you?" Hansen asked.

"He says he protested," Lange said scornfully.

"I protested," Boldt said. "I was arrested by the Gestapo and ordered to be returned to Germany for trial before a court-martial. When you had your way with the train, I saw a chance to get away. Fortunately, I was picked up almost immediately by your underground."

"Fortunately?" Kai Lange repeated. "You may be wrong."

Lange moved closer. "How is it that you speak Danish so well?" he asked suddenly.

"Why were you looking for the underground?" Hansen asked the German.

"I want to trade."

"How?" Lange asked again. "You don't even have a German accent."

"What have you got to trade?" Hansen asked Boldt.

"The latest Wehrmacht code."

"For?"

"Sweden."

"Sweden means internment."

"Pleasantly. The Swedes are too civilized to be wicked."

"How long is the code operable?"

"The entire month of October. We are methodical. We change the code on the first of every month."

"A Vienna baby!" Lange bellowed. He pushed Hansen

away and struck Boldt across the face with such force the officer was knocked off the chair. Lange picked him up as though he weighed nothing and shook him violently. "A Vienna baby!"

"Put him down," Hansen said sharply.

"Where did you live here?" Lange shouted. "Who brought you up?"

"Rolf, put him down," Duul said.

Lange held the German for another moment and then he lowered him slowly onto the chair. Through it all, the German's expression never changed.

"Thank you, Pastor," he said to Duul. "Odd business you're in, isn't it?"

Lange backed away a few steps and pounded his fist into his hand. "I can remember it so clearly," he said gratingly. "You were all so hungry in Germany and Austria after the last war. Little children mustn't be made to suffer even if their parents were the enemy. Take our children, they begged, feed them, they'll starve." Lange walked closer to Boldt, who looked up at him calmly. "And so you came here and we fed you and you went to our schools with our Danish children and you learned our language and you must have been here a long time because you still speak it so well. And when we sent you home, you thanked us and told us you would never forget us and that one day you would return. And you returned, you Nazi prick. You have returned, haven't you?"

Lange turned away. His face was heavy.

Hansen felt something in him reaching out to the big man. He wanted to tell him that he understood him, that he regretted what he had to do to him and his authority.

"How many people must have died on that train," Lange said. "Our own people. And you come away alive."

The room was silent and then Kai Lange said, "Kill him. Kill the bastard now."

"I'm a soldier," Boldt said evenly. "I didn't choose my assignment. It was just in the routine way I was assigned to Norway. It could have been anywhere."

"Denmark," Lange said.

"If I had told them I could speak Danish, it most certainly would have been Denmark," Boldt said.

"Give me the code," Hansen said.

Lange turned swiftly on him. His fists clenched and his face got dangerous.

"First, your parole on the bargain," Boldt said to Hansen.

"I could take the code from you," Hansen said.

"It's not written down."

"We could still take it," Lange said.

"I could give you my parole and then have you shot," Hansen said.

"You could. You could and you probably should," Boldt said. "But you won't."

"You have my parole."

"And them?" Boldt asked.

"They'll do nothing to harm you," Hansen said. He turned to the Langes, father and son.

Kai looked questioningly at his father, whose lips worked against themselves. Then Rolf Lange asked, "How do you know the code will be legitimate? What if it's a fake?" He saw the expression change on Hansen's face. "God damn it, Hansen, we're both trying to accomplish the same thing!"

18.

GEORG SIEBERT was putting his papers into his attaché case, trying to get away from Dagmar House in time to join his wife for a dinner party, hoping he could leave the party early to catch up on his work, when the call came from Dr. Best. Siebert snapped the case shut, told his secretary to call his wife and say he would be late. Late, he thought, walking to Best's office. If Best was in one of his moods it would be never.

When he entered his chief's office and saw Dr. Best staring at the picture on the wall, he knew. No dinner.

"Come in, Georg, come in," Best said, without turning around.

The tone in Best's voice confirmed Siebert's worst fears. Best, he knew from experience, was soul-searching again.

"I never meant it to work out this way," Best said moodily.

Siebert was used to his superior's habit of approaching a subject crabwise and he knew the quickest way to find out what this was all about was to keep silent.

Best swung around and Siebert was startled to see that he was on the verge of tears. This was a bad one.

Best struck the desk. "But you know how the Führer is about Jews," he said.

Siebert sat down. "What about the Jews?"

"Here, in Denmark."

"I've always understood that was not one of our concerns."

Best twisted around slightly so that he could again look at the picture. "You know how often I urged Berlin to ignore the Jews here—forget them, forget them, I told Himmler, forget them. There are only a few thousand of them here, minding their own business, forget about them. Things are peaceful here. Let them remain that way. I kept urging that, Georg, as God is my witness."

"I've seen copies of your communications to Berlin," Siebert said.

Best turned back quickly. "Of course you have, Georg. You know I'm telling the truth." He became silent. "Jews. The word itself is like a red-hot needle to the Führer. Simply for him to hear it. . . ." Best covered his face with his hands. "But I never thought it would turn out this way." He looked at Siebert. "You'll agree with me, Georg,

I know you will; my thinking was sound; listen to me, with things the way they are all over, North Africa, Russia, the Allied bombings, I thought this would be the perfect time to end the Jewish problem here once and for all. You would think so, wouldn't you?"

"What happened, Dr. Best?"

"It was the perfect time, I thought, to put the situation to rest. Ten days ago I sent word to the Führer. I advised him that if he were planning any action against the Danish Jews now was the time, or else to put the entire matter aside, until at least after the end of the war. I was certain he would take no steps now, with all else that is occupying his mind. I felt it would close the book, for the time being at least. Wouldn't you have thought that?"

"I think I would have advised you otherwise," Siebert said quietly. "I think I would have suggested your reasoning might prove too subtle. But you have not as yet told me the result." Though by now, of course, he knew.

"My intentions were of the highest, Georg."

"But the ingeniousness of your tactic escaped the Führer."

Best nodded heavily. "He has issued the order. The evacuation and resettlement of every Jew in Denmark. He is sending two ships and a special Gestapo Kommando." A shadow of fear crossed Best's face. "As though he didn't trust us to do the job ourselves."

Whatever reply Siebert would have made never was uttered. The door was flung open. A thick-set officer whose field-gray trousers wore the red stripes of a general officer strode into the room. He looked at Best with consummate contempt. "You damned idiot!"

The voice belonged to the parade ground and in an enclosed room could shatter glass. Siebert, who had stood up when the general entered the room, now tactfully closed the door.

"General von Kobe," Best said, rising slowly. "This is an unexpected honor."

He said it calmly and with the faintest touch of sarcasm

and Siebert thought, with the mild pride of a dedicated civilian, that his chief had managed that quite well.

For Generaloberst Eugen von Kobe was an elemental force. He was almost too true. He could have been invented by Hollywood if he were not in fact a genuine East Prussian junker, raised on blood and iron and stone. A shaved head sat on a barrel-chested body with only the hint of a neck to separate them. The jaws bulged from years of clamping them shut, the mouth was a slash, the voice addressed the world as though the world were a German regiment.

The general, whose face, florid by nature, now was empurpled by rage, walked to the desk. He studied Best for a moment as though he was looking at something in the zoo. "You swine-dog. You should be shot."

Best's shoulders twitched. "General von Kobe, I must remind you . . ."

"Remind me shit! You stupid fool!"

Siebert, in a far part of the room, wished he had thought quickly enough to slip through the door while he was shutting it. He had no overpowering love for Dr. Best, but this was something he could have easily done without.

"Now, Best, just answer me," von Kobe ordered. "Is it true? Are you going to start trouble here with the Jews? Don't give me any of your damned long-winded explanations. Just answer me yes or no."

Best resumed his seat, arched his hands into a steeple. "The Führer has ordered that Jews in Denmark be regulated by the same laws that apply to Jews everywhere in the Reich."

"Because you demanded it, you lap-dog!"

Best's voice rose in a sudden, shrill scream. "General, I'll thank you . . ."

"You'll thank me to pull your balls out of the fire!" von Kobe rasped. "I know all about you, Best. You started as a lawyer and they should have shot you for that right off. Then you decided you'd look pretty in a uniform but you didn't have the guts to get into a real one. No, it was the SS. Instant officers for the scum of Germany."

70

Best's sallow face was taking on a tinge of green, and once again Siebert wished he were somewhere else.

"General von Kobe . . ." Best started.

"In your pretty black uniforms with the pretty little daggers and your silly secret oaths by moonlight. Brave enough to fight old Jews and shove children into ovens. But when it comes to fighting the enemy, the real enemy with guns, the enemy that can fight back, then you all find you have business somewhere else."

"The Waffen SS has fought bravely," Best said.

"Can't get the fancy uniforms dirty," von Kobe said as though Best had not spoken. "The dirty work is for the army, the soldiers, the poor, stupid, simple soldiers who are dumb enough to believe it's an honor to fight for their country. Well, Dr. Best, I don't give a damn about Jews. I don't give a damn about you and the rest of the SS cunts. The only thing that concerns me is this country, Denmark, and how to defend it against the enemy. This country and my men. Can you understand that or is it too simple?"

"Have you quite finished, General?" Best asked.

There was something in Best's voice that caught Siebert's attention. It was a strength and Siebert wondered where it came from. It took something to pose that against von Kobe and now Siebert no longer was sorry he was there.

"No uprisings," von Kobe said. "No revolts, no more sabotage than what I have to cope with now, no new problems, no troubles with the Danes or the Jews or anyone else. I don't have your tricky lawyer's mind, Best, but I'll tell you this: my men are all facing the sea and I won't have their backs exposed to anything." He straightened. His shoulders snapped back. "Send word to Himmler. Tell him to cancel the orders."

He started out of the room. Siebert moved to open the door. "I'm afraid that is impossible," Best said.

Siebert caught it again.

Von Kobe paused and turned. "I gave you an order, Best. And in case you're so panicked by Jews that you've lost your memory, I command in Denmark."

71

"I am afraid that is no longer correct, General," Best said.

Von Kobe looked at Best silently. He did not appear surprised. Best picked up a piece of paper and studied it for a moment with deliberation. Siebert had his answer now.

"The Führer has issued a new directive," Best said. "Denmark has now reverted to civil authority. I am in command."

He held out the piece of paper. Von Kobe disregarded it, walked to a chair, sat down.

"Because you gave him his Jews," he said.

"I am not required to discuss it," Best said.

Von Kobe looked at Siebert and seemed to see him for the first time. "What a time we live in." He took a silver cigarette case from his pocket, selected a cigarette, accepted a light from Siebert. "Who are you?"

"Georg Siebert, sir."

"What do you do?"

"He is one of my aides," Best said. "He is in charge of shipping."

"To risk an entire country," von Kobe said through the cigarette smoke. "To jeopardize the war because of a few thousand Jews." He looked at the glowing tip of his cigarette. "You make your battle plan and you dispose your men and you pray to God they will be sufficient for the task, brave enough, lucky enough.... And then an insignificant prick who thinks only of his own skin, his own career, becomes an enemy to his country and tries to destroy everything you have done."

"General von Kobe, my orders to you . . ." Best said.

"Not one German soldier, Best, not one," von Kobe said in a distant voice. "If you are determined to hunt down innocent human beings, do so. But not one of my soldiers, Best. I will not permit you to degrade honorable men in an honorable profession."

"You will obey my orders, General," Best said.

"Dragging people out of bed in the middle of the night, that's a Gestapo speciality, Best. Soldiers don't know how to do that. Not part of their training. They're just soldiers, not bloodhounds. All they are prepared to do is to die for their country. I know by your standards that's not very much, but I'm afraid that's the best they can manage."

He mashed out the cigarette and rose to his feet. He pulled down his uniform and straightened his back.

"And when you send your sniveling little report to Berlin," he said quietly, "put it down exactly as I said it: not one German soldier. And if they want to remove me from my command, they can send someone to arrest me—from the Gestapo." He laughed harshly. "That's my little joke, Dr. Best."

After von Kobe left the room, it seemed very still. Siebert wondered how he could leave gracefully.

"Georg," Best said. His face was taut but not from shame. There was a glow of elation in his eyes.

"Yes, sir," Siebert said.

"September thirtieth."

"Is that the day?"

"It's some kind of Jewish holiday, the New Year or something. The Jews will either be in their synagogue or at home."

"Very clever," Siebert said.

"It makes it simpler all round. That's why that day was chosen."

When Dr. Best was alone, he turned to the picture. It now was quite dark in the room but he did not turn on his desk lamp and in the twilight the face was almost obscured.

Being a lawyer and a German, or perhaps a German and a lawyer, Dr. Best believed in orderliness and finality. Of all the things von Kobe had said, one remained with him. The insults, the contempt, that was part of von Kobe's Prussian nature and training. The villification at the end— well, the general had been outmaneuvered and defeated, so bitterness was understandable.

But had von Kobe been correct when he accused Best of doing what he had done to save himself?

73

It was true that until Best had sent the communication there had been difficulties with Hitler. The August strikes, the resignation of the Danish government, had greatly disturbed the Führer and had required that martial law be imposed, the supreme authority given to von Kobe. And there were those who charged Best with responsibility for the unrest because he had the authority before.

But had his position been precarious? Had he given the Führer his Jews, as von Kobe put it, to retrieve that authority? Was he deluding himself when he told himself he had had only the welfare of the Jews for motivation?

When he left his office much later that evening, his hours of introspection had not provided him with the answer he sought but he had come to understand something else. He had come to understand that he had lived for so long in a world of distortion and lies, a world he had helped create and define, he had committed himself so often to dissimulation and deviousness and the changing of even the meaning of words, that words had finally come to lose meaning for him, and, as the final station of the process, he had lost whatever had remained of any talent for truth.

There was no clarity any more, no illumination, nothing but the murk of impure hours. He would never know why he had done what he had done, and, if he were still capable of bearing burdens, he would have to bear that.

19.

SITTING IN THE DARKNESS on the bench at Langelinie, Georg Siebert looked like a statue, left unfinished by the sculptor to suggest something more primitive than today, tonight, here, now.

Why was it, Hansen thought, that big men, really big men, seemed to belong to another time? "Why me?" he asked again. "Why tell me?"

"Even the alteration of the language," Siebert said, his hands gripped, staring at the sea, at the dark outlines of the ships tied up along the long dock. "Did you know, Mr. Hansen, we have evolved something we have named the 'language rule' by means of which new meanings are given to words? We have invented a lie and have presented it with a title."

"You aren't answering me," Hansen said.

"I am, Mr. Hansen, and it is not easy." The hands writhed like fat white doves. "I am not only answering you but I am trying to answer myself. I am a German, Mr. Hansen, and a trusted official of my government."

The slapping of the water against the dock held a sound of protest. Here in the Sound, the sea was not open, Sweden was just a few miles away; it was locked, land water, but it was water and it came from the sea, and not too far away it was free of the embrace of land and what men had done on the land.

"We play etymological games," Siebert said. "We speak in code. We never talk of slaying, killing, murder. We do not even use the more literary expressions—extermination, genocide. No, we refer to it as evacuation, resettlement, even that masterpiece of euphemism, 'special treatment.' Special treatment, Mr. Hansen. That was how Dr. Best spoke of it tonight, the evacuation and resettlement of those people. Even Dr. Best who wrote a primer for torture that is still being used by the Gestapo—instant knowledge so that any German country policeman can overnight become an expert interrogator for the Gestapo—even Dr. Best can't talk about shipping Jews to their death."

Siebert stood up suddenly as though the turmoil in his mind was too violent to be contained. He started to walk. Hansen followed at his side.

"It is something new, isn't it, Mr. Hansen? Not to be able to face the reality of words. To alter the act by altering the word describing it? To be able to work it out in some complicated German way that we are not killing anybody, no one at all, but simply changing their address?" He paused and watched laborers unload a freighter.

"You speak about your facility for changing the meaning of words, Mr. Siebert," Hansen said. "I have to keep remembering that. There's a hell of a lot else I have to keep remembering, but you've given me that now."

Siebert nodded. "Naturally. I expected this."

"Have you seen the latest work sheets?" Hansen asked coldly.

"No."

"I believe we've raised production three and one half per cent since our last meeting."

"God in heaven!" Siebert exploded. He controlled himself. "I understand, Mr. Hansen." He turned swiftly to Hansen, his vast body suddenly unencumbered. "I understand and you must understand. You must listen and believe. I have assumed a certain risk."

"That's just it, Mr. Siebert," Hansen said. "That risk. An officer of the German Consulate giving out a warning that the Jews are going to be rounded up and shipped to concentration camps. That's the whole point. What you said about—what did you call it?—the 'language rule,' that's interesting, Mr. Siebert. It's more than that. It's fascinating. But the thing is that anybody else who wanted to could have told me that, anybody from your side, for whatever reason they thought good. Best could have told me about it, Buhle, Greiner. Why does that mean I should trust you? And who am I to wonder about trusting anybody? I'm a business man, Mr. Siebert."

Siebert resumed walking. "I don't know." He shook his head slowly. "I wish I had a plain, simple, understandable reason, reasonable to me before you. I wish I could say that my conscience bothered me and let it go at that, but why hasn't it bothered me before? I know what's going on in the Reich and I've known it for some time and I've been able to live with it, live quite easily with it, and I've been even

76

able to avoid the truth that I lived with it only because I'm not there but here, and I don't see it, the worst of it. But I work for that government, Mr. Hansen, and I'm part of it, all of it, just the same as the business men who make the gas for the chambers. I don't know why I had to tell some-one, but I had to tell someone."

"Then you started at the wrong end, Mr. Siebert," Han-sen said. He felt suddenly clammy. The sea, the night? "You should have gone to Berlin." He looked closely at Siebert. "All right, Siebert, never mind why. Just give me the other one. Why me?"

"I've been seen with you before. It would not appear unusual."

"I believe that much."

"We've had dealings. You're someone I know."

"We've done business," Hansen said evenly. "I've had occasion to point that out before. You don't know me at all."

"God in heaven," Siebert said again.

They walked in silence until they came to the statue of the Little Mermaid. Siebert paused and looked at the figure, now in the night seeming just fresh from the water or ready to enter it.

"I read a report from Berlin recently," Siebert said. "About salvaging the hair from people sent into the ovens and gas chambers. Instructions to the last letter. Women's hair is to be used for slippers for submarine crews and employees of the Reich railways. Don't ask me why those particular two groups were selected to be honored. Men's hair may be used only if it reaches the length of twenty millimeters. Probably something to do with the machines that manufacture the slippers. It doesn't matter much, of course. The hair wouldn't do the poor devils much good after they were dead. But there was something else. There was a specific schedule for the length of time it must take to process people. 'Process,' Mr. Hansen."

"Language rule?"

"Language rule. The instructions were explicit. The

schedule must be kept. But they specify that five additional minutes are to be allowed for the processing of women with long hair."

"Naturally," Hansen said. "A hair cut."

"For some reason I cannot explain, that intrigues me, Mr. Hansen," Siebert said. "I think other people might have found a use for human hair, probably have, probably the same use. But only Germans could have worked on a schedule allowing for those five extra minutes." Siebert stared at the statue. "You must try to do something, Mr. Hansen. Warn somebody."

"You still haven't convinced me that I should trust you," Hansen said.

"No reason."

"You bother me."

"That is not my intention."

"It's simpler to think of all Germans as being the same."

"And Danes? And Jews? You've been paying attention to our Leader, Mr. Hansen."

Siebert walked away. Hansen watched him disappear in the night. It started to drizzle. He turned up his collar.

20.

As HANSEN APPROACHED his car parked near Langelinie, he saw a man standing by it, and as he got closer he saw the man was in uniform. He felt it again in his stomach. Siebert and now the Gestapo. He turned quietly and started back in the direction from which he had come.

He heard Erik Melchior's dry voice. "Don't run away, Peter. I won't bite."

78

Hansen stopped short, feeling the beating in his heart. He turned again and walked slowly to the car. Melchior was examining the vehicle casually, a policeman's inspection.

"You're parked illegally," Melchior said.

"Giving me a citation?"

"For clairvoyancy. For prognostication. Beyond the call of duty."

"Then you've heard something?"

"Are you that good at the races?"

"What have you heard?"

"Something."

Melchior turned an old and knowing face. And even in the night Hansen could see the tired amusement in the policeman's eyes.

"Is it true?" Hansen asked.

"What did your friend just tell you?"

"A roundup. Total action. On the Jewish New Year."

Melchior nodded.

"Then it's true?" Hansen asked.

"It could be. Let's say it wouldn't be out of character."

Hansen rubbed his face. He leaned against his car. "Ever since he started talking to me, I've been wondering. All kinds of things. It didn't make sense, coming from a German, a Nazi government official. I kept trying to figure out what kind of complicated scheme it might be. But it might be just the simple truth."

"What are you going to do, Peter?"

"I have to warn somebody. I can't sit on this. You can tell me who. You can come with me in case he has the same doubts that I have."

"And I," Melchoir said.

"But you have heard the same thing."

"That could be part of the scheme, couldn't it, if it is some roundabout Gestapo plot? But one thing we know, the Gestapo never bothered before. They just acted. We know something else."

Hansen looked at him sharply.

"If it is true," Melchior said, "then they've pulled the

rug out from under you. Take a look at your excuse box, Peter. You'll find it's empty now."

"You won't be able to stay on the job. They'll be looking for you."

"Eventually. But it'll take a little time. I can see how excited you are. It warms me." Melchior smiled peacefully. "In any case, I'm going to be spared one thing. You're not going to tell me you're happy to have me aboard."

21.

SEVERAL SCORE of pious worshippers were waiting to begin the Selichot service when Rabbi Bent Rasmussen entered the Copenhagen synagogue just after six o'clock on the morning of that September twenty-ninth. The men were in the main part of the synagogue, which had been consecrated exactly one hundred years before. There were a dozen or more women in the balcony, separated from the men, as was required in the Orthodox congregation.

These were to be prayers of penance, asking divine forgiveness for sins, and they were especially meaningful, for sundown of that day would see the commencement of Rosh Hashanah, the New Year.

The men, old and young, were in prayer shawls, fringed with silk, and black skull caps. The cantor was waiting at the reading table near the Menorah. The great chapel, painted in white and gold, with high, austere mahogany pews, breathed an air of freshness and purity in the early morning.

The men looked at their watches as the tall, straight-backed rabbi walked down the center aisle. They were surprised at his tardiness. Few of them noticed that Captain

Erik Melchior, in civilian clothes, arrived with the rabbi and remained at the rear of the chapel. The congregation was even more surprised when Rabbi Rasmussen walked past his own private pew and halfway up the steps and faced them in his ordinary street clothes, a black homburg on his head.

The rabbi raised his hand. He said, "There will be no service this morning."

Incredulous murmuring broke out in the great room.

Rabbi Rasmussen raised his hand again. "A short while ago I was given some information," Rasmussen said. He was a man in his early forties, clean-shaven, with a strong, purposeful face and penetrating eyes.

"Important information," he continued, "that I must in conscience pass on to you. I have received word that the Germans are planning an action against all persons of our faith . . ."

The sounds in the chapel rose again, this time to a higher pitch. But on the faces of many there no longer was surprise.

". . . to round up all Jews and ship them to concentration camps," Rasmussen went on. His eyes lighted on Morten Torres. The thin, ascetic face of the community leader was impassive. "I have been informed that they have chosen tomorrow for this action because they know it is a holy day for us and that Jews will either be here or at their homes."

Now there was silence in the synagogue and then a voice cried out, "What shall we do, Rabbi?"

Rasmussen recognized the voice as that belonging to Mendel Cohen, a German refugee from the first days of Hitlerism who had lost his parents early to the gas chambers. He knew the question would come and it was fitting that it come from Mendel Cohen, to whom the concentration camps were not something in another country.

And what should he answer Mendel Cohen, and the others? Standing there on the steps, the cantor looking down at him, the congregation facing him, the women leaning over the guard wall of the balcony, Rabbi Rasmussen again was assaulted by the memory of Hansen's doubts. Hansen had no choice but to relay the warning, of course, but he had reservations, serious reservations, and he had communicated these to the rabbi. Hansen had his own conflict, ambivalence toward Georg Siebert, confusion. Melchior's convictions were no stronger.

He, the rabbi, had no alternative either. The word had to be passed on. But what would happen? Panic? How many suicides? And what could happen with eight thousand people in the twenty-four hours left to them, even if they believed and wanted to act and it was true? And what if it were a Nazi trick of some kind after all?

"What shall we do. Rabbi?" Cohen asked again.

The question was taken up by others—Rasmussen held up his hand.

"We must move very quickly," he said, his eyes still on the unyielding face of Morten Torres. "We must warn all our relatives, friends. By tomorrow the Jews of Denmark must be in hiding."

"Hiding? Where will we hide?"

Rasmussen recognized that voice, too. It belonged to Ove Jacobsen, who owned a clothing shop in the city. It was a classic Jewish voice of a kind, half-amused, half-cynical, a voice that belonged to survivors. Rasmussen remembered that Jacobsen's grandfather had settled in Denmark in the middle of the last century. He remembered this because Jacobsen always maintained, in a half-joking way, that Denmark was an illusion, a brief dream between flights. Time has caught up with you, the rabbi thought. It has taken almost a hundred years, but it has caught up.

"We must call upon our friends," Rasmussen said.

"Our friends?" Jacobsen asked. "At a time like this, does a Jew have friends?"

"With God's help, our friends will still be our friends," the rabbi said, wondering if it were true.

"Christians defy Nazis for Jews?" Jacobsen shook his head.

"Why doesn't Mr. Torres speak?" someone asked.

"Yes, Mr. Torres. Advise us what to do."

"Yes," Rabbi Rasmussen said quietly. "Mr. Torres, tell us what we can do."

Erik Melchior walked down the aisle and stopped at the row in which Torres was seated. "Yes, Mr. Torres, tell us, and tell us why you refused to believe this warning brought to us by a good Dane, and why you refused to do anything about it."

The voices rose again and then stopped abruptly as Torres said in a low voice that carried through the chapel, "Because it is a lie." He gripped the head of his cane. "A lie delivered by a Nazi."

The voices rose to their loudest. The women leaned over farther.

"I have been assured by the Foreign Minister that Jews in Denmark will not be molested," Torres said in the same quiet, convincing voice. "I prefer to believe the word of our government. Why should a German Nazi warn Jews?"

"You're a fool," Melchior said.

"Who was this German?" Torres said, turning his head toward Melchior. It was as though he had a witness on the stand.

"You know I can't tell you," Captain Melchior said. "Do you believe he should be repaid by making his name public?"

"Well, well," Ove Jacobsen said. He nodded slowly, a short, plump man with a round, quizzical face. "The rabbi and the police captain say it is so. The head of the Jewish community says it's not so. What is a poor, simple little Jew like me to believe?"

"We are Danes," Torres said. "We are Danes and our government will not permit any measures to be taken against any of its people."

"True," Jacobsen said. "I believe you, Mr. Torres. Only, unfortunately, it happens that at the moment there is no Danish government."

"There is the King," Torres said in a quiet voice.

The relief could be felt. That word, the "King."

83

"The King once entered this synagogue," Torres said. "For the first time in history. And he gave his word that nothing would ever happen to us."

"That's true," a man said. "I was here when he said it."

Ove Jacobsen nodded soberly. "Yes, the King, may God look after him. There is the King, the most wonderful man in Denmark, and our friend. But Mr. Torres, the King is a prisoner of war himself. He has said that publicly. He is a prisoner in his palace, surrounded by German soldiers. The King's soul is filled with light, Mr. Torres, but the King is helpless."

"I do not believe the Germans would dare," Torres said.

"Germans? Dare?" Jacobsen raised his eyes to the heavens. "Then you believe this is only a rumor the rabbi is passing on and that we should forget it and get about the business of saying prayers?"

"We are Danes," Torres repeated in a whisper.

"We were Germans!" Mendel Cohen said, terror behind his voice. Eyes turned to him, a slight man with a permanent limp, the result of Gestapo questioning years before. "We thought the Germans believed that, too. Pogroms? Killings? That was in barbaric places, Russia, Poland, Rumania. Not in our Germany. Germany was a civilized country and we were Germans. Yes, we knew about the fate of our fellow Jews in the east, but we did nothing about it because we were happy and proud to be Germans and we didn't want to do anything to suggest to Germans we were anything else." He was silent for a moment. "I have often thought that Hitler is God's punishment for our selfishness, our smugness, our indifference."

There was no sound in the synagogue when he finished. Then Melchior asked, "Well, Torres, what do you have to say to that?"

"I have considered this possibility," Torres said at last. "I have studied it from all sides."

"This isn't a court case," Melchior said.

"Yes, in a way it is, Captain Melchior. I've weighed the evidence, what was told to me by the Foreign Minister after he spoke to Dr. Best, what has been told to all of us by the King, the way the Germans have conducted themselves here for almost four years. Against all this is a warning from a nameless German to an unimportant Dane." He shook his head gravely. "Gentlemen, I would give that case to a jury in a moment, without hesitation, confident of the verdict."

"We're not dealing with a jury, Torres," Melchior said. "We're talking about lives. People. Human beings."

"I've thought beyond that, Captain Melchior," Torres said. "I have asked myself, is it not possible that the Germans themselves are spreading this rumor to cause us to do something violent, rash, something that would give them the excuse to bring down upon our heads this very thing?"

"He's right," a man said. "Mr. Torres is a brilliant man."

"He's right except for one thing," Melchior said, remembering Hansen and the sea air at Langelinie the night before. "The Nazis never bothered about inventing an excuse before. Why now?"

"Because of our country," Torres said with quiet pride. "Our country and our government and our King. Perhaps this is a time they feel they need provocation." He leaned upon his walking stick and closed his eyes for a moment. "But I will tell you something else. I could be quite wrong about all this. It may very well be that the Nazis are planning an action against us and that everything you have heard is authentic, even to the unlikely extreme of a humane German Nazi. But even if it all were true, then I still say we must not run, we must not abandon our little country in its distress. And if the Nazis want to find me, then they shall find me, and if they kill me, they will kill a Dane."

Torres' words and manner were impressive. Even Melchior was silent.

Then Ove Jacobsen shook his head. "To die as a Dane? A very nice thought, Mr. Torres. Only I don't believe the Nazis would extend the honor. I think when the time comes, you will be in the eyes of the SS men just another Jew, a tall, skinny Jew, and the fact that your family has been speaking Danish for five hundred years will make no difference at all."

"He's right," Mendel Cohen said, the years, the old thoughts, the fears returning at last with tired fatality. "To Nazis we're Jews, no matter where they find us." The lines of remembered pain were carved on the thin face. "You say, Mr. Torres, whether the Germans arrest us or not is not the important thing. You're right, but not for the reasons you give. It really does not matter whether they plan to round us up now or later. Because where can we go? Where can we hide? And if by some miracle of God we could escape to another country, what good would that do? They would catch up. Sooner or later they will occupy that country, too."

Torres' lips tightened and he spoke with uncharacteristic passion. "Then die of conviction, not resignation."

"I'll tell you something, Mr. Torres," Jacobsen said. "Death is death."

Torres rose and walked to the aisle. He paused there for a moment, resting on his cane. "Listen to the rabbi," he said. "If you go, go with God."

He walked slowly up the aisle and out of the synagogue.

22.

A LITTLE LATER on the same morning, Peter Hansen was finishing breakfast with his wife, Kate, in their home in Charlottenlund, a fashionable suburb to the north of Copenhagen. Lise, their nine-year-old daughter, had gulped down her breakfast, late for school as usual, and had fled.

Kate Hansen was not a beautiful woman in the ordinary

sense. Her nose was too strong, her mouth too wide, her eyes set far apart. The bone structure, the planes of her cheeks, showed breeding. It was not the face that appears in fashion magazines but perhaps it was something beyond that. It was the face of a woman just turned thirty, a complete woman, a woman who normally had a splendid, sensual body to go along with the face. At this moment, she was very much pregnant, the baby due at any time, and while this condition disguised the lines of the body it also, with its special alchemy, gave the skin and the eyes and the full lips a quality that was rich and luminous and abundant.

The breakfast had passed in silence, as was occurring more and more these days. Hansen ate abstractedly. She watched him finish his coffee, wipe his lips, take out his pipe and pouch.

"You haven't answered me," she said.

He looked across the table. "I'm sorry, Kate."

"You didn't even hear me."

"I'm really sorry." He got up and walked around the table and kissed her on the neck. It started as a perfunctory, apologizing-type kiss but quickly turned into the real thing. Hansen loved the smell of her skin and he pressed his lips to it. "What did you ask me?" he said, as he straightened.

"Nothing important," she said. The kiss meant something else to her. It meant their times together, suspended for the moment by the squirming, kicking thing in her belly. It meant she was short-changing him.

He started for the door. She followed him with her eyes, thinking that another time he would have insisted on her repeating whatever it was she had said.

"Peter!" she called out.

He paused. "Yes."

"Doesn't anything matter any more?" she asked, watching his fingers work the tobacco into the pipe.

"Matter? What do you mean?"

"Nothing. I'm being pregnant-silly."

"You have a right to that," he smiled.

She returned the smile. It was as though a light was turned on her face. "When will you be home for dinner?" "I'm not sure. I'll telephone."

He waggled the stem of the pipe at her and then she heard the door close and a few moments later she heard the car back out of the garage and turn down the street. She poured herself another cup of coffee, remembered that Dr. Hurwitz had told her to cut down until after the child was born, started to push the cup away, remembered it wasn't real coffee anyway, or very little of it was, and she sipped it and wished she could have real coffee and a real cigarette. She shook her head. She wasn't going to have that kind of day.

Peter Hansen drove into Copenhagen to an office building just off Frederiksborgade. He went into the building and walked down the hall to a door marked DENTAL CLINIC. He opened the door and entered. A woman receptionist looked up, pressed a button under her desk. He went past the receptionist, turned the knob on a heavy, thick wooden door, entered an inner room.

In this room, fully equipped for dental work, five men were operating a small printing press, turning out the daily edition of one of the underground papers.

The foreman, a man named Andersen, a jockey-sized foreman in the composing room of a regular Copenhagen newspaper, wiped his hands on a rag, picked up the top sheet from a stack of papers, held it out to Hansen. Hansen ran his eyes over it rapidly, nodded his approval.

"Gunnar's ready to run it down to the airport," Andersen said.

Hansen removed a small piece of microfilm from his pocket and fixed it to the newspaper with adhesive tape. He folded the paper carefully, protecting the film. "This is important," he said to the youth, Gunnar. "If anything goes wrong get rid of it."

The microfilm, with the German code supplied by Major Helmut Boldt, would be transported in the hollow chock, delivered to the British within fifteen minutes after arrival in Stockholm, and, if all went well, would be relayed to London immediately. A yes or no would be returned in code on a BBC broadcast. In Hansen's pocket was a second microfilm with Boldt's code. This would be affixed to the underpart of a certain dray being sent with other drays to Sweden to pick up supplies for the Germans. That week, it was the fourth dray in line on the little shuttle boat that would be inspected for messages by the agent in Sweden.

Gunnar set out immediately on his bicycle, the newspaper and film rolled and slipped into the bicycle pump. The remaining four men returned to their work. Hansen sat down, lit his pipe, crooked his arm to glance at his watch, and presently said, "Now."

The four men went into action. Andersen pressed a hidden button, and a section of the wall under a cabinet slid open. Two of the men carried the press and slipped it into the opening. Andersen pressed the button again and the wall shut. One of the other men was hiding the founts of type in a cabinet containing dentures and material for dentures. The ink and paper were hidden. The men put on long white coats and began to work on false teeth.

"Forty-four seconds," Hansen said.

"Pretty good," Andersen said with satisfaction.

"Not good enough."

"Peter, nobody's ever bothered us."

"We won't be lucky forever." Hansen puffed his pipe calmly while the men reassembled the press. "Now."

Andersen turned, irritated. "Peter, we've got a paper to get out, for God's sake let's not get started on this again."

"I'm going to call it again," Hansen said.

It was shortly before noon, two and a half hours later, after ten or eleven more practice drills, with the time finally shortened to twenty-eight seconds, when Peter Hansen left the dental clinic and drove to his office.

There were a number of calls awaiting him, including one from Georg Siebert. He returned Siebert's call, was informed by Siebert's secretary that the consular official was out to lunch. He thought about having some lunch himself, but he was not hungry.

He paced back and forth restlessly, pausing now and then to look down on the square. One of his foremen called to see him and the two men conferred on a production change. Kate called and he told her he thought he would be home early and he heard the sound of pleasure in her voice.

Georg Siebert called again just before three o'clock. "I tried to reach you this morning, Mr. Hansen," he said.

"I know. I called back as soon as I got here."

"Those figures we discussed. Have you got moving on them?"

"Yes, Mr. Siebert. I believe you will be satisfied with the results."

"Good. There's great interest in the matter here."

After Siebert hung up, Hansen tried to remember the names of any Jews he knew. He knew the rabbi slightly, and Melchior of course, but who else? Dr. Hurwitz. He called Hurwitz's office. The nurse said the doctor was out on his rounds. He remembered a lawyer, called his office. The lawyer was in court. Then he recalled a man named Katzenstein, Otto Katzenstein, and he tried to think who he was, and then he recalled Katzenstein was a sub-contractor with whom he had done business some years before. He asked his secretary to call him.

When he had Katzenstein on the line, he said, "Mr. Katzenstein, this is Peter Hansen, I don't know if you remember me."

"Yes, Mr. Hansen, I remember you quite well," Katzenstein said. "As a matter of fact, your name was mentioned only this morning." Then he said, without changing his voice, "You've caught me at rather a bad time, Mr. Hansen. You see, I'm going on a little holiday today and there are several last-minute things I must do."

"I see," Hansen said. "Well, I'll talk to you when you return. And have a pleasant time."

"Thank you, Mr. Hansen," Katzenstein said.

A few moments after he hung up, Hansen received a call from the manager of one of his Copenhagen plants. A machine had broken down. Hansen told the manager he would be right over, told his secretary to call his wife and tell her he might be a little late, hurried out.

Ordinarily a breakdown of one of the machines would have irritated him, but today he was almost glad it had happened. It gave him something to do that was basic and simple.

It was after six o'clock in the evening when he returned home. His next-door neighbor was seated on his porch enjoying the last of the afternoon sun. The neighbor looked at the car Hansen was granted by the Germans for his cooperation. He always looked at the car.

Hansen entered the house, caught Lise in his arms, and bear-hugged her, kissed Kate, feeling the welcome on her mouth, and then saw a small man with a gray goatee and a pince-nez standing at the far side of the room. Hansen turned anxiously to Kate. "Are you all right?"

"Of course."

"Couldn't be better," the small man said, crossing the room. He shook hands with Hansen, adjusted his old-fashioned eyeglasses, surveyed Kate. "Any second now and she'll provide the world with just what we need, another Viking."

"What the hell are you doing here?" Hansen asked.

"The reason is sufficiently self-evident."

"You know what's going on?"

"I've heard talk here and there."

"Then what are you doing running around like this? You must be at the very top of their list."

Dr. Emil Hurwitz, gray hair parted in the middle in the style of another time, the time of the pince-nez, his face, his clothes, his manner, his imperial all of another time, rocked back on his heels and smiled. " 'H.' 'H' for Hurwitz. You know Germans. Method. System. It will take a little time to get to 'H.' "

Hansen went to the liquor cabinet and poured drinks. "You'll have to go underground, Emil. Now."

"And Kate?"

"We'll get another doctor."

"So?" Hurwitz pursed his lips. "Lise, let me see, she's eight now, almost nine." He took a drink from Hansen. "And, since Lise, three miscarriages, that wild ride to the hospital." He raised his eyes in memory. "I remember that bad one, the hemorrhaging. And now after all these years we have one that seems content to remain in the oven until he's done. Another doctor, Peter?" He held up his glass in toast to Kate.

"You must get out of sight," Hansen said.

Hurwitz sipped from the glass, moved his lips in appreciation, finished the drink, put down the glass, picked up his black homburg. "You mean that, don't you, Peter?"

"I mean exactly that. I'll work out some way to get you to Sweden until all this is over."

Hurwitz fiddled with the brim of his hat. "It's in your voice, Peter. I never heard it there before. Something's changing in you. About leaving Denmark, that must be my decision."

"I'm afraid not," Hansen said curtly.

Hurwitz bowed to Kate, started for the door.

"Emil," she said. "Stay for dinner."

"Dinner?" Hurwitz smiled. "Your husband just ordered me to find a hole and crawl into it."

"You may as well stay," Hansen said gruffly. "You've already run the risk."

"No, if I'm a wanted man, I'm dangerous to have around," the doctor said. "Besides, I still have some calls to make. You know, with the curfew, there are more babies than usual on the way. It appears people are rediscovering basic values."

"Emil, when you leave here I want you to get out of sight and stay out of sight," Hansen said.

"Until when, Peter? For how long?"

"I don't know."

"And what will you do with me?"

"I don't know that either. But I don't want you to fall into the hands of the Gestapo. I'm clear on that."

Hurwitz adjusted his glasses again. That far away, he

seemed quite small. "I must have the privilege of choosing, Peter. You can't rob me of that."

"What the hell are you talking about now?"

"It can't be charity."

"Who's saying anything about charity?"

"Something for something, Peter. A bargain. Jews are bargainers, you know." He raised his head slightly, peering through the glasses, the black ribbon dangling down his cheek.

"What kind of bargain?" Hansen asked.

"You want me safe?"

"I very much want you safe."

"It's important to you?"

"Get on with it, Emil."

"You must pay for the privilege of saving me. Thirty-seven times."

"Emil, for God's sake, stop talking riddles."

"No riddles. Quite clear. I have some relatives around, a few, thirty-seven at the last count, one of them pregnant, but she still has a little time. Thirty-seven persons, Peter, most of them quite insignificant, none of them as famous as I am. Peter, when you've got everyone of them safe somewhere, then come for me."

"Thirty-seven!" Hansen said. "What am I going to do with thirty-seven people?"

"That's the point, Peter. Think of something to do with them. Every last one. Then I'll do whatever you say."

"I don't know them, where they are."

"You've missed some of life's most charming pleasures. Wait until you meet my Aunt Minnie." Hurwitz waved his hand, whistled silently. "I'll prepare a list, Peter. When every name is crossed out, every single name, then come for me." He walked over to Kate, kissed her hand. "Thirty-seven Jews to run down. I'll make a little wager I'll still be here to introduce the Viking to the world."

As he turned to go, Lise bounded into the room. Hurwitz took her hand gravely and kissed it, bowed to Hansen, left.

Hansen went to the cabinet to pour himself another drink. He looked questioningly at Kate. She held up her glass to show him she had not finished. "Did you have a good day today?" he asked.

"Not bad."

He gestured with the glass to her belly. "How's he?"

"You're so sure it will be a he."

Hansen scooped up Lise in one arm and sat down with her. "Already have a she."

"And if it turns out to be another of the same?"

"You mean three women in this house?" Hansen wrinkled his nose at Lise. "I'm outnumbered now." He kissed Lise. "And what kind of day did you have?" he asked the child.

"Intermediate," she shrugged. She was a sober-faced girl with her mother's coloring and Hansen's features.

"Intermediate?"

"Yes, lying or being in the middle place or degree. Between extremes or limits."

"I see," Hansen said, sipping his drink. "Not great."

"But not bad. Perhaps the best kind of day, following a peaceful middle course."

"Is this new vocabulary?"

"Just a new lesson."

"In what?"

"Human relationship." She slid off his lap. "Will you excuse me now, Daddy? I have homework."

After dinner, when Lise went to bed, Hansen and Kate talked of this and that and he knew something was lying there waiting. He made a fire and poured her a glass of aquavit, the brown kind she liked. She stared into the fire, holding the glass between her hands. He looked at her long fingers, the nails clipped close and round, and he thought how he loved her hands and how he knew them and how they knew him, how he knew all of her, the long fingers, the long legs, the body now bursting with child.

"It's true then," she said. "What you told Emil."

94

"Yes."

"And of course you're involved."

"Yes."

"And it's going to get worse now, now with the Jews?"

"I don't know what's going to happen."

She raised the glass to her lips and lowered it without drinking. "Is there anything I can say?"

"You can anything, always," he said gently.

"Would it do any good?"

"Would it make me walk away from my responsibility? Is that what you mean?"

"Why is it your responsibility?"

"It just worked out that way."

"I know it's a question of humanity. I know that, but why you?"

"It's not a question of humanity, Kate," he said quietly. "It's not that at all. It's a question of politics."

"I don't understand. I pity those poor Jews and what's going to happen to them. It is a question of humanity."

"It's a question of Germans taking action against Danes. The fact the Danes happen also to be Jews has nothing to do with it."

"But that's why the Nazis are doing it, because they're Jews."

"That's why they're going to do what they're going to do," he said. "It's not why we're going to try to do something about it. As far as I'm concerned, as far as the rest of us are concerned, it's exactly the same as if the Germans decided to arrest all Danes who wore glasses, or all Danes who parted their hair on one side. In this case it's that they have decided to arrest all Danes who are Jews."

"Do you really believe that?"

"Yes."

She rolled the glass around in her hands. The firelight wove across her face. "All right, Peter. I can see that. But I'm frightened. I'm terribly frightened."

"So am I."

95

"There's so much fear around. Do you have to look for a special kind?"

"I haven't looked for anything, Kate. I inherited something."

"You can disinherit. There are many others. Someone else can do it."

"At the moment, I'm the someone else."

She looked at the fire, tilting her chin slightly, and he saw the hollow in her neck where so often in the years he had buried his mouth and smelled her skin and felt the throbbing and listened to the sounds of her satisfaction and the press of her flesh against him, against his belly, his thighs, and then the deepest sigh of all, the sigh that came from the deepest part of her and which he always heard and felt and loved, no matter what was happening to him. He had never got over the splendor of possessing her love and being informed of her in every way, that way, sleeping in the morning, waking sleepily, smiling, the early yawn, the intimacy of breakfasts and dinners and the time afterwards in the evenings, in this room, with the things they had come to own, the paintings, the books, the gramophone, the truth, the safety, the completion of living. They had achieved that miracle of joining so that the wholeness existed only when they were together, and he knew what was happening was interfering, but it had escaped him in some insidious manner and it was something they had to ride through to the end and then pick up what was left and hope, hope to God, that nothing had been spoiled.

"Peter," she said in a very low voice. "When you started with this, I was frightened then, but you told me it was only for a little while and then you'd stop, and you didn't, and now this with the Jews. Whatever you want to call it—politics—I still see it another way—pity, compassion. I don't have any feeling against Jews, you know that. I don't know many Jews. I don't think so anyway. I never thought about it." She paused and turned her face to him. "Don't look at me quite that way, darling. Yes, Emil. I know. Please don't give them names and faces."

The whole day suddenly lay on his back. "It's only a small point," he said. "But it's something they share with the rest of the world. Names and faces."

"Peter, I don't want to make a scene, you know I never make scenes." She stopped abruptly and looked at the brown liquid in the glass as though it held a secret. "Peter, you're getting into something, getting deeply into something, something terribly dangerous, something, and this is the worst of all, something that's taking you away from me and maybe will take you away for good."

There was no reason to soften it, he thought. They both knew what it was and what it could be. "It's not between us," he said, knowing it was.

"It is. A whole world between us. I'm frightened."

"It's our world," he said. "We should all be frightened because we let it happen."

"Peter, don't let this happen to us." Her voice dropped to a whisper. "Can't we just live normally, as normally as anybody else the way it is now, and soon you'll have another child, perhaps a son, and it will all have passed. You want a son, Peter, and I think he'll want a father." She looked at him, her eyes haunted. "Somebody's got to help them all right, but it's not our fault there are Germans in the world and that they're beasts. You can't change that."

"I can do what I can."

"Peter, I'm as human as you are, I'm a woman, I have feelings, but it's moving in on us, it's taking over." She lowered her head and her shoulders shook.

He went to her and took her in his arms. She pressed her face against him and he could see her pressing her lips together to keep from crying more.

"I don't want anything to happen to the Jews," she said presently. "I don't want anything to happen to anybody. But most of all I don't want anything to happen to you. I'm going to have a child, Peter, and I need you. I need you more than they do. I know I'm hitting below the belt and I don't care. You've done enough. Let someone else do this."

"If there was someone else who could manage it better, I'd pass it along willingly," he said. "But I'd still be in it, doing whatever I was asked to do."

She pulled away from him. "Then nothing I've said has meant anything."

"It can't mean anything, I can't let it mean anything."

She said, so low he barely heard her, "It's because I'm fat and ugly now."

"Kate!" He moved swiftly to take her back into his arms, but she raised her head and it was as though she raised a hand.

"Nothing I say now means anything because it isn't any good with us now," she said. "It used to be that when we were together, nothing else was important. But it isn't that way any more. I'm fat now and ugly and it isn't any good for you, and anything I say isn't any good either."

She set the glass on the coffee table, still not having touched the drink, stood up, looked down at her belly with loathing. She turned away from him to hide her deformity and walked out of the room.

After a while he picked up her glass of snaps and drained it. He ached and he felt old.

23.

RABBI BENT RASMUSSEN returned to his apartment near Solvgade shortly after eleven o'clock on that Wednesday morning the services were aborted in the synagogue. His wife, Lotte, and his eldest child, Jorgen, a tall, slender boy of fifteen, looked at him questioningly.

Rasmussen, slightly out of breath after climbing the three flights to his flat, sat down. He waved his hand. "Nothing," he said. "No trouble at all. The city officials will remove the Torahs and will keep them for us until we return." He breathed deeply and made a slight gesture with his head. "They seemed so sure of it."

"I'm sure of it," Lotte said. She was a slightly built, brown-haired woman of thirty-eight, with a trim figure four children had done nothing to spoil.

"And so am I," Jorgen said forcefully.

"Of course, of course," Rasmussen said. "And for that matter, so am I. But it's pleasant they feel that way, too. They even told me where they would hide the Torahs." He chuckled. "They will put some in the archive hall in Town Hall and some in the Royal Library. And then I remembered Pastor Orum of the Lutheran church near the synagogue. I remembered he once made me promise if there were any trouble with the Germans that I had to let him keep some of them. I called him and he said he would be furious if we didn't leave one or two with him." He shook his head. "It was a debate, a debate as to who should have the honor of guarding our Torahs."

"You seem surprised," Lotte said. "After all this time."

"No matter how long he's been exposed to it, there's always some little part of a Jew that feels surprised when he's confronted personally with decency." He was silent for a moment. "Well, somehow, in a way, it won't be as though we're leaving altogether. Jorgen, get me a beer." He stood up. "Now, work to be done," he said briskly. He went to the telephone. "Who knows?" he said cheerfully. "Perhaps things will quiet down and we'll be able to return sooner than we expect, perhaps a week or so."

"It's nice to think that," Lotte said. "But I don't think we'll be back in a week."

"What does it matter?" he said, still cheerful. "We need a little vacation anyway."

Jorgen handed him a glass of cold beer. "I won't have to go to school," he said happily. Then his face fell. "But I'll miss football."

"You'll keep a couple more of your own teeth in your head," Rasmussen said, drinking deeply. "Lotte, where are the other children?"

"Playing, with friends."

"Just so long as you can put your hands on them," the rabbi said. He sat down at the telephone stand and opened his address book.

"You must be careful what you say, Papa," the boy warned.

"So?"

"I mean they may be listening in, the Germans."

"The Germans? Listening to me?"

"Well, you're the chief rabbi, Papa. You're an important man."

"So I am," Rasmussen said. "Thank you, Jorgen."

"They call it tapping the line, Papa."

"Tapping the line. Well." He gave a number to the operator. Presently he said, "Julius? Rasmussen here. How are you? Good. Listen, Julius, we're going on a holiday for about a fortnight. I understand the weather is going to be fine. I suggest that you go away, too. Good, Julius, and a happy holiday." He hung up, put a small check mark next to the name, drank some more beer. "Wouldn't have to bother with this if more people came to the synagogue," he said. "Well, Jorgen, how was that?"

"Just right, Papa."

"Do you think he understood?"

"I'm sure he did."

"And if the Germans were listening in, do you think I fooled them?"

"Yes, Papa, but you must get on with the others."

Rasmussen nodded. "If only more of them came to the synagogue." He raised his brows. "The Danes don't make the best Jews in the world."

It was almost three o'clock in the afternoon when Rasmussen, having made almost fifty calls, having perfected his technique to the point of suggesting to the people he called that they call their friends, sat back to take a rest.

"Another beer, Lotte," he said. "I think I'm losing my voice." He wet his dry lips. Lotte returned with the beer and a fresh glass. He took the bottle. "This is better," he said, putting the bottle to his lips. "Colder. Ah, that's good. My, I'm going to miss our beer." He looked wistfully at the half-emptied bottle.

"Bent," Lotte said.

"I don't know where we're going to land up," Rasmussen said. "But wherever it is, we won't find beer like this."

"Bent, that's just it. Where are we going to land up?"

"Hmm?"

"Bent, I mean us. I know you have to warn as many people as you can. But what about us?"

24.

EVERY WOLFGANG I've ever met has been the same, Colonel Buhle thought sourly, rolling the cigar around in his mouth. I don't know why it is, but when you name a baby Wolfgang he's got to turn out to be a prick. He contemplated Sturmbannführer Wolfgang Becker in his beautifully tailored black uniform with the twin silver flashes of the SS on the tunic collar with a distaste his Gestapo-trained face carefully shielded.

Major Becker had arrived in command of the specially chosen Gestapo Kommando sent from Berlin to take the action against the Jews. As soon as Buhle had heard the name he made a face, and when he saw the major he unmade it, but he thought, this is one of the pretty ones.

Major Becker was a very pretty one, tall, very handsome, with hair even fairer than necessary. Buhle wondered whether the major tinted it.

Becker had marched into Buhle's office in Dagmar House as though he was on parade, stuck out his hand violently and shouted, "Heil Hitler!" Buhle returned the salute, somewhat less extravagantly, put in a call for Greiner, engaged Becker in pleasantries until the police supervisor arrived.

The details for the action were gone over rapidly. They had been worked out by Buhle and Greiner and were quite simple. It was routine Gestapo work and all three men knew their business.

When Becker was made familiar with the city plan of Copenhagen, Buhle passed the box of cigars. Becker refused, as Buhle knew he would, that warm-brother, and he took a fresh one for himself, pierced the end carefully, held the cigar in his mouth until Becker caught on and lit it, moving so fast to make up for lost time he almost tripped.

"Well, that's that," Buhle said, knowing quite well that was not yet that.

"I am certain all will work smoothly, Herr Standartenführer," Becker said.

"Yes," Buhle agreed, waiting.

"It must work out well." Becker's high-pitched voice rose slightly. "The last thing the Führer said was, 'Sturmbannführer Becker, our eyes will be on you. The thought of Jews walking as free men on the streets of Denmark is like a thorn in my throat.'"

"And what did you reply?" Buhle asked politely.

"I said, 'Mein Führer, we will remove that thorn!'"

"Well put," Buhle said heartily.

"And I promise you, gentlemen, their eyes will be upon us. The Führer said to me, 'Let every man know I consider ridding Denmark of Jews as important as winning a battle.'"

"And how is the Führer?" Buhle asked. He glanced at Greiner. The police supervisor's face was wooden. Buhle wanted to kick him on the shin.

"As ever," Becker said in a voice misty with adoration. "Tired from the burdens he bears but the spirit the same, unweakened, undaunted." He paused for a long, theatrical moment. "Somewhat concerned."

Here it is, Buhle thought. All the shit, leading up to this. "Of course he's concerned," he said. "We're all concerned these days."

"The Herr Standartenführer is correct," Becker said. "But this is a particular concern." He smiled winningly. "The Herr Standartenführer must understand I am only repeating what I have heard."

"Bruited," Buhle said.

"I beg your pardon?"

"Used generally with 'about,'" Buhle said, producing his own splendid smile.

"Yes," Becker said uncertainly.

"Continue."

"Well, there was talk in Berlin, about the necessity of special forces, why the mission here could not be accomplished by the forces already here." Becker looked at Buhle ingenuously.

"The answer to that is quite simple, Becker," Buhle said easily. He broke off the ash on his cigar, flicking his eyes at Greiner at the same time. Look alive, you idiot. "There were not enough forces. I don't have the men for the job. I went to Berlin myself to make that quite clear."

"I know that," Becker said. "Everyone is aware of that, of course. Still, there is talk that perhaps there is not enough of the . . ." Becker hesitated.

Like a bad actor, Buhle thought contemptuously. "Not the what?" he asked.

"That perhaps the—zeal, the drive, the dedication has lessened." Again he turned on the smile. "I am reporting this only for the benefit of the Herr Standartenführer."

"That we have become weak National Socialists, is that what you mean?" Buhle asked.

"I have not said that, and I have not said the other, either. I simply . . ."

". . . repeat what the others are saying."

"The Herr Standartenführer understands that," Becker said anxiously. "I don't think . . ."

"Excellent," Buhle said. "Don't think. Just do what

you're told. You will encounter sufficient zeal, and all those other things you mentioned."

Becker understood he was being dismissed. He jumped to his feet and went into a brace. "Heil Hitler!"

"No lack of zeal," Buhle said a little sadly. "No lack of dedication."

"Of course not, Herr Standartenführer," Becker said, his hand still thrust out. "I knew it could not be true."

"Depression, Becker. Depression, dejection, dispirit." Buhle shook his head somberly. "Months, years, seeing Jews walking on the same streets, eating in the same restaurants, attending the same theaters, signs in shops owned by Jews stating German trade was unsolicited. Jews telling us to keep out. Enough to discourage the best of us, Becker."

"I hadn't thought of it that way," Becker said. He realized that his hand was still sticking out and he lowered it.

"Heil Hitler," Buhle said.

"Heil Hitler," Becker repeated abstractedly. Then he remembered to jerk up his arm again. He made a smart about-face.

"Palace prick," Buhle said almost before the door was closed behind Becker. "But we'd better do this right. You made a spectacular contribution to the meeting, Max."

"I will do everything I am required to do," Greiner said.

"But with zeal."

"Oh, Christ, Rudolf, this is a filthy business."

"Don't make any mistake, Max," Buhle said placidly. "That ass was making sense. The Führer would rather have us fail fanatically than succeed without interest."

Greiner rose heavily to his feet. "I will make my arrangements."

"With zeal."

"With absolute zeal."

When Greiner was gone, Buhle swiveled in his chair and gazed thoughtfully out of the window. He remained that way for several minutes. Then he turned back slowly to the desk and thumbed through a small black book, his eyes moving over notations he had made. He carefully checked off one after the other, and he read, "Tel. Exch. Morten Torres & Rasmussen, chief rabbi."

He ordered a car, an SS man, and then left hurriedly.

25.

RABBI RASMUSSEN called another number and repeated the cryptic message. He caught Lotte's eye. "I must get word to these people," he said, his voice tired and slightly hoarse. He called the remaining names in his book, found seven more in the Copenhagen telephone directory, and then looked up puzzled, frowned, pursed his lips. "Lotte, does the name Lars Duul mean anything to you?"

"Duul?" She thought for a moment, shook her head. Then she asked, "Does he have a title of some sort?"

"Title? Councilor Duul? Dr. Duul? Count Duul?"

"No. Pastor! Pastor Duul."

"Pastor Duul?" He thought for a moment. "I believe I lectured with a Pastor Duul in some school, five or six years ago. Why should I think of him?"

"You'd better think about what we're going to do," Lotte said. "They won't find the congregation but they'll have the rabbi."

"Pastor Duul. Let me think for a moment. He had a church, in Randers, I think, Jutland."

The streets were crowded in the late afternoon and the black Mercedes proceeded slowly.

"Get on with it," Buhle said to the driver. He thought again about Greiner and what they had asked him in Berlin and how as a friend he had reassured them.

Rasmussen looked through an old address book, found the name and number of Lars Duul, asked the operator to connect them. "Probably he won't remember me at all," he said to Lotte. "But I remember him now. He used to be a football player in college." He turned to the receiver. "Hello. Pastor Duul? My name is Rasmussen. Rabbi Bent Rasmussen. I don't know whether you remember me."

"Rasmussen, my dear fellow." Duul's voice boomed so loudly over the telephone Lotte could hear it clearly. "How good to hear your voice."

"I'm thinking of taking a little vacation," Rasmussen said. "I understand the weather is going to be fine in Jutland."

"Randers is beautiful this time of year," Duul said. "Why don't you come here?"

The manager of the telephone exchange led Colonel Buhle and the uniformed SS man past rack after rack of switchboards. The girls operating the boards looked up nervously.

"Can't you be a little quicker?" Buhle asked.

"We have thousands of numbers, Colonel," the manager said. "It's not that easy to locate a particular connection."

"The chief rabbi of Denmark is not any connection," Buhle said. "He's as prominent a Jew as you have here."

"I have four children, Pastor Duul," Rasmussen said. "Perhaps we should split up. My wife and smaller children could go to you." Lotte shook her head decidedly. "I'll manage somehow with my oldest son."

"Nonsense, Dr. Rasmussen," Duul said. "You must bring your entire family."

The exchange manager paused in front of one of the boards. He peered closely at it, turned to Buhle. "This is the connection to Dr. Rasmussen's house. The line is engaged."

"Of course it's engaged," Buhle said. "Why else would I be here? Cut me in."

"Are you certain, Pastor Duul?" Rasmussen asked. "All six of us?"

"You are all welcome."

A girl's voice said, "You wish to listen in on Dr. Rasmussen's line, Colonel? One moment, Colonel."

Rasmussen stiffened. Then he heard another voice, with a German accent, say drily, "Yes, miss, thank you."

"So, my friend," Rasmussen said, gripping the telephone, "I wish you a very happy New Year, and if you are feeling better I hope to see you in the synagogue tomorrow."

"If I am unable to be there, Rabbi, you know my spirit will be with you."

Rasmussen hung up. He stared at the telephone. His hands were shaking.

"What is it, Papa?" Jorgen, who just entered the room, asked.

Buhle put down the earphone. He looked at the switchboard girl for a moment. Then he turned to the manager. "The exchange will be closed as of now." Buhle started out of the room, the SS man following silently.

The manager ran after Buhle, protesting. "But, Colonel, this is unheard of, the entire city . . ."

"You will keep it closed until I personally give you permission to reopen," Buhle said.

"We can't take too much, Lotte," Rasmussen said. "It must not look as though we are going anywhere."

"What happened on the telephone?" It was the third time she asked.

"Someone wanted to listen in. A colonel. The girl referred to him as colonel."

"She must have left the key open so you could hear her," Jorgen said.

"I hope no harm comes to her," Rasmussen said. He rubbed his face tiredly. "Please God." He was silent, thinking of the girl. "A strange girl and she knew what it was about because she spoke my name as well. Lotte, just a shopping bag so it will appear we've just been to the market."

"One?"

"All right, two. One for you to carry and one for me. Nowadays even men go to markets. Jorgen, your brother and sisters. Come, everybody, we must move. That girl, a complete stranger, please God, don't let anything happen to her. Hurry, Lotte, and not such a long face, please, you'll trip over your chin."

After the barest necessities for the four children and themselves were stuffed into two sacks, there was room for very little else. Rasmussen's selections were simple, his prayer shawl and his phylacteries. Those he would take. But nothing else. Not the silver *kiddush* cup he used for sacramental wine on *shabbas*, not the Menorah left to him by his father, nor the silver candlesticks presented to him by a rabbi visiting from Palestine. Not any of the books from the library, hundreds of books, of the *Talmud*, old manuscripts, histories of the Jews in half a dozen languages.

Lotte saw him looking at the books and touched his hand. He turned to her with a quick smile. "It doesn't matter, Lotte, not at all. They're only things, and things can always be replaced. The only thing to worry about losing is love. That's the only treasure."

Despite that, Lotte could not bring herself to look at the cabinet containing the two sets of dishes, one for dairy foods, the other for meat. She would not even glance at the large wooden box containing her good silver, a present from the Georg Jensen people on the occasion of her marriage.

The shopping bags finally were filled so that not another toothbrush could be added. Lotte wrapped up the youngest child, Leif, three, who, being wakened from sleep, began to cry. Lotte soothed him. The doorbell rang.

It was a large, peremptory sound.

Rasmussen, kneeling, tying the laces of the next youngest child, Ruth, six, became immobile.

"Who's that, Papa?" Ruth asked.

Rasmussen rose with stiff angularity. He looked at Lotte, who had turned white. Leif, who had quieted under the soft voice of his mother, began to whimper again.

"If it's the worst," Rasmussen said. "We must behave with grace."

The bell rang again.

"Shall I answer it, Papa?" Jorgen asked.

Rasmussen walked erect to the door, his lips compressed. He opened the door and saw a short man with a puckish face adorned with a small black mustache not unlike the famous one. On the man's head was a taxi-driver's cap.

"Are you the rabbi?" the man asked.

"I am Rabbi Rasmussen."

"Olsen here. Mikkel Steffen Olsen. Big name. I never grew into it."

"What do you want, Mr. Olsen?"

"Hurry up. Better get moving."

"Moving? Where?"

"Anywhere you want to go. Only hurry. I can't leave my cab standing too long."

"What makes you think we're going anywhere?"

"Dr. Rasmussen, all I know is, this policeman, he wasn't a policeman, a plain policeman, a police captain, a big man, tough, he told me to get my ass down here, begging your pardon, ma'am, and pick up all of you and take you anywhere you wanted to go. Free. 'Anywhere?' I asked him. 'Anywhere, to the moon, and if anything happens I'll have a little look at your license.'" He hunched his shoulders. "Nothing wrong with my license, you understand, but a police captain!"

They left the apartment. Rasmussen touched his fingers to his lips and then touched them to the *mezuzah*, the little case containing lines from Deuteronomy, fixed to the doorpost, as the passage from the Scriptures commands.

Olsen took the shopping bag from Lotte.

"Mikkel Steffen Olsen," Rasmussen said. "Mikkel, the messenger from God."

Police Captain Erik Melchior finished the last of his coffee in the Central Station restaurant and mashed out his cigarette.

"About time," the man at the next table said again. "If I knew any Jews, I'd turn them in myself."

Melchior looked once more at the man in the bright checked suit and shook his head in silent amusement. If anybody he had ever seen was a caricature of a Jew, it was he. Julius Streicher could have used him for a model. Actually, Melchior thought, he had never seen a Jew look like that.

He got up, paid his bill, and wandered out toward the station, hearing the man say loudly as he passed him, "Never mind what did they ever do to me, the whole damned bunch of them ought to be gassed."

That nose, Melchior thought. The man's entire life had been conditioned by that nose.

Walking through the huge station, crowded as always with German soldiers, arriving, departing, Melchior saw that everything was in good order, neither noisier nor less noisy than usual, a Gestapoman strolling about as always, trying to appear inconspicuous, appearing in the dark suit and dark, snap-brimmed hat as inconspicuous as a baby elephant.

Driving toward Central Station, Olsen twisted his head and said, "Break up, Rabbi. Remember that. And when you get on the train, too. Don't stay together."

"Thank you, Mr. Olsen. But I insist on paying you."

"Nothing doing, Rabbi."

"The police captain shall never know. I promise."

"Oh, it isn't that. And he didn't mean it. It's kind of like a joke between us. He knew I'd do it and for nothing. You must be the tenth family I've hauled today."

"How did you know. . .?"

"Gets around, Rabbi," Olsen said, maneuvering the car skillfully in the evening traffic. "Lots of Germans ride in this cab, Gestapo people, reason I have this mustache, makes them feel good and maybe makes the tip a little bigger, though most of them never tip at all, some of them never even pay. Anyway, you know, Rabbi, person hears things. Here we are, coming to the station now. Remember, break up, break up."

He pulled up and Rasmussen and his family got out. "Have a nice time in the country," he said. He saw Melchior standing in a corner of the main entrance. "No, thank you, it wouldn't be the same thing at all." He pushed away Rasmussen's extended hand holding money and shouted, "Yes, sir," as two German officers walked out of a nearby hotel. He drove toward the officers, rolling his eyes at Rasmussen.

Melchior watched the rabbi and his family emerge from the cab. He saw the rabbi direct Jorgen to go ahead with his mother and the baby while Rasmussen took Ruth by one hand and the other girl, Eiler, by the other.

Melchior turned quickly and re-entered the station. He saw the Gestapoman leaning against a post, his eyes on the ticket windows. Melchior walked rapidly to the Gestapoman and said something to him. The German policeman threw away the toothpick he was munching on and hurried away.

A moment later Melchior saw Rasmussen go to a ticket window and buy tickets, giving three to Jorgen, who scooted off. The rabbi and his two daughters walked toward one of the flights of stairs leading down to the train platform.

At that moment the Gestapoman appeared, pushing the man in the loud checked suit.

"Damn it to hell, I'm not a Jew!" the man shouted.

"Just keep moving and shut your mouth," the Gestapoman said. He shoved the man, waved a friendly finger at Melchior, left the station. Through the window Melchior could see them moving toward the inevitable black car.

Well, Captain Melchior thought, it's a little ahead of schedule, but he'll get "A" for effort.

His daughters on either side of him, Rabbi Rasmussen sat near one end of the platform. Lotte, Jorgen and Leif were at the other end. Close by to the rabbi was a group of German soldiers, young, he saw, and unwarlike. One of the soldiers presented Ruth with a piece of orange and patted her fair hair. Lonely men, the rabbi thought.

The train arrived almost exactly on time and Rasmussen shepherded the girls aboard. He did not dare to look to see whether the rest of his family had boarded. In any case, the platform was too long and too crowded.

As they settled in their seats, Ruth asked, "Are we really going to the country, Papa?"

"Yes, little darling." He cradled his arm around her.

"Oh, goodie," she chortled, snuggling close.

Rasmussen gazed out of the window and watched the houses fly by. It was getting dark and the New Year had officially begun. To be traveling now was against the ancient laws, but he knew he was committing no transgression. In their wisdom, the Talmudic law-givers had granted Jews the right to break any ritual law if it were necessary to save human life.

Rasmussen made Ruth more comfortable in the crook of his arm, saw that Eiler was staring fascinated out of the window; it was a holiday for them. He thought how at this moment the words would have been spoken in the synagogue. *"Oh God, divine Ruler of the universe, as the twilight of the old year fades into the night that marks the birth of another year, we gather together in Thy house with mingled emotions, mindful of the blessings and sorrows Thou has seen fit to lay upon us. . . ."*

Later, when the night closed in, an ambulance stopped in front of the iron gate of the synagogue. The driver and the intern entered the house of worship, and were taken by the sexton to where the Torahs were kept in the Holy Ark facing Jerusalem. They carried out the nine scrolls, each of them containing the first five books of the Old Testament, inscribed by hand by holy men who dedicated their lives to this purpose. They placed the Torahs carefully in the back of the ambulance and drove off to their first stop, the Lutheran church down the street.

26.

ABOUT THE TIME Rabbi Rasmussen and his family were starting their journey west across Sealand, Ellen Oppenheim was riding on a train north from Copenhagen to her home in Holte. She, too, was seated next to a window, her hands clasped in her lap, her face turned so she would not see Anders Jessen seated next to her.

"Ellen," Anders said for the fifth time since they had left the station. He reached over to her as he had before and touched her hand. She did not move it away. The hands remained motionless, cold without life. After a moment he withdrew, his face miserable. "Ellen," he said again, and it was not an enunciation of a name but a call of distress.

It had started early in the day for Ellen, in the store on the Stroeget in which she worked. The day had begun as any other day, people waiting in the street for the doors to open, salesgirls braced behind counters for the onslaught.

Ellen worked in the lingerie department and, as usual, dealt with Germans, some of whom were going home on leave and wanted to take home practical gifts from Denmark, others who were looking for presents for their Danish girls. As usual, her German customers saw in her nothing but a young, attractive Dane. The predictable proportion tried to make dates.

Ellen had coped with all this quite easily and successfully for many months now. She had a fixed attitude of loathing for the Germans. The attitude itself was protective. The wholesale shooting in the square and the death of the small child in her arms had had a traumatic effect on her.

In the days that passed, the trauma became part of the attitude.

It was shortly before noon that the first incident occurred to begin to alter the character of the day. The floorwalker in her section, a man named Schmith, whose marriage and three children had never inhibited him from trying to persuade Ellen to meet him somewhere, anywhere, after work, strolled over to her counter, where she was waiting on a captain in the Wehrmacht.

The officer, a Siegfried type, was trying to decide between two undergarments, one of them sheerer than the other. Ellen stood there waiting, the correct, polite expression on her face. The officer picked up one of the undergarments and then the other, feeling them with a small, sensual smile, as though they were already sheathing that for which they were made. "I cannot make up my mind," he said in tormented Danish.

"They're both lovely," Ellen said.

"Hmm." He ran his fingers slowly over the material. "If it were you, Fraulein, which would you prefer?" His smile just touched the border of a leer.

"They're both lovely," Ellen repeated.

"Yes, but which would you prefer?" It was almost an order.

Ellen glanced at Schmith, lingering nearby, picked up the sheerer—and more expensive—of the two panties. "I think this one."

"You think so?" the captain asked, looking at the almost transparent lingerie and then at Ellen. "You are sure?"

"Any woman would love this."

"Good, then I will have it." He leaned on the counter as Ellen made out the sales slip. "So that is what you would like to wear, Fraulein. Well, I can see it would be most becoming."

Ellen had long ago learned to control her queasy reaction to remarks like that. She thanked the officer. He clicked his heels and left.

Schmith came closer. "You handled that very well, Miss

Oppenheim." His words emerged musically, shaped carefully.

"Thank you, Mr. Schmith." Ellen turned away.

"It must be difficult for you, dealing with Germans."

"As difficult as for any Dane."

"Perhaps slightly more so for you."

Ellen slowly raised her eyes to the floorwalker. The first feeling was genuine surprise, then shock. As far as she could remember, this was the first time since she had started work in the store more than a year before that any reference was made to the fact she was a Jew. After the surprise and the shock, the sickness began to seep in, a new kind of sickness, and for the first time in her life she was aware that she was being reminded by a Dane that she was different from other Danes.

She moved away. He followed on the other side of the counter. "Would you by any chance be free after work today? We could meet at the Palace bar."

"Thank you, Mr. Schmith, but tonight is the beginning of a Jewish holiday. I always spend it at home with my parents."

"Perhaps this is the one time you should not spend the night at home."

She moved farther away; he followed.

"I've heard rumors, Miss Oppenheim."

She turned her back to him and began to rearrange the shelves.

"I've heard that the Germans are planning an action against Jews. Perhaps this will make you grateful you have a Danish friend you can trust."

She turned and looked at him, leaning her back against the shelves. He smiled in a gentle way.

"Palace bar, shall we say?" he asked.

She saw a customer walk up to the counter and she hurried over to her. She was beginning to feel faint. She gripped the counter. The customer made her purchase and left. Again Ellen felt the faintness. Another salesgirl, Helga, sidled up to her.

115

"Are you all right, Ellen?"

"Yes, thank you."

"What was old flat-feet trying to do, date you?"

"Yes."

Helga started to walk away, paused. "Ellen, say, you're Jewish, aren't you?"

"Yes."

"I thought so. I wasn't sure." Helga came closer, looked one way and then another in a conspiratorial manner. "I've been hearing something. One of my customers was saying something about the Germans. . . ."

"I've heard about it," Ellen said, feeling her stomach constrict.

"Probably nothing to it. Thought I'd pass it along."

"Thanks, Helga," Ellen said.

Throughout the rest of the day, other persons, girls working in the store, old customers who knew her, spoke to her about rumors of an impending action. And with each time, something inside of her shriveled a little more. She knew they were trying to help her, were coming to her out of goodness and possibly with some risk, but it went beyond that. New lines had been drawn, new definitions made. She was different from them.

The warnings came to have a dreadful monotony; she wondered who would be the next to admonish her. And each time she was stamped again. They were they, and she was something else. They were together, unassailable. They were Danes and she was a Jew.

When the working day ended and she left the store, she felt as though her Jewishness was something hideous, something that marked her like a disease. The street, her beloved Stroeget, was a place of strangers, filled with Danes. For several moments she could not step away from the store exit. It was like plunging into a turbulent sea. She stood there trembling, and then she saw Anders walking toward her and she rushed to him. She clung to him, fearing if she let go she would be washed away.

People passing saw only a lovely young girl embracing a

good-looking boy. It was not an unusual scene in the Stroeget.

He held her tightly, knowing she knew, knowing she needed something badly now, wondering whether he had it in him to give to her.

"Thank God you're here," she said.

"You've heard."

"You didn't tell me you'd meet me. Hold me, Anders, don't let me fall."

"Ellen, you've got to get away."

"Please, Anders, don't let me fall."

"You can't go home tonight."

"Please, Anders." Then she moved away. "What are you saying?"

"You can't go home."

"It's the eve of our New Year."

"Ellen, listen to me." He led her off the walking street to a bench in front of the church. "Ellen, there's going to be trouble. Sit down, please, and listen to me. Ellen, the Nazis, they're going to make raids. It's going to mean concentration camps." He looked at the bleakness in her face and the stillness in her eyes. "Ellen, you can't go home. You must stay with me."

She stood up, the wall between them now. Without speaking, she started rapidly up the Stroeget toward the square and the station.

He ran after her. "Ellen, I'm trying to help you."

"I don't need your pity."

"Ellen, you're in danger, and it's not pity."

"If it's true, we'll be notified by one of our own."

"One of your own? What are you talking about?"

"If there's trouble, we'll take care of ourselves."

"Ellen, I don't understand you."

She didn't understand herself, not entirely. Yet she knew something had to be retrieved, some pride salvaged.

He took her hand and tried to stop her. "Ellen, listen to me."

"You've said enough."

117

"I love you. I want to help you."

"And you want me just not to go home? So they can find my mother and my father and not me?"

"We'll telephone them."

"Unnecessary. What happens will happen to all of us."

"Ellen . . ."

He walked helplessly at her side, knowing that somehow he had botched it. He followed her onto the train and sat next to her, seeking in her face some remission for a sense of guilt he could not wholly explain. Her face was enclosed in hurt and shame and embarrassment. In her own way, she had accomplished her own unassailability.

He walked her home from the station in Holte. She left him without a word. He stood outside and looked at the closed door, his fists jammed in his pockets, not knowing whom or what to hate, himself for bumbling, the Germans, the stiff-necked Jewish intransigence.

Bernhard Oppenheim was already at prayer when Ellen entered the house. He was a small, bald-headed man, the Danish representative of several firms in Sweden. Business was not normal these days, to say the least, but he was a cheerful little man, with a fund of usable jokes and an unshakable conviction that in the end everything would turn out all right. That applied to everything, even the Nazis.

Looking at her father now, Ellen wondered again at the transformation that took place when he put on his prayer shawl and read words from the Scriptures. In a curious way he went away from her, and yet somehow at the same time came closer than he was at any other time. As she entered the room he raised his eyes in silent greeting. Ellen's mother, Bella, touched her finger to her lips.

Bella Oppenheim was seated on a straight-backed chair. She was a plump, round-faced woman, and the expression on her face now was that of listening to exquisite music. As she listened to the Hebrew words, the sounds that could be astringent, harsh, passionate and unbearably melodic, sometimes all at once, she nodded slowly when she heard passages that were familiar.

118

It was an old scene to Ellen. It always had a unique meaning for her. She did not consider herself a religious person and she did not know whether it was religion at all or just that, at these times, the family, the three of them, were at their nearest to each other. She slipped quietly into another chair and listened. She raised her head slightly as her father came to the closing words. He always read these in Danish. He maintained he did this so Bella and Ellen could participate in at least part of the service. Privately he told Ellen long ago he did this so Bella could be alerted to get ready to serve dinner.

"Standing on the threshold of the New Year, between darkness and dawn, between memory and hope, between the known and the unknown, we feel Thy presence, Oh Thou Who are timeless, Creator of the world and of man. We have come to Thy Sanctuary, Oh Lord, to give utterance to the emotions that surge within us. . . ."

Bernhard Oppenheim lifted his eyes from the prayer book and looked first at his wife and then at Ellen, as he continued from memory, *"Recalling the past year, with its exultations and its disillusionments, its joys and sorrows, and facing the uncharted course of the coming year, we realize that our destinies are in Thy hand. . . ."*

His eyes held Ellen's and she knew he knew, too. She glanced at her mother. She could see from Bella's expression that she was moved by the words and at the same time worrying the chicken would overcook.

"We pray, Oh Lord, that by our deeds we may become worthy of Thy grace," Oppenheim concluded, *"and thus be inscribed in Thy Book of Life. Amen."*

He closed the prayer book. Bella, weeping slightly as she always did when the words were finished, touched a tiny handkerchief to her eyes and then broke into a sunny smile. "Beautiful, Bernhard, such beautiful words."

"Don't flatter me," Oppenheim said, removing the prayer shawl. "I didn't write them."

"But the way you say them." She closed her eyes and moved her head slightly in remembered rapture. Then she opened her eyes abruptly. "Now, if it isn't burned to death

119

we shall have a wonderful dinner, and for dessert I have a special treat. No," she went on, although she had not been queried, "it's a surprise and I won't let you know what it is until I put it in front of you."

She hurried out of the room. Bernhard looked quietly at Ellen as he folded the shawl in the prescribed manner, touched it to his lips.

Oppenheim held his daughter's hand as they walked into the dining room. The table was set for the occasion. On it was the roast chicken and vegetables. On the table as well was a jar of honey and an apple, to indicate the coming year would be fruitful and sweet.

Bella surveyed the table, her husband, her daughter. "Sit down," she said. "Sit down and eat."

Oppenheim carved the chicken carefully.

"Not too much for me, Papa," Ellen said, wondering if she could swallow anything.

"Why not too much for you?" Bella asked. "Does your boy friend think you're getting too fat?"

"A girl has to keep her figure these days," Oppenheim said.

"On the eve of Rosh Hashanah she doesn't have to think about her figure," Bella said. "Besides, men don't like women to be too skinny."

Bernhard handed Ellen her plate. "How do you know about that, Bella? Are you an expert on these things?"

"Only women like to look skinny, the way those women look in magazines," Bella said firmly. "They look starved. I always ask myself how their mothers allow them to get that way."

"Listen," Oppenheim said, handing Bella her plate. "The way Anders looks at Ellen with the eyes of a sick sheep, he wouldn't care whether she was fat or skinny."

"How is Anders?" Bella asked Ellen.

"Fine." Ellen made herself chew and swallow.

"He's such a nice young man," Bella said, eating heartily.

"But not Jewish." Oppenheim winked at Ellen. It was an old gambit.

120

"What difference does that make," Bella demanded, rising to the bait. "It's the same God."

"It is hard for Jews to remain Jews in Denmark," Oppenheim said. "It's so easy to get lost in the lovely Danish culture." He sliced a piece of chicken. "It's a sad thing to say, but adversity is what keeps Jews Jews."

"I think just the opposite," Bella said resolutely.

"Listen to her. First she's an expert on women, and now she knows about everything else," her husband said.

"It's God's blessing that the Danes don't keep reminding us we're Jews," Bella said, ignoring him. "They let us be what we are and they hardly think about it. We think about it more than they do." She looked at her husband's plate and then at Ellen's. "What's the matter with you two? You're eating like a couple of birds. Is there anything wrong with the chicken?"

"No, Mama," Ellen said. "I had a big lunch today. And we were so busy I had to eat late."

"I had lunch with a customer," Oppenheim said. "You know these Danish lunches, even these days."

"Then why did I bother?" Bella asked.

"Because it's the eve of Rosh Hashanah and if you didn't make chicken the world would come to an end," Oppenheim said.

Bella smiled. It was difficult for her to worry for very long. "And now for the special surprise. You won't believe your eyes."

She bustled out of the room and Oppenheim and Ellen looked at each other again. The same question was in the minds of both of them. Who would tell Bella Oppenheim? And how?

She came back into the room, carrying a silver tray. "Look," she proclaimed. "Coffee! Real coffee!"

Oppenheim was jolted out of himself. "My God, Bella! Have you joined a smuggling ring?"

Her surprise a success, Bella smiled in sweet triumph. "Mrs. Petersen, she lives three doors away, you know her. . . ."

"I know her," Oppenheim said dutifully.

"This morning I'm in the market seeing what there is, you wouldn't believe what little there is these days. I remember..."

"Bella, about the coffee, while you're talking it's getting cold," Oppenheim said.

"My goodness, it mustn't!" Bella cried in panic. She poured the coffee and gave a cup to Oppenheim and another to Ellen.

"And yourself, Mama?" Ellen asked, her throat lumping.

"It doesn't matter too much for me," Bella said.

"Coffee?" Oppenheim asked in astonishment. Then he understood. "Who are you saving it for? Ellen and I will not want seconds."

"Drink it while it's hot," Bella commanded.

"Bella, not a drop will touch my lips. I swear it."

"Bernhard..."

"I said I swear it."

Bella nodded and poured a cup for herself. She smelled it. Her face opened with joy. How she loved coffee. How long had it been since that smell had been in the house? The three of them sipped and for a few moments everything else in the world was forgotten. Ellen remembered first, and cast a secret and worried look at her father. Oppenheim caught the look.

He put down his cup. He wiped his mouth carefully with his napkin. He rolled the napkin deliberately and slipped it into the silver ring. "Bella," he said.

"Well, as I was saying," Bella resumed, "I'm in the market and I see Mrs. Petersen and I asked her how Jingle is, that's the name of her dog, such a crazy name for a dog, Jingle. Anyway, last week Jingle wasn't feeling so good and I told her to put him to bed with a plate of hot chicken soup...."

"Chicken soup!" Ellen laughed, her first true laugh of the day. "A dog?"

"Why not, little Miss Know It All, if it's good for a human, even a baby, why not for a nice little brown-and-white dog?"

"Bella, about the coffee," Oppenheim said, relieved to have a moment's respite.

"Anyway, I asked her about Jingle and she said he was better, and then as I was leaving she came to me and she said, isn't tonight a Jewish holiday, and I said, yes, Mrs. Petersen, it's the beginning of the New Year. She said she would have a little something for me. So this afternoon she comes to the house with Jingle, he's all better now, and she has coffee, real coffee. She said, here, Mrs. Oppenheim, here is a little something to celebrate the holiday. At first I didn't want to take it, but she insisted, she has a cousin who has a fishing boat at Espergaerde and he gets over to Sweden and he gets things. So I took it and thanked her and here it is."

Having brought her saga to a victorious conclusion, Bella beamed at her husband and her daughter. "Also she told me that if ever we wanted a little more to please feel free to ask her," Bella remembered. "But such a thing, coffee, I would never ask her for any, I told her. Any time, Mrs. Oppenheim, she said, any time you want to make a dinner into a little party, there'll always be a little coffee for you."

Oppenheim took a deep breath. He looked at Ellen, who was looking down at her cup of coffee. "Bella," he said.

Bella threw up her hands. "Cilia Fried! I promised her I would call her on Rosh Hashanah evening. My mind these days! I tell you, if I don't write everything down. . . ." She got up and rushed into the living room. A moment later she rushed in again, picked up her coffee, ran out.

Ellen raised her eyes to her father. He nodded.

"I think we'll pay a little visit tonight, Ellen," he said. "A Danish friend of mine, he has a villa near Hilleroed." As Ellen closed her eyes, he said, "I forbid you to tell your mother. We'll just say we're going on a little visit." He looked toward the living room and lowered his voice. All day long, all day. I called a lawyer I know, I always had the notion he's mixed with the underground. He said, 'Hurry into hiding. You and your family.'" Bernhard Oppenheim breathed heavily. "Our little Denmark."

"It's not Denmark," Ellen said.

"Of course, of course." He shook his head. "What a way to start the New Year." He was silent for a moment. "Ellen, your mother and I. We're not spring chickens any more."

"Papa, please."

He hunched his shoulders. "Who knows what will happen. Whatever it is, your mother and I have had a good life, thank God. But you, Ellen, you're young, you're just beginning."

"Please, Papa," she pleaded.

"Ellen, this lawyer friend, he said Jews who were married to Christians, they would be left alone."

"Papa, you must stop!"

He raised his hand to quiet her voice. "This Anders boy. Such a lovely boy. Ellen, whatever happens to your mother and me, you must marry Anders, and we'll rest assured, knowing you're safe." He reached to her hand. "Promise me."

She started to reply, shaking her head, when her mother came back into the room.

"The funniest thing," Bella said. "Something's gone wrong with all the telephones in Copenhagen. I can't reach Cilia or Ina Chaikin. I can't even get the operator in Copenhagen." She looked at the coffee pot, weighed, indulged. She poured the coffee and then saw their faces. "What is it? There's something. My heart tells me."

"Bella," Oppenheim said. "We're going to spend the night with a friend of mine. In Hilleroed."

There was stillness. Then it entered Bella's eyes, the ancient thing, the thing never lost, not in hundreds of years anywhere, not even Denmark. Looking at her mother, Ellen recognized it as that which had become part of herself during the long day. And then she felt something else, something unexpected. Seeing it seep into her mother, it left her.

"Mama," she said strongly. "Mama, don't worry."

"The Germans?" Bella asked, the stillness in her voice.

"It will be all right, darling," Oppenheim said.

Bella carefully set the coffee cup on the table. It was an

124

act in slow motion. Not a drop was spilled. She stood up. "And you knew all the time?" Bella asked her husband.

"Yes."

Bella shivered. Ellen moved to go to her, but her mother raised her hand. "Thank you for eating my dinner."

"Who could miss your chicken?" Oppenheim asked.

"When must we go?" Bella asked.

"Now, Mama," Ellen said, hoping she would not cry, not now.

"I'll get ready," Bella said. She walked to the door. "We had this evening." She looked at Ellen. "You knew, too?"

"Yes, Mama."

"Such a family," Bella said. "Secrets." She started out of the room and went suddenly dead-white. "Oh, God in heaven," she said in a whisper. She wiped her face aimlessly.

Ellen and Oppenheim rushed to her to catch her as she fell. But before they reached her, she straightened. She looked past them, frowning.

"I can't leave the place looking like this," Bella said.

"What are you talking about?" Oppenheim asked.

"Dirty dishes on the table? Dirty pots in the kitchen? What am I, a slob?"

"Bella," Oppenheim said, "at a time like this?"

"When the Germans come here, they will not find this place looking like a pig-sty," Bella said.

"I must be going crazy," Oppenheim said. He looked at Ellen and saw that her eyes were filling with tears.

"They'll find a clean Jewish home," Bella said. "A beautiful, clean Jewish home."

The next train for Hilleroed was not due for twenty minutes. Oppenheim bought the tickets and they waited.

Ellen held her mother's hand and gazed around the station, and in the dim blackout light she saw many people and she knew they, too, were Jews moving on. This was the station from which she left every weekday morning and to which she returned every night. It was the same station, with the same tobacco and newspaper kiosk, the same advertisements for the fake wartime soap and cigarettes and the big poster for Carlsberg beer.

She found herself thinking of Anders. She needed him now. Then she smiled. Anders, to help her and her mother and father? Anders pose his mildness against the Gestapo?

The train, with its blacked-out windows, was crowded for this late hour and the passengers sat in the dark like dim ghosts. Ghosts of all ages and all sizes. The new passengers rushed into the train as though afraid it would leave without them. Those who had risked taking luggage shoved it into corners on the train platform to make it as inconspicuous as possible and discovered that those who had preceded them had had the same thought. The newcomers found seats and stared ahead blankly, as the people there before them were staring ahead.

Toward what? Ellen asked herself.

The train moved on in its spectral half-light on its spectral journey.

It is a refugee train, Ellen thought.

27.

AND IN THAT NIGHT, the men in black uniforms with death-heads on their black caps started on their mission and the black cars flowed like dark blood through the arteries and veins of the city.

And Dr. Werner Best, the supreme Nazi in Denmark, having for a time soothed himself that he wanted it one way, now wanted it the other way as well.

He sent a telegram to Adolf Hitler: "DENMARK IS FREE OF JEWS."

126

PART II.

1.

MORTEN TORRES lived alone on the fifth floor of an apartment house on Vester Voldgade. It was a building constructed toward the end of the last century, which meant in Copenhagen it was an infant among structures that claimed four and five centuries, but it was one of the pioneers among skyscraper dwellings, six stories, and was considered an old building of its kind.

It had its own personality. In the elevator, there was a sign forbidding more than three persons to ride at any one time. Nobody ever knew how the figure three was decided on. The Danes obeyed the injunction to the letter. No more than three 200-pound Danes would ever crowd into the tiny lift; if a mother had an infant in her arms and two small children at her side, she would make one of the children wait and ride up alone.

The building suited Morten Torres perfectly. His apartment, which at one time was the home of his wife, Gudrun, and his son, Oskar, now served him alone. His study, once Oskar's room, now was filled with law books, briefs, digests of opinions, legal publications in Danish, Swedish, Norwegian, German and English. In this room, hanging on the wall, was a framed quotation from Marcus Aurelius: "Remember this—that there is a proper dignity and proportion to be observed in the performance of every act of life."

Morten Torres had come upon this advice when he was in law school. Dignity and proportion. To the young law student, those two words supplied a formula for living.

Next to his office was the bedroom with the bed to which Gudrun had been taken as a bride, in which she had thereafter slept, conceived Oskar, delivered Oskar, and finally, after thirty-one years, had died—and left abandoned a man who grieved wordlessly and never again looked upon another woman.

There was a dining room, now rarely used, and a smaller room with a radio, gramophone and a small table where Morten Torres ate his meals, served by an old woman who had once helped deliver his son. Oskar, who had left Denmark when the Nazis invaded, now was an officer in the British merchant marine.

The building was conveniently located for Morten Torres. It was not too far from his office and, except in very bad weather, he always walked. It was close to Tivoli where Torres dined often in the season and where he was familiar to the head waiters in the good restaurants there. Although Torres dined alone most often and was not much interested in food and only a modest imbiber, the sight of the tall, spare, patrician figure, always carrying a cane as in some earlier time a man might carry a rapier, brought the maître to attention. It rarely mattered how long the waiting list. Morten Torres usually was guided to the best table available.

On this morning of the New Year, Torres had wakened with the feeling it would be a strange day. He realized immediately that for the first time in its hundred-year history there would be no Rosh Hashanah services at the synagogue.

Although he was the chosen head of the Jewish community, Morten Torres was not an emotionally religious man. It had never been his nature to get involved emotionally with anything or anybody, Gudrun being the sole exception and then, in a different way, Oskar. Now as he moved toward the Biblical goal of three score and ten, he had a comfortable, understandable and reasonable connection with God. He believed in Him with all his being. He prayed to Him at the prescribed times. He half believed that one day there would be a confrontation.

But he was not an extremist, not a pietist, and he was uncomfortable in the presence of some of the refugee Jews who had come to Denmark. He was embarrassed by the small group of Chassidic Jews, with their side curls and black clothing. He was worried about the Chassidic boys, curled and dressed exactly as their fathers. How could they become part of Danish life?

But if Morten Torres believed that religion, like law, should be accommodating and, if necessary, adjust, if he wanted Danish Jews to be in every way Danish except for the particulars of their worship, he was a devout Jew and he was at an utter loss as to what to do with himself on this first day of Rosh Hashanah.

He rose early and said some of the prayers and then he ate a small breakfast and wondered what he would do with the rest of the day. He supposed he could read through all the prayers for the day, but that was not his nature. Rosh Hashanah meant the synagogue.

The day appeared pleasant. He dressed, impeccably, as always. The streets were neither more nor less crowded than usual. There was no commotion of any kind, nothing in any way out of the ordinary. Hansen was an idiot, Torres thought, and Rasmussen was just as bad.

He found himself near the Glyptotek. He entered. There was permanence here. There also was assurance that time passed and events passed with it. That save for art nothing of man lasts, not Rome, not Egypt, not even a Reich to which the Leader had allotted a moderate thousand years.

On this day, his usual favorites, the mannered Egyptian artifacts, gave him no pleasure. They were too stylized for his mood. He wandered about, pausing now and then to look once more at the power of the great Rodin, continuing on, seeking something, he did not know what, and then finding something new in the great Roman faces which had previously impressed him as being theatrical. He had never quite decided whether they were genuinely so or whether it was the familiar theatricality of their names. But on this day, the countenances which before had seemed to be showy, vain, even in bad taste, now appeared wise and serene.

Before them, he leaned on his cane, a tall, thin old man deeply missing his lost hours with God, finding a measure of comfort in faces and remains of faces in stone, and then knowing he would find nothing else he walked slowly out of the building.

He had a small, unsatisfying lunch, unsatisfying not because the food was bad, but because he was out of rhythm with the day. He realized he was in a state of nerves and was getting worse. He walked directly home, his nerves beginning to make his skin edgy. When he was in his apartment, he undressed and bathed, put on burgundy silk pajamas and a black silk dressing robe, and picked up a copy of Steinbeck's *The Moon Is Down*, which had been reproduced and distributed by the underground. He did not at all approve of the violent activities of the resistance, but he did believe bringing to the Danes this moving account of the Norwegian opposition was a coup. This kind of Danish defiance had more proportion and greater dignity than blowing up a bridge.

He lay down on the couch in his office. He read through the words of Aurelius and, as always, they comforted him. He opened the book and read from it. He was about a quarter of the way through the small volume when he heard a violent pounding on the door. He put down the book, stood up, drew the sash of his robe and asked, "Who is that?" It was, he knew quite well, a foolish question.

"Open the door!" The German accent was unmistakable.

Yet Morten Torres was compelled to walk to the door and ask again, "Who is that?"

"Open the door or we'll break it down!"

Torres would not subject himself to the indignity of watching his door broken. He turned the latch and the door was opened with such force it sent him reeling. Two Gestapomen charged into the room as they might have charged an enemy position. One was short, with several chins; the other was tall and lipless. They looked around warily, their fingers on the triggers, and then, satisfied it was safe, stood back at attention as a tall, blond officer entered the apartment.

Major Wolfgang Becker looked at Torres pleasantly. The old man had by now recovered from the impact of the door and he stood erect.

"You are the Jew, Morten Torres?" Becker asked.

His blue eyes were mild and unangry and Torres thought they were the cruelest eyes he had ever seen.

Becker slapped Torres' face, hard. "Answer me."

It was the first time in Torres' life that anyone had struck him.

"Answer," Becker said.

"I am Morten Torres."

"Then you must come with me." Becker spoke as though he was inviting Torres to join him in a drink.

"I am a Danish citizen," Torres said. "I am not required to obey you."

Becker slapped his face again, this time in the opposite direction. "We don't have time to waste on one Jew," he explained reasonably.

Torres folded his arms. "You are intruders in my home. Leave."

The tall Gestapoman grabbed Torres by the arm and pushed him toward the door.

"Will you allow me to get dressed?" Torres asked.

The Gestapoman shoved Torres into the hallway. Other tenants in the building, wakened by the disturbance, were peeking through narrowly opened doors, which they closed quickly as Torres and the Gestapomen came out of the apartment. But not so quickly that Torres did not see them and feel shame that his neighbors saw him mishandled and in a state of undress.

For the first time since Torres had lived in the building, he saw four persons crowd into the elevator. It creaked no more than normally and it brought them safely to the street. After all these years, Torres thought, to find this out.

The tall Gestapoman gripped his arm again and walked him into the street in the traditional manner of the policeman. Parked in front of the building was a large truck bearing the name of a wholesale fish company. The back doors of the truck were opened and another Gestapoman stood guard with a machine gun.

Torres was thrown against the rear of the truck and ordered to climb in. Acutely conscious that people were watching from behind window curtains, Torres tried to obey. His one desire was to get out of the sight of people who knew him. He struggled to climb aboard, but the truck bed was too high.

"In, Yid!" one of the Gestapomen ordered, poking his rifle into Torres' thin buttocks.

Torres did not know what he would have done if two hands had not reached down from the truck. He grasped them and was hauled up. The doors were slammed shut. The truck pulled away.

In the darkness, Torres could not tell how many others were there. He knew there were many. He heard a baby crying and a mother trying to quiet it. He heard someone weeping. He smelled sweat and stale fish.

The truck made three more stops and a dozen other persons, including three of four children, were loaded. Now, when the doors were closed, the people inside were packed. Torres was trapped with his hands at his sides.

"Where are they taking us?" It was a high, thin, woman's voice.

"The Gestapo is having a little tea party." This was the voice of a man. It sounded vaguely familiar to Torres.

"Is this time for jokes?" another man asked.

"What is it time for, my friend?" the mocking voice asked.

"Where are we going?" the woman asked again.

"Next stop I'll ask the driver," the man said.

Torres tried to place his voice. The woman began to cry, and another woman, a very old woman from her voice, started to wail in the ancient way. Children began to cry and the sounds echoed in the confined van as it careened through the streets.

"Listen to me," Torres said. His voice, trained to impose

quiet in courtrooms, had an effect in the fish truck. "I am Morten Torres."

"Well, well, well," the mocking voice said.

"Listen to me," Torres said. "We must not let them see us afraid."

"Afraid?" the mocking voice repeated. "Who's afraid of a little concentration camp, Mr. Torres?"

The wailing rose at the pronunciation of the dreaded words.

"Quiet!" Torres said. "Whatever else they can do to us, they can't take away our dignity. Only we can give that to them."

"Mr. Torres," the mocking voice said. "You're an old man."

"What has that to do with anything?" Torres asked.

"What have you got to lose?"

"Do you mean that?" Torres asked.

"No."

One of the women started to laugh, half-laughter, half-tears, and another woman started to cry, and then the children joined in again. The sounds stopped abruptly as the truck jolted and came to a stop. The doors opened. "Out!"

"Where are we?" a woman asked.

Torres looked out. "The synagogue," he said.

Major Becker came round to the back of the truck and stood with his hands on his hips and a smile on his face. "Isn't this where Jews are supposed to be today?"

There were two hundred or more persons in the synagogue when Torres entered. He noticed with odd irrelevance that men who had hats were wearing them. Other men had covered their heads with kerchiefs. The Jews, in various states of dress and undress, of all ages, were seated, sprawled, curled in the pews. Children were crying, mothers were rocking babies in their arms. It was the first time, Torres thought, that men and women had ever sat together.

Half a dozen Gestapomen, all armed, lined the walls, watching, listening, alert.

Torres moved to the nearest pew and sat down. It was very strange to be in the synagogue in dressing robe and slippers. It was lacking in dignity. He had been wrong in what he had said to the others in the truck. The Germans had already taken away much of his dignity, and he had not given it to them.

He looked around. So Hansen and the rabbi were right and he was wrong. It was still almost impossible to believe. And if the Germans had started at the time Hansen had said they would then they had been at it for more than twelve hours now. The synagogue must merely be a gathering place, he thought; the rest of them must already have been put aboard the ships.

Nearby, a little boy of five whispered something to his his father, and the father, a thin man with horn-rimmed glasses, led the boy up the aisle to one of the exits. A Gestapoman barred their way. Torres could see the father asking something and the SS man grin and shake his head. The child squirmed. The father pleaded. The guard looked at the child hopping with pain and laughed. The father tried to slip by. The guard thrust his rifle into the father's belly and held him there.

Torres saw a German face, Max Greiner, the police supervisor, dressed for the occasion in his SS officer's uniform, walking rapidly toward the guard. Whatever Greiner might have done, if he intended doing anything, was made impossible by the next move of the guard, who shoveled the father away with his gun as though he was shoveling snow and the father went sailing back and his glasses flew off his nose.

The father lay doubled up, unable to move. The boy, his own needs for the moment forgotten, stood by his father and cried. Greiner, Torres noted, turned and walked away. Torres stepped into the aisle, retrieved the father's glasses and gave them to him. The father put them on, pulled himself painfully to his feet, whispered something to the child. The boy opened his trousers and relieved his bladder against the rubbed, worn wood of the pew. Mortified, the father led the child away. The urine spread in a little pool in the aisle.

No, Torres thought, it's not any of the things, it's the idea. He wanted to say to the child, the synagogue is not made of wood and varnish and brick and paint. The synagogue is in the heart. He thought of Oskar and wondered where he was and if he were still alive.

"Mr. Torres."

Torres recognized the voice as that of the mocking man in the van. "Yes," he said, looking at the smiling man, well and fully dressed.

"Jacobsen, Mr. Torres," the plump man said. "Ove Jacobsen, gentlemen's tailor and outfitter."

"Yes," Torres said, remembering Jacobsen from the last meeting in the synagogue. He tightened his robe.

Jacobsen stood back a foot or two. "A thirty-nine long."

"I beg your pardon," Torres said. The day had been very long and he was getting tired.

"And for such a prominent man, only the best," Jacobsen said. "A fine mohair or perhaps a beautiful worsted such as we used to get from England."

"I'm afraid I don't understand," Torres said. He wanted to sit down again and close his eyes.

"For the head of the Jewish Community to be seen in this undignified manner is a sorry state of affairs, Mr. Torres. We should send a special protest to Hitler. So help me, Mr. Torres, I would give you the suit off my back, only it wouldn't be a good fit and I have a reputation to maintain."

"Mr. Jacobsen, I'm an old man, and I'm tired," Torres said.

"I'm surprised you're here at all," Jacobsen said.

"I'm no different from any other Jew."

"That's just it, Mr. Torres. Many of us thought just that, that you were different from the rest of us."

"I'm sorry to have given that impression." What could he do or say to make him go away?

Jacobsen was silent for a long time and Torres sat down

137

and closed his eyes. To sleep in the synagogue. What was happening?

"Mr. Torres," Jacobsen said.

"Yes."

"I hate to see you here, believe me. I hate to see any of us here. I hate to see you this way. You are an elegant dresser, Mr. Torres, and many's the time I thought how wonderful it would be to have you for a regular customer. You're a very elegant man, Mr. Torres, and I know you must feel embarrassed being here like that."

"Mr. Jacobsen, really, I must ask you . . ."

"Mr. Torres, when something like this comes along, people like me, we expect it. What kind of important friends have we got? But a big shot like you, a man with your connections . . ."

Torres looked at Jacobsen. There was quite another expression on the stout man's face.

"What I'm trying to say, Mr. Torres, is, and please forgive me and try to understand what I mean, what I mean is that I feel a little better, seeing you here. I know you could have pulled a few wires and missed out on this little treat."

He walked away. Torres stared after him. Could he have pulled wires? Would he have, if he had believed?

At the main entrance to the synagogue Major Wolfgang Becker stood with a pleased smile on his face, surveying the large room. There were not as many people there as he would have liked to have seen—they were slippery, these Jews—but he felt exhilarated. At that moment, looking around, hearing the sounds of defeat, he had a kind of love for these people for making him feel so fulfilled. Nothing else could ever give him that, make him so aware of his strength. Everything bad in his life disappeared at times like this.

He saw Lieutenant Colonel Greiner approaching him. He came to attention.

"You look satisfied with yourself, Major Becker," Greiner said.

"Obeying the Führer's commands is always satisfying," Becker said.

"Then why are you not obeying them?" Greiner said.

"Yes, Herr Obersturmbannführer!" He marched away.

Greiner looked around. These were a strange and difficult and ununderstandable people here. Yet all of this was wrong.

He saw Morten Torres, sitting alone. He walked over to him.

Torres stiffened slightly as Greiner looked down at him. He again was overwhelmed with humiliation at his appearance, at the odor of stale fish he felt still clung to him.

"Mr. Torres," Greiner said.

"You have me at a disadvantage," Torres said.

"Our paths have not often crossed," Greiner said.

"Lieutenant Colonel Greiner," Torres said, and he thanked God for permitting him to manage the frosty tone. "I know that Germans are not renowned for tact, but don't you think this conversation is in particularly bad taste?"

"Perhaps," Greiner said. "Mr. Torres, I came over to tell you one thing and then I will leave you. Just outside the main entrance and down a corridor is a men's lavatory."

"This is my synagogue," Torres said.

"I know, but I'm reminding you. I am also telling you that not far from the lavatory is a door leading to the street. If it is of any interest to you, the guard at that door is presently having a fifteen-minute relief."

Torres discovered he was amused. "I thought you people had got past arranging for escapes in order to shoot the man in the back," he said.

"I could have had you shot any time tonight, Mr. Torres," Greiner said. "I don't have to set up fake escapes." He consulted his watch. "You still have twelve minutes."

"Why, Lieutenant Colonel?"

Greiner shrugged.

"You seem to be a man with either the beginning or the ending of a conscience," Torres said. He felt the great weariness again. "Look around you. There are babies here, children, women. Any of these, Lieutenant Colonel Greiner, the smallest child, will help that fly-speck conscience more than I can. Now, I ask you, leave me in peace."

Greiner walked away. Torres leaned back against the hard wood of the pew. His heart was pounding and he was a little breathless. And he thought he might have been a fool. But there was one thing. He no longer thought he smelled of fish.

In the next hour, another fifty or sixty Jews were brought to the synagogue. Torres wondered when they would all be taken to the ships to join the others.

On the other side of the aisle from Torres, a mother was having a problem with her infant. The baby had dirtied its diaper and the mother had nothing with which to replace it. A little boy to Torres' right asked his father when he could have something to eat.

"In the morning there'll be some food," the father said.

"Where are we going?"

"I don't know."

"Then how do you know there will be something to eat?"

"I'm sure there will. Now sleep a little and you won't feel hungry."

"I'm too hungry, Papa."

"All right, let's see what we can do." The father smiled at the child and then gestured for him to remain where he was. He went to one of the guards and spoke to him. The SS man listened, considered, nodded, accepted money, pocketed it. The father stood there, waiting for something. The guard told him to return to his seat. The father said something and the guard hit him with the rifle, a swinging blow with the barrel.

The father staggered back and then rushed to the guard and pummeled him with his fists. The guard struck him again, on the face. Blood dribbled from the father's mouth. A young, husky Jew rushed up to the guard and flattened him with a punch on the jaw. As the guard went down, another guard ran up behind the young man and swung the gun at his head. The youth was bending down to pick up the man he knocked down and the rifle struck him only glancingly. Now the youth straightened with the first guard in one hand. He reached out and grabbed the second guard with the other hand and he held them both up and smashed their heads together, laughing merrily.

He banged them against each other again and again until three or four other guards beat him unconscious. The youth was dragged out of the synagogue.

Colonel Buhle, watching all this from another part of the synagogue, asked Greiner, "Did that amuse you, Max?"

"In a way," Greiner said.

"That statement could be considered treason," Buhle said.

"Could it?"

At that moment the two officers saw Major Becker enter the synagogue, a broad smile on his face, his arm slipped in friendly fashion under the arm of an old, bearded Jew. A small woman, a black shawl over her head, walked on the other side of the old man.

"So you ran away from the Fatherland," Becker was saying in German, in his most amiable voice. "Then you should be doubly grateful. First I bring you to your synagogue and then I shall take you home."

The old Jew looked at the smiling Nazi officer with such naked terror, Becker broke into a loud laugh.

"It will not be as bad as that, old friend," Becker said. "And besides, it will not be for long."

He slapped the old man heartily on the back and walked away. The man staggered under the blow. The shawled woman tugged at his arm but he did not move. He started to say something and toppled like a log. The woman screamed. Someone knelt beside the old man and then shook his head.

The woman got on her knees. "Daniel," she said.

She began to cry, in the old way, nodding her head in her grief. Then she leaned over and kissed her dead husband on the lips. "You're lucky, Daniel," she said. "You don't have to go back."

Torres remembered another line from Aurelius, "Nothing happens to anybody which he is not fitted by nature to bear." He looked up as an SS man leaned over him.

"Are you the Jew Torres?" the Gestapoman asked.

"I am Morten Torres."

"Outside."

"What for?"

The guard jabbed him with his rifle. "No questions, Jew."

Torres stood up and the guard yanked him out of the pew and shoved him up the aisle toward the doors. Torres could see the others looking at him. He saw Ove Jacobsen smile.

"Tell me what this is about," Torres said to the guard.

The guard pushed him out of the synagogue into the outer hall and then shouldered him into the street. Standing at attention at the iron gate of the synagogue were two SS men. Waiting in front of them, smoking a cigarette negligently, was an SS officer. Behind him, leaning against a black Mercedes, was a Danish police officer.

The guard who brought Torres out clicked his heels. "Here is the Jew Torres, Herr Obersturmbannführer."

The SS officer dropped his cigarette and stepped on it. "Put him into the car."

"Tell me what this is all about," Torres said. "I demand to know."

The guard pushed Torres into the rear of the car. The SS lieutenant colonel climbed in after him. The Danish officer got in the other side.

"What is happening?" Torres asked the Danish officer. He fell back as the car drove off. "Where are you taking me?" He looked closer at the Danish officer. "Melchior," he said. He turned quickly. "Hansen." His lips tightened. "What is this?"

Hansen, looking trim and at ease in the SS uniform, grinned. "The Americans have a classy word for it. 'Snatch.' "

Torres shook his head slowly. "You fool. You two fools. You don't know what you have done."

"I know damned well what we've done." Hansen said. "And I think we were bloody clever the way we managed it. By the way, Mr. Torres, you can thank Captain Melchior. He had the notion how to do it and he scrounged the uniforms and the car."

"What's the matter, Torres?" Melchior said. "Are you worried about what the rest of them will say, that you had pull and used it?"

"Yes," Torres said. "Yes. Exactly that."

"Well, stop thinking so damned much about yourself," Melchior said.

"I'm not thinking about myself," Torres said. "I'm thinking of them. They all saw me there. It meant something that I was there, too." He looked at Hansen bitterly. "I was getting it back, Hansen, can't you see, for my foolishness, for my blindness, not believing you in the first place, I was getting it back. And now you've brought disgrace on me."

"Disgrace?" Hansen said. "I hadn't considered that, Mr. Torres. And we didn't take you out of there because you're an important Jew. We chose you because you're going to be needed and you'd be of no use at all in a German concentration camp."

"Hansen, you must take me back."

"Don't be a damned fool all over again," Hansen said. "You don't prove anything, getting yourself stuck into a gas chamber. Now I suggest that you forget your precious self-esteem and start thinking how you can help your unfortunate fellow Jews."

"By going back to them," Torres said. He made a sudden move, past Melchior, grabbed the door, tried to open it.

Melchior caught his hand and took it away from the door. "In your night robe, Mr. Torres?" Melchior asked.

After a moment Torres said, "You're hurting my wrist,

Captain Melchior." He sat back in the seat. "Mr. Hansen, I ask you again, please take me back to the synagogue." "Not a chance," Hansen said. "No time for martyrs." He reached over to the front seat of the car next to the driver and came up with some clothing. "Hope we selected something you like, Mr. Torres, we were in a bit of a hurry. By the way, one of your neighbors said to tell you they'd all watch over your belongings, you're not to worry." He reached over to the seat again and this time came up with a box of cigars. "You do yourself well, Mr. Torres." He raised the lid of the box and sniffed. "May I?"

2.

AT EIGHT O'CLOCK on Thursday morning, a little more than twenty-four hours after the Gestapo launched its roundup, Colonel Buhle and Lieutenant Colonel Max Greiner stood just inside the main entrance to the synagogue, looking slowly around the room.

Some persons were asleep, some awake, some in a stupor. Children were fretting. One group of children, Greiner noticed with bemusement, were gathered together, playing a game with tops. The old Jew who had dropped dead had been dragged to the wall. He lay there in a huddle, like a bundle of old clothes.

"I make it about three hundred and fifty," Buhle said. "No more," Greiner said.

Buhle took his cigar out of his mouth. "Well?"

"There's only one explanation, of course." He saw Buhle looking at him calmly. He shook his head. "No, Rudolf, I'm not a fool. Besides, I wouldn't have had the courage."

"Somebody warned them. And so efficiently they were able to spread the word to all of them—and with the telephone dead. But it's more than that." He looked at the stub, threw it away. "They had to have somewhere to go."

"The Danes received them," Greiner said. "It doesn't surprise me."

They saw Major Becker and his men bring in a dozen or so more Jews. Becker walked over to them rapidly. His face was flushed.

"Every place we went to, empty! They have disappeared into the thin air!" he said angrily.

"We have had the same experience, Becker," Buhle said. "Somebody warned them!"

"We came to that conclusion."

"Who warned them?" Becker demanded, in his frustration forgetting military courtesy. "When the Führer hears of this, heads will fall!"

"Well, my dear Becker, we can console ourselves," Buhle said, taking out a fresh cigar. "We all did the best we could."

"It was not enough."

"It was not," Buhle agreed. "Now why don't you see about getting these people onto the ship?"

Becker cast a malevolent eye around the chapel. "A handful! Eight thousand Jews, and we deliver this handful. We'll be the laughing stock of the Reich!" He held up his hands. "I had such plans. I was going to ask to be transferred to the resettlement camp."

"I didn't know you aspired to that," Buhle said.

"Yes," Becker said. "A new gas. I'm not at liberty to divulge its name. It's still in the process of being tested." He calmed down, thinking about the gas. "The problem has been in manufacturing. Tricky." He straightened his uniform. He was the man from inside, talking to men outside. "One of the largest chemical companies is working on it. Double, even treble efficiency." His brave words against the failure of the night worked a glow into his eyes. "I have other theories. I wanted to test them. With the swine we

145

took from Denmark. I would have felt I entered a project at the beginning and worked on it to its successful conclusion."

Buhle looked at Greiner. The police supervisor's face was turned away. "Well, Becker, you'll get other chances," Buhle said encouragingly. "Europe hasn't run out of Jews."

"You are quite right, Herr Standartenführer," Becker said, as though Buhle had uncovered an eternal truth. "I must tell myself to remember that."

"But meanwhile you will get these people aboard ship."

"Yes, certainly, Herr Standartenführer." He shook his head. "Two ships and less than four hundred people. It is ridiculous." He clicked his heels, jutted his hand, pronounced the sacred words, made an about-face, marched off.

The SS men moved through the synagogue, jabbing people with their guns, waking the sleepers, pushing the people into the aisles. The Jews shuffled out of the synagogue into waiting vans.

Buhle and Greiner watched in silence until the chapel was empty. Except for the body of the old Jew. Buhle saw Greiner looking down at the body, and frowned. Then he put his best smile on his face and clapped his friend on the back.

"What the hell, Max, so we lost the first round. The Jews are still here in Denmark and we'll get them all. And we'll do it together, without that fancy bastard Becker."

Greiner continued to look at the shabby clothes that contained the old body.

"Come on, Max, it's been a long night," Buhle said. "Let's get something to eat. Then we'll work out what to do."

Greiner turned his head slowly. Buhle looked at his face and knew the worst.

"No, Max," Buhle said.

Greiner shook his head. "I don't have the stomach." He started for the door.

"Don't go, Max," Buhle said quietly.

Greiner stopped. "No more, Rudolf. I can't do it any

more. I will submit my resignation. I will ask to be assigned somewhere else, anywhere."

"It's not that simple, Max," Buhle said.

"They can't keep me here." Greiner moved toward the door.

"Max, do not go."

Greiner turned slowly. "You're warning me."

"Just stay here and do your job. We will get out of this mess one way or another."

Greiner walked back to him and looked at him closely. "You brought something else back from Berlin, didn't you?"

"Max, we've failed for the moment. But it can be retrieved. Nothing is final. You've been on the job long enough to know that."

"You had it in your pocket all the time," Greiner said.

Buhle's face hardened. "You have been stupid, Max, and, worse than that, you have been weak. And we live in the same snakepit here. Everybody is spying on everybody else. You know that."

"I should have known," Greiner said. "You have been understanding since you came back. Not like you at all."

"Pull yourself together," Buhle said harshly. "We can still salvage this disaster, salvage something, in time. You have had an excellent record, until now."

"Salvage?" Greiner asked. He smiled. "And they're just Jews."

Buhle breathed out heavily. "All right, Max."

"I'm to consider myself under arrest."

"Yes."

"But because of my rank and my past services to the Reich, I will be trusted to remain under my own custody."

Buhle looked up. "I haven't heard anything just now, Max. You haven't said anything and I haven't said anything. Let us work out a feasible plan and get on with it."

Greiner looked at him for a long time. "What happened, Rudolf? What happened to all of us?"

Buhle flung away his cigar and left. Greiner looked down at the old dead Jew.

147

3.

IN THE CHILLY early-morning hours the captured Jews walked up the gangplank of one of the German ships anchored at Langelinie. A small crowd of Danes was gathered at the pier. Some of them began to sing the anthem, "There Is a Lovely Land." Jews joined them.

"There is a lovely land that proudly spreads her beeches beside the Baltic strand. . . ."

The Gestapomen, who had not attempted to quiet the Danes, ordered the Jews to be silent. Some of the Jews obeyed. Others did not. In the end, the Germans gave up and hastened the embarkation.

4.

BUHLE DECIDED he was entitled to a decent breakfast. He ordered his chauffeur to take him to the Hotel d'Angle-terre. The outside tables had been removed for the oncoming winter and the building appeared barren. He entered the lobby, went into the dining room, saw a group of German officers at a table, declined an invitation to join them, took a corner table by himself. He ordered a glass of snaps and then a large meal, and then discovered he was not as hungry as he had thought. He picked at the food, drank another snaps, and when the waiter looked at him, worried, told him to take the plates away and to bring him another drink. He lit a cigar. What, as Greiner had asked, had happened?

5.

THE DANISH POLICE car drew to a stop in front of Dagmar House. Captain Erik Melchior stepped out and ordered his driver to wait. He hoped he was not being unduly optimistic. He walked past the guard, accepted his salute, entered the building with the usual feeling of apprehension.

Why had Greiner summoned him? He knew Greiner, of course, had worked with him during the years, particularly after he was made captain. He never understood him. He was always disturbed by the intensity he felt in the German. Greiner's eyes always bothered him, always seemed bordering on something.

Well, he'd asked for it. He'd asked for it all along and he'd asked for it particularly in the last few days. He had considered, upon receiving word that the police supervisor wanted to see him as soon as possible, leaving some kind of note for Hansen, but that, on second thought, seemed unnecessarily melodramatic. In any case, if anything went wrong, Hansen would know about it soon enough.

The SS man on duty as Greiner's aide was expecting him. He rang through to the police supervisor and then stood up in respectful attention and opened the door to Greiner's office. He's behaving all right anyway, Melchior thought.

Greiner's appearance startled him. His eyes were in black caves. His skin stretched tautly on his face. His manner as he greeted Melchior was nervous and distant. Melchior could understand all that. After the fiasco with the Jews.

"Captain Melchior," Greiner said. His eyes were lost in their grottoes.

"You sent for me, sir," Melchior said. Then he asked, "Are you all right, sir?"

"I must talk to you," Greiner said.

Melchior waited. He had not often seen Greiner in his SS uniform. With the rest of it, it made a different man.

Greiner was silent. It was as though he went somewhere. Then with a sharp motion, he gestured toward a chair. "Sit down, Melchior, sit down."

Melchior eased himself into the chair. Again Greiner was silent. Melchior had the feeling that he was summoning his mind, from wherever it had gone.

"Melchior, I asked you to come here because there is going to be a change. I wanted to talk with you." Greiner pushed a box of cigarettes toward the police captain.

Melchior took a cigarette and lighted it.

"I'm going to leave this post," Greiner said suddenly. He picked up the cigarette box, looked at it absently, put it down again.

"You're being transferred?" Melchior asked politely.

"Yes."

"I'm sorry to hear that," Melchior said, again politely.

Greiner reached down and took a cigarette and then he spoke very swiftly. "Melchior, I want you to talk to your chief, Larsen. I want you to tell him he must continue to administer the Danish police. I want you to tell him he must cooperate in every way, every way, with whoever replaces me. Do you understand?"

"We've tried to work cooperatively," Melchior said.

"Yes, and you must continue to do so. It may look odd."

"I don't understand."

"It will look odd. It will look odder as time passes. But

no matter what happens you must continue to cooperate."
Greiner looked at Melchior intensely. "Larsen must not
resign, no matter what happens. The Gestapo would take
over the policing."

"I don't think Mr. Larsen has any intention of resign-
ing," Melchior said.

"I know it will seem that he is collaborating with the
Gestapo. More so, as time passes. But in the end it will
help your people. Do you understand?"

"I think so."

"It will be a difficult thing, to appear to be a collaborator," Greiner said. "But it will be the best for all of you in
the end." Greiner mashed out his unsmoked cigarette.

"Is that all, sir?" Melchior asked.

"Yes, Captain."

It was on Melchior's tongue to ask Greiner why he had
chosen to give this message to him, why he had not spoken
to the Danish police chief directly, but something warned
him not to open that kettle of fish. He stood up.

"You must be wondering why I have chosen to speak to
you," Greiner said. "To you, personally."

"Hadn't thought about it." Melchior put on his police
cap and touched his fingers to the visor.

"Yes, Captain Melchior," Greiner said impersonally.
"Good-bye."

6.

COLONEL BUHLE delayed returning to his office. He knew
what he had now to do about Greiner. Well, he tried. You
can't stop a fool from being a fool. Still.

When he reached the office he found Lili Lund awaiting him. He was glad to see her. She looked full of sex and, after the last hours, that was something. "What do you want?"

"This is my day," she said.

"Come in." He held the door open for her, smelling her perfume as she passed. He looked at her long legs with their slim ankles and their slightly overdeveloped calves. He looked at her backside under her thin dress. No girdle, he'd bet. Full of sex and ready. He sighed. Life could be so simple. He followed her in and shut the door. "Sit down."

She sat down, a liquid movement, and stretched her legs. He walked round his desk and sank wearily into his big chair. He looked over the desk. He could see the swelling of her thighs under her skirt.

"Well?" he asked.

"Nothing," she said. She opened her lizard bag and took out a pack of cigarettes. She extracted a cigarette with two long, red-nailed fingers, returned the packet, took out a holder, fitted the cigarette into the holder, reached into the bag again and took out a gold cigarette lighter. She lit the cigarette and dropped the lighter into the bag.

"Nothing?" Buhle asked.

"Nothing."

"Are you wasting my time?" he asked, not displeased that at this moment she was.

"I don't know."

"Perhaps you're wasting your own time."

"No," she said. "I'm not doing that."

"No," he agreed. "But then that's for me to decide."

She drew in a mouthful of smoke, pursed her lips, blew it out.

"I had him in here the other day. He was nothing," Buhle said. "He squealed like a pig."

"I know. His hand. It was a bother for a day or two." He leaned forward slightly. "Just that long?"

"We got round it. Then I made him forget."

"He doesn't seem very much."

152

"No, I imagine he's not. Not to you."

He looked at her, sitting indolently, as though she was at a fashion show, looking over the new fall line. She had something, he thought. Something more than the ankles and the legs and what they led to. "Perhaps you should chuck him and try someone else," he said.

Her eyes widened slightly, so briefly he almost missed it. "I'd rather not," she said.

Something inside him quickened. There were other girls doing what she was doing, she was one of the best but there were others, and it was difficult sometimes to keep them apart, to remember their natures and what they sought and what they needed, they all needed something, beyond the money, beyond the protection, something whatever it was they needed deep within them, and he put his mind and trained memory to work and it came to him quickly, sorted out, what it was with her. It never was simple with any of them and with her it was perhaps more twisted than with most, although, was it twisted? Sex and death, they were close, were they not? The finality in each, each time. They were close in everyone.

She had almost had him fooled, because for a while his mind was elsewhere, with that idiot Greiner. She was cool and there was no faking about that, but today she was very cool, and that meant with her it mattered, and for his purpose that meant it mattered very much.

"You don't think you may still turn up something?" he asked casually.

"I don't know. It's still very soon." Then she said in the same disinterested voice. "How is my father?"

The telephone rang. "Buhle," he said. Then he said, "I'll be right over." He hung up the receiver. "What did you say?" he asked.

"How is my father?"

"Nothing has changed." He took a cigar and lit it.

"Can I get word to him?"

"Of course. The usual?"

"Nothing has changed with me, either."

"I will see you next week," he said.

She stood up, removed the end of the cigarette from the holder and leaned over his desk to use the tray. Again he smelled the perfume and he saw the cat's look in her eyes. She turned and left. He watched her go, the long legs, the carriage.

He sat at his desk for several minutes, smoking his cigar, and then put down the cigar and walked out of the office.

7.

THERE WERE half a dozen men, including Major Becker, in Greiner's office when Colonel Buhle entered. They stood back respectfully.

Greiner had done a professional job, Buhle saw. The bullet hole was in precisely the right place on the left side of his head, slightly above and to the front of his ear. The hole was surrounded by powder burn. The exit hole on the other side was somewhat bigger and messier. Greiner's head was on his desk. His service gun was in his right hand.

"We haven't touched anything, Herr Standartenführer," a young SS *Untersturmführer* said quickly. "Not until you saw him."

"Did he leave anything in writing?" Buhle asked.

"Nothing, Herr Standartenführer."

"You may remove the body now," Buhle said.

He watched while Greiner's body was carried out of the room. He saw that Becker had remained. Buhle sat down in Greiner's chair. "What do you want, Becker?"

"An idea has occurred to me, Herr Standartenführer," Becker said.

154

Buhle raised his head heavily. He saw the excitement in Becker's face and the glitter in his eyes. "Yes?"

"It could be put out that Greiner was killed by the Jews."

"Obersturmbannführer Greiner," Buhle said.

"My error, Herr Standartenführer," Becker said instantly.

"How killed by Jews?" Buhle asked, although he knew and, for some reason he could not explain, it disgusted him.

Becker leaned forward eagerly. "Not in the official report to the Reich, of course, but here, to the Danes. For an excuse."

"An excuse for what, Becker?"

"To make it look better."

"Do you still concern yourself with making things look better?" Buhle asked.

"This action we are taking."

"You believe it is not justified?"

Becker reared as though struck. "Justified! Of couse it is justified, Herr Standartenführer!"

"Then we do not corrupt it with lies."

"Yes, Herr Standartenführer." Becker heiled Hitler and left.

Buhle leaned back. Greiner did it neatly. And he looked peaceful. He could still believe, that much. Well, now he knows whether it was worth it.

Buhle's head ached. He needed a drink.

8.

THERE WAS no question. His small, somewhat vacant face showed it plainly. Obersturmbannführer Adolf Eichmann was upset. "You cannot imagine how inconvenient this is," he said petulantly. "I'm at a simple loss."

He sat in a straight-backed chair in the office of Dr. Werner Best in Dagmar House. It was the day following the debacle with the Jews and he had been dispatched to Copenhagen by Reichführer Heinrich Himmler to find out what had gone wrong.

Present at the unhappy meeting were Dr. Best, leaning on his desk below the picture, his hands clenched; General von Kobe, sprawled in the farthest part of the office; Colonel Buhle, the inevitable cigar clenched between his teeth; Georg Siebert, impassive as a Buddha, and Major Becker, who preferred to remain standing in the closeness of his awesome superiors. Of them all, Becker was most reverential before Eichmann, whose relatively unimportant SS rank of lieutenant colonel meant nothing against the terrifying fact that he came from the innermost sanctum and on this occasion spoke directly for Himmler.

Eichmann looked sadly at Best's sallow, pinched face. The "other Adolf" was demure in his black uniform. He worried his hands in his lap. His manner did not in any way mislead Colonel Buhle, who knew Eichmann was as harmless as a cobra.

"I had everything worked out," Eichmann said. "To the last detail. The trains to pick them up in Hamburg—and you cannot imagine how complicated it is to work out a railway schedule these days." He ignored a derisive grunt from von Kobe. "It was nothing less than coordinating a troop movement. And then the empty cars were blocking traffic. They had to be returned unused. It was quite embarrassing. And the resettlement centers. Doctors prepared to give the necessary examinations, clerks ready to compile records, orderlies on hand to issue clothing. It was most distressing all around. Really, your Excellency, the Reichführer cannot understand your Danish Jews. Everywhere else they have been most tractable."

Best looked up morbidly at "your" Danish Jews.

Von Kobe rumbled in his distant corner. "Get on with

it, Eichmann," the Prussian growled. "I'm not here to listen to your damned problems."

Eichmann turned slowly. He took off his glasses, breathed on them, wiped them, replaced them. His movements were deliberate, almost pedantic. "Yes, Herr Generaloberst," he said. "I am only conveying the incredulity of Reichführer Himmler—and of the Führer."

The words tolled in the room.

Eichmann returned his attention to Best. "There must be order and system, your Excellency. Without that, there is nothing. Days of preparation, all for nothing. Orders issued and then canceled. It is most unfortunate." There was no sound, save from von Kobe shifting in his chair. Then Eichmann, with silky diffidence, asked, "Who informed the Jews?"

Best sighed somberly. "If we knew, Herr Obersturmbannführer, you may rest assured he would now be behind bars."

The faintest flicker passed across Siebert's eyes. It went unnoticed by everyone except Buhle. Buhle looked more attentively at the huge man whom he knew only slightly.

"I am sure, your Excellency," Eichmann said. "Who here in Copenhagen knew of the contemplated action?"

Best waved his hand in a vague, inclusive gesture. "Everybody in this room. And Greiner, of course."

Buhle rolled his cigar from one side of his mouth to the other and contemplated Siebert casually from under lowered lids.

"Obersturmbannführer Greiner," Eichmann said. He pressed his slender fingers together. "Is it possible that is why he shot himself? That he betrayed his trust and regretted it?"

Again Buhle saw the faint flicker cross Siebert's vast face. "No," Buhle said.

Eichmann shifted his gaze. "You are certain of that, Herr Standartenführer?"

"Yes."

"How can you be certain?" When Buhle turned his eyes

157

flatly on Eichmann for this peremptory interrogation, Eichmann said disarmingly, "You must be kind enough to understand, Herr Standartenführer, that I am only asking these questions in the name of the Reichführer."

After a moment, Buhle said clearly, "Greiner was my friend. I have known him for many years."

"Well, Herr Standartenführer?"

"Very well. His record speaks for itself. He needs no defense from me."

"Did he approve of the action?"

"It was not his place to approve or disapprove," Buhle said. "Max Greiner was an officer and a loyal German and at no time in his career has he ever failed in his duties."

"I appreciate your support of your friend, Herr Standartenführer," Eichmann said apologetically. "But I must remind the Standartenführer that in certain circles Obersturmbannführer Greiner made quite another impression."

"He needs no support from me," Buhle repeated implacably. "But since he is not here, I will presume to speak for him. I will vouch categorically and for the record that Max Greiner was in no way responsible for the lack of success of the action and that he did everything in his power to accomplish it."

"God in heaven, Eichmann!" von Kobe said loudly. "Nobody here is a traitor! Stop wasting time!"

"Yet, there was in fact a betrayal, Herr Generaloberst," Eichmann said with profound respect. In the same decorous manner, he asked, "Is it not true, Herr Generaloberst, that you sent a dispatch to Generaloberst Keitel protesting the action?"

The other men looked with surprise across the room. Von Kobe's face darkened.

Eichmann raised his eyes as though to refresh his memory. "The exact words, Herr Generaloberst: 'The implementation of the Jewish deportations impairs the prestige of the Wehrmacht. . . .' Yes, those were the words." He lowered his head and peered hesitantly at the Prussian. "Orders from the Führer impairing the prestige of the

158

Wehrmacht, Herr Generaloberst?" He waited for the general to say something and, when von Kobe did not, he went on with the same faltering relentlessness, "And what else was it you told Generaloberst Keitel? That you could not guarantee order if the raids were carried out? Could not guarantee order?" Eichmann now stood up. He clasped his hands behind his back. "But the reply to your protest, Herr Generaloberst. We must not forget that." He looked at von Kobe. "Do you remember the reply, Herr Generaloberst?"

"Since when," von Kobe asked slowly, "am I required to answer questions addressed to me by you?"

Buhle wished with all his heart at that moment that he had two sets of eyes. He would have given anything to be able to watch Eichmann and von Kobe at the same time. He had never heard anything quite like this before. And he had never realized until this moment just how much power Adolf Eichmann must possess.

"And the reply was this, Herr Generaloberst," Eichmann continued. "And these, too, are the exact words: 'Nonsense. These are matters of State necessity.' State necessity, Herr Generaloberst." The frail-looking little lieutenant colonel pulled down the tunic of his uniform and walked closer to von Kobe and, in the tones of a quiet and assured prosecutor, asked, "Your protest was called nonsense, was it not?"

Buhle waited for the explosion. He was astonished when von Kobe finally spoke, in a voice so low as to be almost inaudible.

"What a day we live in," the Prussian said.

Siebert and Best exchanged glances. Both remembered the general using the same words at another time. It seemed a long time ago.

"What a day we live in," von Kobe said again in a whisper. He looked up and down Eichmann with a kind of weary revulsion. "When a secret communique from a general officer to the chief of staff of the Wehrmacht becomes the property of a turd like you."

Eichmann recoiled. He said, his voice rising to a shriek, "I speak for Reichführer Himmler!"

159

Von Kobe rose to his feet. Eichmann backed away. Von Kobe studied him for a moment as though he was a specimen. "I don't give a howl in hell if you speak for Almighty God," the general said. "You are speaking to a German general officer. You piece of shit, you swine-dog, you ought to be horsewhipped."

Fair enough, Buhle thought. He pulled on his cigar and discovered in his stimulation he had allowed the cigar to go out.

Eichmann composed himself. "I am under orders to inform the Generaloberst that in future he will cooperate."

"Eichmann, I have gone on record before, but for your special benefit I will repeat myself," von Kobe said. "As long as I am in military command in Denmark, no German soldier will disgrace his uniform by hunting down human beings who do not constitute the enemy."

Eichmann folded his arms theatrically. "Then you are in disagreement with the Führer, who holds that all Jews are enemies of the State?"

"Save that bullshit for home consumption, Eichmann," von Kobe said contemptuously.

"Is that what I am to report to the Reichführer?"

"Report whatever the hell you please, you little palace cunt!" von Kobe roared. "And if he doesn't like it, he can get me transferred to someplace where war is not conducted against women and children!" He picked up his cap and slapped it on his head. "Open a window, Best," he said. "This place stinks."

The slamming of the door reverberated in the room, it seemed to Buhle, for several moments. He took the opportunity to relight his cigar.

Best made a business of gathering papers on his desk. Siebert stared at the floor. Becker made a graceful point of not looking at Eichmann.

"We are chagrined, Obersturmbannführer Eichmann," Best said at last, "at what has just transpired. Generaloberst von Kobe is under a very great strain. But with regard to the problem of the Jews, we will rectify matters."

Eichmann, still stunned by von Kobe's outburst, nodded dully. "Of course, your Excellency."

"The Jews have not vanished into the air," Best went on smoothly. "They are still in Denmark. The Führer and Reichführer Himmler may rest assured we will find them."

Eichmann rallied his forces. "Your Excellency's telegram to the Führer, declaring that Denmark was free of Jews, it was somewhat premature." He smiled to make it a joke.

Best responded by turning up the corners of his own lips, a good effort; his face remained pinched. "Let us put it as a promise, instead, Herr Obersturmbannführer," he said. "More than a promise. A solemn guarantee."

Buhle stole a look at Siebert. The big, bald head was still lowered, the eyes fixed on the floor.

PART III.

1.

THE BLACK-CLAD mourners walked gravely in the bright sunlight, along the street of lime trees toward the chapel at the Bispebjerg Hospital. It now was two days after the abortive action against the Jews.

Watching them, seated on a bench with Dr. Poul Klampmann, Dr. Stephan Moller blinked his eyes behind his dense glasses. "Children. I have never seen so many children at a funeral."

Dr. Klampmann, feeding his eyes on a stunning area, rich with the last flowers of the year, said, "Children miss their loved ones, too, wouldn't you think?"

It was strange, Moller thought. The last day. The sudden changing of the names of all the Jewish patients in the hospital. Well, he could understand that, everybody did, the people were sick, some dying, but that would make no difference to the Gestapo. With a few strokes of a pen, a brief clattering of a typewriter, Izak Hertz, ulcer case, became Christian Hviid, ulcer case, and, to Moller's eyes, by some mysterious chemistry, at the same time somehow changed in appearance.

It was all done quietly and efficiently and swiftly, new name tags prepared and substituted for the old. The orders, issued by Klampmann, were received without surprise or question. Overnight, there was not a single Jew registered on any record in the enormous hospital.

Moller had heard of the plan with apprehension. "The whole staff will know about this," he had said to Klampmann. "All the doctors, nurses, orderlies, helpers, even the janitors.

165

Just by the law of averages, there must be some Nazi sympathizers here."

"There are a few pro-German doctors," Klampmann had admitted. "Not that they've ever done anything about it. But it's something we've simply got to do and there's no time to worry about possible informers." Then, as Moller let his worry creep across his face, Klampmann, inexplicably, burst into laughter. "You know, Stephan, when some of the doctors with German leanings find out what we're doing, they'll be more frightened than anybody else."

"Frightened?"

"They know if the Germans get wind of this, they'll be the ones automatically suspected. And even those bastards who have no dislike for Hitler know there'll be no future for informers in Denmark."

Klampmann had been quite certain of this, and perhaps he was right, but only time would show. But now this, this particular and in some way extraordinary funeral. Why had Klampmann summoned him from his work to watch it? And what was it that was out of the ordinary? There was nothing unusual about the people. They seemed unhappy enough. Then it struck him. "It's like the car in the circus," he said to Klampmann.

"Is it?" Klampmann asked. "Is that how you see it?"

"Poul, there have been too many people. There must be more than two hundred who have gone in there. They couldn't all fit."

"You've noticed that?" Klampmann stood up. "Then you must come with me."

He led Moller across the clipped lawn, across a cement walk, to the rear of the small chapel. Moller raised his head in astonishment. The same people were pouring out of the back door of the chapel as steadily as they had entered the front. They climbed into waiting taxis. As soon as the taxis were loaded, they started off.

"Jews," Moller said.

"Now I want you to come to my office with me," Klampmann said.

Moller blinked again in confusion. "Where did the taxis come from? Where are they taking them?"

"These people are all here because for some stupid reason they trust their doctors," Klampmann said. "A friend of mine called yesterday. He asked me whether I could get a few Jews away if he sent them here." Klampmann watched a father pick up a little girl and carry her into a cab. "I told him yes. Do you know why, Stephan? Because I knew it would make me feel good. And do you know something else? I feel good. Now come along."

"But where are they going?" Moller asked.

"In due time."

"Poul," Moller said after a moment.

Klampmann caught the tone immediately. "Where?"

"There. Two of them."

Without looking at Moller, Klampmann said curtly, "They're not mind-readers. They only know what they see, like anybody else."

Klampmann walked up to the two SS officers who were gazing curiously at the people entering the chapel. "I'm Dr. Klampmann, gentlemen," Klampmann said, noticing the Germans could not see the rear of the chapel from where they were standing. "Can I help you?"

The officers clicked their heels. The senior said, "We are looking for a fellow-officer, Obersturmführer Johan Weber. He was injured in a disturbance." His eyes held on the people entering the chapel.

Klampmann walked a few paces in front of the officers, requiring them to turn their backs to the chapel. "Yes, I know of the unfortunate lieutenant. He's in the casualty section." He pointed. "Do you see that building? Just inside, you'll see the inquiry desk. Just ask the receptionist there and she'll direct you."

The Germans clicked their heels again. The sun flashed on the silver darts. Moller lowered his eyes. His hands were damp and he kept them in his pockets.

"Thank you, Doctor," the senior officer said. He turned his head, peered again at the chapel. "So many mourners, no?"

Klampmann nodded gravely. "Yes, he was a very popular man, the one who died. A great benefactor. Much loved."

At that moment, the little girl leaned out of the taxi which had come into view and waved her hand cheerfully. The senior officer frowned. Moller's hands in his pockets pressed against his thighs.

"Children," Klampmann said understandingly. "They're lucky, aren't they? They don't comprehend death."

"So true," the senior officer said. He nodded to the other officer and the two walked briskly toward the building Klampmann had indicated.

"Come, Stephan," Klampmann said. "It's all over and we're still alive. Remember—only what they see. Despite all intelligence to the contrary, they're not supermen."

A tall man in a baggy tweed suit was staring from the window, his head enveloped in a cloud of smoke, when Klampmann and Moller entered the office. When the man turned at the sound of the opening door, Moller saw he was puffing on a stubby pipe. He was no one Moller had ever seen before.

"Stephan, this is Peter Hansen," Klampmann said. "The friend I mentioned. Peter, Dr. Stephan Moller, my colleague."

Hansen extended his hand, his blue eyes taking in Moller swiftly. Moller wiped his moist palm on his white doctor's gown and shook hands.

"Is this the one, Poul?" Hansen asked.

Klampmann sat down at his desk and stretched his legs. "Ask him."

Without preamble, Hansen said, "Dr. Moller, we're shipping some Jews to Sweden tonight. The problem is to keep the children quiet until they get past the Germans. They'll have to be sedated."

Moller backed away slowly, feeling it seep through his body. "Why are you telling me?"

"I want you to do it," Hansen said.

Moller shook his head. "I will not."

Hansen glanced at Klampmann. He took his pipe out of his mouth. "Why not?"

"I will not," Moller repeated, his hands going wet again.

"Why, Stephan?" Klampmann asked. "Because they're Jews?"

"Jews, anybody," Moller said. "I'm not for this."

"Nobody is," Hansen said.

"I'm not for this," Moller said. He looked at Klampmann. "Poul, you know that. I won't risk my neck, for Jews or anybody else."

"Poul?" Hansen asked.

"Don't be silly, Stephan," Klampmann said easily. "Of course you'll do it."

"I will not get involved!" Moller said.

"You are involved." Klampmann smiled affably. "One way and another. Your alternative is to go and inform to the Gestapo."

Moller jerked up his head. "You know I won't do that. I'm not that kind of man."

"Then you don't have a choice, do you, Stephan?"

"No, Poul, I'm not a hero!"

"Who is?" Klampmann asked.

Moller leaned across the desk. His fists were clenched. His knuckles were white. "I'm a doctor, Poul, that's all."

"Exactly." To Hansen, who was contemplating Moller dubiously, Klampman said, "He'll be there, Peter. Just tell him when and where."

2.

A LITTLE LATER on that same day, a hatless, fair-haired man in a trench-coat read the little sign in the window of a grocery store in a residential district of Copenhagen: *"DEUTSCHE SIND HIER NICHT ERWUNSCHT."*

The man entered the shop and waited patiently until the grocer, a pot-bellied little man, was free. Then he asked pleasantly, "Why don't you care to do business with Germans?" Other customers looked up nervously at the German accent.

The grocer said, "It's my store and my privilege."

"Of course," the German said.

The grocer beckoned. He leaned across the counter and said in a whisper, "If I didn't put that sign in the window I might lose some of my Danish customers. You understand, sir."

"Of course," the German said. "But it is not a feeling in your heart."

"I'm a business man," the grocer said. "Your money is as good as anybody else's."

"Spoken like a true Dane," the German said. "Wait on your other customers. I'll just look around."

The grocer nodded, turned to another customer; his eyes widened as he saw Niels Rider enter the store.

Niels, his long face lamenting the sorrows of life, waited his turn and then said, "I'd like some herring. King Christian brand."

"I'm sorry," the grocer said instantly. "We happen to be out of it at the moment."

"Thanks," Niels said. "I'll try again."

He started from the store and found the German standing in the entrance. In the German's hand was a can of herring. "You did say King Christian, did you not?" he asked in a friendly way.

The grocer bustled out from behind the counter. He held up his hands. "How could I have made such a mistake? These days one doesn't know whether one's head is on one's shoulders right side up or upside down." To Niels he said, "How many cans do you want, sir?"

"Two," Niels said, watching the man in the trench-coat.

The German offered the can to Niels. Niels accepted it. Then he saw that the German's other hand held a small automatic. "You will come with me, please," the German said.

A woman in the store gasped audibly. The customers moved away.

170

"Who the hell are you?" Niels asked.

The German reached into his pocket with his free hand and took out the familiar card with the two red lines identifying him as an agent of the Gestapo. As he returned the card to his pocket, Niels slung the can of herring underhand. It caught the German on the right wrist. At the same moment, Niels hurled himself at the German reaching down with his outstretched hands. He jerked the German forward just below the knees, and as the German buckled he brought up his knee at the German's groin. The German caught his breath hoarsely. Niels chopped him hard on the side of the neck with the edge of his hand. As the German staggered back, Niels ran out of the store.

He saw a girl bearing down on a bicycle. He grabbed the handlebar and pulled the cycle to a stop. "Excuse me, darling," he said, smiling lugubriously. He shoved her off the seat, jumped on, pedalled away.

"Wait a minute!" the girl yelled.

She backed away in terror as the German ran out of the store, aimed his pistol at Niels and opened fire.

Niels ducked his head low so that he resembled a bicycle racer, realized the prudent action had raised his rump, thoughtfully brought that back down firmly on the seat. He heard the shots, counted the bullets passing close to him and, when they reached seven, wheeled the cycle round and pedalled back. As the German was slipping a new clip into his automatic, Niels pulled out his own gun and shot him through the heart.

"Wow!" the girl said.

Niels handed back the cycle, bent down over the dead man. As he was removing his papers, he heard Peter Hansen say, "Murder? In broad daylight?"

Niels looked up. His face was sadder than ever. "He tried to murder me first. I'm sorry."

"He's right," the girl said. "I saw it."

"Why?" Hansen asked Niels.

Niels stood up sheepishly. "He never gave me a chance to ask."

The grocer, who now joined them, nodded towards Niels. "He behaved quite correctly."

"He certainly did," the girl said.

Hansen looked at the girl, at the grocer, at the customers now threading cautiously out of the store. "Come along," he said to Niels. "Before some of his friends turn up." He started down the street.

Niels waggled a finger at the girl, said, "Thank you." He saw she was pretty and adoring. He kissed her on the lips and hurried on to catch up with Hansen. "It wasn't my fault with the German, Mr. Hansen," he said earnestly. "He was arresting me."

"You're here," Hansen said. "I have something for you to do. Machine guns."

Niels' face sagged lower. "A raid? Without Arne and me?"

"The guns are not German. They were made in a little basement in Copenhagen."

"Are they any good?"

"I don't know," Hansen said.

"That Gestapoman," Niels said. "No waste."

"How is that?"

"He was a bad shot."

3.

THE LAUGH IS ON MR. SIEBERT

Georg Siebert, one of the most malignant of the Nazi officials in Denmark, is not a happy man these days. Given the task by Dr. Best to assist in the evacuation of Jews to Germany, Mr. Siebert carefully worked out the plans for loading eight thousand Jews on the two ships sent up from Germany. But, as it turned out, Mr. Siebert and his cohorts have been able to put their hands on about 350 of the unfortunate people. Where did the rest disappear to? Mr. Siebert, a vicious, fanatical follower of his Führer, would be hard put to answer that.

Siebert lowered the little underground sheet. "Yes," he said to Hansen. "I've read this. It was on my desk this morning."

The two men were seated at an outdoor table at Frascati's, facing the big square. It was late in the afternoon, two hours after the killing of the Gestapoman. The day was still warm. The square was crowded. The outdoor café was almost full.

Siebert looked at the paper again. " 'Vicious. . . .' 'Malignant. . . .' 'Fanatical. . . .' " He looked at Hansen. "I was congratulated by all my colleagues. Even Dr. Best considered it a distinction." He held up the paper. "May I keep this?" When Hansen nodded, he folded the paper carefully and put it in his billfold. "This may be more useful than you realize, Mr. Hansen," he said. "I'm being recalled to Berlin."

He slipped the billfold into his jacket pocket, picked up his coffee cup. He looked more closely at Hansen and lowered the cup slowly. Despite his diplomatic training, he could not keep the astonishment from coloring his voice. "How did you know?"

Hansen gazed out at the square.

Siebert shrugged, a major movement in the terrace where the tables were not too widely separated. "Yes," he said. "In any case, I should not know."

Hansen stuffed his pipe. It wasn't easy to shift gears. After thinking about Siebert for so long in a certain way. The memory of fear. It was almost as bad as the real thing. And he wasn't all that sure of Siebert, even now.

He switched his eyes to Siebert. Inert bulk. He needed handholds, Hansen thought, to guide him between his normal, naïve instincts to trust, to like, and the wariness he inherited with the job, which still fitted him like a badly made suit.

"When do you leave?" he asked.

"They haven't informed me."

173

"Was it Best?"

"I don't know."

"What will happen to you?"

"I don't know that, either."

Hansen lit his pipe carefully. It would be a risk. But Siebert rated that. But did he? It could still be a complicated German scheme, the warning, everything. He drew on the pipe and stared at the people passing, and he said finally, "Perhaps something can be done."

Siebert altered his position. The small restaurant chair protested. Siebert waited in a state of monumental suspension, a man who was not unfamiliar with chairs surrendering. "Thank you, Mr. Hansen," he said. "I'm afraid not. I have a wife and children here."

"Something could be done about them at the same time," Hansen said quietly.

Siebert smiled. It was a gentle smile, one Hansen had never seen on him before, but he knew it was thoroughly at home in that immense face.

"That is nice to know, Mr. Hansen. But I have family in Germany as well," the German said.

"It goes that far."

" 'Sippenhaft,' Mr. Hansen."

Hansen frowned. "Language rule?"

Siebert shook his head slowly. "No, Mr. Hansen, in this instance the word is quite explicit and means exactly what it says. Quite literally, it translates as 'apprehension and arrest of kin.' " He sipped his coffee. "When the order was sent from Berlin, telling me to prepare to go there for questioning, other orders were issued simultaneously. At this time, Mr. Hansen, the Gestapo without question has my parents, my brother and my two sisters under surveillance, and probably my old grandmother into the bargain."

Hansen studied the stem of his pipe. His teeth had left their mark. "I regret we were the occasion for this."

"You have nothing to blame yourself for," Siebert said. "Quite the contrary. I went to you voluntarily. I almost had to beat you over the head to make you listen to me. And even then you didn't wholly trust me, and properly not."

"I think I trust you now, Mr. Siebert," Hansen said.

"You can, as of now," Siebert said. "Or up to now. But don't make a habit of trust. Not in principle and never specifically. When I return from Berlin, if I return from Berlin, I may be an entirely different man."

"Or it may be a different Berlin," Hansen said.

Siebert smiled again. "Isn't that a pleasant thought? I shall remember it."

At that moment a stone sailed through the air, struck Siebert's cup, shattering it. A young man in the square shouted, "Nazi swine!" and darted away. The others on the Frascati terrace looked briefly and disinterestedly toward Siebert, turned back to their coffee or beer. Passersby in the street did not break step.

Siebert took a kerchief seeming large as a bedsheet and wiped the spilled coffee from his trousers. "You're all so very cooperative," he said to Hansen.

"I can't take credit for that," Hansen said.

"You should," Siebert said, tapping his breast pocket. "The little paper gets around, does it not?"

A waiter appeared, dabbed the cloth with a towel. His face was without expression, absolutely. "Would you like another cup of coffee, sir?" he asked Siebert. His voice was impeccable.

"No, I think not," the German said. When the waiter went away, Siebert said to Hansen, "I must go now. I will report that you have lived up to your promises to increase the production level and that you will endeavor to achieve even higher production in future."

"Absolutely," Hansen said.

"Good-bye, Mr. Hansen," Siebert said. "And once again, my thanks for the credit rating you gave me in your little paper. I have always found pleasure in reading it, but I assure you I never was as pleased as I was today." He stood up and everyone else in the street-side café suddenly seemed small. "One day when all this is over, if we manage to survive the stupidity, perhaps you will be good enough to tell me how you became *au courant*—and so quickly—with a secret order known only to Dr. Best and myself."

The enormous man bowed with his own distinctive grace and then set out across the street in the direction of Dagmar House. Hansen finished his coffee, watching Siebert walk, slowly and light-footed under the mass of body. He supposed if Siebert really wanted to know, it would not be too hard to follow the trail from the cipher office to the ordinary Gestapo files to the Danish police liaison to Captain Erik Melchior, who had now made it a question of personal honor to be worthy of his position as Hitler's only Jewish police captain. At least the only one who admitted it.

However, Hansen was confident Siebert would not bother. It was something he would prefer not to know. For Hansen had decided in the end that Siebert was quite a man. A man with dignity as huge and durable as he was. Hansen hoped there would be that time when they could sit and talk as human beings. If the world ever was that way again.

Hansen looked at his watch. It was after five. He had a lot yet to do. He paid the bill and walked to his car and started for home. He wondered about Kate and how she was. What with the hospital and the business of Niels Rider and then Siebert, he had not spoken to her since early in the day. He might be a father again. Kate. He hoped so. She detested the unborn child. Just for the moment, of course. She blamed it for her appearance, which was quite natural, he supposed. She was convinced she was a complete mess. Also natural. Almost every woman got that way toward the end. But with Kate it was linked to other things, related to what she feared and hated more than anything else. It wasn't anything that could be talked about. Something came down over her eyes and the neck he loved so much got ropy with tension and he could see the same tension in her hands. They always had to get somewhere else fast.

But the baby couldn't stall forever. And then she'd have back the body she offered him always and endlessly with love and pleasure and delight and gratitude. The marvelous body and the marvelous nature within it. No woman he had ever known performed the act of love as Kate did. It was their mutual gift, and that was part of it now, beyond the mood about her appearance; she was a highly sexed woman and, no matter what the modern doctors said, the last month or two of pregnancy was hell on sex. Even when you did it as they said you should.

He wondered about Moller and whether he would show up tonight. Klampmann said he would, but still. Moller was frightened. Well, Hansen knew all about that. But why had Klampmann chosen him?

He wondered about Georg Siebert and what they would do to him in Berlin if that was the way it was going to be, and if it was that way how would he stand against it? Siebert was like a rock. But in time they could break rocks. Would they go that far?

It occurred belatedly to Hansen, as he made his way through the evening traffic, that he had more than a friendly anxiety about Siebert's future. With all that was happening during the day, he hadn't bothered to realize that if Siebert went bad in Berlin that would only be the beginning.

The ending would be here in Copenhagen with him.

4.

THERE WERE DANES who still visited Kronborg Castle in Elsinore these days, finding sustenance in the majestic pile at the mouth of the Sound, not so much for its connection with Hamlet as for its reminder of a less onerous and prouder time.

In the basement of Kronborg, according to the old legend, dwelt Holger Danske, Holger the Dane, the protector of Denmark, who wakened and went forth only in time of danger. Holger Danske was afoot again, it was said, embodied in one of the resistance groups that called itself by his thunderous name.

By now the night was on Elsinore and the wind was coming chillingly from the open sea and the visitors were gone, even those who had remained until dark so they could look across the narrowest part of the Sound and see the lights twinkling in Sweden, free Sweden, less than two miles away.

By now the big railroad station, the long platforms, were host to other visitors. These were people who sat quietly, in desperation or despair, who nursed babies, soothed children, smoked, stared, thought; there were those who smoked and gazed in apathy and thought of nothing. But most of them were thinking about what had happened to them, where they had been for the last three or four days, and where they were going. And how it would be if by some miracle they got there.

Standing in a corner of the station, puffing on his pipe, Peter Hansen watched the steps leading up from the street. It now was after eight o'clock and he had told Moller to be there at eight, at the latest. From the corner of his eye he saw a uniform approach. He waited for a moment and said, without taking his eyes from the entrance, "That better be you, Erik."

"Where the hell is he?" Melchior asked.

"I don't know."

"What about the doctor in Snekkersten?"

"Too late. And he wouldn't have the drugs. That's why I went to Klampmann. He has the hospital supply." He looked up at the station clock. "God damn it!"

"I'll kill him," Melchior said. "Personally. If that son of a bitch messes things up, I'll find him and kill him."

Hansen craned his neck suddenly. "All right," he said. "But wait until after he's done his job."

He walked rapidly across the station to where Moller was mounting the steps. The doctor looked around vaguely. He started when Hansen bore down on him.

"Where have you been?" Hansen asked.

"There was a German convoy on the Strandvejen," Moller said. "It held everybody up."

178

"Have you got everything?"

"In my bag," Moller said, looking around. "More in the ambulance."

"Did you park it where I told you to?"

Moller nodded. "My God, how many are there here?"

"There are more outside on the platforms."

"But the Germans, the Gestapo . . . how can they fail to notice them?"

"This is a railroad station," Hansen said. "The Germans are logical and it's logical to have people waiting in a railroad station."

"Where will they go from here?"

"To Sweden. In empty freight cars. Now, Doctor, you've got to go to work and you've got to work fast. That freight train leaves on a schedule and we can't do anything to alter that."

Moller nodded. He wet his dry lips. "Where shall I start?"

"Here. Right here. And then the people on the platform." Hansen took Moller by the arm and propelled him toward a group of Jews. "And remember, there's something else you can administer, Doctor. A little cheer. A little hope." He looked at Moller's face. "Try not to worry too much," Hansen said. "There are quite a few of us around."

A mother, about thirty-five, looking ten years older now, suckled an infant. An older child huddled against her. Her husband, a thin man with a stubble, stood close by. The mother and father looked at Hansen and Moller through dulled, indifferent eyes.

"All right, Doctor," Hansen said.

The mother's eyes flickered in numbed puzzlement. "Doctor? What for?"

"Just a little precaution," Hansen said. "We don't want the children to make a noise at the wrong moment." He jabbed his elbow into Moller. "All right, Moller, for Christ sake move!"

Moller opened his bag and fumbled around and took out a hypodermic. The mother started to shiver and she held the baby closer to her breast.

"No," she said. "You're not going to do anything to my baby."

179

She spoke in a whisper, but Moller's doctor's ear detected the hysteria.

"I promise you, madam," he heard himself say, wondering how all this was happening in Denmark, how he was involved in it, "I promise you this won't hurt the child." He heard the shaking in his voice and he wondered whether it would be in his hand as well. "It will just sedate the child, make him sleep." He reached out with the needle and the mother pulled the baby away.

"Please," Hansen said sternly. "There are so many and such little time."

The mother looked up at Hansen and then she held the baby toward Moller. The doctor inserted the needle. He thanked God his training did not desert him. His hand and fingers were steady.

He injected the other child and moved on to another group. While Moller went about his work, a man asked Hansen, "Do you really think we can get away from the Gestapo by crossing a couple of miles of water?"

"At least you can be sure of one thing," Hansen said. "Once you're in Sweden, the doctor can't collect his bill."

With Hansen at his side, Moller moved among them like some magic monster in a fairy tale, touching little people with his fingers and putting them to sleep. As he worked, he saw the drugs take effect. As the children went under, he saw young Danes, most of them hardly older than children, move the people out of the station. When he finished with the last child three hours later, the station was empty.

Moller wiped the sweat from his face as he had wiped it a dozen times that cold night, and he looked at Hansen. "Is that it, Mr. Hansen?"

"Come with me," Hansen said.

He led Moller across the tracks, across another platform, across several tracks. Ahead of them, Moller could see the freight train.

"Brings in stuff from Sweden," Hansen said. "Returns empty. Officially, anyway."

When they reached the train, Moller could see many of the

people still waiting. As he watched, the young underground workers broke open the seals on the closed doors and slid the doors open. Then they helped the refugees aboard.

A woman saw Moller. She held out an unconscious baby. "He'll be all right, Doctor? When he wakes up, he'll be all right?"

"Yes," Moller said.

"You swear it, Doctor?"

The woman's husband helped her into the train. "He's a doctor, isn't he? He knows what he's doing." He turned to Moller from the door of the car and waved his hand. "Thank you, Doctor, may God bless you, Doctor."

The last of the Jews was loaded on the train and then Moller was startled to see four Danish customs men go down the length of the train and reseal the doors. He looked at Hansen. "Everybody?" he asked. "The whole country?"

"No," Hansen said. "But quite a few."

The seals again intact on each door, the customs men gave the engineer the word and the train moved slowly to the pier. A ferry was waiting in the slip.

Hansen led Moller to a secluded place where they could see the train and the ferry with its tracks awaiting it. Then Hansen saw Moller stiffen as German customs people joined the Danish officials and began a careful inspection of every seal on every car.

"Now's the time your sedative had better be doing its job, Doctor," Hansen said.

Moller nodded, shivered in the damp wind. He turned up his coat collar, wiped his sweating face. One cry, one whimper, one small sound from inside the cars.

Hansen saw Captain Melchior join the customs inspectors. "Let's go," Hansen said. "They'll be a little time at that. The Germans, as we all know, are very thorough."

Moller took a last look at the train, at the ferry, at the lights of Hälsingborg in Sweden across the narrow, dark water.

"Come," Hansen said. "We need a drink."

5.

THE BAR in the little inn at Snekkersten a few miles down the coast from Elsinore was not crowded at this late hour. The owner of the inn, a jolly Jutlander named Pedersen, was behind the bar. As he poured the snaps, he looked briefly at Hansen who, as briefly, nodded.

Moller's hand, which had been steady enough, shook slightly as he lifted the glass to his mouth. Hansen watched him drink all of it, set the glass down again. He saw the sweat break out on Moller's face again.

Moller stared at his empty glass.

Hansen finished his own drink. "What is it?" he asked. "Do you regret what you've done?"

"No," Moller said.

"What's bothering you? Fear?"

"That," Moller said. "Other things."

Hansen waved to Pedersen, who refilled their glasses, started away, returned and left the bottle of aquavit on the bar.

"Fear?" Hansen asked. "Are we talking about fear?"

"Yes," Moller said. "That and other things."

"You're just beginning to know about fear," Hansen said. "You had the sweats and you have them now and the turning over inside. And you think it's going to get better and it never gets better."

"You?" Moller asked. "You have it, too?"

He poured snaps into Hansen's glass and into his own, and Hansen saw his hands were steadying and he looked at Moller's face and for the first time liked what he saw. He was beginning to know why Klampmann had picked him. He might be worthy.

"There's a German I know," Hansen said. "From the beginning, he was trying to tell me something. But I was always so scared I couldn't see it. All I knew was that when I saw him, something inside me started to crawl." He emptied his glass and again Moller refilled it, his hand quite steady. "It wasn't him," Hansen said. "Not him personally, not entirely. But it was as though he was the poisoned end of the spear, the end of the line, that behind him were all the Germans, the Gestapo, the concentration camps, the ovens, the gas chambers. Everything. It was a long line stretching all the way back to Germany and he was the end of the line or maybe he was the beginning. I had to see him a lot and it was always the same, and the terrible thing was that it was nothing he said or did. It was just there. He had been given it like a weapon, and he had it and they all have it, that is their true weapon, and that's what we have to do, to show they all don't really have it, that it's a trick, a kind of legerdemain. They're strong and so far they're ahead, but that's because they prepared and then moved first. But they're people and they can be whipped by people, and they're clever but they can be fooled by others who are clever. But only if everybody else doesn't lie down and play dead."

Hansen emptied his glass. The snaps was taking hold now, in a good way. The cold was going away, and his own fear.

"I could never feel that way," Moller said. "To want to whip them. They frighten me. They frighten me the way they frighten you. But you have something that I don't have. I'll try, Mr. Hansen, but I don't think I have it." He breathed deeply and drank his snaps, more slowly now.

"If you haven't," Hansen said, understanding Klampmann more and more. "If you haven't, you've got something that works just as well."

Moller wiped his glasses and smiled shyly. His glasses had steamed a little in the room but his face no longer was sweating. And, Hansen thought, after three solid snaps that was damned good.

"One thing, Mr. Hansen. May I ask you something?"

"Yes," Hansen said. "Sure."

"If everything goes all right up there and the train gets on the ferry and they get across—how do you know the Swedes will admit those people?"

"They will," Hansen said.

"You know that?"

"Yes. They'll take them all, as many as we can get over there, they'll take every one."

"And they're not concerned about the Nazis?"

"They are, Doctor, they're very much concerned." Hansen refilled his glass. "You said fear and other things, Dr. Moller."

"Other things," Moller said.

"Such as what?"

"Will we know, Mr. Hansen?" Moller asked suddenly. "About them?"

"Yes. Now, what other things?"

"Those children. There was no time to learn anything about their medical history. No time to find out whether any of them had any medical problem—something that might contra-indicate sedatives. Allergies, for instance." He fingered his glass. "In certain extreme instances, the drug I administered might cause death."

Hansen picked up the bottle and poured some snaps into Moller's glass.

"Monstrous," Moller said. "Grown men chasing down children."

"They've been doing it for years," Hansen said. "Shouldn't surprise you."

"That was somewhere else. These are ours." Moller drank some of the snaps. "After I left the hospital tonight, all the way up, I kept asking myself, how much shall I give them? I never sedated a baby before. If I gave too little, it could have the opposite effect—make them jittery, noisier, more restless than if nothing had been given to them."

"How did you decide in the end?" Hansen asked.

Moller emptied his glass. "I gave them just half of what I thought would kill them."

184

Hansen was reaching for the bottle again when he heard Pedersen ask, in what seemed an unnaturally fruity voice, "How may I serve you?"

He understood when he heard the question, in German, "Do you speak German here?"

Hansen carefully poured a drink for Moller and another for himself, moving deliberately and unhurriedly, and set down the bottle before he turned to look. He recognized Major Wolfgang Becker.

Pedersen shook his head. "I speak a little English, if that would help," he said cheerfully.

"Why English?" Becker asked. "Why English and not German?"

Pedersen shrugged. "Before the war our chief source of income was from tourists, and most tourists came from England or America."

"Of course, it will be different in the future," Becker said, in passable English. He smiled, revealing brilliant teeth. "You see, I speak the English as well. But we have been instructed in English to another purpose."

"So?" Pedersen said.

"The future. There will be a need for trained men to administer affairs in both England and America after the war."

"Wise planning," Pedersen said. "And what may I offer you?"

"Snaps," Becker said.

"What brings you to Snekkersten, Major, if I am permitted to ask the question?"

"The same thing that brought me to Denmark," Becker said. He drank the snaps in a swallow and nodded approvingly. "Jews."

Hansen glanced at Moller. The sweat was creeping across his face again.

Becker poured himself another drink. "We have heard rumors about the transporting of Jews to Sweden," Becker said. "Have you heard anything about that?"

Hansen slowly pushed Moller's glass closer to him. He took out his pipe and filled it.

"One hears everything," Pedersen said.

"Are Jews being smuggled across the Sound?"

"So I've heard," Pedersen said.

Moller glanced startled at Hansen who was tamping the tobacco nicely and who appeared not at all perturbed.

"From whom?" Becker asked Pedersen.

Pedersen shrugged. "In this business one hears everything, here, there, behind the bar, in the lobby. One hears and one forgets."

"You should have reported this immediately," Becker said.

What was Pedersen about, Moller asked himself.

"Report what, Major?" Pedersen asked. "If I went running to the authorities every time I heard a piece of gossip, I'd be locked up myself." He smiled disarmingly. "Major, at a bar one hears about love, lost love, unhappy love, unrequited love, about infidelity, about cars parked illegally, about clever business ventures, about cheating, lying, and the fact that somebody heard from somebody that a fishing boat took a couple of Jews to Sweden. Are you suggesting I make a report on everything that floats through the air here, Major?"

Becker was silent for a moment and then broke into a boyish grin. "You're quite right," he said. "Now I shall ask you a question."

"I am honored, Major," Pedersen said grandly.

"What is your attitude toward Jews?"

Pedersen crossed his arms around his ample belly and pursed his lips thoughtfully. "I love them slightly less than I do others."

"Good!" Becker said heartily. He lifted his glass in salute to Pedersen and emptied it. "Excellent!"

Pedersen leaned closer. "But only because Jews don't drink as much as other people," he said. "And in this business you make your most money at the bar."

Becker frowned for a moment and then burst into laughter. He reached across the bar and clapped Pedersen on the back. He refilled his glass and, still chuckling, turned and saw Hansen and Moller and, seeing two upright Aryans, he raised his glass to them. Hansen and Moller lifted their glasses.

The telephone rang at the end of the bar. Pedersen shuffled down and answered it. He walked back and nodded to Hansen. Hansen got up and went to the phone.

"His wife," Pedersen said to Becker before he could think to ask. "She's always nagging. Nagging, nagging, nagging. Do you have a wife, Major?"

"No."

"You're smart," Pedersen said. "Very smart." As Hansen passed on his way back to where he was sitting, Pedersen asked, "What did you tell her?"

"What I always tell her," Hansen said. "To hang up and leave me alone."

"Wives," Pedersen said. "Major, you're smart."

"Captain Melchior," Hansen said to Moller in a moderate, casual voice. "The shipment of potatoes, every sack, arrived safely. Not a single little potato was damaged."

Moller was astonished at the wave of relief and pleasure that swept through him. Not even the presence of the Gestapo officer interfered; perhaps it even helped.

"Potatoes," Moller repeated, feeling the snaps, the satisfaction, the well-being, the triumph.

"Melchior," Hansen said. "He's romantic."

6.

ON A WARM evening, in Jutland, Rabbi Rasmussen followed Pastor Lars Duul out of his house in Randers to where Duul's bicycle was parked. As Duul straddled the bicycle, Rasmussen restrained him with his hand.

"I must insist," Rasmussen said.

"Nonsense," Duul boomed. "I haven't had such a good time

in years. Best chess I've played in a long time. Good talk. You must stay as long as you can."

"It's been wonderful," Rasmussen agreed. "Another time you'd have a job getting rid of us. But right now it's dangerous. For you and for us. I don't know how one goes about it, but we must leave here as soon as possible."

"You're right about one thing, you know," Duul said. "You are dangerous. All of you Jews."

Rasmussen looked worried. "Has anyone said anything?"

"The Germans. They've had quite a lot to say. Have you seen the afternoon paper?"

Rasmussen shook his head. "I'm afraid not."

"Well, when you go back inside, read it. Meanwhile, I'm off."

Rasmussen stepped back. He had a very good idea where the pastor was off to. "You will remember what I said."

"Yes, my dear fellow. If only to be allowed again to eat something besides fish." He put his foot on the pedal. "A kosher house is something of a bore, isn't it?"

In deference to his guests and against Rasmussen's protests, the Lutheran pastor had insisted on establishing a kosher regime. Since there were no kosher butchers in Randers, that meant vegetables and fish.

Rasmussen grinned. "Never. Someday Lotte will prove it to you."

Duul looked at Rasmussen intently. "Matters are being taken care of, Dr. Rasmussen. I assure you of that." He started down the country road, waving his hand.

Presently Rasmussen turned and walked back to the house. It was a good house, plain, honest, unpretentious, set in a large orchard. The house itself was on a hill and there was a lower section, facing onto a valley. This was where Duul had installed the Rasmussens.

In the living room of the house, Lotte and Asta Duul were sitting with their heads together, thick as thieves as usual, smoking cigars, as usual. Rasmussen shook his head. He still could not quite get used to seeing Lotte with a cigar. A cigarette now and then, yes. But look at her.

The women didn't interrupt their conversation, the current instalment of their life stories. As Rasmussen looked around for the paper, smelling the cigar smoke, hearing the chatter, he wondered whose turn it was tonight. He couldn't tell. The two women even were getting to sound alike.

He found the paper, looked for a place to sit, saw the comfortable chairs were occupied by the women. He sat down gingerly on a small, cane-backed chair, and looked at the paper. The article was on the front page.

The German occupation officials in Copenhagen had announced that Jews had been responsible for all acts of sabotage in Denmark, the Danes being too loyal and too cooperative and too Aryan to have committed any such crimes. And now the Jews were being rounded up in order to restore peace and tranquility to the land.

There was more. In their love for their fellow Aryans, and now that the provocateurs were being arrested, the Germans were releasing all the prominent Danes who were arrested on the previous August twenty-ninth when Danish and German relations broke off.

There was a final local touch from Hauptsturmführer Lutz Kroll, the head of the Gestapo in Randers. Hauptsturmführer Kroll personally hoped that this action of his superiors would inaugurate a new era of good will between Danes and their German protectors. It was a matter close to Hauptsturmführer Kroll's heart and he pledged he would do his part.

Rasmussen put the paper down. Well, he thought, isn't that something, we really are naughty. And who, he asked himself, did the Germans think they would fool? He looked at the paper again. It would be fine if it were true, even in a little part.

7.

As PASTOR DUUL rode his bicycle through the main section of Randers, he heard his name called and he recognized this particular German accent without any difficulty. He pulled up to the curb and exchanged a friendly greeting with Hauptsturmführer Kroll, a scrawny little man whose rickety body was not ennobled by his smartly tailored uniform. Pastor Duul had often wondered how Lutz Kroll had managed to wangle his way into the élite corps. He had decided it must be because he resembled Goebbels.

With Kroll were two other Germans, one in black uniform, one in civilian clothes. He recognized Colonel Buhle. The other man was a stranger.

"How are you, Pastor Duul?" Kroll asked in the hearty style he had reasoned would endear him to Danes.

"As well as one can be these days," Duul said.

"Pastor Duul, this is Standartenführer Buhle," Kroll said.

Duul nodded politely, remembering it was a good rule never to acknowledge a previous meeting with anyone from the Gestapo.

"And this is Sturmbannführer Becker," Kroll said.

Duul nodded to the man in uniform. It was easy to see why this one got into the corps.

"What are you about?" Kroll said amiably.

"A parishioner, an old friend. He is coming to the end of his time and he thinks I can help him make the transition. Optimistic, I'm sure."

"I didn't quite get all of that," Kroll said, putting on an engaging smile. "I'm trying to learn your language as fast as I can, but I have a long way to go."

190

Well, that was for Buhle's benefit, Duul thought. He found a responsive smile. "Danish is not a language, Captain Kroll. It's a throat disease. What I said then was that I'm going to offer my services to an old friend who is dying."

"Ah, sad. But that is your function, Pastor."

As Duul slipped back onto the seat of the bicycle, Buhle asked carelessly, "The sabotage of that train. Nothing you would know about, Pastor?"

"I'm afraid not, Colonel."

"Nothing? No rumors, gossip?"

"Nothing, Colonel."

Buhle stuck a cigar in his mouth. "Remember, you're a man of God." He struck a match. "You must not lie. At least not get caught." He held the flame to the cigar, his keen eyes on Duul.

After a moment, Duul said, "Truth is love, Colonel, and love is truth. To say something that will hurt someone, that is telling a lie."

He inclined his head courteously, but before he got away Buhle said quietly, "A great many Germans were killed on that train, Pastor. German soldiers, on their way to Norway, to the fighting. You must understand, this cannot be tolerated."

"I have dedicated my life to Jesus Christ," Duul said. "He taught us all life is valuable."

"You might just pass that word, Pastor," Colonel Buhle said.

"To whom, Colonel?"

"Pastor, this is a small section of a small country. Any word of good advice would sooner or later reach the interested parties."

Duul nodded again and rode off. Becker looked around. "Provincial town such as this, one wouldn't think there could be many Jews here."

"My dear Becker," Buhle said. "In time you will come to realize that the Jews are only one of our problems."

"The Führer . . ." Becker started.

"Yes, I know," Buhle said. "Only one."

Twenty minutes later, Duul reached the White Hart Inn. He parked his bicycle in the rack and entered. Nina Lange was tidying the bar.

"They're waiting for you, Pastor," she said, pouring him a drink.

"They can wait." He liked to look at her. She always made him feel peaceful and proud. She was everything that was good in Denmark. "I'm out of breath," he said. "And I'm a little chilled from my long ride in the night."

"And with them waiting below?" This was their way together.

"They can wait," he said.

But he finished the snaps in a gulp. He looked at her again. His cheeks were pink from the ride and his eyes glowed at the sight of her and with the snaps.

Three men were in the wine cellar, together with Lange, his eldest son, and the German officer, Boldt. The Danes were in a cheerful mood. There was beer and cigarettes. Lange greeted Duul and handed him a box of cigars. "For Asta," he said. "With my compliments."

"Compliments of the RAF," one of the men said.

"By way of me," Lange pointed out. "Don't forget that, by way of me."

"When was the drop?" Duul asked.

"Less than an hour ago."

"Trouble?"

Lange shrugged. "Two of the lads ran into a German patrol. There was a little shooting but nobody was hurt." He lifted a bottle of beer to his mouth and emptied half of it. "Well, we're all here." He switched his eyes to Major Boldt. "The important word is this, I've heard from Peter Hansen. The code given to us by this German swine has proved authentic. It is now in use."

"That almost makes me an Allied hero," Boldt said.

"You shut up," Lange said. "I was looking forward to killing you."

"Politeness," Boldt said chidingly. "Politeness and courtesy in dealing with a fellow accomplice."

"I said shut up. I might kill you yet."

192

"He's right, Rolf," Duul said. "He's done his part."

Lange finished the rest of the beer and set the bottle down hard. "Being honorable with a Nazi," he said. "It's enough to turn your stomach."

Boldt held up his manacled hands. "Since we've all become good fellows and jolly pals. . . ?"

Lange looked dourly at Duul. The pastor shrugged. Lange removed the handcuffs.

Boldt rubbed his chafed wrists. "Thank you, Pastor. Would you dare go a step further and give me a cigarette?"

Lange handed the German a cigarette. "The plans I had for you," he said.

Boldt dragged deeply and appreciatively. "RAF never drops anything like this on us." He looked at Duul with interest. "Isn't this a strange world for you, Pastor?"

"Is it, Major?"

"How do you make it right with yourself, all this blowing up of trains and killing people?"

"I haven't made it right with myself, Major."

"But you do it."

"Yes, Major, I do it."

"And what about me, Pastor? How do you work out dealing with the devil?"

"That's easier. Lives will be saved."

Boldt nodded approval. "You're a realist, Pastor. I like that."

"Who the hell cares what you like?" Lange said.

"Among those lives," Duul said, "perhaps even yours, Major."

"That is my intention, Pastor, to remain alive, as long as possible."

"I did not mean saving your life that way."

Boldt smiled. "I feel the pulpit closing in."

"There must be some decency in you, Major, or you wouldn't be here."

"Hadn't occurred to me. But you may be right."

"Good is like evil in a way. Given a chance, it may grow. When this war is over, there will be a new Germany."

"I thought we already were blessed with that," Boldt said.

"A new Germany," Duul said. "And there will have to be Germans to take over. Perhaps you will be among them."

Boldt shrugged. "If that satisfies your conscience, Pastor, you're welcome to believe that. I think it more sensible just to face the truth. There are times you have to walk with the devil when you cross a bridge."

"A philosopher," Lange said. "A German philosopher. Just what the world needs."

8.

NINA LANGE leaned on her elbows on the bar and read the Copenhagen newspaper left by a customer. Farther down the bar, a young salesman from Randers was sitting next to a girl. They were the last of the evening crowd.

It was two hours after the meeting in the cellar. Lange and two of his sons had departed to dispose of some of the kits from the RAF drop. They had returned and had gone off to bed. Nina had asked Lange to have a drink with her but he said he was too tired. She forbore from saying that was the first time she ever knew him to be too tired for a snaps. She watched him walk away, fiercely fighting sorrow in her, seeing yet another step in the diminution.

Lange was changed since the confrontation with Hansen. He did everything he was supposed to do, and he did it well, and perhaps only Nina had noticed that something had gone out of him. The edge was a little dulled and there were moments of abstractedness, as though Rolf Lange did not quite understand what had happened around him.

Nina looked down the bar at the salesman from Randers and the girl he was trying to get into bed, and she wished they would get out. She wanted to go downstairs and lie next to her husband. The thing with Hansen had done damage there, too, in the bed, but it didn't matter, anything with Lange was all right, just lying next to him and smelling him, the sweat from his labor dried on his skin, his great body seized in sleep, his face released from the doubt that had attached itself during the waking hours.

She wanted to be able to lie next to him and think, and by thinking make him believe, that he had been a hell of a man and by anybody's standard except perhaps his own he was a hell of a man still, and that he would be the old way again. It would take time for the slow, stubborn, proud mind to grow into acceptance, but it would. Because he had the virtues and they would win.

"Mrs. Lange!" the salesman called out. Nina looked down the length of the bar. "Two more, Mrs. Lange, and another beer."

He hasn't made the sale yet, Nina thought. These young girls. They know what they're going to do when they accept the date but they have to make a production about it. How many drinks had she made him buy? The little idiot, doesn't she know what drink does to a man in that department? She ought to by now. It didn't take this long last night when she was in with the lorry driver, or two nights ago with the Randers policeman.

Nina refilled the little glasses with snaps and opened another bottle of beer. If the aquavit doesn't take the starch out of his pecker, the beer will keep him running all night.

"Why don't you say yes?" Nina asked the girl.

"I beg your pardon?" the girl asked.

Phony, middle-class, sniveling, deballing prissiness, Nina thought. Take the man, take him and glory in it, and squeeze every drop and feel him next to you all night. Don't sit there with your legs crossed and your mouth prim, looking as though the sight of a stiff prick would make you faint. Come off it.

"Business hasn't been that good with him," Nina said. "You're drinking up the boy's lunch money."

"Nina," the salesman protested.

"It was only a joke," Nina said. She went back to her paper. It was a moment or two before the sound of the automobile braking in front of the inn made any impression on her. Then she thought it was late for new customers and then she thought the automobile sounded like an automobile, not a firecracker. By then the three men were at the bar. Then she heard the sounds of another car.

"Captain Kroll," Nina said. "An unexpected pleasure."

Kroll bowed gallantly. "Mrs. Lange, my colleagues from Copenhagen: Standartenführer Buhle and Sturmbannführer Becker."

Nina inclined her head. Becker clicked his heels and appeared at the point of kissing her hand. Buhle chewed on his cigar and looked at her lazily.

"It is not too late, Mrs. Lange?" Buhle asked.

"It's never too late when the Gestapo wants a drink," Nina said.

Again Kroll bowed, Becker clicked his heels. Buhle looked more thoughtful.

The salesman and the girl got up abruptly and left. Well, Nina thought, our Nazis have accomplished something. If the boy could still make it with the Gestapo on top of everything else.

"What would you like, gentlemen?" Nina asked.

"Your excellent snaps, Mrs. Lange," Kroll said. He smiled proudly. His superiors were celebrities he had brought to this rural inn from the great world.

She poured the drinks, left the bottle on the bar.

"Aren't you curious as to what brings us here at this hour, Mrs. Lange?" Buhle asked.

"I'm not very bright, Colonel," Nina said. "But one thing I've managed to learn—never ask questions of the Gestapo."

Becker and Kroll looked at Buhle for a clue how to react. Buhle looked at Nina pensively and then he smiled. The other two relaxed.

Buhle tasted his aquavit, approved, finished it. He put his glass down carefully. "You must not feel that way about us, Mrs. Lange," he said. "We are only policemen, simple policemen, and when we hear rumors then it is our duty to check on them. And usually we find it's just that, rumors."

He pushed his glass toward Nina. She refilled it and felt the first sense of danger. A colonel of the Gestapo, from Copenhagen, on a rumor?

"That's why we're here, Mrs. Lange," Buhle went on. "The usual thing. Underground. Sabotage."

"I have taken the liberty of telling the Standartenführer that he must be misinformed," Kroll said. "I have told him if there were an active resistance here, surely I would know of it."

"Yes," Buhle said, his eyes idly on Nina. "Hauptsturmführer Kroll is of the opinion that sabotage here is committed by outsiders."

"How can I help you?" Nina asked.

"Your husband, Frau Lange?"

"Asleep. He starts the day."

"And you finish it," Buhle said. "You have sons?"

"Three. They are asleep as well."

"What do they do, Frau Lange?"

"Help. We could use more hands. Is there anything else, Colonel?" She folded her arms.

"Just one thing," Buhle said. "Standing behind the bar, listening to scraps of conversation, did you by any chance hear anything this evening about an air drop?"

"What is that, Colonel?" she asked.

"An air drop. Surely you know the RAF drops supplies to saboteurs in Denmark?"

"I have heard talk about that, Colonel."

"Just talk? At meetings, Mrs. Lange?"

"I'm a working woman, Colonel. I have no time for meetings."

Buhle looked up and down the length of the room. He put his cigar in an ashtray although it was only partly smoked, and walked slowly to the end of the bar and back, his eyes as bright and alert as a bird-dog's. "Tell me, Mrs. Lange," he said. "Do you have a wine cellar here?"

She pressed her hands harder against her breasts. "It's usual, Colonel, in every inn."

"Would you be good enough to show it to me, Mrs. Lange?"

She had felt easier when he called her "Frau" Lange. She shrugged. "If the colonel wishes." She saw lines forming around his eyes, pleasant lines that should have reassured her and did not.

She led them down the stairs to the wine cellar, turned on the light, stepped back to let them enter. Her eyes whipped across the room. She relaxed a little. Everything had been tidied.

Buhle walked around the room slowly, his hands clasped behind his back. "You have quite a good stock," he said.

"If the colonel could tell me what he is looking for, perhaps I could help him," Nina said.

"Who knows?" Buhle asked, reading the labels on the wine shelves. "A secret meeting place?"

Kroll laughed as though Buhle had said something funny. Becker was puzzled and he did nothing.

Nina watched Buhle, moving about, taking his time, and everything in her was wary now, wary and animal, wild and wanting to run and summoning all her will not to run.

Buhle meandered here and there, pausing now and then to remove a bottle, examine it, grunt approval, and then he bent down and picked something off the floor under the mouth of a bottle of champagne. He walked back to Nina and the laugh lines were etched deeply on his face and she was more frightened than she had ever been in her life.

"The British are sentimental," Buhle said. He took a fresh cigar from his case and allowed Kroll to light it for him. He blew out a rich mouthful of smoke. "Everyone says we Germans are sentimental, but under that stiff upper-lip the British are riddled with tenderness. Along with plastic explosives, fuses, small arms, ammunition, radio transmitters—something of a personal, friendly nature. Something that brave men, living dangerously, want more than anything else." He smiled at Becker and Kroll. "Didn't either of you gentlemen smell it?"

They shook their heads uneasily. "No, Herr Standartenführer," they said simultaneously.

198

"I have the nose of a bloodhound," Buhle said to Nina. "From the moment almost that I entered the inn I could smell it. A little faded upstairs, then stronger at the head of the stairs to the wine cellar. The pleasant aroma of smoke, Mrs. Lange, real smoke from real cigarettes." He opened his hand. A tiny, rolled-up wad of paper was in his palm. "Before I look at it, Mrs. Lange—Players? Senior Service? Or one of the American brands—Camels, Chesterfields?" He shook his head pityingly. "Sabotage is a game for professionals, Mrs. Lange. Enthusiastic amateurs always make mistakes. Wake up your husband and your sons, Mrs. Lange. And in the event they have second thoughts, the inn is surrounded."

"Well, Mrs. Lange?" Buhle asked.

Nina Lange looked at her husband and her three sons standing against the wall of the parking lot illuminated by the headlights of the Gestapo cars, and in the side-lighting from the headlights the four men with rifles. They were like steps, she thought. Rolf, still the tallest and the broadest, and then the three boys, blond, sturdy, and, until this moment, alive and without ailment.

"The names of everybody involved, Mrs. Lange," Buhle said.

She saw the four of them standing there already removed, and she made herself remember what Rolf Lange had said to her again and again, made her swear to, once on the family Bible, made herself remember now, not that she had forgotten, but to remember as strength, as faith. "Never speak," Rolf Lange had said. "It buys nothing. In the end they would destroy me anyway, only by then you'd have all the others in and they'd get it, too. Remember this, Nina, if anything happens, you must let me go."

She remembered that from the days when he had his power. That's what he'd said, "let me go," but that was then and did it mean her three sons as well?

"The names of everybody involved, Mrs. Lange," Buhle said quietly, puffing a cigar. "Who blew up the train?"

She sought her husband's face, seeking a message, a sign— did the rules still hold, Rolf, she said to him, I'm so frightened. Her husband's face was like steel and the faces of her sons were like steel.

"For the last time, Mrs. Lange," Buhle said. Then he said quietly, "Hauptscharführer."

The warrant officer in command of the firing squad said, "Ready!"

"Herr Standartenführer." It was Becker.

Buhle turned toward him. Becker was staring at the men against the wall, his eyes glittering. "Yes, Becker?"

"May I suggest something to the Standartenführer?" Becker asked. His voice had a flat manic excitement as though he was drunk or on drugs.

Buhle felt a curious sensation. He raised a hand to stop the warrant officer. "What is it, Becker?"

"One at a time," Becker said.

Buhle heard Nina Lange catch her breath and saw Rolf Lange stiffen. Buhle turned again and peered at Becker. In the dark he could see little more than the febrile light in his eyes. He felt the sensation again. He put a finger under his collar and loosened it.

"We would have a better chance, one at a time," Becker said. "She wouldn't be able to go through that."

Buhle ran his tongue over his lips. "Thank you for the suggestion, Becker. But I think it is not necessary." To Nina Lange, "A final chance."

She looked at her family and again at her husband and she knew they had all heard Becker and she saw the steel in Rolf Lange's face and she saw more, the power, the old power, all of it, there, where it had been, and she folded her arms and raised her head and she thought how blessed she had been and she did not hear the two succeeding commands, and then the four bodies slumped in their blood.

9.

SUNDAY, THE THIRD DAY of October of that year, started bravely in Randers with a clear sky and a cautious sun, but the clouds came early and by the time the parishioners gathered at Pastor Duul's small white church a light drizzle had started. Despite the uncertain weather, the attendance that morning was very good, Duul was pleased to notice. The Danes were not ordinarily famous for going to church, but the times had done something to some of them.

When he finished the service, the congregation settled back for the sermon. Pastor Duul's flock appreciated his sermons. They were frequently entertaining and always short.

Duul faced the members of his parish. His cheeks were bright and prominent. His eyes widened slightly when he saw Captain Kroll seated in the rear of the church. So he knew, Duul said to himself. Duul was glad Kroll had the tact at least to wear civilian clothes. It appeared to Duul that the Gestapo captain appeared subdued, but from the distance he could not be certain.

Having looked fondly upon the faces of his friends, his confidants, his neighbors, Pastor Duul held up a piece of paper. "I have in my hand a letter from the bishop of Copenhagen," he said in an even voice that touched all parts of the church. "This letter has already been forwarded to the German authorities."

There was a slight stir in the church. People frowned curiously; several glanced at Kroll. The Gestapo officer sat composed.

"Bishop Fuglsang-Damgaard has further requested that this

letter be read from the pulpit of every Danish church on this day," Duul went on in the same calm voice, "so that the German authorities may know the official position of the Danish Church on the subject of the Jews."

The stirring in the church became general. Duul could see the confused emotions on the faces in front of him, puzzlement, surprise, nervousness and, here and there on features as he could have foretold, resentment. Again some people looked toward Kroll; others made a point of not doing so. The Gestapo captain continued to look straight ahead, directly at Duul, his face without expression, his hands folded passively in his lap.

Duul lowered the letter. He said, more slowly, "Before I read the letter to you, I want you to know that I concur with its contents to the fullest degree. I consider it a privilege to read it to you. Here is the letter from the bishop:

" 'Where Jews are persecuted as such, on racial or religious grounds, it is the duty of the Christian Church to protest. Because we can never forget that the Lord of the Church, Jesus Christ, was born in Bethlehem by the Virgin Mary in fulfillment of God's promise to Israel, His own people.' "

Duul paused and raised his eyes. There was no sound in the church.

" 'The history of the Jewish people up to the birth of Christ is the harbinger of the salvation God holds out to all men by Christ. . . . Christ knows no distinction between persons, and He taught us that every human life is dear to God. . . .' "

The thin rain had stopped. A sliver of pale sunlight crept softly across the pulpit, enhancing the pink in Duul's cheeks and the bright sky-blue of his eyes.

" 'The leaders of the Danish Church are fully aware of our duty to be law-abiding citizens who will not untimely oppose those exercising authority over us, but we are also by conscience bound to maintain what is right, and to protest against any transgression. Therefore we shall, if necessary, live unambiguously by the words of the Scriptures. We shall obey God rather than man. . . .' "

The silence was ennumbing as the pastor continued.

202

The parishioners filed slowly out of the church. Kroll had left immediately on Duul's last word. The members of the congregation walked past their pastor at the door and on this morning there were none of the usual smiles and pleasant exchanges. Many of the Danes openly endorsed the bishop's letter. Others shook Duul's hand a little more firmly than usual. All of the worshippers, business men from Randers, farmers, laborers, their wives and children, looked thoughtful and serious.

When the last of them was gone, Duul went to the small room he used as an office and place to change. The words of the bishop had filled him with exaltation. He felt a deep sense of pride in the courage and integrity displayed by his superior.

He found Nina Lange awaiting him. He smiled broadly and held out his hands. "Nina, I didn't see you at services." He stopped. He said in another voice, "Nina."

She took his hand. Her fingers were icy. She pressed his hand against her cheek. She said, "They're still lying there, Pastor, like garbage."

10.

ON THAT SAME Sunday morning, Peter Hansen entered the chapel at Bispebjerg Hospital with a small bunch of fall flowers. Another "funeral" had been arranged by Dr. Poul Klampmann, and the Jews, in dark clothing, holding the hands of their children, carrying babies, walked gravely past the empty casket and out the rear door to the waiting taxis.

The taxis, Hansen reflected with amusement, were doing a land-office business at Bispebjerg these days. It seemed half the cabs in Copenhagen collected daily at the parking rank in front of the sprawling medical complex. The drivers, getting into the spirit of things and well knowing the risk, were coming to regard themselves as direct descendants of the valiant men in Paris whose taxis had delivered another army in another war.

The swarm of cabs had startled Dr. Stephan Moller when he first saw them. He told Hansen and Dr. Klampmann he was sure they would bring the Gestapo down on their heads if nothing else did. "Everybody will know about it," Moller protested.

"Everybody has to know about it," Klampmann said equably. "Everybody in the hospital. Every doctor in Copenhagen, every Jew. I want this place to become known as a refuge."

It had become a refuge all right, Hansen thought, scanning the faces of the Jews. Between funerals Klampmann shoved them into hospital beds and fed them from the hospital kitchen, and if they needed something done for them while they happened to be there they got that, too. When the woman in charge of the commissary asked who was to pay for the food, Klampmann, in his private euphoria, said airily he would. And he would have, too, Hansen chuckled to himself, if Hansen hadn't heard about it and passed along some of the funds siphoned to him regularly now by Danish business men, trade unions and wealthy Jews, funds mounting all the time, paying for this, for the taxis, for the fishing boats that were beginning to transport the refugees to Sweden.

The line of mourners was starting to thin when Dr. Emil Hurwitz entered the chapel, clasping the arm of a small, slender woman weighed down with enough flowers to open a shop. She was wearing a flowing black gown and a hat brimmed as large as a parasol. Hurwitz removed his dark velour homburg, tilted his goatee, held his glasses to his eyes, peered around. He saw Hansen, dropped the glasses on their ribbon and guided the woman to the casket.

By the time Hansen joined them, the last of the mourners was gone and the little woman was busy arranging her flowers around the closed coffin.

"This is my Aunt Minnie," Hurwitz said in a matter-of-fact voice.

Hansen always remembered that; Hurwitz had introduced his Aunt Minnie as though she was the same as anyone else.

Aunt Minnie turned her head, peered up from under the awning of her hat and acknowledged the introduction. Close up, Hansen saw she had beautiful skin, that she was weeping, that the eyes behind tears were bright and chirpy, like a small bird's, and that she was very, very old. And among the rich odors of the banks of flowers around the coffin, Hansen also detected the smell of lavender water.

Aunt Minnie took out a lace-bordered handkerchief and dabbed her eyes gently. The tears came on in force. The little body twitched and the mouth quivered piteously.

"She's a good actress," Hansen said. "She's overdoing it."

"She's not acting," Hurwitz said.

"The crying."

"It's real."

Hansen again looked at Aunt Minnie, who, having finished arranging her flowers, pushing away others which interfered with her grand design, now knelt before the casket, tears pouring down her face.

"But there's nobody inside that coffin," Hansen said. "Doesn't Aunt Minnie know that?"

Aunt Minnie looked up and spoke for the first time. "I cry for all the dead," she said.

Hansen was startled at her voice. It was melodious and, despite the wrenching sobs, clear and distinct.

"She does, too," Hurwitz said placidly.

"All the forgotten dead," Aunt Minnie said.

"She loves funerals," Hurwitz said. "When I told her I was going to meet you here, she insisted on coming. I told her it was a fake but she said she didn't mind."

Aunt Minnie reached out and timidly touched Hurwitz with a tiny hand. "Oh, Emil," she said in that musical voice. "This is a good one. I have gobs of tears."

"I think I'm losing my mind," Hansen said.

Dr. Hurwitz tugged his goatee. "She weeps for the dead, Peter. One can do worse than that." Gazing lovingly at Aunt

Minnie he asked, "What is the progress of our little bargain, Peter?"

"Excellent."

"Let me have the list."

Hansen gave Hurwitz his small bouquet. The doctor carefully unwrapped the paper around the stems. He laid the flowers on the casket, folded the paper and slipped it into his pocket. Without disturbing in any way the rhythm of her sobs, Aunt Minnie hauled herself to her feet, shaking her head at the intrusion of Hansen's flowers on her own arrangement. She picked them up and laid them elsewhere, then resumed her performance at the casket.

I will remain calm, Hansen counseled himself.

"I'll get in touch with you, Peter," Hurwitz said.

"Never mind that," Hansen said. "I want to know where to find you."

"You know where I'm staying."

"Where you were staying. Don't you sleep in the same place two nights in a row. For God's sake, tell Aunt Minnie to stop!"

"Impossible," Hurwitz said, looking benignly at the old lady. "Aunt Minnie is a natural force. Like rain. Once the water is turned on, it has to keep flowing until it's used up."

"She'll float us out of here. Where are you staying, Emil?"

"Isn't that what you told me? To become elusive?"

"Damn it, not from me!"

"I must look at the list, Peter. You're not going to play any tricks on me."

"I gave you my word," Hansen said. "Thirty-seven. Until then, you're safe."

"There are a couple more," Hurwitz said. "Four, or maybe five."

"Emil," Hansen said warningly.

Hurwitz stroked his goatee and shrugged. "We Jews proliferate. One of life's joys we've managed to retain, no matter. Can you believe it, I found three cousins I never knew I had?"

"Emil," Hansen said again.

206

Hurwitz sighed. He slid his hand along the ribbon until he had the glasses, held them up. "Oh dear, that tone again, Peter. I hardly know you these days. I'll add the new names to the list."

Hansen raised his eyes to heaven.

"Anguish," Hurwitz said admiringly. "You do well, Peter. This situation is making professionals out of all of us."

"How is Kate?" Hansen asked. "My God, this is ridiculous."

"She is very well," Hurwitz said gravely.

"When will she have the baby?"

"Any day."

"That's what you've been saying."

"I'm consistent." He touched Aunt Minnie very gently on the shoulder. "All right, little darling, start drying up," he said.

The quivering began to lessen immediately; the sobs spaced themselves out. Hansen shook his head in fascination; it was, he thought, exactly like a machine running down.

Hurwitz tugged his arm. Hansen saw the doctor had a folded packet of money in his hand. "So you're still making your rounds," Hansen said.

"My patients have become used to me," Hurwitz said.

"What am I going to do with you?"

"At the moment, take this." Hurwitz held out the money.

"Keep it," Hansen said. "You'll need it."

"When I need it, I'll have more."

Hansen looked for a long time at the small man, at the almost completely white imperial jutting forward as arrogantly and defiantly as a dagger, at the gently unyielding face that at that moment was ageless, timeless, eternal. "Emil," he said at last, slowly and with a careful clarity. "Emil, you have already turned over every last crown you had in the bank. For the love of Christ, hold onto that. I don't need it."

With a quick and graceful gesture, as a magician might perform an act of prestidigitation, Hurwitz deftly slipped the money into Hansen's coat pocket. "Then find someone who does," he said. He took Aunt Minnie by the arm. "Come, little darling," he said softly. "It's time to go."

Aunt Minnie whisked away the last of her tears and looked shyly at Hansen. Her eyes were radiant. "Oh, this was a beautiful time, Mr. Hansen," she said. "Thank you."

"My pleasure," Hansen heard himself say.

"Thank you, Emil," she said, like a lark. She peered up at Hansen again. "Do you think it helped, Mr. Hansen?"

"I'm sure it did, Aunt Minnie," Hansen said.

"Bless you, Mr. Hansen." Aunt Minnie stood on her toes and kissed Hansen lightly on the cheek, a brush from a nestling's wing, and he smelled the lavender water and she was gone.

After a moment, he took out his pipe and walked to the front door of the chapel. He saw Dr. Hurwitz adjust his ancient velour at a rakish angle and then extend his hand in a courtly manner. Aunt Minnie rested her hand on Hurwitz's arm and, escorting her as he would royalty, he led her down the avenue of lime trees toward the stand of taxis.

Hansen lit his pipe. By now hospital orderlies were piling the flowers in the chapel on carts to distribute among patients. Then, in that place of death, he suddenly smiled. It was going to work. It was all going to work. He felt good. It was more than that. Something of Dr. Emil Hurwitz's indomitable jauntiness had rubbed off. He plucked a white carnation from one of the carts and slipped it into the buttonhole of his lapel, and he wished he had a marvelous, brushed velour hat and possibly even a marvelously brushed imperial.

He went to his car, springily, drove to the doctors' quarters, collected Dr. Moller, whom he greeted cheerfully, and started up the coast to the village of Snekkersten.

11.

As THEY EMERGED from the train and heard the doors close and the train rattle on, the peaceful, harmless, clattering of wheels on tracks on a Sunday afternoon, Ellen Oppenheim felt her mother's fingers tighten on her wrist. Ellen did not lift her eyes until the two German soldiers strolled past. "It's all right, Mama," Ellen said. "It's all right."

The day had turned out fine. The sun finally had had its way. The shadows lay pleasantly and lazily in the pretty village. The air was almost sultry. People sauntered by idly. Even the German uniforms were not oppressive amid the falling leaves and the smell of the country. It was a good time of the year, after the summer, before the winter, the time some people believed to be the best of all.

Bella Oppenheim watched after the departing soldiers. "Whenever I see them I think, and they were once babies."

Ellen looked swiftly at her mother. There was sympathy and pity on the soft round face. Ellen realized incredulously that, in some extraordinary manner, at this of all moments her mother had dipped into herself and had found compassion for German soldiers.

"Little babies," Bella said. "And their mothers loved them and fed them and changed them—and to grow up like that."

"Hatred," Oppenheim said, craning his neck and looking around the station.

"Yes, hatred," Bella said. "But where does such hatred come from?"

"Hitler," Oppenheim said definitely.

Bella nodded. "He has enough for the world. But it

wouldn't have spread if the others hadn't felt the same way," she said, veering on another tack.

"Now, Bella," Oppenheim said, in a voice of reason. "You can't condemn all Germans."

"I condemn nobody. All I say is that in their hearts this is what they wanted or Hitler could have broken his head against a stone wall and nothing would have happened."

"Then how can you feel sorry for them, Mama?" Ellen asked, bewildered.

"Not for them now," Bella said patiently. "For when they were innocent babies."

"Papa," Ellen said, the subject made clear. "Papa, I wonder what we're supposed to do. What did they tell you?"

"I've told you," Oppenheim said.

"Tell me again. We just can't stand here."

Oppenheim sighed. "I was instructed to go to Snekkersten and that when we got there, there would be somebody waiting to take care of us."

"Who, Papa?"

"They didn't tell me."

"Where is he?"

"Why should they arrest Anders?" Bella asked curiously.

"What are you talking about, Mama?" Ellen asked.

"There, in the police car. Now what could he have done?"

The Danish police car pulled up to the railroad station, with Anders Jessen sitting next to the police officer at the wheel.

"He was always such a good boy," Bella said.

Anders jumped out of the car and walked rapidly toward the Oppenheims. Even then, that quickly, in the manner of his walking, Ellen saw something new.

"Sorry I'm late," Anders said. "Hello, Mr. and Mrs. Oppenheim."

"Don't run away from the police, Anders," Bella said. "I'm sure it's just a little mistake you can easily explain."

"Anders," Ellen said, seeing a very known and understood face that was somehow subtly altered, so that while everything was the same nothing was.

He took her hand. "Everything is going to be all right."

"What are you doing here?" Ellen asked.

"Taking care of you, all of you."

"Anders, you mustn't get mixed up in this," Ellen said quickly.

"I am mixed up in this," he said.

There was the new thing in his voice as well, Ellen heard. She peered at him. There were traces of the old shyness, in the soft eyes, in the set of the lips. "You, Anders?" she asked.

"Why not?" He grinned.

Once, Ellen knew, he would have bristled at a question like that. And now he smiled. And when was it she had last seen him? Four days ago, five? "I'm sorry," she said. "It's just that I never thought of you that way."

"Please, would someone tell me what this is all about?" Bella asked.

"Of course," Oppenheim said in the triumphant voice of a man who has solved a difficult riddle. "Anders is the one who is going to take care of us."

"Come," Anders said, taking Ellen's arm.

Oppenheim glanced around the sleepy Sunday village. "So many German soldiers."

"They won't bother us," Anders said. "Only the Gestapo."

"Only the Gestapo," Oppenheim said, jutting his lower lip.

"There aren't that many of them, Mr. Oppenheim," Anders said.

"Would you like some more?" Oppenheim quipped in his old salesman's manner. "We have plenty at the factory and they come cheaper in quantity."

Ellen felt Anders' fingers press on her and she followed him. She followed him without question. As they walked away from the station, she felt, on this day in Snekkersten—this day when she was going to leave her home and her country and the young man with whom she was in love, the depth of which love she was just dimly beginning to realize—a certain light-headedness. She had just to obey the pressure of the fingers. She glanced at him, almost timidly. How could the tip of a man's nose in profile have such authority?

They reached the Strandvejen, the lovely coastal road that runs between Copenhagen and Elsinore. There was traffic on the road, wood-burning private cars, taxis, German military vehicles and, of course, a stream of bicycles, going in both directions.

"It's a lovely day, isn't it?" Anders asked conversationally.

"Anders," Ellen said. "You're mad."

"Isn't it nice?"

"It's very nice," she said, wondering how she had ever been able to find her way without those fingers, how she would during whatever was to come.

The police car which had brought Anders to the station now entered the Strandvejen and the police officer stopped it in front of a small, leafy lane leading down from the highway to the Sound. The police officer, a tall, blond man, got out of the car, walked into the middle of the highway, stopped traffic from both directions, waved to Anders and the Oppenheims and others who were waiting with them to cross. Anders walked past the police captain without looking at him.

"Isn't that your friend?" Bernhard Oppenheim asked.

"In a manner of speaking."

"You walked right past him," Bella said.

Again Ellen glanced at Anders and she saw the small smile twitching on his lips. She shook her head. It was too much and too fast and too impossible. She moved just a little closer to him, to the source of the fingers, and then, being a woman, and Ellen, she paradoxically felt a fleeting sense of loss. Just for a second. She could not fault the change in him, but in a tiny, private way, it was a loss. That had been to her one of his most endearing qualities, a boyishness, one of the things she had loved in him, the fact he allowed her to feel wiser, more adult, almost motherly. And that was gone now. She could never again feel motherly to Anders. Not for real, anyway. Perhaps just as a joke, a personal, nostalgic joke.

"Why are you smiling?" he asked, leading her down the path toward the water.

"I was just thinking I could never again tell you to buy new socks or change your tie or get your shoes shined."

"That's only for now," he said tranquilly. "Because you're scared. When this is all over, you'll be the same old Ellen."

"Who is the same old Ellen?"

"A pain in the neck," he said.

At the foot of the shaded, woody path was a large, open area used as a parking lot and, behind that, built over the water, a large, old open-air restaurant, now closed for the winter. On the expansive terrace which in the season was filled with little tables covered with brightly colored cloths and small vases filled with foreign flags and glass-shielded candles, looking onto the Sound and small boats and white and yellow and red and blue sails and across the narrow strip the low outline of Sweden, were fifty or sixty people, now integrated into the classic image, the clothing which had been slept in, the crying children, the paper sacks, the suit-cases, many tied with rope, and, beyond everything, the common, heavy weight of defeat and disruption and loss, and the overpowering sense of the inevitable that collected them and framed them so that moving, talking, they were yet a picture, a canvas, fixed and immutable, the face of the day.

Anders felt Ellen stiffen as she saw her companions in flight, seeing herself and her parents with a dreadful finality to be what they were, the Sunday afternoon, the warmth, the soft, quiet splashing of the untroubled water, the boy holding her arm all an illusion, a trick of a tired and bruised mind.

"It's all right," Anders said.

"Stop saying that," she said.

"He's right," Bella pointed out.

"Please, Mama," Ellen said.

"You wait here, Mr. and Mrs. Oppenheim," Anders said.

He led Ellen away. She didn't ask him where.

Leaning indolently against his police car, Captain Erik Melchior saw Peter Hansen and Dr. Moller drive up and park

213

behind him. Before Hansen could turn off his engine, Melchior pointed to a small side-road across the highway. Hansen swung into the road and a moment later crossed over to Melchior, Moller trotting behind him. Melchior looked with interest at the carnation.

"Is everything all right?" Hansen asked the police officer.

"How many people did you expect here?" Melchior asked.

"About fifty."

"I think you have a few more."

"Oh, Lord," Hansen said. He gestured to Moller and started down the path.

"Peter," Melchior said.

Hansen paused, turned.

"You were worried about the Langes in Jutland," Melchior said, looking at the carnation. "All you have to worry about now is the widow."

Hansen saw the fear that filled Dr. Moller's eyes, enlarged all out of proportion behind the glasses. "Go down and get started on those people," he said to the doctor. He went back to Melchior.

When Dr. Moller got down to where the refugees were waiting, young men and women, members of the underground, many of them students, were passing coffee made in the restaurant kitchen. Dr. Moller went about his work quickly and efficiently, wondering about the Langes and who they were and how it had happened, the old fear rummaging inside him. He gave injections to the children and sedative pills to the adults, something he had thought of at the hospital, a new step in his present education.

He offered the pills to Bella and Bernhard Oppenheim.

"What is that?" Oppenheim asked.

"Just something to quiet you," he said.

Oppenheim shook his head. "I don't need that," he said strongly. "But perhaps Mrs. Oppenheim can use one."

"If you don't take one, I won't either," Bella said.

"Don't be stupid, Bella, take what the doctor offers."

"Each of you take one," Moller said.

Each took a pill and washed it down with coffee. Moller

moved on. Oppenheim looked around as a theater manager might observe his house.

"So many of us wherever we go," Oppenheim said. "You know, Bella, I never thought about it before, how many Jews there are in this country."

"Hitler shouldn't have thought about it, either," she said.

"You're a wit, Bella," he said. "Where do you think of these funny things?"

"It's a funny time," she said. "So I'm funny."

Straightening from having given a baby an injection, Moller saw Peter Hansen walking slowly down the path. The white carnation was gone.

A few hundred yards away from where the Jews were waiting, Ellen Oppenheim watched Anders Jessen and half a dozen other lads steal a boat. On the way there, Anders had explained that German regulations specified that all craft not used for fishing had to be beached 150 meters from the water. The boys, none of them older than Anders, most of them obviously younger, all of them apparently under his command, had first filled the tanks with gasoline from jerricans, passing the cans from one to the other with the rhythm of a ballet, had then stripped the little craft of its protective canvas, and now were engaged in dragging it down to the water.

"Heave," Anders said.

She watched as the others moved in unison at the level voice with its assertive timbre. Anders? She shook her head. Of all the strange things in this strange time, this was the strangest. Then she stiffened as she saw a Danish policeman, not the tall one who brought Anders to the station, but another one, heavy and red-faced and out of breath from running.

"What's going on here?" the policeman demanded.

Anders pulled something from his pocket and in the dying light of the day, Ellen saw it was dark and filled with death.

"Are you a good Dane?" Anders asked, pointing the gun directly at the policeman's face.

"Yes," the policeman said.

215

"Then help us get this damned thing into the water," Anders ordered.

Bernhard Oppenheim left the toilet at the side of the restaurant and started back to the terrace. Two Danish youths ran up to him.

"Are you going to Sweden?" one of them asked.

"Of course not," Oppenheim said in his best bluff salesman's voice. "What a silly question. I live near here."

"You're a Jew and it's dangerous for you to be here," the other boy said.

"That's no business of yours," Oppenheim said, his belly tightening so fast and so much he thought with manic irrelevancy that surely his pants must fall.

"You can trust us," the first boy said. "Don't go up to the Strandvejen. It's full of Germans."

"Worse," the other boys said. "Danish collaborators."

The two boys ran up the path leading to the highway. Oppenheim rejoined his wife.

"Who were those two boys?" Bella asked. She was feeling peaceful and relaxed from the sedative.

"What boys?" he asked.

"Those two boys who just spoke to you." It was like after a little wine, really.

"Nothing," he said, patting her hand. "They told me the restaurant was closed for the season. I said I knew."

Captain Erik Melchior, smoking a cigarette, resting again against his car, drew himself up as the familiar black Mercedes stopped alongside him. A handsome SS major, riding next to the SS man driving, pulled out his identity card. "Sturmbannführer Wolfgang Becker."

Melchior assumed a more military stance. "Yes, sir," he said, casually not mentioning his own name.

"There have been reports that people have been seen going down there," Becker said, pointing to the pathway.

"Lots of people," Melchior said, as casually dropping his cigarette and grinding it under his heel. His hand fell carelessly on his holstered gun.

216

"Do you know who they are?" Becker demanded to know.

"Jews," Melchior said.

He watched Becker galvanize into action, swinging open the door of the car, leaping out.

"Escaping to Sweden," Melchior said.

"What the devil are you doing just standing there!" Becker shouted.

Melchior looked at him, deadpanned, and then broke into a hearty laugh.

"Why are you laughing?" the German shouted.

"You Germans," Melchior said through his laughter. "You are so reasonable until you hear the word 'Jew.'"

"Are you making fun of me?"

Melchior shrugged apologetically. "It was just my little joke."

"I don't like jokes," Becker said angrily. "What is your name, Captain?"

"My apologies, Major." Melchior said. "It's been a good joke, all day."

"What do you mean, all day?"

Melchior waved his left hand, the one not touching the holster, in a weary gesture. "Major, have you ever had to deal with the Loyal Sons of Prince Hamlet?"

"Who?"

Melchior leaned a little closer. "You have heard of Prince Hamlet?"

"Of course I have," Becker said impatiently.

Melchior raised his eyes. "Since before noon, Major. Those idiots. Have you ever drunk mare's milk?"

"What the devil are you talking about?"

"You know what a mare is?"

"Yes, certainly."

"It's a female horse."

"I said I know that!"

"Well, like all female mammals, it gives milk."

"God in heaven! Get on with it!"

"This organization, the Loyal Sons of Prince Hamlet—you know about Kronborg, Hamlet's castle? Somewhere these fools have found an old manuscript, undoubtedly spurious, in which it is stated that Hamlet's favorite drink was mare's milk."

"Captain," Becker said warningly.

"I think the manuscript, even if spurious, states that something was mixed with the mare's milk, something a little stronger, probably snaps, but they have ignored that. In any case, every year on this day, they celebrate the twenty-first birthday of Prince Hamlet and they spend the whole day down at the water there, swilling mare's milk. It gets harder each year finding enough mares for enough milk and I think they must stop or else switch to the snaps part of the recipe." He took Becker by the arm. "Come with me, Major, the chairman of the society is an old friend of mine. That's why I'm here, in fact. He would consider it an honor to have an officer of the SS, of your imposing rank particularly, join him in a glass of warm mare's milk."

Becker pulled away roughly. "Take your hand from me!"

"I'm sorry," Melchior said, touching his cap and making it seem like tugging his forelock. "I only thought since you were in Denmark it might amuse you to participate in a local Danish custom."

Becker looked at Melchior disgustedly and got back into the black car. He glared up at him, gave a curt order to the driver, settled back in his seat as the car moved away.

Melchior's hand dropped from the holster. His fingers were stiff. He flexed them. He looked down at the cigarette stub. He had hardly started it. What a waste, he thought, taking a pack out of his pocket and lighting another. He pulled on the cigarette and watched the black car head north.

Evening arrived as a gift. The setting sun had laid its last light on the Sound, pointed out the chop, giving a final illumination to the Swedish coast, finding windows here and there to reflect signals of welcome.

On the Danish side, the shadows were gathering comfortingly. With the sun gone, the wind from the Sound took on a new chill. The refugees at the restaurant huddled together, for warmth, for a shield against the blow off the water, and to know they were there. As Ellen Oppenheim walked back to the terrace from where the little boat had been launched, it seemed to her that the people seemed to lose dimension in the deepening twilight, became silhouettes against the vanishing light in the eastern sky.

She walked up the steps to the terrace and located her parents and made her way to them as Anders and those who were helping him brought the craft alongside the terrace and made it fast. The first of the refugees were helped aboard and were distributed carefully so the weight on the small vessel would be evenly spread.

Ellen and her parents moved slowly toward the boat. There were many more Jews behind them. She held her mother's hand and wondered whether she would ever see Anders again, here or ever. He had made it all seem like a schoolboy prank, this coping with the Gestapo. All the boys and girls had that, acting as though if they were caught they faced nothing more serious than a reprimand. She looked around wearily in the gloom. Was this how it was going to end? Where was he?

They reached the boat and the underground boy extended his hand and helped Mrs. Oppenheim aboard and then Oppenheim, and a voice called out from behind the boy, "That's all!" The boy, in the act of helping Ellen on board said, "Sorry, miss, but there's no more room."

Mrs. Oppenheim turned quickly. "Ellen!"

"That's our daughter," Oppenheim said to the boy.

Ellen, back on the terrace, felt her arm gripped, and she recognized the fingers. "It's all right," she said.

"I'll take care of her!" Anders called out to the Oppenheims. "Don't worry!"

"No," Bella said. "No."

"Well go together or not at all," Bernhard said.

"Please, Mama, Papa," Ellen said. She was safe with the fingers on her arm.

Oppenheim led his wife back to the side of the boat. "We're a family," he said. "We'll all go together."

Anders, feeling Ellen quicken, said, "Don't worry. You'll be moved out tonight."

The Oppenheims climbed out of the boat and two other refugees climbed aboard in their places. The lines were untied and the boys on the terrace gave the boat a shove. Manned by three boys of the underground, the oldest, a twenty-two-year-old humanities student at the University of Copenhagen, at the tiller, the little craft chugged into the darkness of the Sound.

The Jews aboard looked back at the coast. Denmark was smothered in the same darkness and it vanished instantly and it was as though it had never been there. The refugees turned their faces away from their home and looked east, where Sweden lay like a necklace of light.

They were startled to hear one of the underground boys shout, "The bilge hole is open—we're shipping water!"

"Plug it up," the boy at the tiller said.

"Plug's missing!" the other boy said.

"Then shove in your thumb."

A moment later the other boy asked, "How long do I have to keep this here?"

"Until we reach Sweden, naturally."

Then, a little later the boy in the hold said, "Slow down, I think I have a bite."

The Jews left behind watched the boat until they could no longer see it and then they moved closer together and, even in the night, the terrace seemed empty.

Peter Hansen looked at the remaining rufugees and tried not to think about Rolf Lange and the three sons. It was one of the things he had yet to learn: there could be no love, no friends, no regrets, no shock. It was the currency of the business, and lives were ciphers and had only to be replaced so the books balanced. He could not even feel an anger against Buhle. The Gestapo chief had lost before and had won now and would lose and win again, and each time it would involve lives, and if it lasted long enough maybe one day he could accept it.

"What will you do with these people?" Moller asked.

"What?" Hansen asked irritably, remembering his first

meeting with Lange and how the big man was the second time and he had done that and now Lange was dead and his three sons were dead and he had to stop thinking about it.

"These people who are left," Moller persisted. "What will you do with them?"

"What would you suggest?"

"Take them to the hospital. We can hide them there."

"No," Hansen said.

"Why not?" Moller tugged Hansen's sleeve. "They'll be safe there."

"They've come this far," Hansen said. "I can't send them back to Copenhagen. How much do you think human beings can take?" He looked around in the darkness. "Anders," he said. "Anders Jessen."

Anders left Ellen immediately. "Yes, Mr. Hansen."

"Come with me, will you?" Hansen said. "The rest of you kids, go home. Thank you and go home." To Moller he said, "Stay here and watch them. Help them if they need it."

Hansen and Anders walked rapidly across the terrace and down the steps and up the path to the Strandvejen.

12.

THE NIGHT was overcast. The sky was a solid black. There was no light except the thread stretched tantalizingly along the coast of Sweden. The night wind turned raw and without the young students the terrace was emptier than ever and the Jews drew together even closer and stared as though hypnotized at the lights twinkling in the free land two miles away.

"Lights at night," a man said. "Just like that."

"I can almost touch them," another man said. "I can almost reach out and touch them with my hand."

"The boat must be in Sweden already," a woman said.

"Why did it have to be a boat that could only hold that number of people?" another woman asked.

"God knows what He is doing," a woman said firmly and Ellen Oppenheim, lost in dreams and memories and wonder and despair, was startled to realize that the voice belonged to her mother.

"I didn't know you were a philosopher," Bernhard Oppenheim said.

"Philosophy?" another man asked. "Stupidity. Ignorance. Who can believe in God at a time like this?"

"Are there times to believe in God?" Bella asked. "Is there a right time and a wrong time?"

She sounded, Ellen thought, like a poet in the Bible.

"Look around you," Bella said. "You see God everywhere."

"In black uniforms?" the man inquired. "With swastikas on their arms?"

"In the people who are taking their lives in their hands to help us," Bella said.

They sat for another half-hour and listened to the sounds of the night in the woods behind them and on the water, and the dampness made the terrace wet and they heard the vessels in the Sound and heard foghorns as the night thickened and then Ellen raised her head as she saw two thin lights like the eyes of a monstrous cat approaching the terrace and then heard the sounds of the wheels and the uneven puffing of the motor. By now all the others saw and heard, and one old man began to mutter a prayer to prepare himself to meet Him Who made him.

The truck with the cat's eyes black-out headlights rumbled to a stop on the parking lot in front of the restaurant terrace and Dr. Moller wondered what he would do, would he face it, could he run, where could he run, what was he doing there in the night on the coast with thirty or forty Jews, and then two men jumped down from the truck and everybody heard Hansen say in a low voice, "It's all right. This is Hansen. Everything has been arranged."

Hansen climbed the stairs and the refugees moved toward

222

him in a dark mass. "You will all be taken to a little church in Gilleleje."

"Gilleleje?" a woman repeated. "That's away from Sweden."

"Just temporarily," Hansen said. "Just for a little while, until I can arrange for another boat." As the voices rose around him, he said, "Please, don't be concerned. More of you arrived here today than we had planned for. But it often happens and there's nothing to worry about. I promise you, I shall find another boat and you'll all be in Sweden before morning. Now please, just get inside the truck, and don't worry."

The Jews filed down the stairs to the truck. As Ellen, led by Anders, walked past she saw it was a garbage truck.

"I know," Anders said cheerfully. "But it's funny in a way."

It was very funny, Ellen thought, as she was helped into the truck, and she thought again how quickly he sensed what she was thinking, feeling, and that was funny, too, after all this time, funny and too late. She was pushed back into the interior of the truck by the others getting in and she heard her mother call her name, but at that moment the doors were slammed shut and the truck was in total blackness and she could see nothing.

The truck lurched forward on the unpaved ground and climbed the path leading to the highway. Ellen felt it pause for a moment and then turn right and then she felt the smooth pavement of the Strandvejen.

It was very funny, she thought again, and quite appropriate. They had become that, debris, excrescence.

At the highway Hansen and Moller dropped from the cab of the truck. "Just take it easy," Hansen said to Anders, who was at the wheel. "I'll get there as quickly as I can locate a boat."

He watched the truck move up the coast and then, with Moller at his side, went to his car. Inside, Hansen took out his pipe and filled it.

"Now what?" Moller asked.

223

Anders Jessen drove slowly through Elsinore. The truck seemed to him to make a great noise in the quiet town, but nobody seemed to notice it. He drove out of Elsinore along the road embracing the northern tip of Sealand, through Hellebaek. He encountered the German patrol just before he reached Hornbaek.

The squat patrol car was parked on the side of the road. The sergeant and two soldiers stood in the middle of the road, the soldiers with rifles in their hands. The sergeant was waving a flashlight up and down. Anders stepped on the brake and felt under his belt and took out his gun and shoved it behind him into the crack of the seat. He brought the truck to a stop and looked down at the sergeant's heavy, jowled face.

The sergeant poked his light at Anders and held it on his face for a moment and then moved the beam around the interior of the cab. He directed it on Anders again and, without having said a word, started toward the rear of the truck.

Anders felt for the gun. Three of them. If he did it quickly, he might be able to. He would have the advantage of surprise. It would be the first time, killing anyone, but he had practiced on dummies and he was a good shot and he knew one day he would have to and maybe this was the day. The main thing was, they wouldn't be expecting it. The gun felt cold in his hand, and then hot.

Inside the truck, a man asked, "Are we there already?"

"I hope so," another man said. "This isn't exactly a perfume factory."

They all heard someone working on the door handle and then the door was pulled open and a woman said, "Oh, God."

The sergeant stood in the road, flanked by his two soldiers. He moved the light very slowly through the interior of the garbage truck.

"Oh, God," the woman said again. The others were stunned into silence, excepting the old man who again began reciting the words of his prayer.

The small, pale light lingered briefly on each face. "Abraham!" the sergeant said in a bark, as though calling the roll

224

of his platoon. "Isaac, Joseph . . ." The light fell upon Ellen. "Even a Ruth." He laughed hoarsely and slammed the truck door shut.

He walked round to the front and waved Anders on.

13.

GILLELEJE IS ON the northern tip of Sealand and its water is not the Sound but the Kattegat and at night in the fall of the year the air is new and sharp and full of the green smell of the sea.

It is a fishing village and its church is a fisherman's church, plain and simple, without pretense. Its tall, sharp spire with its large clock dominates the village and times Gilleleje in the hours of the day and the seasons of the year. In the winter, it is the spire that takes the first brunt of the northern wind, and when spring returns to the land after the long darkness it is the spire that first reports the renewed visit of the sun.

The church is located in the center of the village amid a cluster of small, austere houses. The only green is the green in the graveyard next to the church. The only other color is the color of the flowers put on the graves. The streets are narrow and cobbled and all lead to the waiting church.

On this twentieth hour of this Sunday, the garbage truck moved slowly along the rutted gutter and finally came to a stop in front of the church. Anders turned the ignition key and glanced around cautiously. A small man in a neat, dark Sunday suit stepped out from the shadow of the entrance to the church and raised a reassuring hand. As Anders slipped down from the cab, the small man climbed up behind the wheel. The small man felt out of place and ill at ease. It was the first time in his life he had been in his truck in his good suit.

Anders paused for a moment and listened. There was not a sound in the village. There was no one on the streets. He knew the arrival of the strange vehicle at the church on a Sunday night had not passed unnoticed and that there were those who were peering from behind curtains or closed shutters, but on the streets Gilleleje was deserted.

Anders walked to the tailgate and opened it. For a moment he could make out nothing in the darkness and silence. Then he could discern the faces, guarded, withdrawn.

"It's all right," he said in a low voice that dispelled doubt. "You are all quite safe."

He helped a woman down. Others followed, sucking in the clean, pure sea air.

"It's all right," Anders repeated. "You're safe."

Bernhard Oppenheim climbed down and held out his hand for Bella. "What happened with those German soldiers?" he asked Anders.

"They weren't interested," Anders said.

"Did you hear that, Bella? They weren't interested." Oppenheim glanced around at the close, Gothic village with its dark, enclosed houses and its twisting streets.

The entrance to the church opened and a tall, spare man with a disciplined face stepped out. With a tight gesture, he beckoned to the refugees to enter. They moved to the door, stiff from the truck, silent as ghosts. A child wailed suddenly; it was a large sound in the night.

Anders put his hand on Ellen's arm. "Stay with me," he said.

She glanced at her mother and father, walking softly with the others. Her mother nodded and smiled. She watched them enter the church and then Anders led her round the side of the building to the graveyard. She heard the garbage truck roll away.

"I am Pastor Olesen," the tall man said. His voice to the Jews from Copenhagen sounded constrained; his speech had almost a foreign sound. "You are welcome to my church," he said with formality. "You will please follow me."

He led them into the building, a Danish Moses leading the people who had been chosen by the Nazis for another purpose. The interior of the church was in darkness. He struck a match and lit a candle. He opened a slender door that was almost lost in the wall, revealing a narrow staircase. He started up the stairs and the Jews followed him.

Bernhard Oppenheim peered down the center aisle of the church and looked at the shadowed altar.

"It's funny," Bella said.

"Make me laugh," he said.

"The feeling. A church, a synagogue. It's the same feeling." She took his hand and led him through the door and up the stairs.

The stairs opened into a small room. The pastor opened a second door. This disclosed an even narrower, spiral staircase. The line of refugees followed him up these stairs and emerged finally into a large, bare, timbered room that formed the interior of the lower part of the steeple. The room smelled of clean wood and freshly from the untainted air that flowed in through half a dozen tiny windows that dotted the unfinished, unpainted walls.

As the last of the Jews entered the room, dropping their paper sacks and battered suitcases, sinking to the floor in torpor and exhaustion and loss, they were all suddenly assaulted by a terrifying noise, a whirring, creaking, agonized sound that might have been the death throes of a mastodon. Some closed their eyes in despair and clapped their hands over their ears. Others looked wildly toward the sound and, at the far end of the cavernous room, saw a gigantic apparatus, a collection of wheels and gears and springs that in the dim light that trickled through the open windows resembled a malevolent instrument of medieval torture.

As they stared, they heard behind the torment of the machine a steady, even beat, a ticking, a ticking that was like paced electric shocks. The steeple clock struck eight.

"Please," Pastor Olesen said in a dry voice. "It is only the machinery for the clock." Then he said in his archaic manner and alien North Sealand accent, "I know it sounds like some kind of time bomb, but I assure you I have not the slightest intention of detonating my church."

14.

ELLEN STRAINED her eyes in the dark, reading from the gravestone, " 'Ib Skov, good father and husband, may his soul rest in peace. 1844–1885.' Forty-one years old. And he succeeded in being a good husband and a good father." She reached out with her slender fingers and gently touched the flowers that grew along the edges of the grave. "I hope Ib Skov is resting quietly in his lovely home."

She raised her head and drank of the briny air and looked about her. The places change, she thought, but the graveyards remain the same, all of them little gardens, formal, sober little gardens, quiet, with dignity, tended, careful and very beautiful.

"It looks like a nursery," she said. She paused and looked again at the weathered stone. "I wonder who Ib Skov was. I wonder if he knows we're here and if he minds." She raised her eyes to the clock on the steeple. It was ten minutes past eight.

"It won't be too long," Anders said. "Mr. Hansen knows what he's doing."

"You say that as though you want to get rid of me."

"Ellen."

She laughed. "I think I believe you. I'm beginning to feel better. I'm beginning to feel like teasing you."

He grinned. "I told you."

"You and I and Ib Skov in a lovely graveyard." Then she said in the same voice, except it was not the same voice at all, "Do you really think Mr. Hansen will be able to get a boat?"

"Yes," he said.

She nodded, leaning against the stone. It was astonishing. It was so easy to believe him. "How long have you been involved in this?"

"The underground? A while."

"How long?"

"A long while."

"With a gun?"

"Yes."

"Have you ever shot anyone?"

"No."

"But you would?"

"I think so."

"Those German soldiers, if they hadn't let us go?"

"I think so. I would have tried."

She turned her head and looked closely at him. Even in the dark of the graveyard, she could see the gently featured face and the lashes curling over the mild eyes.

"Will we go to Sweden, even from here?" she asked.

"Yes."

"Have you been to Sweden?"

"Yes."

"And I never knew." She touched the indentations that marked the arrival, passage and manner of stay of Ib Skov. "It frightens me."

"If you're careful, there isn't too much risk."

"That frightens me, too," she said. "But that wasn't what I meant. To think you could be doing this when we were so close, and I hadn't the slightest inkling, a whole part of your life a secret to me and you kept it so well. It's only that I don't think I could carry that big a secret. I think you would sense something. Is that being stupid, or insensitive?"

"Neither," he said.

She nodded slowly. Again she had heard the calm assurance, the quality of making something so because he said it.

229

"Neither," he repeated. "It was just that you had a picture of me and a picture of yourself and a picture of us together. And with all those pictures, it was hard to fit in anything else."

"And you understood all that and let me go on playing my little game, treating you as a child?"

He made a ball of a blade of grass.

"Why?" she asked.

He tossed away the ball of grass. "I don't know."

"Why?" she asked.

He plucked another blade of grass and chewed it. "I guess when you love someone, you don't want to disturb them."

She leaned against the stone again, sheltering herself from the night wind from the sea. "Will we ever see each other again?"

"Yes."

"You're sure?"

"Yes."

"That sure?"

"Yes."

"Why are you sure? How can you be sure?"

"We have a life to live."

"There were other people who had lives to live, who have been separated, killed, forgotten."

"We can't believe that about us," he said quietly.

"Why not?" she asked, harshness creeping into her voice. "What is so special about us?"

He was silent for a moment, chewing on the grass. "We have to believe in the end we will accomplish what we are trying to do," he said at last. "And that, in accomplishing it, we will then be able to get on with our lives, doing what we were given life to do. If we don't believe that, then we're dead now, just as dead as though we had faced a German firing squad." He was silent again, and then he spit out the grass. It was a long speech for him and he had to recharge. "They've done that, instill fear. But they're people and some of them are damned stupid people and they're going to lose."

She turned to him again, peering at the young profile, the

girlish lashes. "How did you come to know all this? Did you learn it making ashtrays?"

He chuckled and his teeth picked up the low reflection of somber light. "You're right. You've stopped being scared and you sound like the old Ellen."

"I'm not teasing you," she said in a low voice. "And I'm more scared than ever. Not so much for me, because you tell me we'll all be taken where it's safe and I believe you. But I don't know whether you do know everything and I ought to be ashamed of myself or whether you're still a dreamer, looking into the future like a wide-eyed child." The harshness corroded her voice again. "It may be just that, fantasy, the same fantasies you put into clay, doing the same thing with life, our lives, other peoples' lives, fashioning them the way you want them to be, the way you want to see them." She turned away again. "Oh, Anders, don't be a fool! The chances are that one of us will die, the terrible game you're playing with its built-in ending. Me, a Jew in a world that considers itself enlightened if it tolerates Jews. I'm leaving you, if I'm lucky, and you're staying here playing Russian roulette with the Nazis, and you talk as though I were going away on a holiday and you were going to play with your clay until I returned." Her voice was swept by cold wind. "You could get odds from any gambler that our future is behind us. You'd get odds that we've lived our lives, whatever that's been."

"I don't believe that," he said.

"How do you know what to believe?" she said angrily. Then she closed her eyes for a moment and opened them and put a gay smile upon her lips. "Then we don't agree," she said brightly. "But then, we seldom have. The key to our romance, our unfailing ability not to agree."

"We can agree on one thing," he said. "We have now."

"A few minutes?" She gave a short laugh. "An hour or two if we're lucky—or unlucky?"

He turned his face toward the cold air from the Kattegat. "It isn't time," he said. "It isn't even how long it lasts. It's what you have and what you do with it."

Presently she took his face into her hands. "It's fitting," she said. "In some wonderfully exact way, it's fitting." She kissed his lips. "In a graveyard." She felt his arms close around her. "You and I and Ib Skov. Do you think he will forgive us?"

15.

INSIDE THE ROOM, the refugees waited. More than an hour passed since Pastor Olesen had bade them be at ease.

As they sat, sprawled, talked in low tones, quieted their children, looked from time to time out of the small windows, seeing little more than darkness on one side, the frivolous play of the rising moon on the water on the other, the grotesque ticking from the infernal machine reminded them with banal insistence of the inexorable passage of the time. And in the event the message was not made pertinent or was dulled in the repetitiveness, at each quarter-hour the machinery wound itself up again in its wheezings and groanings, sounding to the inanimate listeners, depending on their point of view, as the gestation of all humanity or the death of the world, and resolving itself finally in a mournful, doomed toll. And to sum up these fifteen-minute strikings, the apparatus had its supreme gesture, the counting of the hour, each single chime hammering insistence that time was indeed moving along and that they were still there.

16.

ELLEN OPENED her eyes. Anders started to withdraw from her, but she clung to him. "Don't go," she said. "Don't leave me."

He looked down at her, frightened. "Ellen, you're not sorry. I love you."

She shook her head slowly. "I'm not sorry, no."

"Why are you crying?"

"All the wasted time." Her lips trembled. "All of this we had and we waited so long." She held him even more tightly and pressed his face against hers. "It was so pure, Anders. That's why I'm crying. I don't know what I expected, but it was so pure." She looked up at him, feeling him still in her body, the fury subsided. "Nothing has even happened to me that was so pure."

17.

THE SECOND HOUR had passed, with its Chinese dripping of sound in the room inside the church, when they heard footsteps and a moment later the door opened and a shadowy figure appeared. "It's Hansen," he said. "I have good news." To the persons in the room, the voice was disembodied.

"The important thing," Hansen said, "is that I have located a vessel large enough to take all of you to Sweden."

"Thank God," a woman said fervently. There was a rippling in the dark room, a sound like trees whispering in a breeze.

Bernhard Oppenheim waited. He had detected a strained note in Hansen's voice, and the manner of his phraseology suggested to him there was less good news to follow.

"The reason we are not moving you out to the boat immediately is this," Hansen continued. "There are a number of German patrol boats in the harbor."

There was another sound in the room now. Oppenheim felt Bella take his hand.

"There is nothing we can do about them," Hansen went on. "But you must understand, they are there only in the normal course of their patrol. Their being there has nothing at all to do with you. In due time they will move elsewhere. We are watching at the shore and as soon as they are gone we will come for you."

It was eerie, Oppenheim thought, a bodiless voice speaking to bodiless listeners. It could be the trademark of the time.

Hansen was silent for a moment as the machine went into its unique convulsions and regurgitated a chime. "Well," he said. "You can't be lonely."

There was the sound of him leaving and then the sound stopped as he turned. "Waiting here in the dark, alone, with that damned clock ticking away, you must be having all sorts of ideas. Just remember, you are not abandoned, you are not alone." He smiled, although none could see it. "We've been doing this for several days now. We haven't lost a client yet."

There were one or two chuckles, obliging, and then there was the soft click of the closing of the door, and then there was nothing but the machine, slicing the hours into minutes and the minutes into seconds, crisply and precisely.

18.

SHE FELT a little drunk now in the night with the stars scattered thinly and the smell of the sea, and she was still in that new place she had found with him and she had forgotten where she was and the church and the people in it and why they were all there. All she could think of and feel and know was the way her body was now and that her body could do this to her.

"It's like you," she said to him.

"What's like me?" he asked.

"My body. The secret it's kept from me. It feels so precious now."

They were lying side by side staring upward at the sky, and in the wetness of the night air the flowers smelled cleaned and washed.

"I love it so much now," she said. "For what it did for you and for me. Is that terribly conceited, to love one's body?"

"No," he said.

"I love to ask you questions," she said. "You are always so detailed in your replies. You speak like a telegram, as though you were paying for each word."

"I didn't think we would do this," he said.

"Do what? Make love? How foolish. What else could we have done to kill a little time in a graveyard?"

"I mean just at this time, tonight," he said. "What I'm trying to say is that I didn't use anything."

"Use anything? You mean I just imagined the whole thing?" She laughed, a lovely low laugh he had never heard from her before. Then she said, "You mean you may have made me pregnant?"

"I'd like that," he said defiantly.

"You'd like that? You'd like to send me off alone some-where with your baby in my belly? You'd like that."

"Well, then maybe you'd finally marry me."

"How could I marry you if I'm in Sweden and you're in Denmark?"

"I go over there. I told you that."

She turned over and kissed his cheek and let her head fall upon his breast. She could hear the beating of his heart. "Anders," she said.

"I didn't mean to frighten you."

"Frighten me? About giving me a child?" She found his hand and held it between hers. "Do you have any idea how much I want your child?"

"You do?"

"Then it wouldn't matter so much. Then I would have that, no matter how much longer it took to end this dreadful war."

"Ellen," he said, as though in prayer.

"And if, God forbid, something stupid or foolish happened to you, I'd still have you."

"Nothing is going to happen to me," he said. "Not now."

"Nothing is going to happen to anyone. Not now," she repeated. Then she said, "Anders."

"Yes?"

"How long do we have to wait?"

"To make a baby?"

"How long do we have to wait until you can make love to me again?"

19.

THE THIRD HOUR passed and the Jews in the church waited. The ticking had become like a nagging friend, a pitiless, never-ending reminder, gathered up and distilled into a stern warning on the quarter, impatient, nervous, almost angry on the hour.

There was a single toilet on the landing. Now there was a fixed line in front of it. The sedation had worn off, for the adults as well as the children.

There was a faint sound as the door opened, and again in the instant silence the ticking resumed its remorseless obbligato.

"It's the pastor," a man near the door said.

Pastor Olesen set down two wicker baskets. "Some people living near here," he said. "It's not much. Some cheese and bread and a little milk for the children."

Bernhard Oppenheim held his portion of bread and cheese hidden from his wife as he stared down from the window. "Eat, Bella," he said to her. "You need your strength."

"Did you eat?" she asked.

"Yes," he lied.

She peered down. "You haven't."

He sighed. "I can't."

"Ellen?"

"Yes," he said quickly. "I'm not hungry, I swear it. Anyway, I don't care for this kind of cheese."

Bella smiled. "Did you taste it?"

"Of course. How could I know I didn't like it?"

"Of course," she said. Then she said, "Bernhard."

"I hear it, too," he said, excitement rising in his voice. "Mr. Hansen was as good as his word." To the room he said, "My friends, automobiles. They're stopping here."

A low, spontaneous cheer reverberated throughout the room, defeating the ticking. Oppenheim pushed his way to a window and looked down. He saw the slit eyes of the head-lamps, a pride of tigers, he thought, or was that only lions?

"Folks," Oppenheim said in his best, cheery salesman's manner. "Folks, there are plenty of cars down there. So don't push and don't run. Remember, there are two flights of stairs going down and we don't want any accidents, do we?"

"Bernhard," Bella said in a low voice.

"Remember," Oppenheim said, "like the man said, women and children first."

"Bernhard," Bella said again and now the deadness was plain in her voice.

Oppenheim saw it then, the men getting out of the cars, the guns cradled in their arms like babies, and he forced his way to the door, past people who were laughing and kissing each other, past the old man who again was giving his attention to God. He reached the door as the heavy jackboots clattered up the stairs and turned the key in the lock as a gun was jabbed against it.

"Open the door!" a voice said in guttural Danish. "Open the door, or do we break it down?"

Now Bella Oppenheim looked down again and, in the night that was brightened by the slit eyes, she saw that men were setting up machine guns on tripods. Not an order was given. Perhaps that was the special quality of the terror. Nothing had to be said. The men knew exactly what to do because they had done it so often before.

20.

ELLEN YAWNED and stretched luxuriously. "It's like a marvelous featherbed. It's like a featherbed and a thick, downy
cover and soft pillows, and now it would smell of love and
all the sounds would still be in the air, and it's like morning.
Isn't that crazy?" She laughed the low, throaty laugh again.
"It's not crazy. It could be morning with heavy curtains
drawn, and a lovely old lady will come in and sniff around
and know what we've been doing and she'll set a big tray on
the bed with coffee and cream and marvelous bread, just
baked, and butter. She'll open the curtains and the sunlight
will stream in and I'll have a good look at the young man
who has ravished me. Twice." She laughed again.

"I think I hear cars," Anders said.

"Then it's over and we're here," she said. "But we have our
answer now."

"About what?"

"About how it is, each time, you goose." She twisted towards him. "It's the same except it's as though it's the first
time." She stroked his cheek. "It's exactly as I remembered it
the first time, except it's as though it never happened before.
Do you know what I'm talking about?"

"I think so," he said.

"You're embarrassed," she said. "You mustn't be embarrassed."

"I never talked about it," he said.

"Did you ever do it?"

"No."

"Then how could you have ever talked about it? You are a
goose."

"You don't mind?"

"That you never had another girl before?"

"Well, I don't know. I suppose I was clumsy. I don't really know if I did everything all right."

"You did, Anders. I'm here to tell you. You did." Her eyes crinkled. "I'm happy you never did it before."

"Are you?"

"I wouldn't have minded. I promise you, I wouldn't have minded. But it's lovely that it was the first time for both of us. The first and second time. It's almost as though we discovered it."

"We'd better go." He stood up and helped her to her feet.

She straightened her dress. "And now we have a double chance to have a baby. Perhaps we made twins."

"Quite a few cars," he said, straining to see. "Come, they'll need me."

"Yes," she said, making certain she was presentable. "For the first time in days I'd forgotten. I forgot. But it wasn't a sin, was it, Anders?"

"It can't be," he said. "We love each other."

"I don't mean what we did. I mean losing ourselves so much in it that I forgot about everything else."

"If we forgot, it's because God wanted us to forget."

She looked at him. "How dear that you thought to say that," she said.

She wondered whether it was written on her, if just by looking at her her mother would know what had happened. It didn't matter. As soon as they reached Sweden, she would tell her mother anyway and then she would hope and pray that she had conceived. As he took her hand and led her round towards the front of the church, she looked back and said, "Good-bye, Ib Skov, God bless you and I hope we didn't disturb you too much."

She turned to Anders and said, "I'm beholden to you, Anders. I'll never forget tonight, as long as I live I'll never forget tonight, no matter how many times we make love. You made such funny sounds. Did I make funny sounds, too?" And then she felt her hand jerked violently and she was pulled down behind another gravestone and she started to speak and his fingers tightened on her hand and she saw him staring and she saw what he was seeing.

"Oh, God," she said. "Oh, my God."

The people walking slowly out of the church were like dark spirits and there was still no sound, not from them and not from the men behind the guns, each man a perfectionist in his job, and, in the faint light of the stars and the moon and the hungry eyes of the cars, the dark spirits climbed into a large open truck.

Peter Hansen and Dr. Moller walked rapidly up one of the narrow streets.

"How do you know?" Moller asked.

"They're like automatons," Hansen said. "They operate on schedule. Believe me, the harbor is clear now."

They turned a corner and then Hansen pulled Moller back into the entrance to a grocery store.

Suddenly Ellen tore herself away from Anders and scrambled to her feet and ran towards the front of the church. He leapt up and ran after her, hearing her sob, praying they wouldn't hear it, and he threw himself at her, grabbing her waist, and pulled her down and rolled over with her behind another stone and covered her mouth with his open hand, squeezing the cheeks tightly. She fought, trying to break away, scratching at him, trying to free herself, her face, and then she quit struggling and he thought she had fainted, mercifully, but when he looked at her her eyes were wide open.

Major Wolfgang Becker stood slightly to one side, his arms akimbo, a calm expression of pleasant satisfaction on his chiseled face. A good haul, he thought, watching the people lurch past, stupefied as zombies. And from a Danish farmer, of all people. A farmer who had been puttering about in the early evening and who had been puzzled by the unlikely sight of a garbage truck pulling up to a church and then people pouring out. He'd be entitled to a reward, the farmer had asked, wouldn't he? He would indeed. A generous reward. A very generous reward to encourage other Danes to do the same thing.

"How do you suppose they found out?" Moller asked, shaking. "How?" You said everything would be all right." He clutched Hansen's arm. "How did they find out? Answer me."

"For Christ sake," Hansen said, "shut up."

Ellen was silent and quiet and then suddenly she stiffened and tried again to pull away, and Anders tightened his grip on her and again covered her mouth.

Bella and Bernhard were coming out of the church, holding hands like children. They peered uncertainly for a moment and were jabbed with rifle muzzles. They moved along with the others, Oppenheim still carrying in his free hand his uneaten portion of cheese and bread.

As Ellen and Anders watched, Oppenheim got into the truck and then helped Bella up, and he looked around, seeking someone, and then he appeared to recall himself and he stopped looking and followed his wife inside.

The rest of the Jews climbed in and the gate was raised and the chain hooks were slipped into rings and the truck moved away. Becker went to his car. One by one, the black cars were driven away from the church.

21.

ANDERS TOOK his hands away. He looked at Ellen. Her face was calm. He helped her up.

"What's that funny word for 'whore?' " Ellen said.

"Ellen," he said.

"Field-mattress. Isn't it?"

"Ellen, for the love of God!"

"And all the while we were fucking like animals in the field," she said.

He slapped her face. She looked at him, bewildered, her eyes enormous.

"What happened?" she asked in a child's voice.

"Come," he said.

"But what happened?" she asked. She looked around and saw the church. She screamed, "Mama! Papa!" She ran to the church and pounded on the door.

Anders caught up with her and tried to take her away. Hansen and Moller ran across the street.

"Get her to my car," Hansen said.

"Mama," she said, lost. "Papa." She leaned against the door and crumpled.

Anders caught her and carried her away. Hansen stared after them.

"You should have sent them all to the hospital," Moller said.

Hansen said nothing.

"They would have been safe there," Moller said.

Hansen closed his eyes.

"None of this would have happened!" Moller screamed.

Hansen grabbed Moller by the lapels. Moller pushed him away.

"I'm sorry, Moller," he said. "Go to the car."

Moller closed his mouth and opened it again.

"Don't say anything," Hansen said. "Just go to the car."

Moller looked at Hansen for another moment and then hurried away. Hansen looked at the church, thinking of the people who had been taken away to a concentration camp, of the Langes, of Nina Lange, of the Danes that were killed on the train blown up in Jutland, of Kate in her new isolation.

He walked out of the churchyard toward his car.

PART IV.

1.

ARNE JOHANSEN and Niels Rider worked their way down the aisle of the clothing factory, squirting itching powder on the German uniforms.

"In the crotches," Niels said. "Be sure you get a lot in each crotch. I have that picture in mind, those bastards smelling of cabbage and scratching their balls."

The factory, which turned out cheap men's suits in ordinary times and which had been commandeered by the Germans, was empty and still in the dark of the Sunday evening.

"Arne," Niels said, wielding the squirt gun gracefully, "Arne, where are you?"

"Helping the war effort," Arne said. "Playing a classy little trick Mr. Peter Hansen dreamed up."

"No, Arne, you're not. The nuisance is here but you're not. Where are you, Arne?"

"You talk too much," Arne said. He directed a thin stream of powder as though he was squeezing the trigger of a machine gun.

"You're begrudging again," Niels chided him. "You're thinking of Lili again."

"Let's get on with it."

"Arne, we're dedicated, don't forget that."

Arne paused for a moment. "It would be fun."

"To be able to watch? To see them standing at attention with some officer growling out the orders of the day, and then they start to scratch?"

"To be able to tell her," Arne said.

"Oh, boy," Niels said unhappily. "Oh, boy, oh, boy. And what would Mr. Hansen say to that?"

"Fuck Mr. Hansen, as the British say."

"Arne, we're the hope of Denmark," Niels said. "Don't forget that. The necks, Arne. They sweat and that's when it gets a chance to work in. So you want to tell her all about it. You want her to know you're a hero."

"Don't worry," Arne said.

"I should report that to Mr. Hansen. I should tell him you want to be a hero to your girl."

The uniforms were stacked in neat piles, having just been given a final check by the inspectors. It had been just after seven o'clock when the night watchman let them in. It was shortly before midnight when their work was done.

Niels gave a final artistic squirt. "The only thing I regret is that they're all soldiers' uniforms. It's the officers I'd like to fix. These poor bastards are suckers anyway."

"You're making me cry," Arne said. "Now come along, hero, our leader has something else to keep us happy."

2.

THE MEETING PLACE was the Asiatisk Plads near the harbor, under one of the high old buildings with the sharply peaked roofs whose façades descended in proportioned steps. It was early morning, the moment of false light. Arne stood in the chill with his hands in his pockets and he thought of Lili and how that last time she had stirred as he slipped out of bed carefully not to waken her and how she had reached out in her sleep and he had touched her hand and her fingers had tightened and she had tugged gently and how much he had wanted to get back next to her. It was pleasant to think on this cold morning near the waterfront that with a little luck he could have that for the rest of his life.

He sensed rather than heard or saw someone approaching and he pressed himself hard against the building, gripping the gun he had taken from the cache in his flat, his tempered body now ready to do one of three things—greet, remain hidden, strike. He relaxed when he saw it was Niels.

"It's going to be a little difficult," Niels said.

"Why?"

"I could only put my hand on one car."

"We'll manage," Arne said. "Who's the man?"

"Hansen says it's someone named Frandsen."

"Do you know him?"

"No."

Niels peered down the quiet street and then moved quickly. At the corner, Niels held up his hand and looked around again and then slipped into the entrance to a chandler's shop. Arne followed. They remained silent for a moment and then Niels opened the door and the two youths went in.

The shop was lighted only dimly from the dawn. They smelled the oilskins. Niels went to the rear of the shop, Arne at his heels. There in the weak light of a guttering candle, they saw a score of adults and children. In a small wooden box lay a drugged baby. Niels and Arne lifted the box by its handles and nodded for the people to follow. Niels led them through the rear exit of the shop into an alley. A car was parked there.

Niels gestured for the older people and small children to get into the car. One of the men got behind the wheel. Holding the wooden box between them, Niels and Arne started down the alley, trailed by the other adults and older children. The car crept behind.

Niels led the group to a small, deserted square. He pointed to another alley and the man pulled the car out of sight. Niels set down the wooden box behind a corrugated iron shed and waved to the people to get behind the shed as well.

"You stay here," he said to Arne. "And remember, you're dedicated." He slipped away.

One of the refugees, a wispy-haired old woman, moved closer to Arne. "Do you think everything will be all right?"

He shrugged. "Never can tell."

"Do you do this often?"

"All the time, mother."

"Why?"

He shrugged again. "Better than the movies."

She peered at him. "How old are you?"

"Twenty-three, almost."

"God in heaven!"

"Take it easy, mother, it's going to be all right." He raised his head alertly as Niels ran back.

"Okay," Niels said. "This Frandsen is waiting, just as Hansen said."

"See him?"

"Of course."

"Do we know him?"

"He's all right."

"How do you know that?"

"I don't know anything except it's going to be high noon if we don't move."

Niels and Arne picked up the wooden box again. The woman who had questioned Arne kept close to the box. Arne saw she was not as old as he had thought. She reached into the box and drew the blanket higher.

"Don't worry, mother," Arne said. "Nothing will happen to your baby."

"Not with the living legends here," Niels said. "Have you ever met living legends before, madam?"

"What's he talking about?" the woman asked Arne.

"He's mad," Arne said confidentially. "Stark, raving mad."

"The whole world," she said.

They all hurried along the alley. The man called Frandsen was awaiting them at the appointed place. A small man in seaman's clothing, he beckoned for them to follow him.

Although they could not yet see the water, they could hear it now making itself felt against the docks and pilings and the air was freshly washed by the night and the morning exploded with machine guns.

Frandsen, in the lead, spun around and, before the screaming started and the panic, Arne had the crazy impression Frandsen had been cut in half by the bullets, sliced across the middle as though by a monstrous knife, but he didn't know for certain and perhaps never would, and by then everyone was yelling and crying and running in all directions. There was as yet no voice from the enemy; just bullets coming out of the morning mist.

Still clutching the handles of the wooden box, Arne and Niels ran with the others, Niels thinking, how can anyone outrun a bullet, so many bullets?—and then he felt a blow on his back, a pain colored with heat as though he had been stabbed with a flaming poker, and he stumbled and Arne said, "Watch your step, you silly fool," and Niels fell, remembering to hold onto the handle until his side of the wooden box was on the pavement.

"Niels," Arne said, the box now at a rake. "Niels, you silly bastard."

Niels, lying on his belly, raised a hand and sent Arne on. There was a fresh outburst of bullets. Arne picked up the wooden box and slung it on his shoulder and ran on.

Niels slowly began to drag himself across the street, toward the buildings where the shadows were deeper. He didn't feel too weak, his arms and legs still did what he told them to do. But there was something funny about his breathing.

Well, he thought, pulling himself over the cobbles, well, you're going to die, clawing at the cobbles, pulling, pushing, you're going to die, wondering why he thought things at a time like this so clearly he could almost hear his voice, what's that funny noise every time I breathe? He listened carefully to the sound, over the scrabbling on the cobbles, and he heard the gurgling and he thought, that's blood. I'm breathing through my back. Breathing through a hole in his back, breathing blood through a hole in his back, and by now he had reached the curb and he pulled himself onto the sidewalk, breathing blood through my back, what a curious thing, what a curious way to die, and he rested now, feeling a little safer under the shadow of the building, a dedicated man breathing blood through a hole in his back, and he was aware of someone standing over him and he thought, a German, the Gestapo, and if that were true he'd probably die quite another way because no German would have the humor to allow him to die uniquely by breathing through a hole in his back, and then he heard the whisper in Danish, good Danish, "Can I help you?"

He looked up and in the morning mist which still clung to the street he could make out the bulk of a human being. "No," Niels said. "Just go away."

"Where are you hurt?" the man asked.

"In the back. Now for Christ sake go away. You'll bring them here." The words came out through the bubbling of the blood.

"But there must be something I can do," the man insisted.

The gurgling was getting louder and Niels thought, I'm drowning, I'm drowning in my own blood, which was something—how many people drown in their own blood, dedicated or not?—and he heard the man speak again.

"I just can't leave you," the man said. "For the love of God."

"All right," Niels said. "For the love of God. In my pocket. My wallet. Throw it into the water."

He felt the man go through his pockets, take out the wallet, rise and hurry away. And then for the first time Niels heard the voice of the enemy. "Everybody in this street, go!" the voice shouted in German. "In two minutes there will be shooting!"

That figured, Niels thought, wondering how long one could not drown in one's own blood, giving the warning after the shooting, in the sentences with the built-in exclamation points, and then he heard footsteps and saw some people running down the street and at that moment it started to rain and Niels thought, that's nice, I won't be breathing pure blood any more—blood and water, sounds like a drink, a drink for German heroes. Two of the people running down the street headed toward him and he waved them away. He dragged himself farther along on the pavement and found himself at the base of a street lamp.

If it's lit, he thought, they'll see me and that'll be the end for the most dedicated man in Denmark. He considered it for a moment and then, his neck stiffening now and his head heavy, he raised his eyes. The light was not yet lit. Wrong, he corrected himself. It had already been turned off. You're a lucky man, Niels Rider, he complimented himself, a lucky living legend, nice flow that, and he dragged himself toward the building and to a staircase leading down to a shop.

He made his way down the stairs, slithering like a snake, and he found the door was not locked. He pulled himself into the shop, a second-hand furniture store, he made out. He worked himself onto a couch and passed out.

The wooden box got heavier with each step and Arne kept waiting for the baby to start crying with the noise and everything, they really must have given it a load or maybe the stuff killed it or maybe a bullet hit it and he hadn't felt it, carrying a dead baby and maybe getting killed himself because he couldn't move fast.

Sweat streaming down his face and neck, he ducked into doorways and alleys as black Gestapo cars searched the streets, unable to take the time to see whether the baby in the box was live, wounded or dead, and he felt his arms were going to fall off. He saw the window of an apartment just below the level of the street and a man and woman looking out.

He dropped to his knees, jerking his elbows for them to open the window. They glanced at each other and he rapped an elbow on the glass. They opened the window. He shoved the box through. "Take care of it," he said.

"Jewish baby?" the woman asked. Her face was still creased with sleep and she wore an old-fashioned sleeping-cap.

Arne nodded and turned away and, as they slid down the window, he turned back. "Have a look," he said. "Is it still alive?"

The woman bent low over the box and then she raised her head and nodded and Arne ran back in the direction he had come from, back to where Niels had been shot down. Two crossings later, he dodged into a doorway. He saw the Gestapo had sealed off the street. The gate leading to the pier was closed and the little black cars blocked off everything.

The voice came from a long way away, muffled, and the hand shaking him was at the end of an arm a mile long.

"What are you doing here?" were the words, but Niels could not have answered because he did not know where he was or why he was there. He felt a dull weight on his back and his eyes wouldn't open and his mouth wouldn't open either.

"What are you doing here?" The question was posed again, petulantly, angrily, and with some fear.

Niels managed to open his eyes, perhaps it was only one eye, and he saw a small face with a fringe of hair around a bald, egg-shaped head, the fringe scattered as though wind-blown, and a little, pursy mouth opened revealing bad teeth, and the voice said, "You're spoiling my furniture."

There must be some reply to that, Niels thought, and he put his mind to it, a nice problem to pass a rainy morning. He heard the voice say plaintively, "You're dirty."

That was simpler, Niels thought. He ought to be able to answer that one. "If I am," he said clearly, although he didn't say it all all, "that's what comes of lying in the street in the rain." That was a sensible explanation to a sensible observation, he thought, wondering if the blood had dried and he wasn't enjoying that famous German drink any more.

"I'm wounded," he said. "Call an ambulance."

A boy ran into the shop. "Turn out the light!" he said. "They may shoot through the window!"

The room got darker instantly and Niels felt his mind wandering off with the departed light. "I think I'm dying," he said. "Call an ambulance." He couldn't say anything after that. He thought he could hear the man on the telephone but he couldn't be sure.

Arne crossed the street and walked up to one of the Gestapomen. "What's happening?" he asked conversationally.

"Trying to smuggle out some Jews," the German said. "Well, that's one boatload that won't make it."

"What will the Gestapo do when they see the ambulance?" the man asked Niels.

Niels had the feeling the man had asked that several times and this was the first time it had got through. "I don't give a damn about the Gestapo," he said, giving a small blessing to the man who had removed his wallet. "I'm a Danish citizen and I've been wounded by those damned German swine and I want an ambulance."

He was able to raise his head slightly this time and see the man go to the telephone and place the call, and he heard him say, "Hurry, he's dying."

There seemed to be a long wait, although how long Niels didn't know, and then the door opened and a Danish police officer entered the shop.

The little man said instantly, "I don't know anything about this. I don't know who he is. I just came into my store and found him lying here this way."

Captain Melchior leaned over Niels and examined him. He put his cheek above Niels' heart.

"Never mind that," Niels said. "Just get me an ambulance."

"He asked me to call for an ambulance and I did," the little man said. "You can't blame me for that. It's something anyone would do for a wounded man."

Melchior went to the telephone. "This is Police Captain Erik Melchior," he said with authority. "I want an ambulance immediately." He gave the address. "I'll give you five minutes." He listened for a moment. "Five minutes," he repeated and hung up.

"The voice of command," Niels said happily. "God bless it." He wanted to tell the police officer that he was a dedicated man, too, but he decided against it.

It may have been those five minutes or five hours, but presently Niels felt himself being placed on a stretcher and carried out of the shop. There was more light outside now and he felt the drizzle on his face. He opened his mouth and let the cool rain fall on his lips. He saw another uniform bend over him, black uniform this time, with the familiar and perhaps now appropriate death's head on the cap, and he heard a voice ask in the other kind of Danish, "Who is this?"

"An innocent Danish passerby," Melchior said savagely. "You people ought to be more careful."

"A thousand apologies, Herr Captain," the Gestapo officer said with correct sincerity. "It is a shame, a good Dane, but the Jews bring trouble everywhere, yes?"

"Don't they," Melchior said.

The intern and the ambulance driver carried Niels to the ambulance as the two officers saluted each other, returned to their cars and left. The intern and the driver lifted the stretcher into the ambulance and placed it on the cot. The driver got out and shut the door.

The intern put a blanket on Niels and tucked it in. Then his eyes went peculiar. He slid open the vent in the front panel and said to the driver who was just seating himself behind the wheel, "I think this man is a member of the underground, a famous one. The Gestapo may want to know about this."

"How do you know that?" the driver asked.

"I think I recognize him."

The driver twisted his head to see Niels better and Niels had a feeling that the driver's eyes narrowed slightly, that he was trying to convey something to him, but the intern slid the little opening shut and Niels could not be sure.

The ambulance moved off. Niels felt cautiously down his right trouser until his fingers encountered the bulge of the very small pistol strapped to his leg. The effort bathed him in sweat. His back throbbed. He pulled back his hand and loosened his belt.

"What are you doing?" the intern asked. He was a narrow-faced man with small, ferret eyes.

"Belt's too tight," Niels said, hearing the gurgling again when he breathed. When the intern moved off his seat toward him, Niels said, "Stay the hell away, you Nazi-loving swine."

The intern sat down again and stared out the rear window of the ambulance. Niels unbuttoned his fly. His fingers were thick and clumsy and his back was on fire. The ambulance wheels bumped on a rutted road and then turned a corner and he felt the weakness coming over him. He willed his fingers to free the next to the last button and then the last. His face was pouring sweat. He slid his hand down inside his pants and he went unconscious again.

He was wakened by the jolting of the ambulance and the ding-dong of the bell. The intern was still facing the rear window. Niels brought his mind together, collecting all the scattered parts, and pushed his hand down farther until he felt the gun butt secured by the holster clip. He bit his lips against the pain and the weakness and got the gun into his hand. He closed his eyes in exhaustion and then he forced them open.

"You prick," he said.

The intern turned his head. His little eyes moved nervously as though they had lives of their own. "You better shut up," he said. "You're in bad shape."

"What are you worried about, you swine? Afraid you'll lose the reward?"

The intern wiped his mouth with the back of his hand.

"Is it that you believe?" Niels asked, his voice going hoarse.

"The more you talk, the weaker you'll get," the intern said, his eyes fixed on the window.

"Do you actually believe in them, you sorry son of a bitch?"

"I believe in myself," the intern said, rubbing his hands together.

"And money."

The intern's head spun round. "Why not? Who the hell are you to me?"

The driver braked suddenly and then accelerated. Niels felt washed with weakness. "You bastard," he said to the intern.

The intern sprang from his seat, his hands clenched together, and he raised them like a cudgel.

"Fuck off," Niels whispered. "They'd spank you if you hurt me any more."

The intern stood there for a moment trembling in the rocking ambulance and then he sat down, his eyes sparkling with hatred.

"I have more respect for them," Niels said. His voice was very faint now. "They believe in what they're doing. But a Dane—turning in other Danes. . . ." He ran his tongue over his parched lips and fought to hold his mind in one piece. "Water," he said.

"In the hospital."

"In the prison ward at Vester? Get me some water, you mother's prick."

"There is none, keep quiet!"

Niels kicked at the partition separating them from the driver. It was a massive effort and a feeble result. He tried again. Had he seen something in the driver's eyes or had he just imagined it?

The little vent slid open and the driver moved his ear to it, keeping his eyes on the road. "What is it?"

"Water," Niels croaked. "This Nazi bastard . . ."

"There is no water," the intern said.

"I'll get you some," the driver said.

"I forbid it!" the intern shouted.

A few moments later the ambulance slowed and then stopped. The intern opened the rear door and shouted, "I'll report you for this!"

Through the open door, Niels saw the driver running into an apothecary.

"This is out of order!" the intern shouted.

The driver ran out of the apothecary, carrying a glass of water. The intern spread his arms across the door, barring the way. "I forbid it!" he shouted again.

Niels pulled his hand from under the blanket. He aimed the small pistol, a toy almost with a single bullet. His hand was weaving and he brought out his other hand and steadied it. The intern was raising his foot and aiming a kick at the glass of water as he squeezed the trigger. The small sound of the gun was loud in the ambulance and the intern toppled forward, and the driver caught him and pushed him back into the ambulance so quickly and spontaneously he spilled very little of the water.

He climbed in after him and shut the door and raised Niels' head and held the glass to his lips.

"I thought I recognized you," he said to Niels.

Niels fell back on the pillow. "Most famous face in Denmark. Is he dead?"

The driver turned the intern over. "Yes," he said. There was awe in his voice.

He was, Niels saw, very young; but then, he thought, he could not be very much younger than himself. It was simply that he looked newer.

"What shall we do now?" the driver asked.

He couldn't go home, Niels knew, and he couldn't go to Arne's home. "There's a place in Charlottenlund," he said. "I'll think of the address."

"What about him?" the driver asked. He was very frightened.

"I'll think of that, too," Niels said.

"I never saw a man shot before," the driver said.

"That's very interesting," Niels said. "Get moving."

The driver started out of the ambulance. "I'm proud to have helped you," he said.

"Let's sit here and talk about it," Niels said. "We've got nothing else to do."

The driver got out and shut the door. He leaned against the ambulance for a moment. He looked around. The people were walking by, glancing incuriously at an ambulance in front of an apothecary. The sound of the shot had gone unnoticed in the snorting and wheezing of the perishing vehicles in the street.

He got into the front and drove off, leaving the divider open. "Are you all right?" he asked.

"I'm splendid," Niels said.

"Have you thought of the address in Charlottenlund?"

"No."

"Have you thought of what to do with the body?"

"Dump it," Niels said wearily.

"Where?"

"For Christ sake, anywhere."

"I'll take you where you're going first," the driver said defiantly. "If you don't mind riding with him."

"It's a distinct pleasure," Niels said.

He closed his eyes, wondering just what was going on in his back, wondering what Peter Hansen's address was, wondering whether it was right to go there, where else could he go, and then Hansen's address came to him and he took that as a sign that it was the right place to go. "Driver," he said.

"Yes."

Niels gave him the address. It stayed clear in his mind, so it must be the right place to go.

The ambulance jolted along, but Niels was on a private journey of his own and he hardly noticed it.

Presently the driver turned his head slightly. "I have an idea what to do with him," he said.

"Yes?" Niels asked, no longer interested, no longer interested in anything, not his back, not Peter Hansen's address, not how the driver was going to dispose of the body, not anything in the world.

"I'll take the body to the Gestapo," the driver said, feeling the bravery of associating with the great Orange. "I even worked out a good story how he was shot. Since he's a collaborator, they'll be grateful and that will give me an in with them. Won't that be useful?" The driver smiled happily. He was pleased and proud to be brave with a man like the Orange.

Niels was gone once more and made no reply.

Kate Hansen stood in the doorway and looked at the young driver and then at the ambulance. "Who is he? Why did he ask you to bring him here?"

The driver considered revealing the identity of the Orange and decided it would be more professional not to do so. "He just told me," he said, politely keeping his eyes averted from Kate Hansen's belly.

"My husband is not at home," she said.

"He gave me this address," the driver said, thinking if she didn't make up her mind soon he'd have another client for the ambulance.

"I don't know who he is," Kate said. "I don't know who you are. I must try to reach my husband."

"No time, lady," the driver said. "I can't keep the ambulance here forever. You see, I've also got a dead body in there."

Kate Hansen leaned against the door. When she could, she nodded her head and the driver carried Niels out of the ambulance and into the house.

3.

Colonel buhle pushed a cigarette box toward the ambulance driver. "Help yourself," he said affably. "What did you say your name was?"

The driver hadn't said; he did so now. "Alf Damm," he said, helping himself to a cigarette. Colonel Buhle flicked a lighter and held it across the desk. The driver drew in the smoke luxuriously. His bravery was still with him.

"And now let us hear about this," Buhle said, sitting back in his chair, a fresh cigar between his lips, the small laugh lines prominent around the eyes. "Where did all this happen, Mr. Damm?"

"Near the Asiatisk Plads," Alf Damm replied.

"Yes." Buhle nodded. "There was a disturbance there this morning. An attempted transport of Jews."

"That's when we received the call," Damm said, thinking how simple this was.

"And how was the intern, Dr. . . ?"

". . . Bertelsen."

"Yes, Dr. Bertelsen. How was he shot?"

"Well, we went to the place the call came from. There was still shooting in the street. We both got out of the ambulance and started toward the building. Then he was shot. I carried him back into the ambulance and saw he was dead."

"And brought him here. Why?"

Alf Damm hunched his shoulders. "Doesn't seem the Danish police are doing very much about things like this these days."

The telephone on Colonel Buhle's desk buzzed and he picked up the receiver and listened for a moment and he hung up without saying a word. He turned back to Alf Damm.

"Let me make certain I understand, Mr. Damm," Buhle said. He stood up and walked around the desk and behind Alf Damm. "Dr. Bertelsen and you were going from the ambulance to a building from which you had received a call. There was shooting in the street by Gestapomen aborting an illegal transport. Dr. Bertelsen was shot. You carried him to the ambulance, discovered he was dead, brought him here."

"Yes, sir," Alf Damm said vehemently, beginning to believe it happened exactly that way.

"Because you don't trust the Danish police?" Buhle asked.

Alf Damm twisted around to look at Buhle. "Yes, sir."

"And you trust us?"

Alf Damm twisted his head again, discovered Buhle had moved to the other side, twisted his head that way. "Yes, sir," he said sincerely.

Buhle struck him in the face with the flat of his hand. It was not a hard blow, but unexpected, and Alf Damm almost fell out of the chair.

Buhle walked slowly back to his chair and sat down. He leaned across the desk. "All right, Alf Damm," he said. "We'll start all over again."

"Start what?" Damm asked, his bravery beginning to drain away.

"Dr. Bertelsen was killed by a very small-caliber bullet fired into the base of his skull," Buhle said placidly. "Now, are you prepared to tell the truth?"

"I have told the truth," Alf Damm said, trying to find it again, that feeling he had when he was close to the Orange.

"Did you know that Dr. Bertelsen sympathized with our cause?" Buhle asked.

"No, sir," Alf Damm said.

"I think you did," Buhle said easily. "I think you killed him. . . ."

"I didn't kill him," Alf Damm said loudly.

". . . And you knew he worked with us and you had the bright idea to bring his body here to win our confidence. Now, Mr. Damm, why does a Dane want to win the confidence of the Gestapo?"

He was not born for this after all, Alf Damm was telling himself. It was fine in the ambulance with the Orange to share his bravery, but it was different here. He had not even been fazed when he had entered Dagmar House, thinking how he would share it all with the Orange one day, one famous man to another, but now he realized as though he had just woke up that he was in Gestapo headquarters and that facing him was one of the highest officers.

"Why did you shoot him, Alf Damm?" Buhle asked.

"I didn't. I swear I didn't!"

"Who did then?"

"I told you how it happened."

"The German police does not use toys for guns," Buhle said. "That bullet was fired from less than ten feet. Who?"

"I told you," Alf Damm repeated. Please, God, he prayed, please, God, give me strength.

"Who?" Buhle asked again. When Alf Damm did not reply, he pressed a button on his desk and a moment later the driver was being escorted out of the room by two Gestapomen.

He asked God again for strength and once again when he was taken to the little room. He was denied. It took less than thirty minutes for the professionals to persuade him to speak, although by that time it was difficult to say anything out of a broken jaw. When he satisfied Buhle he had told him all that he knew, he was taken away and shot.

4.

KATE HANSEN wiped Niels' face with a damp cloth. "You must try to be quiet."

"Did I do wrong?" Neils asked.

"Of course not." She looked at Hansen, peering into the street from behind a drawn curtain.

"I think I did the wrong thing," Niels said.

"No."

"I shouldn't have come here," Niels said.

"You're damned right," Hansen said harshly.

"Peter!" Kate raised her head.

"He knows that as well as I do."

"He's right," Niels said.

"Where else could he have gone?" Kate asked.

"Anywhere. Anywhere in Copenhagen or Denmark or the whole bloody world. But not here. He knows that better than I do. He's been in it longer."

"He's right, Mrs. Hansen," Niels said. "I wasn't thinking clearly, Mr. Hansen."

"Never mind all that!" Kate said violently. "He's here and he needs a doctor."

"He'll get one," Hansen said, staring out of the window. "Courtesy of the Gestapo."

"Stop being cruel," Kate said. "Peter, I don't recognize you."

Hansen turned from the window and walked to the bed. He took Kate's hand. She tried to pull it away, but he held it. "Niels," he said.

"What's got into you, Peter?" Kate asked.

"I'm sorry, Mr. Hansen," Niels said. "I'll go before they get here. You can tell them it was all a big mistake." He struggled to get up.

Hansen pushed him down. "The Gestapo is here." He felt Kate's hand tense. Niels tried again to get up. "No use," Hansen said. "They're all around the place. Now listen. Can you understand me?"

"Yes."

"I'll have to surrender you." Again he felt the tension in Kate's hand.

Niels nodded. "What else?"

"But they won't do anything to you," Hansen said. "Not right away. Not until you're stronger. Can you remember that?"

"Yes."

"They must have an idea who you are or they wouldn't be out with the reserves," Hansen said. "So they'll want to question you. They have to get you well for that. Remember that."

"Yes."

"And before that, I'll try to work something out."

"Yes."

"Just let them get you well. I'll do the rest."

"Yes."

"You believe that?"

"Yes, Mr. Hansen. And please forgive me for coming here."

"Just keep believing it," Hansen said, and at that moment the front doorbell rang. "You stay out of sight, Kate."

"Peter, I'm sorry, too."

"Everybody's sorry," Hansen said. "The only people in the world who aren't sorry about anything are those men out there."

The bell rang again in a manner, or so it seemed to Hansen, that it had never rung before, a magnificent Teutonic clanging. He ran down the stairs and crossed the foyer, and opened the door to find a uniformed SS man in the act of driving his rifle butt against it.

Colonel Buhle smiled. "Just in time, Mr. Hansen," he said.

265

He rapped the door with his knuckles. "Very hard wood. Might have damaged the rifle. May we come in?"

"What do you want?" Hansen asked.

"Whatever it is," Buhle said, walking past Hansen into the house, "we usually get it." He looked around. "Lovely home. Where is he?"

"Upstairs," Hansen said. There was no use; there never was any use, not with this kind.

"Upstairs," Buhle said to two of the Gestapomen. "In there, Mr. Hansen," he said, indicating the living room. "This is a lovely room. What do you know about all this?"

"Nothing."

Buhle picked up a Sèvres vase, examined it, sighed. "Nothing. It always starts that way, always."

Lise Hansen, walking up the street with a school friend, saw the black cars in front of the house. She knew whose cars they were, as did every child in Denmark by then, and she started to run toward the house.

She opened the door and ran into the house, and she dropped her books and screamed as she saw a man being dragged down the stairs by the feet. "Daddy!"

The two SS men hauling Niels Rider away marched down the stairs. Niels' head thumped on each step like an errant basketball. The wound from his back left a smear of blood.

"Daddy!" Lise screamed again and she saw it was not her father and by then Hansen had come running out of the living room and scooped her in his arms.

"Lise, Lise," he said. "It's all right, darling, it's all right."

Kate appeared at the head of the stairs and saw the body being pulled like a bundle and the head thudding on the steps and the blood and she swayed and gripped the newel.

"Get back into your room, Kate," Hansen said. He held Lise tightly. "Lise, darling, it's all right. Kate, go away!"

"Yes, get back into your room, Mrs. Hansen," Buhle said, stepping out of the living room and gazing up the stairs. He paid no attention to the body being dragged past him. "I had no idea of the condition you were in, Mrs. Hansen. Please get away from the stairs." He turned to Hansen. "Lovely child," he said. "Everything here is lovely. I'm afraid, Mr. Hansen, you must come along as well."

5.

IT WAS JUST past 7:30 in the evening when Hansen and Buhle arrived at Dagmar House. Buhle had made several amiable attempts to question him during the drive back from Charlottenlund, but Hansen had said nothing.

He now was taken to a small empty cubicle, hardly larger than a clothes closet, and was ordered to stand facing the wall. The door was left open and an armed guard was posted to watch him.

Buhle hated eating alone. He wished Greiner hadn't been such an idiot. He considered seeing if Becker was around. He decided against it. He didn't relish having to listen to a detailed account of Becker's already famous exploit at Gilleleje. He had heard that Becker was planning to write a special report to Eichmann.

He went alone to a good restaurant, had several snaps to ease the rigor of the day and then ate an excellent meal.

He went to his home, a small flat, ruefully compared his meager surroundings with the luxury he had seen at Hansen's house, had a soothing bath and went to his bed for an untroubled night's sleep.

6.

PRECISELY AT NINE o'clock on Tuesday morning, Hansen was led away from his cell. He had stood with his face to the wall for more than thirteen hours. His legs wobbled as he followed the guard. He felt a little drunk.

He had spent the long hours of the night in intricate and exhaustive study of himself. He had been alone with Peter Hansen without distraction for a longer period than he had ever been in his life. He had been compelled to remain motionless. He had not bothered to ask for so much as a glass of water, knowing it would be refused.

The purpose of the petty barbarism was obvious to him and through the night he had willed himself against its taking its effect.

To counter the passage of endless time, he had reviewed his life from his earliest memories. He had thought back to his childhood and his parents and schooldays. He recalled the names of poems he had had to memorize and tried to remember the words. He thought of his meeting Kate, on the fishing party in the little boat on the Sound, of his years with her, of Lise, of friends, acquaintances, enemies. He had tried to bring back to mind the second and third stanzas of "King Christian," one of the two national anthems, and had spent a pleasant few minutes mulling over the irrelevant oddity of it having been translated into English by, of all persons, the American poet, Henry Wadsworth Longfellow.

Somewhere around three o'clock in the morning—just a guess, he hadn't been allowed to raise his arm to look at his watch—he remembered the experience of one of the underground men. The man, who worked for the Carlsberg breweries, had been arrested and confined for six months in a windowless, unlighted cell in Vester Prison. After a few weeks, he felt he was beginning to go mad. He was permitted a fifteen-minute exercise period every day in the prison yard, and it was during one of these periods that he had had his large idea.

He managed, during the course of bending and stretching, to collect five pebble-size pieces of gravel and carried them back to the cell. When the door was shut and bolted and he was again in total darkness, he scattered the pebbles and then crept about the cell on his hands and knees and collected them.

He kept the five pebbles in a corner of the cell and gave himself this problem every day upon returning from his exercise. In time he refined the play, counting evenly until he found the five pebbles, then setting himself to beat his best time.

It was the only thing, he had told Hansen, that kept his sanity. Upon his release, he had taken the pebbles with him and still carried them for luck.

Now as Hansen followed the guard, he repeated to himself in the airiness of his hunger that he was not Peter Hansen, involved with the underground, but Peter Hansen, business man, involved with the Germans. His attitude and answers must reflect that Peter Hansen. No matter what Buhle said or did, he must not forget that.

He had worked off most of the stiffness of his body by the time he was led into Buhle's office, but he still felt lightheaded. He must not let that play tricks on him.

He found Buhle at his desk and the desk covered with enough food for a party. Beer, sandwiches, pastry, coffee, even a bottle of snaps. Buhle, an enormous white linen handkerchief tucked under his chin, waved a bottle of beer.

"Come, come, sit down, Mr. Hansen," Buhle said heartily. He raised the bottle to his lips and drank off half the beer. He swept his hand back and forth over the table. "You see, I am becoming a good Dane," he boomed, wiping his lips grandly with the napkin. "What would you like? Help yourself."

The sight and smell of food made Hansen feel dizzier. Buhle's unlikely expansiveness did not reassure him. He gripped the top of the chair and felt the old knot of fear in his stomach. "You've got your own damned nerve," he said coldly. "Just what kind of monster are you?"

Buhle, about to take a large bite of a herring sandwich, gaped in astonishment. The guard opened his mouth, closed it, opened it again.

Hansen walked over to Buhle's desk and leaned on it, his insides shaking. "You've got a right to arrest anyone, question him about anything. But there's a civilized way to do that. You're acting like a Mongolian savage."

The guard moved forward courageously to protect his chief in the event Hansen had it in mind to attack him. Buhle, his mouth full of herring, waved the guard away. "Go on, Mr. Hansen."

"You're damned right I'll go on," Hansen said, hoping it was sounding right, his head ringing, unable to tell. "I don't know who you think you're dealing with, but you're supposed to be civilized people."

This was the first time in many years Colonel Buhle had heard that adjective applied to his race by a non-German. It intrigued him. Hansen, he thought, was either a fool or a very clever man. For some inexplicable reason he found himself hoping Hansen was not just being smart. "Please sit down, Mr. Hansen," he said solicitously. "You must be quite tired."

"Never mind about me being tired," Hansen said, with an icy fury that was almost genuine. "I don't know what this is all about. I'm a business man. I've done business with you Germans. Check your records. You'll discover you've made a bloody damned fool of yourself."

Colonel Buhle was becoming more and more interested, but in the interests of discipline he could not continue to permit the guard to hear a person of his rank described in those terms. He ordered the guard to wait outside. The guard departed with reluctance. He was fascinated and would have liked to have heard more. But he'd seen enough to captivate the guard room.

270

Buhle inspected the array of food as though the desk top was a master control designed to deliver a man to the moon. He pounced on a fresh pork sandwich covered with slices of cucumber and went to work on that. "I know all about you, Mr. Hansen," he said. "I know all about your business with us. With Georg Siebert."

The name was dropped gently. It sounded a tocsin to Hansen. "That's quite correct," he said.

"Mr. Siebert presently is in Berlin," Buhle said, emptying the bottle of beer, belching pleasantly. "Being interrogated."

"Let's hope a little more sensibly than I am," Hansen said.

Buhle's eyebrows shot up, down. "Do sit down, Mr. Hansen," he urged. "And have something to eat. You must be starved."

The smell of the food was driving Hansen wild. "I'll sit down when I bloody well want to." He realized he had not eaten since breakfast the day before. "Now let's get this nonsense over with. I'm wasting your time and you're wasting mine."

"Perhaps," Buhle said, finishing the pork sandwich, wiping his mouth again. "Who is this wounded man?"

"I don't know."

"Why was he taken to your house?"

"I don't know that, either."

"Have you ever seen him before?"

"I don't think so."

"Why should he ask to be taken to your house?"

"I haven't the slightest idea. Maybe he works for me, in one of my factories."

"Didn't you talk to him before I arrived?"

"He was delirious. He didn't make sense."

"How did he get to your house?"

"I wasn't home. Some ambulance driver drove up to the door and told my wife he had a badly wounded man who asked to be brought there. I don't think my wife is making much sense these days, either."

"A woman that close to having a baby," Buhle said with understanding. "They rarely do."

271

"Well, instead of telling the driver to take the man to the hospital, she let him bring him into the house. She finally located me. I went home immediately. He seemed pretty far gone to me, and I was just going to call for another ambulance when you got there."

Buhle cut off a piece of pastry. "We believe him to be a saboteur."

"I wouldn't know," Hansen said.

"It is even possible he might be the notorious saboteur known as the Orange," Buhle said, cutting off another piece of pastry. "The one who works as a team with the other saboteur called the Blaze."

"Oh, Christ," Hansen said scornfully. "Orange, Blaze. . . . You disappoint me, Colonel. You sound like a schoolboy. This wounded lad, he can't be more than twenty-two, three. Are you seriously suggesting he could have fooled all of you for years?"

"Please sit down, Mr. Hansen," he said again. "I would take it as a favor."

Hansen accepted the invitation this time, and the coffee Buhle poured for him.

"Have some pastry," Buhle said.

"Thank you, no."

"A sandwich?"

"Thank you, no."

"Perhaps some roll and butter."

"Just the coffee."

"On an empty stomach? It might make you heady."

Hansen sipped the coffee. It hit his stomach like a shot. Nothing had tasted as good in a long time.

"So you believe this young man is not the Orange?" Buhle asked, sitting back in his chair.

"I'm not sure I believe anybody is the Orange," Hansen said. "Did you ever hear of a story called 'The Scarlet Pimpernel?'"

"I do not think I have."

"That was a work of fiction," Hansen said. "The story of a dozen men rolled into one. Well, every time there is an act of sabotage you Germans run around yelling, 'Orange! Blaze!'"

272

Buhle lit a cigar, his eyes never leaving Hansen. "What will you do when the Germans win the war?" he asked unexpectedly.

"I don't think you have a prayer in hell," Hansen said, setting the coffee cup and saucer on the desk.

"Would you like some more coffee?"

"That was fine."

"Are you frightened, Mr. Hansen?"

"No," Hansen said.

"Why not?"

"I know you Germans have your own kind of honor," Hansen said. "You may threaten to torture me, but you won't."

"Why not?" Buhle asked again, wanting truly to know.

"You have me completely in your power," Hansen said. "But you know damned well I haven't done a thing against you."

Buhle opened the cigarette box on his desk and offered it to Hansen. Hansen would have preferred his pipe but he was afraid of that with his head and his stomach. He took a cigarette and lit it and pulled in deeply. "You know something, Colonel Buhle," he said, relaxing. "When I was a small child, my father was bailiff for the King and he was not paid very well and there were six of us children. And yet we also had staying with us at one time or another six Vienna orphans. Starving Germans. There was hardly a Danish family that didn't at one time or another make a home for those children. I've always believed that one of the reasons you Germans have treated us so decently since you've been here is that you remember those days when things weren't going so well in your country and we took your children into our hearts."

Presently Buhle said, "I think that will be all, Mr. Hansen. You are free to go. Would you like to ring your wife first and tell her nothing has happened to you?"

"I'll call her from my office," Hansen said, rising. "If you don't mind." He started for the door.

"So you believe we will lose the war?" Buhle said, almost to himself.

"Yes," Hansen said.

"I like this country," Buhle said.

"Yes," Hansen said. "Many people do."

Buhle ordered the food removed from the desk. It had not, in any case, accomplished his purpose. Perhaps there was no purpose to accomplish. Perhaps Hansen was exactly what he said he was and nothing more. A Dane making money out of the Germans, with a magnificent home and a magnificent wife who was about to produce what would undoubtedly be a magnificent child.

He would like to have had Max Greiner to talk to now. He wished he had listened more closely to Greiner.

He put down the cigar and walked to the window. He looked down. He saw Hansen leave Dagmar House and walk across the square. He saw the swarming pigeons and he thought, as he had thought before, a German village could subsist on what was fed to those pigeons every day.

He returned to the desk. He picked up the dead cigar. He started to light it, tossed it away, lit a fresh one. The buzzer on his desk sounded. He flipped the switch and listened and said, "Send her in."

The door was opened immediately and Lili Lund entered. He felt an excitement and tried to remember when last he had had a woman.

"You sent for me?" she asked coolly.

"Obviously."

"This isn't my day."

"It may be nobody's." He opened a drawer and took out a photograph and slid it across the desk. "Do you recognize that man?"

Lili picked up the photograph. She looked at the face of Niels Rider, taken in Vester Prison. The head was out of shape, as though reflected in a mirror in a funhouse. The eyes were closed. The cheeks and jaw were bruised. The mouth was twisted.

"I don't think his mother would recognize him," she said.

"Have you ever seen him with Arne Johansen?"

"I hardly ever meet any of Arne's friends. We spend most of our time alone."

274

And I know exactly where, and how you spend it, Buhle sighed to himself, thinking of his own barren bed. "But he could be a friend of Johansen's?"

"He could be anybody." She put the picture down. "What happened to him? Was he hit by a tank?"

She opened her purse and took out her cigarettes and holder. She fitted a cigarette into the holder. Buhle gazed at her thoughtfully. He made no move and she lit the cigarette herself.

"You're in rather a frivolous mood this morning," Buhle said unangrily.

The tone did not deceive her. She picked up the picture and looked at it again. "I don't believe I've ever seen this man before."

"But you are not certain?"

"Take me to the hospital. I can't tell much from this."

Buhle pursed his lips around the cigar and thought for a moment. He shook his head. "If this man is the one we think he is, his friends will be watching Vester Prison. Someone might see you and then your usefulness with Johansen would be ended."

7.

PETER HANSEN and Arne Johansen stood off to one side of the little *polser* wagon in the Stroeget, at the corner of Koebmagergade. It was a little more than three hours after Hansen left the Gestapo headquarters.

Arne was alone in his own world. "Why not?" he demanded. "It would be easy. Let's just grab this swine Buhle and hold him until Niels is turned free."

Hansen took a bite of sausage. He had forgotten how good it tasted. "We can't do that."

"Why not? Tell me, why not?" Arne's sausage was clamped in his hand.

"It would focus attention on Niels."

"He needs that. He needs a little attention."

"The Gestapo may suspect who he is, but they have no proof. If we made a big effort, that would convince them," Hansen said, hearing his own voice, aware how weak logic always sounded against emotion. "That's reason number one. Eat your sausage."

"Fuck my sausage," Arne said.

"That's what we're here for, to eat sausages," Hansen said. Reason number two. If we kidnapped Buhle, which might not be too difficult . . ."

"I'll do it myself," Arne said.

"So you said. If we kidnap Buhle, when we release him your position and Niels' and perhaps even mine would be destroyed."

"Why release him? Why not get back Niels and then kill the swine?"

He's a weapon, Hansen thought, a deadly weapon in himself, a weapon ready always to be used for the simple solution.

"Kill him?" Hansen asked. "And what do you think the Germans would do? A clearing murder to end all clearing murders. Eat your sausage."

Arne bit into the *polser*.

"You forgot the mustard," Hansen said.

Arne looked at him and then dabbed the sausage into the mustard on the little piece of paper on the *polser* wagon's counter. "Then what can we do?"

"At the moment, nothing," Hansen said.

Arne raised his eyes.

"He can't be moved yet," Hansen said. "The bullet's lodged in his lung."

"They'll let him die," Arne said.

"I think not. They'll do everything to get him well."

"And what are you doing?"

"Trying to think."

"Trying to think. Jesus Christ." Arne almost choked trying to make himself swallow the sausage.

"Just that. Meanwhile, you need a change of scenery."

Arne's eyes paled until they were without color. "I'm not going anywhere."

"Just south of Ringsted there's a little village called Hoem," Hansen said.

"Fuck Hoem."

"Below the village there is a crossroads."

"Fuck the crossroads."

"As the British say."

"As I say."

"Be there at four o'clock this afternoon. Exactly at four."

"No chance," Arne said. "I'm not leaving Copenhagen. Not until I know something's being done about Niels." He held up the sausage, looking around to throw it away.

"Arne," Hansen said very quietly.

"No chance," Arne said. "No chance at all."

"Four o'clock."

Arne's washed-out eyes turned to pinpoints and he cocked his arm as though to hurl the sausage at Hansen.

Hansen felt he was looking into the muzzle of a gun. "Eat it," he said. "It's getting cold."

Every muscle in Arne's body tensed. He made no move and yet he seemed to go into a crouch, ready to spring.

"Four o'clock," Hansen said, struggling to keep the exhaustion out of his voice, the hours of facing the wall, the ordeal with Buhle, all of it out of his voice. "Let me worry about Niels," he said.

8.

THE TRAFFIC had never been so heavy; the drive home had never seemed so long. Kate was waiting at the door when he drove up. He looked at her quickly and breathed thanks. She watched him drive into the garage and walk to the door.

"Peter," she said.

"Well, you look the same," he said. "Fat as ever."

"I told you that when you called." Her eyes searched his face as though something was hiding there. "I told you."

"I had to see. You're famous for lying."

She reached out and touched his cheek. "Peter." Her wide mouth broke into a grin and then she bit her lip.

"Aren't you going to invite me in?" he asked.

She stepped back, her eyes on him, her lips pressed between her teeth. He put his arms around her.

"I'd like to squeeze you," he said.

"I know."

"But you're like a beer barrel."

"I know."

He patted her belly. "Still refuses to get born."

"He's smart," she said. "They didn't do anything to you?"

"A yoga lesson and then a cup of coffee. Where's Lise?"

"Visiting her friend."

"Why isn't she home at this hour?"

"I wanted to have a look at you first."

"In case I was a mess? I told you when I called."

"I had to see. You have a small reputation for lying."

"Only therapeutic lies," he said. He glanced at the stairs. There were wet, dark stains where the blood had been cleaned away.

"How is he?" she asked.

"I don't know."

"The way they dragged him down the stairs."

"Don't think about it."

"Do you know him well?"

"Yes."

"He's one of your boys, isn't he?"

"Let's not talk about it, Kate."

"I know. It's none of my business."

"We've been all through that, Kate."

"I hope he lives."

"Don't think about it."

"He was so sorry he had bothered you."

"Don't think about anything but a drink."

"I have the glasses chilled. Peter, do you think he'll live?"

"I don't know."

He walked past the stairs with the stains on the carpet into the living room and sat down in his chair and put his feet on the ottoman and leaned back. She fixed a martini and gave it to him and went back to the cabinet to pour herself an aquavit.

"The way they dragged him down, like a bag of laundry," she said.

"Don't think about it," he said. He tasted the drink. It seemed years since the last one.

"But he was making war against them," she said.

"Please, don't go on."

"It's what they do to people who make war against them," she said. "It's what they do to everybody who makes war against them."

When he said nothing, she turned from the cabinet and looked across the room. She walked quickly to him and saw he was asleep in the chair, the glass in his hand. She took away the glass and covered him with a throw. She looked down at his face and she wanted to cry.

9.

A COMPLETE and accurate account of the roundup of the Jews at Gilleleje was carried in the Tuesday edition of the underground newspaper printed in Randers.

Rabbi Bent Rasmussen read through the story slowly.

Each word was a hurdle to be crossed. When he finished, he lowered the paper as though it was made of lead. He blinked his eyes and turned his strong, beardless prophet's face toward the orchard.

Presently he said, "May God watch over them."

Pastor Duul nodded. "Amen."

The two men walked slowly among the orderly rows of apple trees, the leaves turning, fluttering down. There was a sweet, winey smell in the air. A bird sang.

"So much peace here," Rasmussen said. "So much beauty. How can it happen in the same country, Pastor Duul?"

"My dear Dr. Rasmussen, ask yourself how it can happen in the same world," Duul said. "I have news for you as well."

"Those poor people," Rasmussen said. He took out a handkerchief and blew his nose. "Those poor, poor people."

"I have news for you," Duul said again.

Rasmussen nodded. He wiped his eyes with the handkerchief. "Yes, we must go." He looked around. "But we have been privileged to have had this for a little while. We've been lucky." He returned the handkerchief to his pocket. "What happens now, Pastor Duul?"

"You will go to Falster," Duul said. "To the home of the bishop there. Everything has been arranged."

Rasmussen picked up an apple. He looked at it as though he had never before seen an apple. "It's all arranged, you say. As simply as that. A miracle is performed and you say calmly, it's all arranged." He contemplated the apple and then set it down gently exactly where he picked it up. "How does one say thank you, Dr. Duul?"

"I prefer you to say nothing," Duul said. "I prefer to think you know that I understand how you feel and that you need say nothing."

They started walking back to the house.

"The bishop of Falster," Rasmussen said. "You know, when the King visited our synagogue he told us we would not be forgotten, that we were Danes as all other Danes. I suppose after that nothing should surprise us."

10.

To REACH FALSTER, southernmost of the Danish islands, it was necessary to return to Copenhagen and board a southbound train there.

The Central Station was thronged as always, and as much German was heard as Danish. Lotte and the children waited while Rasmussen bought the tickets.

"It's so strange," Lotte said to Jorgen. "To be in Copenhagen just to pass through. Not to be able to find out about our friends. Not to see our home."

"It is strange," Jorgen said. "But so is everything else these days."

She nodded and then looked at him sharply. For a moment it had seemed it was not Jorgen but his father who had spoken.

Rasmussen returned with the tickets and they walked to the head of the stairs going down to the new platform. The platform was so packed with German military, it seemed some of the soldiers would be pushed onto the tracks.

Lotte looked at Rasmussen anxiously.

"Have to expect that," Jorgen said. "You see, the train goes on to Gedser and then crosses by ferry to Warnemünde in Germany."

Rasmussen shrugged. "Is it all right with you if we divide as before, Jorgen?" he asked politely.

"Yes, Father," Jorgen said. He picked up Leif and started down the stairs. Lotte watched him, then turned to Rasmussen. She gazed at him and then turned and hurried after Jorgen.

Jorgen and his mother walked to the forward part of the platform. They boarded the train when it pulled into the station and walked down the corridor. They found a compartment empty except for a pleasant-faced woman. Jorgen opened the door and looked in inquiringly. The woman, middle-aged and motherly, with thickly plaited golden hair twisted in a ring on top of her head, smiled and nodded.

"Good day," she said as Lotte and the children entered. She had a faint accent Lotte could not place. Lotte and Jorgen returned the greeting and made themselves comfortable. Several persons, including a German captain, peered into the compartment and continued on.

The train departed on time. The woman, who had not spoken after her greeting, smiled to Jorgen and asked, "Where are you bound for?"

"Falster," Jorgen said.

"A little holiday?" the woman asked.

Lotte glanced at her, trying to identify the accent. It might have been one of the accents of Sweden.

"We have family there," Jorgen said.

"A lovely time of the year," the woman said. "But don't you go to school?"

"I don't mind missing a few days," Jorgen said cheerfully.

"Just like a boy," the woman said. The woman opened a black bag and took out a newspaper.

Lotte saw that it was a copy of the *Völkischer Beobachter*, Hitler's own newspaper.

As Lotte tried not to stare, the woman settled herself and began to read. Now and then she smiled faintly and nodded.

Without realizing what she was doing, Lotte found her fingers touching her face. It seemed to her her Jewishness was written all over it. Her fingers touched her nose and her lips and her cheek. She had never been conscious of her face before, but now she felt the word "Jew" was stamped on it and that at any moment the woman would raise her eyes from the newspaper and, alerted in some mystical way by her present connection with her Führer, would see Lotte for what she was.

She pulled her eyes from the woman and the paper, and forced herself to look at Jorgen. He, too, was staring at the newspaper. Then he glanced at his mother and, seeing what was there, touched her hand.

At that moment, the woman looked up. Lotte felt she would faint.

"It is a pleasant journey, not?" the woman asked, and now Lotte had no difficulty placing the accent.

"Yes," Jorgen said.

"It is a lovely country," the woman said. "I am very happy to be going home, but I shall miss this lovely country."

"Thank you," Jorgen said.

"I see that you are looking at my newspaper," the woman said.

Lotte stiffened. Her stomach was churning.

"I was just interested to look at it when you're finished," Jorgen said.

Lotte looked swiftly at her son. Where had that come from?

"Do you read German?" the woman asked Jorgen.

"A little," Jorgen said. "I'd like to learn more."

"It is a beautiful language," the woman said. "And when one listens to the Führer use it, is it like hearing a symphony."

Jorgen leaned forward. "I have heard him on the radio."

"Then you know," the woman said dreamily. "Then you know." She held out the paper. "Here, little man, take this and read it and whatever you manage to understand will be good for you."

"Thank you, ma'am," Jorgen said gravely, accepting the newspaper.

Lotte watched her son settle back in his seat, cross his legs, and try to read the paper. Where had it come from? she asked herself again. And how recently had it been that she still thought of him as a child?

When the train reached their destination Jorgen offered to return the newspaper but the woman told him to keep it and study it. Jorgen promised to do so. The woman exchanged farewells and Lotte, from pride in her son, found the strength to return the farewell as cordially as it was given.

Rabbi Rasmussen's eyes widened when he saw the newspaper in Jorgen's hand.

"When I tell you," Lotte said, "you won't believe it."

She started to laugh. It began as a nervous laugh, a laugh of relief, and Rasmussen looked at her quickly, but then it changed to a merry laugh and Rasmussen saw Jorgen begin to laugh and then Lotte and Jorgen hugged each other, laughing, until the tears came to Lotte's eyes.

"Tell me," the rabbi said plaintively. "Please tell me so I can laugh, too."

11.

WHEN THE RASMUSSEN family arrived at the residence of the bishop of Falster, they were astonished to see some fifty-odd Jews enjoying lunch at trundle tables under the shade trees in the bishop's front yard.

The rabbi was welcomed by members of his congregation. Most of the refugees were strangers to him.

As he looked at the peaceful scene, at the long line of tables covered with food, at the people eating and chatting as unconcernedly as though they were attending the annual picnic of their lodge, he heard his name called shrilly and he turned to see limping toward him Mendel Cohen, the German Jew who worshipped at the Copenhagen synagogue and who now was making his second flight from the encroachment of Adolf Hitler.

Cohen, in a highly distraught state, threw his arms around Rasmussen and clung to him. "I'm so happy to see you,

Rabbi," he said. "I cannot tell you what it means to me to see you here. For the first time, I allow myself to believe that perhaps they will not capture us."

Rasmussen was shocked by Cohen's appearance. It was less than a week's time since he had last seen him in the synagogue, but the small man seemed to have aged ten years. His skin was pasty and drawn. He had developed a nervous gesture, a twitching of the mouth. As he spoke, he glanced behind him as though he was worried someone was eavesdropping.

"You've heard about Gilleleje, Rabbi?" Cohen asked.

"Yes."

"It could have been us, just as easily."

"Yes, it could have been us, Mr. Cohen," Rasmussen agreed. "But God chose it otherwise. That's why you're here and why you soon shall be safe in Sweden."

"When I heard about them, Rabbi . . ." Cohen looked behind him. A small thin woman was walking toward them, holding the hand of a tiny ten-year-old girl. Cohen ignored them. "When I heard about them, it was all there again." His fingers dug into Rasmussen's arms. "The inside of a concentration camp, Rabbi. It's something one doesn't easily forget."

"Calm yourself, Mr. Cohen," Rasmussen said.

The woman and the little girl reached them and stood there silently, the girl staring up from somber eyes. Cohen saw them and continued to talk to Rasmussen, but when they remained there he introduced them as his wife and child. Recognized and identified, the woman slipped her arm under Cohen's.

"Come," she said quietly.

"I have not finished talking to the rabbi," Cohen said.

"He has just arrived here and he's tired," the woman said. "You can talk to him later."

"Later, Rabbi," Cohen said as she led him away. "I have many things to tell you. I cannot tell you how happy I am to see you here, Rabbi."

Rasmussen nodded. He sighed and looked around. The

bishop, as befitted his more exalted rank, lived in a much more imposing manner than did Pastor Duul. His house and spacious grounds with beautifully cultivated gardens formed a small estate. With most of the property walled off, it had a reassuring atmosphere of isolation and privacy.

Bishop Oxlund, a cheerful, hearty, energetic man, on being informed that the chief rabbi of Copenhagen had arrived, came rushing out of the house. He greeted Rasmussen warmly and then beckoned him to one side. "My dear Dr. Rasmussen," he said in a conspiratorial manner, "I have a problem. You must help me solve it. It has to do with food."

Rasmussen looked at the tables and nodded. "I can imagine. I don't know how you've managed it up to now."

Oxlund frowned, looked at the tables, shook his head vehemently. "No, no, no," he said. "You misunderstand me completely, my dear fellow. We don't lack food here. Heavens, no, not at all. The local farmers, the nearby fishermen . . . gracious, they never stop sending food here. My worry is to get it all eaten before it spoils. No, that's not the problem at all."

"Then what is this problem, Bishop Oxlund?" Rasmussen asked.

"It's this, just this," the bishop said. "I have been told that this coming Friday is the beginning of your most important holiday, Yom Kippur." He smiled beatifically. "Have I pronounced that properly?"

"Exactly right, Bishop Oxlund," Rasmussen said.

"Now what I want to know, and this is my problem: what is it Jews eat specially on that day, so that I can have it prepared for all of you? I know what it is, it's on the tip of my tongue, but for the life of me I can't put the word to it."

"My dear Bishop . . ." Rasmussen said.

"I'm really quite embarrassed," Oxlund said. "One should know about these things. As a matter of simple knowledge, if for no other reason. However are we going to come to understand each other unless we do start by learning a few basic facts?"

"Bishop Oxlund . . ." Rasmussen said.

Oxlund snapped his fingers. "Matzohs!" he exclaimed. "Is that it? That is it, isn't it? Oh, I'm genuinely delighted I remembered it."

"My dear Bishop," Rasmussen tried again. "Matzohs is for Passover."

Oxlund's face fell. "Oh, dear," he said.

"I hope that of all the problems you have to face in life, however, this is the most serious," Rasmussen said.

"That's very kind of you," Oxlund said.

"On Yom Kippur, Jews eat nothing."

"Nothing?" Oxlund asked, astounded.

"The Day of Atonement is the holiest day of the year for us, Bishop Oxlund, and we observe it by fasting."

The bishop shrugged dejectedly. Then he brightened. "Well, you'll be quite hungry the day after Yom Kippur," he said with new cheer. "We'll have to think of something special for that."

It was not intended that any of the Jews spend the Day of Atonement at the bishop's establishment. On the evening of the same day, word was received by Oxlund, in the still, mysterious way of the underground, that two vessels were now ready to transport all of them across the Sound. As soon as it was dark, the ubiquitous taxis and ambulances arrived and took the Jews away.

Bishop Oxlund stood at the gateway to his home and waved the last of them farewell.

12.

THE RASMUSSENS and thirteen other Jews, including Mendel Cohen, who would not let Rasmussen out of his sight, and his wife and child, were taken to a small coastal village and put aboard a fishing boat that appeared not to have yet reached its full size. The captain, a heavy-set Dane in his early thirties, ordered everyone below.

"It stinks of fish," he said. "But you can be grateful for that. Some of the German patrol boats have bloodhounds aboard."

Even in the dark, Rasmussen could see Mendel Cohen's face blanch. "Bloodhounds," Cohen repeated.

"Specially trained to smell you out," the captain said. "But there isn't a dog in the world, bloodhound or not, that could make out anything but old fish from the inside of this boat!"

The Jews climbed down into the hold and the hatch was closed, and the boat moved out into the Sound. The water was rough, but not too rough; a few persons became ill. Soon most of them were asleep.

Rasmussen leaned back and closed his eyes. Sleep was denied him. He thought of the manner of his departure from his native land and the old question passed through his mind: why?

Then he thought of the effort it had taken to put him and the others inside this boat—the effort, the trust, the love—he had an answer to the question. He closed his eyes and slept.

He was awakened by a tugging of his hand. He opened his eyes. His son, Jorgen, looked at him excitedly. Then Rasmussen realized he could see Jorgen's face, that it was not totally dark, that light was filtering through, that it must be morning.

Moving carefully not to waken the others, Rasmussen and Jorgen worked their way to the hatch and pushed it open a slit. They saw the captain at the wheel, smoking a pipe; he nodded to them and they opened the hatch and climbed onto the deck. It was first light.

Rasmussen breathed deeply. The air, after the night in the hold, was like perfume. Suddenly Jorgen grabbed his arm and pointed. Straining, Rasmussen tried to see.

"Land," Jorgen whispered. "Father, it's land."

Rasmussen squinted. He shook his head. "I think it's just a cloud, a low cloud."

288

"It's land, Father," Jorgen insisted. "It's Sweden." Then he shook his head. "No, Father, you're right. It is just a cloud."

"But we can't be far, can we, Captain?" Rasmussen asked.

"No," the Dane said.

"You must be tired," Rasmussen said.

Again Jorgen clutched at his father's arm. "Father," he said. "Papa, look there."

Rasmussen followed his son's pointed finger and he saw the lighthouse in the distance.

"Thank God," he said in a low voice. He closed his eyes. "Dear God, please accept our thanks for Thy generosity and Thy love. We shall strive to be worthy of it."

"Maybe they'll turn on the light for us," Jorgen said.

They stared at the thin, white lighthouse, and then the sun rose and they could see more clearly. Now they could make out the coast, low and still distant.

Rasmussen put his arm around his son. "In just a few hours, please God, we shall all be safe."

There was a puzzled expression on Jorgen's face. "Father."

"Yes?"

"Sweden is east of Denmark, isn't it?"

"Of course."

At that moment three of four other men poked their heads out of the hold, among them the harassed face of Mendel Cohen.

"Where are we, Rabbi?" Cohen asked nervously.

"There, look ahead," Rasmussen said. "You can see land and a lighthouse."

The men broke into cheers and climbed onto the deck, stretching, looking around, breathing deeply of the fresh air.

"Father," Jorgen said.

"Yes, son."

"Father, if we're heading east, then the sun should be rising on our faces, not on our backs."

Rasmussen frowned and then looked at the coast approaching.

"He's right!" Mendel Cohen cried out. "We're on our way back to Denmark!"

"That's the Gedser Light," another man said. "That's the tip of Falster Island!"

"What's happening here?" Rasmussen asked the captain, who had listened stoically to all the shouting.

"He's betrayed us!" Cohen shouted. "I knew we would never get away!"

The angry voices, the cries, brought others to the deck. The women joined their voices to the men's. In a very short time the people were close to panic. Rasmussen tried to restore quiet.

"In any case," he said clearly, "we must not attract attention."

The terrifying implication of the warning brought on a sudden silence. Rasmussen, who had watched the captain's face, who had seen him maintain silence, opening his lips only to emit small bursts of smoke from his pipe, had an instinct that, of all the persons aboard, the captain was the most frightened.

"Captain," Rasmussen said, "what is happening here? Why are we returning to Denmark?"

"He's betrayed us!" Mendel Cohen shouted again.

Rasmussen raised his hand to silence him. "Captain," he said, "I'm not a mind-reader, but I believe I can recognize a good face. There is something you want to tell us."

The captain took his pipe out of his mouth. "I got lost." He put the pipe back.

The statement brought on the hubbub again, and again Rasmussen held up his hand for quiet. "I believe you owe us an explanation, Captain," he said.

The captain was silent. He looked at the questioning faces and then he tore off his cap and flung it on the deck. "You might as well know the truth!" he said loudly.

"You betrayed us!" Mendel Cohen screamed.

"No, I didn't sell you out! As God is my judge! I'm an honest Dane!" The captain bit his lips and appeared on the verge of tears.

"What happened, Captain?" Rasmussen asked gently.

"I'm not a fisherman," he said miserably. "I just help on the docks, unloading."

The voices rose again. The captain picked up his cap and slapped it on his head and looked miserably at his pipe.

"Then why did you undertake this transport?" Rasmussen asked quietly. "After all, there are nineteen people here."

The captain took off his cap again and wiped his nose. "I just got out of jail," he said. "Nothing serious. A woman, you know. But I needed money to pay my fine. The fisherman who owns this boat took sick." He dug into his pocket and pulled out a small hand compass. "I bought this yesterday and I don't even know how to use it."

"Perhaps we could try again," Rasmussen said. "I have had experience on boats. I could help navigate."

The Dane shook his head. "The boat took a bad beating out there last night. It's leaking."

It was just after eleven o'clock on a brilliant morning, so bright they were all sure that every German eye for miles around must surely see them, when the nineteen Jews were landed back on the shore of Denmark. A few minutes afterward, they were whisked away to a farmhouse and two hours later they were picked up by taxis and taken to a hotel near the railroad station in Nykoebing.

By now Mendel Cohen was almost in a state of nervous collapse. He was put to bed in the hotel and a local doctor injected him with a sedative.

The Rasmussens were given a large double room. They were hardly settled in it, when the manager appeared with breakfast on trays. He refused all thanks and hurried off.

"Well," Jorgen said to everyone, "at least we are getting a first-class tour of Denmark." He bit into a sandwich. "The operative word, as they say in our grammar class, is 'first class.'"

13.

Dr. STEPHAN MOLLER finished his rounds in the wards at Bispebjerg Hospital and returned to his office. He sat down at his desk, removed his glasses and rubbed his eyes tiredly. He reached out to the telephone when it rang, identified himself, leaned back in the chair when he heard Dr. Poul Klampmann's voice.

"Stephan," Klampmann said, "I'm afraid I've heard some bad news."

Moller sat up straight. "What is it, Poul?"

"Do you remember the man who owns that little inn at Snekkersten? Fat, jolly little chap."

"Yes. Pedersen."

"Picked up this afternoon. Gestapo."

Moller's mouth went dry.

"Pop round to my place this evening," Klampmann said. "We'd better have a talk."

"Yes," Moller said.

"Make it late," Klampmann said. "I have some business to take care of first."

When Moller reached his flat, he saw the bullet scars remaining from the clearing murder. He bathed and shaved and changed his clothes and opened a can of sardines and a bottle of beer. He could not manage to eat any of the sardines, but he got down the beer. He followed that with a snaps. Although Klampmann had told him not to go to his apartment until late, Moller could remain alone no longer.

He left his flat and walked the short distance to the building in which the Klampmanns lived. The street was dark.

The rooms were hidden behind their blacked-out windows.

Gerda Klampmann told him Poul had just telephoned he would not be much longer. She shooed their two sons off to bed and offered Moller a snaps.

"You heard?" he asked.

"I'm not supposed to hear anything," Gerda said. "But if you mean Pedersen, yes."

Moller's hand, holding the snaps, trembled slightly. "I wonder how they found out about him."

"Perhaps Poul will know more about it," she said. Then she said, "Drink your drink, Stephan."

"Yes," he said. "Skoal." He emptied the glass. He felt better. "Where is Poul?"

"I'm not supposed to know," she said. "But he's treating a wounded saboteur at Nyhavn."

Moller smiled. "How do you know all these things you're not supposed to know?"

Gerda refilled his glass and poured a glass for herself. "Do you think after all these years I don't know how to read his mind?"

There was a sharp rapping on the door. The bell rang simultaneously. Moller became rigid. Gerda Klampmann put down her drink and walked to the door. She opened it and Major Wolfgang Becker entered, flanked by two uniformed SS men carrying sub-machine guns. Moller tried to stand up. He found he could not.

Becker walked up to Gerda Klampmann, clicked his heels and bowed curtly. "Sturmbannführer Wolfgang Becker," he said. "You are Frau Klampmann?"

"I am Mrs. Klampmann," Gerda said.

Becker's eyes flickered. He turned to Moller. "Is it not good Danish manners to rise when a guest arrives?"

Moller put down the empty aquavit glass and made it to his feet.

"We have met before," Becker said.

"What is your name?"

"Dr. Stephan Moller."

"We have met. It will come to me because I never forget."

He turned back to Gerda. "Mrs. Klampmann, it is your husband I wish to see."

"He is not home."

"Where is he?"

"Making calls."

"Medical calls?"

"He's a doctor."

"He is in the hospital?"

"No."

"Then he has a private practice."

"He has patients outside the hospital."

"When do you expect him back?"

"I don't know, Major. I should think almost any time."

"Then I will wait." He sat down in Klampmann's deep leather chair and studied Moller, who was staring at the black-curtained window. "Have you remembered yet, Dr. Moller?" Becker asked.

"No," Moller said. He had the sudden sickening feeling that all this was connected with Pedersen and the inn at Snekkersten, and that the Gestapo officer knew exactly where he had seen him before.

"Why were you looking out of the window, Dr. Moller?" Becker asked.

"No special reason," Moller said.

"You will lie down on the floor. Frau Klampmann, you will lie down on the floor."

"And why must we do that?" Gerda Klampmann asked coolly.

"I will not risk your sending a signal."

"Through the black-out curtain?" Gerda Klampmann asked.

"You will lie down, both of you and at once," Becker said.

Gerda Klampmann stretched out on the floor on her side. She did it gracefully and unhurriedly.

"Moller," Becker said.

Moller lay down on his belly. He realized the positions had nothing to do with sending signals. They were impositions of ignominy and the beginning of the breaking down.

294

"Over here," Becker said.

Moller crawled like a large animal to the feet of the Gestapo officer.

"Snaps," Becker said. One of the Gestapomen looked around the room. He saw the bottle and went to it. He poured Becker a drink and handed it to him. "Why is it?" Becker said, looking down at Moller. "Why is it I have this strong impression I have seen you before?"

"I don't know, Major," Moller said, bereft of dignity.

"Do you meet many German officers?"

"Sometimes, in the hospital."

"No," Becker said. He drank the snaps. "I associate you with the sea."

It was the most degrading moment in Stephan Moller's life, lying there like a dog, knowing now for certain the Gestapo major was toying with him.

Gerda Klampmann saw Moller's despair. "Why do you want to see my husband?" she asked Becker, making it sound, despite her position, a perfectly normal question.

"It is I who must ask the questions, Frau Klampmann," Becker said, finishing his drink, holding out the empty glass. "After all, that is what I am paid for." His flawless face broke into a smile and the SS men chuckled along with him.

"Snekkersten," Becker said, accepting a fresh drink. "Does that mean anything to you, Dr. Moller?"

"I have been there," Moller said. He wondered how he could feel such fear and not cry out. He looked at Gerda Klampmann and drew some comfort from her composure.

"The bar with the fat bartender."

"I remember, Major," Moller said.

"Of course you remember. The little fat man, he spoke with such an open manner, such candor, such good spirit."

"I didn't pay too much attention to him."

"How well do you know Pedersen, Dr. Moller?" Becker asked.

"I don't know him at all."

"Did you know he was involved in this illegal business of smuggling Jews out of the country?"

"No."

"What were you doing in Snekkersten that night, Dr. Moller?"

"Having dinner."

"Just that?"

"It gets a little close here at the hospital. One tries to get away now and then."

"And nothing else? Such as the sedation of children?"

"I don't know what you're talking about," Moller said.

"Jews, Doctor. And their children who have to be quieted during the transport. That takes a doctor, doesn't it?"

Moller felt more and more like an animal, trapped, in a cage, and the voice of Becker was the voice of the trainer, demanding, exacting, patient, never harsh, never cruel, relentless and inescapable.

"It takes a doctor, does it not, Doctor?" Becker asked.

"I would think so."

"What are you doing here, Dr. Moller?"

"I am on the staff."

"I don't mean here at the hospital. I mean here, in Dr. Klampmann's flat."

"We are colleagues. We are friends. We often meet in the evenings. I just live up the street."

"You are a close friend of Dr. Klampmann's?"

"We have known each other some time."

"Then it would be difficult, perhaps impossible, for Dr. Klampmann to maintain a regular activity without your being aware of it?"

"I don't know what you are talking about."

"Then let us commence at the beginning, Dr. Moller. What were you doing at Snekkersten that night?"

"I told you, I went there for dinner."

"And Pedersen, how well do you know him?"

"I don't know him."

"You know we have arrested Pedersen?"

"Yes." Moller knew with despair that was a mistake.

Becker pounced on it. "How did you know? How did you find out?"

296

"I don't remember."

"From Dr. Klampmann?"

"No."

"Is that why you are here?"

"No."

"Then how do you know about Pedersen? How do you know about Pedersen? How do you know about Pedersen?"

Becker's voice was like a delicate hammer. Moller felt his brain was being broken, piece by piece. He raised his head and through his dense glasses he saw Becker's face very close, and he heard Becker ask the question again and once again with the compulsive montony of a broken record, and he sprang up and ran across the room to the window.

"Stephan, don't!" Gerda Klampmann screamed.

Moller grabbed the black-out curtain for leverage and clambered onto the sill and as the SS men with no signal from Becker opened fire, he plunged through the window to the street.

14.

HAVING AMPUTATED the leg of a saboteur injured in an explosion, Dr. Poul Klampmann got a lift from Nyhavn as far as Central Station. He was unable to find a taxi and boarded a tram that would take him within a few blocks of where he lived.

He got off at his stop and walked toward the hospital. When he was two blocks away from his apartment building, he saw a light in a window and when he walked closer he saw the light was coming from a broken window in his own flat. At the same time he saw two automobiles parked in front of the entrance and two men standing there in the classic position.

In the darkness, he was unable to see the stain that remained in the street after Moller's body was taken away.

Klampmann turned and walked back briskly in the direction from which he had just come, thinking how the circumstance of not being able to find a taxi had saved him, that the taxi would have driven him directly to the house and he never would have been able to see the broken window. As he walked, he heard a car door slam behind him and a motor start.

He heard the car approach and he walked faster and then started to run. He saw a thick hedge and dived into it. The car with its slits for headlights passed by slowly. He waited behind the hedge until he saw the car return to the building. He slipped back into the street and hurried toward the nearest telephone booth.

15.

THE CHILDREN, who had come running into the room when the SS men started shooting, had been persuaded to return to bed. When Gerda Klampmann finished tucking them in and returned to the living room, Becker asked her, "Where is your husband?"

"I haven't the slightest idea," she said. "I just wish to God he was somewhere other than Denmark."

She looked at the torn black-out curtain, at the shattered window. It was curious, she thought; Becker seemed to have forgotten all about that.

"But he is in Denmark," Becker was saying. "And so in the

end he will return home and so we shall wait. Frau Klampmann, please be so good as to get down on the floor."

"Go to hell," Gerda said, sitting down on a chair.

Becker was having another snaps when the telephone rang. "Be very careful what you say, Frau Klampmann," he said.

She walked to the telephone and picked up the receiver. "Hello," she said.

"I know you can answer only yes or no," Klampmann said at the other end. "Germans?"

"Yes, this is the residence of Dr. Klampmann," she said.

"Should I stay away?"

"Yes. I expect Dr. Klampmann at any time."

"Are you all right?"

"Yes. I shall tell him you called."

She hung up and saw that Becker was examining the torn curtain and broken window as though he had noticed it for the first time. He must be drunk, she thought.

"Who was that?" Becker asked, looking down into the street.

"A patient."

"Not your husband? I do not suppose it was."

"I said it was a patient."

Becker turned away from the window. "You are under arrest, Frau Klampmann."

Gerda nodded, unsurprised. "As a point of interest, on what charge?"

Becker shrugged. "Is it important?"

16.

ARNE JOHANSEN pedalled the bicycle leisurely along the lovely country road. He was in good time. The air was brisk and clear and spoke of the oncoming winter. Farmers were gathering fallen leaves for garden mulch. Ruminating cattle turned their heads to watch him ride past.

The land around him was flat and well tended. But all of Denmark was flat and well tended. The loftiest peak in Denmark, the Everest of the land, was a towering hillock a few hundred feet high.

He saw a barnyard grunting with pigs, pigs which had been bred for years to suit the taste of the British, bred long and lean and as free from fat as possible, and which now were being bred for the Germans, who wanted them exactly the opposite, thick and fat. Interesting. By their pigs shall ye know them. Poor pigs, he reflected, moving his legs up and down rhythmically, being skinnied and lengthened and then blown up and stuffed to suit the whims of first one and then another. The pigs of Denmark, weather vanes of the times.

Hansen had been right after all. He had needed a change of scenery. He would have liked more. He would have liked to be able to stop and take a walk through one of those fields. To lie down under a tree and chew on grass and smell the earth and listen to the humming of insects. Hansen had been right. He would have gone out of his mind hanging around Copenhagen.

He felt alone without Niels. He always felt alone without Niels. Except when he was with Lili.

He had taken Niels for granted and he had taken Lili even more for granted. Now that he was separated from Niels and might continue to be for some time, and separated from Lili as well, he felt alone, more alone than he had ever felt in his life. That's why it was good to get away; it helped fix values.

Although he hated to admit it and could never admit it to Hansen, he had faith that Hansen would move heaven and earth to get Niels away from the Nazis. He had to. He'd said it himself. They were the best he had. The Orange and the Blaze. A lot of horseshit in a way but not every way. They were the best he had and he'd break his ass to keep it that way.

But there were so many imponderables. Niels' life was the first, and if the wound were bad enough there was nothing Hansen could do about that. Arne's lips tightened and the muscles of his legs felt suddenly tired. When he started to think about it, there were so many factors necessary to be exactly right before Niels could be spirited away from the Germans that it seemed it would take a miracle to make them all happen and fall into place.

And yet they did have to happen and fall into place. It was unthinkable that he and Niels would be separated permanently.

Lili. It was altogether different with Lili. He was all mixed up about Lili. They were getting closer and at the same time moving apart. Because for a small time they had had a connection they both understood and accepted. They were healthy and they liked to make love and that was all they had asked of each other, to work on each other until they could bring about the magic convulsion, and as frequently as possible.

But now it was like all the old standards were going. For some reason he didn't understand, she was no longer the woman he had been screwing the last few months, the woman he had lied to constantly about everything, who he was and what he did, acceptable lying because it was about secret work and friends, but lying, chronic, consummate lying, and if there had been another woman he would have lied about that. There hadn't been, the way things had worked out, but he would have lied.

And now for some crazy reason Lili was undergoing a mysterious change. She was, in some way he could not only not explain but not even comprehend, more valuable.

He thought of all the things he wanted to do with her now, places he wanted to take her, things he wanted to tell her, about himself, things milling around in his head—where did they come from? How he could scarcely wait until he was with her again, the times he had been away from her for days and never gave it a thought, how did it happen this way now?

He passed a large field, innocent-looking now as a dowager aunt, pastoral enough for a mushy painting, but it was a field used often by the RAF for its drops and that peaceful sward had served as a carpet for the packets that fell upon it, and how often in the night the men had worked, rolling up the chutes, loading the vans, scattering in all directions with gifts from men they had never seen.

He reached Hoem and rode through it and reached the crossroads Hansen had spoken of and he saw another cyclist trying to fix a flat. Arne glanced at his watch. He had timed it exactly.

The other cyclist was someone Arne had never seen before and probably never would again. Arne dismounted to help him and was told the difficulty was with the pump, which would not inflate the tire. Arne removed the pump from his own cycle and gave it to the other youth, and when they parted shortly thereafter Arne had the faulty pump strapped to his cycle and the youth pedalled away with Arne's.

A half hour later, before entering another small village, Arne extracted a rolled-up slip of paper from the pump. In the dim light from a kerosene lamp in the village inn, Arne read a few coded words on the slip of paper. He twisted the paper, used it to get a light for his cigarette from the lamp, smoked the cigarette and drank a glass of beer.

In the early hours of the next morning, by bus, train, the cycle and a lift on a van, Arne reached Randers and, as he had been instructed to do in the coded message, he went directly to the church of Pastor Lars Duul, who now was serving as Hansen's chief in Jutland. He parked the cycle in the rack outside the church, went round to the rear, descended a flight of stairs, rapped on a door in a rhythm and count prescribed in his orders.

The door was opened almost immediately. Pastor Duul's cheeks were as rosy and his eyes sparkled as though it was high noon and not four o'clock in the morning. In the room Arne saw a handsome, full-bodied woman and a man in workman's clothes.

"Have you met Mrs. Nina Lange?" Duul asked Arne.

Nina Lange raised her eyes briefly and lowered them. Arne remembered seeing her once or twice before at the inn. He had thought she was plenty of woman. She was still plenty of woman, but the light was turned off. He knew why and he knew there was nothing to be said.

"This is Major Helmut Boldt," Duul said in his benign way, as though he was host at a party.

Arne saw instantly the man was handcuffed. He looked more closely at him, the brownish hair, the blueish eyes, the ordinary face. Not quite. A certain expression around the mouth. Amusement?

"Norwegian?" Arne asked. There had been a number of quislings passed through for passage to London.

"German," Boldt said. "A German officer anticipating a quiet leave in Sweden."

"Anything I should know about him?" Arne asked Duul.

"He has performed a service. He is being paid."

"Accomplices," Boldt said cheerfully. "All together."

Niels passed through Arne's mind and the question of whether he was alive or dead. The cellar room was suddenly close.

"Have you arranged for a vehicle, Pastor?" Arne asked.

Duul's eyes became even livelier. He said there was a local farmer who was known to be sympathetic to the Germans and who was also suspected of informing. Since he never knew anything of any importance, he was left alone by the resistance except that now and then he was fed some false information. This farmer, either because of unparalleled husbandry or companionship with the Gestapo, had a truck. It was in excellent condition. It still operated on gasoline and the farmer even managed to scrounge a gallon now and then.

"Are you coming away with us?" Arne asked.

Duul's eyes now were positively twinkling. "Oh, no. I have to remain here and see. I tell you, when it rains it isn't his grain or his cows or even his children he worries about. And when that truck goes. . . ." He held up his hands and grinned fiendishly. "I wouldn't miss it for the world."

Presently the four of them left the cellar and made their way on foot through back roads and country lanes. As they walked away from the church, Boldt held up his manacled hands.

"If anyone saw this, wouldn't it look odd?" he asked.

Without a word, Duul unlocked the manacles and handed them and the key to Arne.

"No conditions?" Boldt inquired. "No solemn parole that I won't attempt to escape?"

"Unnecessary," Arne said. "I'd kill you before you got five yards."

Nina Lange trudged on the dirt road and stared ahead into the darkness. "Killing. It settles everything so easily." She looked at Arne as though she had not quite recognized him before. "Have you ever shot anyone?"

Pastor Duul, loping along like a frisky stallion, said, "Nina."

"Have you?" she asked again.

"Yes," Arne said.

"How many?"

"Nina, I will have no more of this," Duul said.

"What did it do to you?" she asked Arne, ignoring the pastor and the tone in his voice. "What did it do to you when you put an end to life? When you realized it? When you realized it was irrevocable?"

"He patted himself on the back and assured himself it was for the good of the country," Boldt said. "The universal panacea. Patriotism."

"Don't judge me by yourself, you German swine," Arne said.

Boldt cocked his head and then nodded with interest. "You are even getting to sound like us. That timbre. Everybody's taken to using the German book."

"Shut up," Arne said.

Boldt moved closer to Nina Lange. "I remember I was in Paris once on a mission. Before the war. I was posted as an observer during French military maneuvers. As you know, there are no two languages in the world less similar than French and German and yet I swear when those French officers were shouting their commands they sounded more Prussian than the Prussians." He put a peculiar smile on his lips. "It's what the German language is most suited for," he said, speaking directly to Nina Lange. "To give exquisite military commands and to sing marvelously sentimental songs. What a range for a language to encompass."

Nina Lange looked at him for a moment and then turned away.

"Sentimental songs," Boldt said. "You don't realize what you have missed, Mrs. Lange. If it had been a German inn you owned, you would have had the nightly privilege of listening to that incomparable sound—German beer-hall harmony."

She looked at him again and then she reached over to Pastor Duul and took his hand. "Forgive me, Pastor," she said. She looked at Arne. "One day perhaps you will tell me how many people you have killed and how it made you feel and what it left you with and how you came to feel later on. I don't want to know now, but one day you will tell me, and if God has forgiven me for whatever wrong things I have done I will perhaps not want to know then, either."

They reached the farmhouse when the first light was beginning to betray the eastern sky. Duul pointed to the barn where the truck was kept.

305

"Wait here," Arne said. He started off, turned round and returned, taking the manacles out of his pocket.

"I was rather hoping you wouldn't forget that," Boldt said, holding out his hands. "It would have been quite unprofessional."

Arne snapped on the cuffs. He started for the barn again, when he was arrested by the sound of a heavy vehicle coming down the paved road that fronted on the farmer's house. He slashed his hand downward and all four fell on their faces. Arne took out his gun. He raised himself slightly. Then he said, "Just a farm truck."

Nina Lange was staring at the gun. Arne looked down at it and then slipped it under his belt.

"It's like a penny-thriller," Boldt observed. "Even to the beautiful woman."

"Shut up," Arne said.

"I've always thought that must be the most difficult thing if one were a writer—working out acceptable ways of getting the women in. And here we are."

"I said shut up," Arne said.

"Or what?" Boldt asked. "The good people never strike the bad people when the bad people can't strike back."

Arne backhanded him across the face.

"That will be all of that," Duul said.

"I'm the one who's got to steal that truck," Arne said coldly. "The way that Nazi pig is blabbering, he'll wake up the whole house."

"I though I was talking rather quietly," Boldt said. "Perhaps it's just that you object to my accent."

"That's what makes me so mad," Arne said. "You don't have an accent."

He raised his head again and, seeing that the way was clear, he ran at a crouch toward the barn. There he waited for a moment and then he opened the door and slid inside. Again he waited. It was at a moment like this that he most missed Niels. It was always easier with Niels, and when someone like that German prick got under his skin Niels would be ready always with something that would snap the tension. Now he was by himself and didn't know whether Niels was alive, being tortured or already dead, and all he could do about it was slap the face of a man who couldn't slap back. Something to be proud of.

The inside of the barn was in almost total darkness. Faint early-morning light was beginning to drift down from a skylight in the loft. He looked at the truck. It was a lovely thing. It would have been lovely at any time but now it was gorgeous. Not too large, not half falling apart. A personality. A gift.

He opened the cab door, took a small piece of wire from his pocket and worked his hands under the dash. The motor caught on. He checked the gasoline gauge. Only a quarter full. The Gestapo must have been chintzy lately. But enough for what was needed.

He went back to the door, swung it open, ran back to the truck, jumped up into the seat, threw the gears into reverse. He backed out of the barn, swung round in the yard, drove to where the others were waiting near the side of the road.

He paused just long enough for them to climb aboard and then stomped on the accelerator and laughed out loud as the truck leaped just ahead of the blast of a shotgun. The next shot sounded far away, as far away as a second-story bedroom window where a Danish farmer was having apoplexy.

Arne drove rapidly and expertly and turned off the main road at the first opportunity, and took a circuitous course on the back roads until he had Pastor Duul within walking distance of his house. He pulled up.

As Duul dropped down from the truck, Arne unlocked one of Boldt's handcuffs and snapped it around a steel brace in the truck.

"You don't seem to understand," Boldt said. "I want to go with you."

"Just so you don't misunderstand, Major," Arne said. "In case I have to abandon the truck for any reason, for Gestapo reason, say, I have a small plastic device that can blow a locomotive off its tracks. I'll leave it behind in the truck, with you."

"Do you hear that, Pastor?" Boldt asked. "He's planning to murder me."

"It's like brushing teeth these days," Duul said. "And who do we have to thank for it?" He reached up and took Nina Lange's hand. "Good-bye, Nina. God bless you." He released the hand reluctantly. Then he said, "Major Boldt, perhaps our paths will cross again."

With his peculiar smile, Boldt said, "No blessing for me, Pastor?"

"No time," Arne said. He waved a hand to Duul and drove away.

Arne followed back roads for another few miles and then swung into the main highway leading south to Aarhus. On the outskirts of the city, he left the highway again and drove to a garage.

Within two hours, a wood-burner was mounted on the truck. The truck was repainted. The name of a farmers' supply house was printed on its sides. The paint was dried under heat lamps and then the truck was given a bath with dirty water.

Arne and the others were fed breakfast of rolls, cheese and coffee while the work was being done. No one spoke to them. No questions were asked, not even when Boldt was again handcuffed to the truck.

The morning was clear and the air blew in on fresh wind from the Kattegat when they drove away from the garage. Nina Lange lay down on a piece of tarpaulin and fell asleep.

Boldt saw some folded canvas near the tailgate. He tried to reach it. He was inches short. He turned to speak to Arne. Instead, he reached again. The manacle bit into his wrist. His fingers closed on the canvas and he pulled it toward him.

He covered Nina Lange. She didn't stir. He lit a cigarette and gazed at the sleeping woman.

17.

THE FOUR JEWS sat composedly in the taxi. Two men, a boy, and the middle-aged woman who just got in.

"There is now only Aunt Minnie," one of the men said.

"I have her address," Hansen said. At the wheel, a taxi-driver's cap on his head, he twisted round and surveyed his passengers. Entirely all right; four Danes in a cab.

He started off.

"Do you know Aunt Minnie?" one of the men asked.

"Yes," Hansen said.

"Do you know the woman she lives with?"

"No," Hansen said. "But we'll manage her, too."

"She's not Jewish," the man said.

"She's crazy," the boy blurted.

"Shhh," his mother said.

Aunt Minnie lived on the fourth floor of an apartment building on a small street off Kristianagade. Hansen told the four to remain in the cab while he went up and fetched her.

He went up on a creaking elevator and rapped lightly on Aunt Minnie's door.

A voice behind the door inquired, "Who is it?"

Another voice behind the door answered, "It is Micah, who is like God."

"It's Peter Hansen," Hansen amended.

The door opened and Hansen went in and was enveloped in two arms and lavender water and bussed on the lips.

He disentangled. "Hello, Aunt Minnie," he said and did a double-take. Aunt Minnie had put on about fifty pounds.

"The messenger brings tidings," the other voice said.

He looked toward it and saw, kneeling on the floor, her hands clasped in prayer, another very old woman with pink hair and a white face.

"Yes," Hansen said. "And the tidings are that we don't have a hell of a lot of time. Are you ready, Aunt Minnie?" He looked at her again. She *had* put on about fifty pounds. She was wearing several dresses and two fur coats.

"Yes," she said with a resplendent smile, "I'm ready."

"Only the pure in heart are ready," the woman on the floor announced. She weaved from side to side, staring at the ceiling, unclasping her hands only to brush back strands of strawberry hair that fell over her face.

"Isn't she marvelous?" Aunt Minnie asked, trying to fold her small arms, defeated by bulk.

"Aunt Minnie, I must ask you to come now. There are four of your relatives waiting in a taxi downstairs. I can't expose them too long. And we've just got time to reach the boat."

"Mette," Aunt Minnie said, looking fondly at the woman on the floor. "Her name is Mette."

"Thanks, thanks, gentle Lord of all mankind, for the deliverance of Thy loyal servant known far and wide to everyone as Aunt Minnie," Mette said.

"It makes you want to cry, doesn't it?" Aunt Minnie asked.

"We have to hurry," Hansen said.

"I'm ready," Aunt Minnie said. "Except for my face."

"For the love of God, Aunt Minnie," Hansen said.

"Love is God and God is love," Mette explained.

Aunt Minnie went into her bedroom and sat down at a small dressing table. It was not simple, with the layers of dresses and the two coats. She applied powder to her face. Mette entered the room on her knees.

"It had been said the eye of the Lord is upon even a falling sparrow," Mette said. "Thank you, dear Prince of Heaven, for keeping one of Your eyes on Aunt Minnie."

"Stop," Aunt Minnie said. "I shall cry and my mascara will run."

Hansen gazed helplessly around the living room, which was like an antique shop, filled with silver, brass, copper, china, and said feebly, "Aunt Minnie."

Aunt Minnie finished without haste. "Good-bye, Mette," she said.

"Good-bye, blessed Aunt Minnie," Mette said.

"Good-bye everybody, any minute now," Hansen said.

He went into the bedroom and took Aunt Minnie firmly by the arm, finding it difficult to find it through the fur, and propelled her toward the door.

Mette followed on her knees. "Calm sea and peaceful voyage," she said. "God will watch over you, Aunt Minnie, friend of lost souls."

"I want to weep," Aunt Minnie said lovingly. "Whenever she starts that way, I want to weep."

"Your mascara will run," Hansen reminded her.

"Thank you, Mr. Hansen," Aunt Minnie said, fluttering her eyes. "So you noticed."

At the door, she stopped. Hansen tried to push her over the threshold, but she took root.

"What is it now?" he asked.

"I forgot something."

"What?"

"My corset."

"The devil with it," Hansen said, trying in vain to move her.

"Yes," Mette shrieked. "The Devil is present, too!"

"I just bought that corset this afternoon," Aunt Minnie said.

"War!" Mette shouted. "Between Good and Evil!"

"Why don't you leave the corset with Mette, for a farewell present?" Hansen asked, considering this a diplomatic ploy of the first order.

"Wouldn't fit," Aunt Minnie said.

"Then get the damned corset and let's go," Hansen said.

"The Damned!" Mette cried out. "The Damned are present, too!"

Aunt Minnie disappeared into the bedroom again. Hansen

looked at the museum around him, his head reeling, and when he realized Aunt Minnie had been gone an unconscionable time he went in there, and found her naked. She was struggling into the corset. Mette was on the floor, reciting the names of the ancient Viking gods.

Aunt Minnie smiled affectionately. "I won't be but a minute, Mr. Hansen," she said.

Hansen leaned against the door. For the life of him now, he could not take his eyes off Aunt Minnie as she tugged and jerked and yanked the corset into place, then carefully redressed, putting on, by Hansen's count, six separate dresses and then the two fur coats. Accompanied by Mette, who now was chanting the lexicon of the saints.

Having disarranged her coiffure in the process, Aunt Minnie sat down again at the dressing table, tidied her hair, repaired her face as well, added some scarlet lipstick and splashed herself with lavender water. She stood up and presented the bemused Hansen with a glorious smile. She held out her hand and he found himself taking it as Emil Hurwitz had taken it outside the hospital chapel, as he would take the hand of a grand duchess, and he escorted her out of the apartment. Mette followed them to the door on her knees, reciting the names of the minor prophets of the Bible.

None of the other four members of the family seemed in the least surprised at the time it had taken Hansen to collect Aunt Minnie, nor was there a single eye raised at her appearance. She greeted each of them with the pronunciation of the name and a tender kiss and then sat back in the taxi without looking, knowing, as Queen Victoria had always known, there would be a seat awaiting her.

Without actually doing so, she seemed to gesture to Hansen, giving him her permission to depart.

He drove to a fishing village south of Copenhagen. The boat was at the point of leaving. Hansen got them all aboard and cut short their thanks. Aunt Minnie refused to go below until she kissed Hansen once more. She took a lace kerchief out of her purse and wiped off the lipstick.

"We must not make your wife jealous," she said. Then she said, "You're shivering."

"It's getting chilly," Hansen said.

"Here, take one of my coats," Aunt Minnie said instantly. "I'm wearing two of them."

She began to peel off one of the coats. Hansen tried to dissuade her. He saw nothing would stop her and he jumped off the boat to the landing.

By this time the boat was moving, and Aunt Minnie had the coat off and she was preparing to sling it ashore. One of the fishermen stopped her. There was a brief struggle, but by the time Aunt Minnie freed herself the boat was too far way from the dock. She contented herself with beating the fisherman with the coat, and when he ran away she waved the coat back and forth in farewell to Peter Hansen.

It was after three o'clock in the morning when Hansen returned home. He entered the house quietly, poured himself a scotch, sat down on the sofa to drink it and for the second time that night fell asleep with a drink in his hand.

It was just after eight o'clock when the telephone rang. He reached out sleepily for the phone. "Hansen here," he mumbled. He looked up to see Kate enter the room.

"This is Aunt Minnie," the voice on the phone announced.

He sat bolt upright. "What!"

"Aunt Minnie. What's the matter with you?"

"What are you doing here?" he demanded.

"I'm not there, I'm here, in Ribe. Peter, are you sure you're all right?"

"What happened?"

"Nothing happened. What is the matter with you? I'm just calling to thank Kate for the basket of fruit she sent."

"I'll tell her," Hansen said.

"Peter, have you been working too hard?"

"I'm just fine." He settled the receiver in the cradle.

"Who was that?" Kate asked. "And why aren't you in bed?"

"That was your Aunt Minnie. And I'm not in bed because

313

I have to go out." He stood up, stretched, yawned, kissed her. "How could I have forgotten you have an Aunt Minnie, too?"

18.

HANSEN'S FIRST STOP was police headquarters in Copenhagen. There he returned the taxi and the driver's hat he had borrowed through the good offices of Captain Erik Melchior. In return, at his request, he was outfitted by Captain Melchior in the uniform of a Danish policeman and was given the necessary identification papers and a warrant for the arrest of Dr. Emil Hurwitz.

While Hansen was putting on the uniform and admiring the developing result, Melchior telephoned Vester Prison and, by way of the Danish police authorities there, ascertained that Niels Rider was still very much alive. He had been operated on—the bullet had been removed from his lung. He was still unconscious. It was believed he would survive.

With one or two acid comments from Captain Melchior on his appearance and demeanor as a police officer, Hansen left the police building, went to Central Station, took a train to Birkeroed, found that Hurwitz had transferred to another house in Hilleroed, found there he had gone to live with some friends in Hornbaek on the north coast of Sealand. He proceeded to Hornbaek and showed his arrest warrant to the station master, commandeering a private compartment for himself and his prisoner on the next train to Copenhagen. Then he ordered the station master to get him a car to fetch the prisoner.

The station master, a gangly man with a rooster neck, listened to all this and then asked politely, "Were you always this way, or only since you've been working for the Germans?"

Hansen considered he was a success.

Twenty minutes later, Hansen was delivered by local taxi to the beach hut where Hurwitz was living, or was last known to be living. An elderly woman opened the door at his ring.

"I'm a police officer," Hansen said, getting now almost to believe he was. "I have a warrant for the arrest of Dr. Emil Hurwitz."

"He's not here," the woman said instantly.

"I'm here," Hurwitz said. "Come in."

Hansen entered the house. Hurwitz shut the door and calmed the woman. "He's a fake," he said. To Hansen he said, "The list."

"Every bloody name has been crossed off."

"The list please," Hurwitz repeated.

"Even Aunt Minnie," Hansen said.

"Has Aunt Minnie gone?"

"Yes."

"Your word?"

"My word."

Hurwitz sighed. He looked at the bewildered woman and smiled gently. "So the time has come?" he said to Hansen.

"The time has come. I've kept my part of the bargain."

"And I shall keep mine. Somehow I think it's a bad bargain." He took the woman's hand and squeezed it. "Watch yourself," he said. "Go easy on the salt and as little starch as possible." To Hansen he said, "I'm ready." It was the tone of a man about to face a firing squad.

When the taxi returned them to the station, Hansen had the normal impulse to pay the driver but he knew that would be totally unrealistic so he dismissed the driver with his thanks.

"Thanks," the driver repeated. "I'll have a bottle of beer on that."

315

The station master, having a little snooze in his office, looked up without surprise and without pleasure as Hansen walked in with the doctor. Hansen ordered the station master to keep Hurwitz locked up in the office until the train arrived.

When the train pulled in, it had a normal quota of German soldiers. Hansen, moving Hurwitz ahead of him, found the compartment he had reserved. Four soldiers were sprawled in it. Hansen flagged down the conductor, showed him his papers, his tickets for the compartment.

"I demand that you remove those soldiers from my compartment," Hansen said.

The conductor looked at the soldiers. "It's not customary," he said.

"I demand it," Hansen said.

After another moment's hesitation, the conductor opened the door of the compartment and asked the soldiers to leave. They obeyed immediately. The conductor was astounded.

"They're Germans," Hansen said cheerfully. "And I'm the police."

Hansen closed the door of the compartment and he and Dr. Hurwitz made themselves comfortable. Presently the train started.

"How was Aunt Minnie?" Hurwitz asked.

"Aunt Minnie was splendid."

"That bad?"

"She was marvelous," Hansen said. "Someday I'll tell you how your Aunt Minnie took leave of Denmark."

"And how is Kate?"

"Impatient."

Hurwitz nodded. "I'll miss the grand entrance, after all." He adjusted his glasses and looked closely at Hansen. "Why this masquerade, Peter?"

"I would think that was obvious."

"Why couldn't you come as plain old Peter Hansen? Or have you always harbored a secret longing to be a policeman?"

"Your face and your name are too well known for plain

316

old Peter Hansen. In the event we're intercepted, I want first draw."

"You actually have a warrant for my arrest?"

"Bona fide. Issued at police headquarters."

Hurwitz sighed. "All arranged, all arranged," he said. He slumped in his seat and stroked his imperial and looked morosely out of the window. "Everything I love in this world is contained in this small land," he said. "I feel I'm in the patient's room. I don't want to leave. I feel if I turn my eyes away, the patient will die." He looked across the compartment at Hansen. "If the patient dies, then I prefer to be here and die with her."

19.

THE LIVING ROOM of Standartenführer Rudolf Buhle's flat was devoid of any sign of human habitation. The furniture appeared not new, but unused. There were no newspapers, magazines, books, old mail, no pictures anywhere. It might have been a room in a middle-class hotel before anyone moved in for the night.

Buhle, pacing back and forth thoughtfully, a cigar in his mouth, his hands clasped behind his back, saw Hansen glancing around curiously. "It is sterile, yes?" Buhle asked.

"I'm sorry, Colonel," Hansen said. "I didn't mean to gawk."

Buhle placed himself in front of Hansen, who was occupying the only comfortable chair in the room. "It must seem specially so to you, Mr. Hansen. You have a most beautiful home, with most beautiful things in it."

"What I don't understand, Colonel, is why you don't live

at the d'Angleterre or any of the other good hotels with the rest of your colleagues?"

"I dislike hotels," Buhle said. "I dislike hotels and I dislike hotel rooms. I am a family man."

Hansen, filling his pipe, looked up. "Odd. I've never thought of you as being connected with anything but the Gestapo."

"My wife thinks the same," Buhle said. "She is very proud of that. She is a very good Nazi." He smiled. "Women make the best Nazis, Mr. Hansen. It is a political philosophy designed specifically for the emotions."

"She's not here with you?"

"No, Mr. Hansen. My wife is one of the leaders of the 'Strength Through Joy' movement. I have a son and two daughters. They are all in the Hitler Youth. So you offer me money to free this saboteur?"

Hansen, lighting his pipe, saw his hand tremble slightly. He still felt it. "I'm not making the offer, Colonel," he said steadily. "I represent people who make the offer."

"Yes," Buhle said. "You have taken pains to make that clear." He paused again in front of Hansen and looked down. "Then this wounded person must be the person we believe him to be."

"I haven't the slightest idea who he is," Hansen said.

"And why were you selected to offer me this bribe?"

"The people know I have dealings with the Germans. They know that you and I have met. They approached me to approach you."

"Who are these people?" Buhle asked.

"I'm not at liberty to say."

"I could make you say, of course," Buhle said.

Hansen felt it again. "I thought we were past that point, Colonel."

"Past what point, Mr. Hansen?" Buhle asked pleasantly. "You have come to me asking me to betray my trust for money. Am I not justified in taking every measure to get to the bottom of this plot to secure the release of a notorious gangster?"

Hansen made himself puff on his pipe for a moment. "Are you serious, Colonel?" he asked.

"Quite serious, Mr. Hansen. I should have suspected something such as this when you requested a meeting here in my home."

Hansen reached into an inside pocket and took out a piece of paper. "This is a production report, Colonel. What I have delivered to the German authorities during the last twelve months. If you remove me from the business, Colonel, these figures will drop by half."

"That is not my area of responsibility," Buhle said.

"Of course I will deny this conversation."

"Your word against mine?"

"Valueless, I know." Hansen held up the paper. "In other quarters, this might have some weight."

Buhle considered, nodded, resumed his pacing. "It will be a vast risk," he said.

For the first time since he had arrived, Hansen began to feel a breath of hope. "My friends are willing to pay for the risk. Not vastly, but well."

"Have you worked out a plan?"

"An order signed by you, releasing the prisoner to me."

"To you?"

"I shall be attired properly as a Gestapo officer."

Buhle turned toward him abruptly. After a moment, he asked, "And when the hoax is discovered?"

"It probably never will be discovered," Hansen said. "This man is simply one among many prisoners the Gestapo has in its custody—in Vester Prison, other prisons, hospitals, Dagmar House. Who will comment on the fact that one of them has been removed from a prison ward by an officer of the Secret Police?"

"But if a comment is made?"

"It stops with you, Colonel. You disclaim the signature on the release order. The underground is credited with a coup. That is the end of it."

"How much, Mr. Hansen?"

"One hundred thousand Danish crowns."

Buhle walked to a table, contemplated an ashtray decorated with a figure of the Little Mermaid. He broke off the ash from his cigar. "Have you the funds with you?"

"Fifty thousand when you give me the release order. The balance when the man is free."

Buhle straightened. "I will think this over, Mr. Hansen. I will give you my decision in a day or two."

"Not after you've had a chance to wring him out, Colonel," Hansen said. "My people want him the way he is, not the way he'll be when your people get through with him. I want the papers tomorrow."

"Impossible."

"There is a small tobacco shop off Falkoner Alle, just past the Fredericksberg Town Hall. I will be there at four o'clock tomorrow morning with fifty thousand crowns."

Buhle turned slowly. His face was still. He spoke in a mild voice. "You are being high-handed," he said. "This man is an enemy of the State."

Hansen felt it again, stronger than before. He recognized the manner and the voice and the danger. "Whatever you believe he has done in the past, Colonel, you won't have to worry about the future," he said earnestly. "He's badly wounded. It will take a long time for him to recover. He'll be out of the country and out of your hair within forty-eight hours. I give you my word."

Hansen waited for Buhle to reply and when he did not, he picked up his hat and left.

20.

THE CAFÉ near the university was packed with students and their girls. Arne Johansen stood inside the doorway and tried to penetrate the crowd and the smoke.

He saw her. She was at a table surrounded by students. Her head was back and she was laughing and he saw the line of her neck and the flush on her face. One of the students raised a glass of beer to her and the others joined him in a toast Arne couldn't hear and he felt a stab of jealousy.

He looked at her as though he had never seen her before. It went through him like a wind. He made his way toward her, pushing people aside, and halfway across the room she saw him and got up quickly and rushed toward him.

"It's the same with you," he said wonderingly.

"Yes."

"My God, Lili, what's happened?"

"You know."

"But all this time."

He took her hand. It was a different hand. Why had it taken him so long to know all this?

"I've missed you," she said as they seated themselves at the bar.

"I know." He ordered two snaps and beers.

"Was it a good trip?" she asked.

"Yes." If only he could tell her; if only he could explain that he had not been selling material for ladies' dresses, but what he really had done.

The bartender set the drinks in front of them. Arne lifted his glass and nodded it to her and emptied it in a swallow. He washed it down with beer and pushed the glass toward the bartender.

"Don't get drunk tonight," she said.

"No," he said.

"Please, not tonight," she said. "Oh, I've missed you!" She took his hand and pressed it against her cheek. "I'd reach out in the middle of the night and realize I was alone and I'd wake up, shaking. I get so frightened when you're not there."

The bartender set the second drink in front of him and he drank it.

"Please don't drink too much, Arne," she said.

"I won't. I'm just a little tired from the trip. I just want to unwind."

"Let's go home," she said. "Let's go home and be alone and go to bed, it seems like so long and I've missed you so much. I need you so much, Arne—I need you to love me, it's the only time I feel safe."

He had a third drink, not noticing she had not finished her first. He looked around and listened to the noise.

"Who are your friends?" he asked, looking at the table where he had found her.

"Just some students. I never saw them before." She took his hand again. "Arne, they were just having fun."

Just having fun. He wondered whether the students in Norway and France and Holland and Belgium and England were sitting around just having fun.

"This must seem a little sick-making to you," he said.

She felt a chill, a shudder of fear, a cold breath. And the beginning of an excitement—and for the first time in her life she didn't want that excitement. "Arne," she pleaded, "let's go home. Arne, please don't drink any more and let's go home."

"After your country, what happened there," he said. "After what you saw in Norway."

"Don't talk about it," she said, knowing it was no use, that things worked themselves out and this was working itself out. And now, just now, at this time, naturally at this time, when what they had had finally come to have value. It is the world, she thought, it is the fucking world, as Arne and the British say, and we're all fucked when we're born in it and sooner or later it catches up, and always at the wrong time, at the wrongest, wrongest time.

He looked at her and she could see the drinks had bitten and she could see he wanted to tell her something and she knew what he wanted to tell her, that picture of Niels Rider hadn't been that unrecognizable, she hadn't seen him often, only once actually, and that was an accident and she knew why now, but who could forget that long, sad face even after the mauling? She knew what Arne wanted to tell her and she didn't want to hear it, and she didn't want to feel what she was feeling more and more; he was alive and she wanted to feel that, the way other women felt.

322

He looked at her that way for a long moment and then turned abruptly and ordered another drink and finished it and finished his beer. "Let's go home," he said.

"Yes," she said. "Yes."

He paid for the drinks and took her hand and led her from the café.

He had dodged it himself, she thought, but it would come again, and he might dodge it again, but in the end he couldn't because he loved her now and she loved him and that had betrayed and defeated them. He loved her and he wanted to give to her his truth, his secret, his power, himself and, in the end, his life. That was the fuck-up and that was what happened when you let yourself in for love in this world.

Outside the café, in the clean night, she turned to him swiftly. "Let's go away, Arne."

"Away? Away where?"

"Anywhere. Let's go away from Copenhagen, from Denmark."

He looked at her. "Wouldn't that be fine?"

She took his arm. Her fingers bit hard. "Anywhere, Arne," she said.

"I can't," he said.

"Of course not," she said. That would be too simple and too good and that wasn't the way things were.

21.

PETER HANSEN, sitting next to Anders Jessen in the small pickup, looked at his watch again. It was five minutes past four in the morning. Anders shifted uneasily.

"Do you think something's gone wrong, Mr. Hansen?" he asked.

"I don't know." He looked at Anders and he wondered about him. Niels, even if they managed to get him away, was going to be useless for a long time. "How is Ellen?"

"All right," Anders said. "Still under sedation, but not so much of it. Dr. Klampmann is keeping his eye on her."

"Dr. Klampmann won't be keeping his eye on anybody," Hansen said, trying in the dark to fathom Anders' reaction.

The boy's head turned swiftly. "Gestapo?"

"Almost. They tried and they missed," Hansen said. The fear was in the boy all right, but how much and could he handle it?

"What's going to happen with Ellen?" Anders asked.

That was a good sign. "We'll move her."

"But if they're onto Klampmann, they may go through the hospital."

"Wouldn't matter," Hansen said. "She's Ellen Jessen now."

Anders smiled wanly. "I wish it were true. But it sounds nice anyway."

Would he work? Hansen wondered. Those curly lashes, the almost feminine face. The artist's hands. Would he? Could he? Lord, should he? Turn him into something special, like Niels, like Arne? The way they took dogs and made killers out of them?

He looked at his watch again. Ten past four. The street was empty.

"Why did you bother with Buhle at all, Mr. Hansen?" Anders asked. "Couldn't we have forged the papers?"

"I thought of that," Hansen said. "I didn't know what they might have found out about Niels. I still don't know. They might have been sitting there waiting for us." He looked at his watch again. "I'll give him another five minutes. I thought I had him hooked. I believed it."

"Mr. Hansen, there, walking down the street," Anders said.

"Forget it," Hansen said without looking. "Gestapo colonels don't walk down streets, not even to pick up fifty thousand crowns." He saw the pedestrian walk past the corner and vanish up the street. Then he stiffened as a black Mercedes moved slowly toward them. "Here he is," Hansen said.

Anders' hand went to the stubby carbine fixed out of sight under the overhang of the seat.

"He's alone," Hansen said. He rapped his knuckles against the wood ceiling of the cab. There was an answering rap instantly. Hansen felt for a folded newspaper in his pocket and dropped from the truck as the Mercedes stopped near the tobacco shop.

Colonel Buhle lowered the window and peered out, saw Hansen, opened the door and got out.

"Good morning, Colonel," Hansen said.

"Good morning, Mr. Hansen."

Buhle took an envelope out of his inner pocket and gave it to Hansen, who in his turn took the newspaper out of his pocket and handed it to Buhle. Hansen lit a pencil-thin flashlight and held the tiny beam over the newspaper. Buhle unfolded the paper and riffled a packet of money hidden inside, closed the paper. Hansen opened the envelope, removed the official paper, played the pin-point of light over it, standing so his back was to the truck.

"It is in order," Buhle said. "And now we are enemies."

"We always have been," Hansen said.

"Officially. Now we are personal enemies, Mr. Hansen." He slipped the folded newspaper into his own coat pocket and got back into the car. He looked up through the open window. "I don't know what I would prefer, that everything went well and I received another fifty thousand crowns, or that everything went wrong, and I received you."

He wound up the window and drove away. Hansen returned to the pickup and then that was gone.

22.

IN THE DAYLIGHT on the bright, crowded, noisy streets, everything seemed different to Lili. She didn't have to tell Buhle anything. She could hold him off, and with time anything might happen. Was that love, she wondered, thinking of Arne—being optimistic, having hope?

She remembered the night and she went weak. Just the thought. What had happened. What had happened.

The way he turned to her and took over her world. The promise, she had thought, the promise, the incredible promise that never quite paid off, until the time of the end, until the other thing was there, watching, waiting.

But it was her world, her world in bed, and he took over as a pilot takes over a plane, all the controls under his control, knowing where to go and what to do, except by then nothing could be wrong as long as it was touch, because now, as always at this moment, her whole body was sex, it had spread from between her legs, from her breasts, from her lips, to everywhere, so that her toes were sex and the tips of her hair were sex, the promise, the grand, incredible promise, the unfulfilled promise, the climax that never climaxed anything but itself, that left only the need for the next and the next.

But it was something, now dissolved in sex, bathing in sex, alive and open and vulnerable with sex, it was something to reach that point, to get that far, even if it only beckoned always to something farther on, the addiction, and then he had entered her and she had cried out only because at this time she always cried out.

He had begun the movement in her, the slow stroking that brought on the madness without ever easing the madness, and she settled for that as she always settled for that, only it was not to be that way this time. It was to be the other way, the way it had been only four times in her life because until then there had been only four men who had made love to her just before they were going to die.

But it had not reached there yet with Arne, they hadn't got that far in the play, they might with luck never have to go that far, that was what she was hoping now, in the day. But it had been there in the night, she was like any other woman, as she had been only four times before, and when he had finished, largely, calling her name, for the first time where he had gone she was there, too, and she didn't know whether it was Arne, the new thing they owned, or whether it was because they were reaching the other place, because they were closer to it than she knew.

She had cradled him afterwards. He seemed smaller than ever. So fragile to have been doing what he did. Such a small body and the demands he made on it. He was breathing easily. There was a small smile on his lips. He was breathing easily, she had thought, perhaps because he did not as yet know he was dead.

But that was in the night and belonged to the things of the night, and now it was day and easy to be brave and easy to move through streets filled with people and have people pass you and bump into you and smile and apologize and remember that they all had lives and some of them had love and that maybe one could somehow get lost among them and have life and have love, too.

A little after 9:30 on that morning, Lili Lund entered Dagmar House and asked to see Colonel Buhle. She was informed Colonel Buhle had worked until all hours, until past four in the morning, and that he would be a little late coming to his office. If she had an appointment with Colonel Buhle, it was advisable that she wait.

At ten o'clock Major Wolfgang Becker reported for duty. His eye was caught by the stunning woman. He made inquiries about her and, learning something of her history, he ordered that he be given the complete file on her. He studied the papers with his usual thoroughness in these matters and then he asked that the young woman be brought to his office.

23.

THE VESTER PRISON was an ugly, mustard-colored building, no better nor worse than any other similar institution in Denmark, save for one thing—its unfortunate location. It was almost directly opposite the buildings that made up the Carlsberg breweries.

This, to Danes hapless enough to draw Vester Prison for their period of incarceration, was torture that bordered the demoniac. It was tormenting enough for a Dane to have to subsist on the bleak prison food made even bleaker by war and occupation. But it was unmitigated hell to know that only a few hundred yards away was being brewed one of the great beers of the world, millions of gallons of it, and that not one drop would make its way to the prisoners' larder.

The section of the prison taken over by the Gestapo, which included the hospital ward, was on the side of the prison facing the breweries. Men held in that section swore they could smell the beer. It was almost unendurable. It was, they said, just another filthy Gestapo trick.

It was at the main gate of this unfortunate institution that a black Mercedes arrived at precisely 10:10 on this same Thursday morning.

Peter Hansen, glowering suitably in an SS uniform with the rank of *Obersturmbannführer*, his face under the death's head cap sporting a small, dark, squarish mustache, instantly nostalgic, lolled in the rear of the car. He did not bother to look at the prison guard.

Anders Jessen, at the wheel, in similar black uniform but with the more modest rank of *Hauptscharführer*, merely raised his eyes. The guard opened the gate and Anders drove to the office of the warden.

He jumped out of the car, opened the rear door, froze to attention as Hansen got out unhurriedly. Hansen glanced incuriously around the prison yard and walked up the three steps to the office. The door was opened for him before he reached it.

Speaking in Danish with a German accent it had taken him a little time to master, Hansen informed the Danish official who greeted him that he was there to remove a prisoner of the Gestapo and requested that he be taken to the section of the prison occupied by the German Secret Police.

Hansen and Jessen followed the official through the dreary building. The cells were built around an open area. Each cell had a solid door. There were two openings, one on the bottom through which food was passed, the other at eye-level with a one-way peephole.

The two men were taken through doors into the Nazi area of the prison. There the Danish official left them and they were taken in hand by an SS man who sprang to his feet and shouted "Heil Hitler!" in a voice to shatter the rafters. He escorted them to the Nazi commandant of the prison.

Hansen took one look at this official and braced himself. Hauptsturmführer Ludwig Mannheim was a small, bony man with the face of a bookkeeper. He wore rimless glasses on a thin nose that came to a point above rimless lips.

After accepting Captain Mannheim's salute and heiling Hitler in return, Hansen produced papers which identified him as Obersturmbannführer Karl Hengst, after which he proffered the order signed by Standartenführer Rudolf Buhle for the release of Prisoner 4539, provisionally known as Niels Rider.

Captain Mannheim read through the order twice, slowly

and deliberately. He lowered the paper and raised a face that fought a tenuous way between military manners and astonishment. "If the Herr Obersturmbannführer permits, this order comes as a surprise. I have been given to understand this prisoner is a special case."

"He is," Hansen said indifferently. "That is why he is being removed."

Captain Mannheim removed his glasses, went through the motions of an unnecessary wiping. He spread the order under two neatly manicured sets of square-tipped fingers. "It is," he said with cautious respect, "something I cannot understand."

"I am not aware there is any need for that," Hansen said. "Is the prisoner capable of being moved?"

Captain Mannheim pushed the order aside, pulled it back and read it for a third time to see if there was some possible explanation he might have missed.

Hansen glanced at Anders, who was standing at attention. "My question, Mannheim," Hansen said, allowing the faintest sharpness to enter his voice.

Mannheim stiffened in reflex action. "The prisoner is doing well, sir," he said. "It was only yesterday that Standartenführer Buhle made inquiry about this particular prisoner. He left orders that he be informed directly the prisoner was strong enough to be questioned. I was going to call the Standartenführer this morning to apprise him the prisoner had recovered sufficiently for preliminary interrogation."

"Then that is a call you will not have to make, Mannheim," Hansen said easily. As the captain appeared ready to speak again, Hansen went on. "Have him put in a wheel chair."

Mannheim touched the order again, breathed deeply, and then picked up the telephone. "The Prisoner 4539 is to be made ready for removal," he said. Small white spots appeared on his upper lip. "Put him in a wheel chair." He replaced the telephone carefully. "If the Herr Obersturmbannführer will take a seat while he is waiting."

Without looking at Anders, Hansen strolled to the window and looked at the Carlsberg breweries.

"Herr Obersturmbannführer," Mannheim said.

When Hansen did not respond, the Gestapo officer called out again. Hansen turned slowly, did not reply.

Mannheim took off his glasses and replaced them without wiping them. "Forgive me, sir, but I must repeat I am quite amazed by this order from Standartenführer Buhle."

"Of what possible interest could that be to me?" Hansen asked politely.

"It is only that the Standartenführer was so emphatic about guarding this man."

Hansen smiled pleasantly. "Are you suggesting you would like to telephone the Standartenführer and question this order?"

Mannheim began to mount a reply and then the temerity of his attitude smote him like a blow. "No!" he said loudly. In a more controlled voice he said, "No, sir." He ran his tongue over his absence of lips and said, "With the Obersturmbannführer's permission, may I ask where he is taking the prisoner?"

"No." Hansen turned to the window. He could trust the back of his head to betray no expression.

Sturmbannführer Wolfgang Becker toyed with the dagger upon which he had, on a black midnight, sworn a blood oath to his Führer. "It is extraordinary, Fraulein Lund, that in all this time you have learned exactly nothing."

"Perhaps it is because there is nothing to learn," Lili said. She wanted another cigarette; she wondered if the blond Gestapo officer had noticed she had smoked four of them in rapid order and whether he had attached anything to it.

Becker again looked down at her file, turning the pages delicately with the tip of the dagger, running the point along the lines, jabbing lightly here and there. His brow was serene. His clean-cut face was correct. He lifted his blue eyes and fixed them on her. "You may smoke as much as you please, Fraulein," he said agreeably.

Lili was frightened. She did not know how to cope with Major Becker. She had gaited herself for her usual role with Buhle. The society woman with chronic hot pants. Let him look her over as he always did, both frankly and surreptitiously. Cross and uncross her legs. Hint with her eyes and mouth of future and more intimate occasions. Hints which would not be altogether spurious because Lili was always ready to deal in futures with men. For amusement, if nothing else.

But she was not prepared for Major Becker. For the recruiting poster face; the flat, cold, impersonal eyes; the high voice; the detachment. Her strength was between her legs and she knew the moment she saw Becker she had no muscle against him. He was beyond her, beyond any hints or promises she could make. She could strip in front of him and he wouldn't blink an eye. It wasn't a question of whether or not he was a homosexual. He might well be. But whatever else, he had a higher love. And in competition with the Führer, she knew she didn't have a prayer.

"If there is nothing to learn from this young man with the vivid red hair, then why do you waste our time?" Becker asked.

"I have understood that it was for Colonel Buhle to decide," Lili said.

Becker pushed the point of the dagger against the flesh of his thumb. He appeared interested in seeing how far he could go without drawing blood. "Standartenführer Buhle is somewhat lenient," he said.

In the Nazi world, where ruthless toughness was the avowed ideal, more, the demanded goal, this was almost an accusation against a superior officer. The major must have connections. She was more frightened than ever.

"You have done this kind of thing before," Becker said. He traced the dagger across the pages of the file. "Four times. It never took this long. Why are you persevering with Arne Johansen?"

"I am doing the best I can," she said. It was a losing fight, she knew. The most she might manage was a delaying action.

But that was the story of her life, she thought, with a sudden upsurge of cheer.

"Have you fallen in love with this man?" he asked.

"No," she said.

He pointed with the dagger. "Standartenführer Buhle has noted here that it is his opinion you have fallen in love with this man and that your conscience disturbs you." He scrutinized her, reversing the dagger. "Conscience!" His voice rose. "Where does a person such as you come to have a conscience!" With the last word, he stabbed the desk and left the blade quivering there.

"I am not responsible for Colonel Buhle's opinions," she said, staring at the shining steel.

"Conscience!" Becker repeated shrilly. "Consience is for men of faith! How dare a whore have a conscience!"

Lili took her eyes from the dagger. She opened her purse. It didn't matter now. She took out a cigarette and fitted it into the holder. "I wish I was a whore," she said. She lit the cigarette. "I wish to God I was an honest whore."

Becker removed the dagger carefully, walked round the desk and sat on the edge. He tapped the flat of the blade on his open palm. "Did you hear of the shooting at Asiatisk Plads, where the saboteur Niels Rider was wounded?"

"I heard something about it," Lili said.

"A small man with red hair was seen there," Becker said.

"I don't know anything about that," Lili said.

He reached behind him and picked up the telephone. "Connect me with the commandant of the rehabilitation center at Stavanger," he said.

"No," she whispered.

"Priority call," Becker said.

She shook her head slowly. "No."

"We'll find out what we want to know, Fraulein," Becker said. "But by then, your father will be dead."

Hansen looked away from the window. "What is causing this delay, Mannheim?" he asked.

Mannheim reached for the telephone and repeated the

query. He listened, hung up. "The doctor in charge of the case has changed the dressing since the prisoner was to be moved, Herr Obersturmbannführer."

"Excellent," Hansen said.

"He has just finished. The prisoner will be brought here directly."

Becker nodded with profound satisfaction. "Is that all?"

Lili nodded. "Yes."

"Perhaps it is not all," Becker said. "But we have time, no? We have all the time in the world." He spoke into the telephone. "You will cancel the call to Stavanger for the moment. You will get Hauptsturmführer Mannheim at Vester Prison."

He cradled the receiver and picked up the dagger. He looked across the desk at Lili. He smiled at the sight of the huddled figure, at the dry, racking sobs. He felt powerful. It was all in the technique. The new technique. The young and modern technique. Buhle had been diddling for weeks. And now here in just a few brief minutes. He anticipated the report to Reichführer Himmler.

He answered the telephone. "Sturmbannführer Becker," he said in his voice of power and authority. "Mannheim? Good. Listen carefully. This is important. I have just received information confirming the identity of Niels Rider. You will take every extra precaution."

Lili heard the exultancy in his voice and looked up and saw the pleasure on his matinee idol's face. Nothing could defeat them. Nothing that was human could touch them and nothing could defeat them.

But then she saw a change come over Becker's face.

"When?" he demanded. "By whose order? Impossible! Are you certain? You have the order? Yes, immediately!" He jiggled the telephone key. "Has Standartenführer Buhle arrived? Please inform him I wish to see him." He stood up. He straightened his tunic and slipped the dagger into its sheath. He said to Lili, "It is my belief the Standartenführer will want to see you as well."

24.

COLONEL BUHLE peered at the order with astonishment. He shook his head. "It is perfect," he said, astounded. "I tell you these people are becoming impossibly proficient." He looked up at Mannheim, standing terrified. "You have nothing to blame yourself for, Mannheim. These papers would have fooled anyone."

Mannheim almost sagged in his relief. "I wondered at the order, Herr Standartenführer," he said eagerly. "I had the instinct to telephone you and verify it. But I have witnessed your signature so many times, and the papers were in order and the bearer wore the uniform of an SS officer and arrived in an official car."

Buhle rolled his cigar in his mouth. "This officer, what did he look like?"

"Tall. Light hair. Mustache. Papers identifying him as Obersturmbannführer Karl Hengst. Everything was correct, sir, I give you my oath as an officer."

"I'm sure it was," Buhle said. He ran his eyes admiringly over the order again. "If I didn't know better, I'd swear I signed these papers myself." He looked at Becker. The silly fool with the eternal uniform and the toy dagger. But dangerous. "Well, Becker," he said heartily. "Because of your competence we have learned of this abduction very quickly. They cannot have gone very far. The man Rider will need medical attention. We have that much to go on."

"Thank you, Herr Standartenführer," Becker said, his mind framing the precise words of his report to Berlin.

Buhle was studying Lili. For the first time since he had

known her, her face was sexless; bleak, empty, sexless. She had really cared. Childish. In this business, always such a nuisance. "And if we have lost one for the moment," Buhle said, "we have finally found the other."

"We could have had them both," Becker said angrily.

Buhle blew out a cloud of smoke. He shrugged. "In this business, Becker, one learns half a loaf is better than none. Lili, I'm afraid we shall have to put you under detention. After that, we shall consider another arrangement."

She nodded. Of course. Not that it was necessary. It had to be done and she had done it, but she was not happy. But one had to live. Even in this world, one had to live one way or the other. She would not have hurried to die with him. Outside of bad books and films, did anyone ever do that?

"I am at your disposition, Colonel," she said.

"We could have had them both," Becker said. "She should be punished."

"You are always so prepared to punish," Buhle said. "It is when you come closest to bestowing yourself."

"She should be punished," Becker repeated stubbornly in his new power.

"She should indeed," Buhle said. "But it is better for her to still be useful." He regarded Becker thoughtfully. "It is something you do not understand, Becker. That is her punishment."

25.

ARNE JOHANSEN woke that morning to find Lili gone. He yawned, smiled, stretched, thinking of the night. The smell of sex, of her perfume, her body, was in the bed, on the sheets, on the pillows.

It was the best night they had ever had, and that was saying something. He lit a cigarette, remembering, feeling the happy tiredness in his groin. It made a difference. You could joke all you wanted to about it, but it made a difference. It had been great before but now, now that they knew, it was something else.

He remembered how much he had wanted to tell her about himself, about everything, and how he had not. With all the booze. Something. He was, he was forced to admit, a remarkable fellow.

Full of himself, he dressed. He telephoned Peter Hansen at his office to see if he could find out anything about Niels. Unable to reach Hansen, he went out and had a breakfast worthy of a dedicated man and living legend. He called in at the dental clinic to see if Hansen was there. Hansen was not, but he was told there Niels was alive and apparently recovering nicely.

From the dental clinic, he went to his own flat on the third floor of an apartment building in Jaegersborg Alle. He paced back and forth restlessly; he tried to read; smoked. Then he had another idea. He went to a closet in the bedroom and slid back a false ceiling. He took down a sub-machine gun, one of the new ones being manufactured in small Danish metal works. Niels, who had hidden three of the guns in their cache, had said they were marvelous and Arne had been wanting to have a look at them for himself.

He dismantled the gun, which had been painstakingly copied by hand from a captured German weapon. Niels was right. It was a beauty. He was putting the gun together again when he heard the jackboots on the stairs and the pounding on the door and the unnecessary command, "Open up! This is the German police!"

He was not at all surprised. He had been expecting them off and on for a long time.

He shoved the machine-gun parts under the bed and ran to the front window. He saw the black beetle cars and the Gestapo in the street. He ran to the back window as the thudding on the door and the shouted orders were repeated.

337

"I am coming!" he called out, looking down from the rear window. More Gestapo. "I'm coming!"

He took from under his belt a new pistol, a Walther P. P. obtained from the Danish police, and slipped it into the right-hand pocket of his jacket. Holding his finger on the trigger of the Walther, he opened the door. He said "Good morning" to his two guests and fired twice through the pocket, dropping them without fuss. He chucked their rifles into the flat, rolled their bodies to the landing, kicked them down the stairs. People living in the building already were hurrying out.

He returned to the flat and locked the door. He went back into the closet and took down all the weapons hidden there, the two other machine guns, seven rifles, nine pistols, ammunition for all of them, and five hand grenades. Crawling on hands and knees, he carried his arsenal to the window.

He heard his name called through a bullhorn in the street. He peered cautiously over the sill. He saw Major Becker holding the bullhorn to his mouth. Near him stood Colonel Buhle, smoking a cigar.

"Johansen," Becker intoned. "Arne Johansen. The building is surrounded. You will come down with your hands held behind your neck."

Arne surveyed his weapons judiciously as a man might look over his ties to choose one for the day, picked up one of the newly acquired German rifles, hefted it, sighted, fired.

The bullhorn spun out of Becker's hands.

That's for starters, you mother's prick, Arne said, looking respectfully at the rifle.

Becker looked with shock at his empty, tingling fingers and ran behind one of the black Volkswagens. Buhle followed him as quickly as dignity permitted.

Arne dropped back to the floor laughing as bullets tore into the room. Then there was quiet from below and he heard a shout. He looked down to see SS men carrying out the two men he had shot at the door.

From behind the Volkswagen, Becker watched the dead men being taken away. He squinted at the window. "How many do you suppose are up there, sir?" he asked Buhle.

338

"One." Buhle puffed calmly.

"One?"

"Order more troops."

Becker turned to him in surprise. "We have thirty men here now, Herr Standartenführer. Will we not appear foolish, summoning still more for one single Danish saboteur?"

"We already appear foolish," Buhle said.

There was a crack from the window. A Gestapoman racing across the street for a better position clutched his throat and fell down, making strangling sounds.

Buhle glanced at Becker. The major slipped away.

The order from Major Becker to Arne Johansen to surrender peaceably had been delivered on the bullhorn at ten minutes before noon. At 12:25, two hundred additional SS troops arrived from a nearby barracks.

By that time, the original Gestapo force had suffered eleven casualties, including the three deaths. By that time, too, all the tenants in the building and nearby buildings had streamed out and fled, and now there was nobody in that part of Jaegersborg Alle except two hundred and nineteen Waffen SS and Arne Johansen.

The reinforcements came equipped with two small artillery pieces. The riflemen took shelter behind whatever they could find and the artillerymen began to level the building.

As the building was razed systematically, brick by brick, window by window, floor by floor, Arne Johansen disposed of his ammunition thriftily and with style. A sportsman, he tried always to select moving targets. He took aim at a German attempting to better his position. From the manner in which the man doubled up and dragged himself to safety, Arne considered he had hit his target, which was the man's balls, or had at least come close to it.

His own face was creased by a bullet at the same time. He regarded it as a fair exchange. A Heidelberg cheek. Very smart these days. He wondered whether Lili would approve. Probably not. But then Lili was not going to be able to approve anything any more, not with him.

By 3:20 the building was a shambles, neatly dropped like a

collapsed soufflé between the buildings on both sides, and the artillerymen now set out to reduce it to rubble.

It was five minutes after four, more than four hours after the Gestapo had arrived and Major Wolfgang Becker had demanded his surrender, when Arne Johansen staggered out of what was left of the apartment house on Jaegersborg Alle.

One side of his face was streaked with blood. His red hair was powdered white with dust. His left arm, wounded above the elbow, dangled at his side, a grenade in the hand. His right hand clutched another grenade.

He stood in front of the pile of brick and broken glass and pulled out the pin of the grenade in his right hand with his teeth and lobbed the grenade over a Volkswagen, killing another SS man and wounding still another, bringing his grand total to five dead and fourteen wounded.

More than a hundred men took aim at him. He would not give them that at all, not him, not the dedicated man—whatever would Niels say? As the German rifles spat like firecrackers, he lifted his useless left hand with his right hand and bit off the pin of the last, the final grenade, and fell upon it in the debris of the demolished building and, without bothering to grace his enemies with a "Fuck you," blew his small body to bits.

Colonel Buhle stood up, rubbing his aching back, and walked over to what was left of the body of Arne Johansen. He looked at it for a long time. He went to his car without saying a word and departed.

After the rest of the Gestapo left with their dead and their wounded, the people returned. They gathered around the remains of Arne Johansen and stared until a woman who lived across the street brought down a blanket and covered him. Still, the people stood there and stared at the blanket.

26.

THE SWEAT stood on Peter Hansen's lip as Colonel Buhle accepted the envelope containing fifty thousand Danish crowns. Sweat of hatred and pride and contempt but, most of all, of the need to kill.

"It had to be done that way, Mr. Hansen, you can understand that," Buhle said. He put the envelope in a drawer in a sideboard in the living room of his apartment and locked the drawer. He turned back to Hansen, drawing on his cigar. "After the stink of losing Rider, we had to put on a big show with the other one."

"Yes," Hansen said.

Buhle clasped his hands behind his back. "The way it worked out with Rider, there will be questions asked, reports. I had to make the other appear outstanding."

"And you consider it outstanding?" Hansen said. "Almost five hours for an army to bring about the death of a boy, and then only after he shot down almost twenty of you?"

Buhle's face set. "You have excellent sources of information, Mr. Hansen."

The face, the voice, the eyes would have shot fear into Hansen before; but not now, not after Arne Johansen. "Your élite troops they were, too," he said. "Your best."

Colonel Buhle walked slowly to the sideboard again and tapped the cigar against the edge of a tray. When he had himself under control, he turned to Hansen. "It was a successful action. It destroyed a legend."

"You destroyed a building," Hansen said. "And during the course of that heroic act, a smallish man destroyed himself. The legend, Colonel? I'm afraid it's escaped you. There might have still been a few people in Denmark who hadn't heard about the Blaze. Before today."

"In any case," Buhle said after a moment, "that is not our present concern. We have come to a satisfactory conclusion to our own transaction."

"And now proceed to another," Hansen said.

"So soon?" Buhle smiled. "It reassures me to see that above all else you are a business man, Mr. Hansen. What is it you want now?"

"The name of the person who informed on Arne Johansen."

Buhle shook his head. "You disappoint me."

"Who was it, Colonel?" Hansen asked quietly.

"Negative, Mr. Hansen." Buhle hunched his shoulders. "After all, I have my honor." He smiled roguishly, walked to the door and opened it. "Think of something else. I believe I like doing business with you."

"I am not leaving," Hansen said. "Not until I know who betrayed Arne Johansen."

Buhle slammed the door, his face flooding with blood. "Who do you think you are?" he whispered. "What do you think you have on me?" He rushed back to Hansen. "Nothing has happened," Buhle said, his voice stretched tight. "I am still who I am and you are still you. Nothing has happened."

"But something has happened," Hansen said, feeling the memory of the knot again, despite the newer memory of Arne Johansen.

"Nothing," Buhle repeated. "Nothing. Tomorrow you are in Dagmar House again and anything can be done to you and nothing has happened between us. Now get out."

Hansen took an envelope from his pocket. He went to the sideboard and opened the envelope and removed some small photographs. He laid the photographs on the sideboard as though they were the winning cards in a poker game.

"You see they are quite complete, Colonel," Hansen said. "This little one, where you are checking the money in the folded newspaper. You can't see it clearly here, but when this picture is enlarged the date on the newspaper is quite legible, the day Niels Rider was released. And here, Colonel, you can see me holding up the release order. When this is enlarged, everything on it is clear, including your signature."

Colonel Buhle studied the photograph. His face became impassive again and his attention was impersonal. "Infra-red and a telephoto lens?"

"Yes," Hansen said.

"From your lorry."

"Yes."

Buhle shook his head chidingly. "That was not sporting, was it, Mr. Hansen? I thought we trusted each other."

"You expressed it very well, Colonel. Enemies. Officially to begin with. Now personally."

Buhle threw back his head and laughed jovially. "Of course, as a compliment!" He jabbed a finger at Hansen's chest. "It was to say we would have a cordial relationship, untainted by friendship."

He opened a sideboard drawer and took out a magnifying glass. He studied the photographs, nodding admiringly. Presently he said, without looking up, "Professional, professional. . . . I will have the negatives, Mr. Hansen. The negatives and all the prints." He raised the glass slightly to increase the magnification of one of the pictures. "Yes, if you were to retain any of these and brought it to light, it would certainly injure me. Of course, I would have killed you first."

27.

THE BLACK MERCEDES moved cautiously through the black-out on the road to Kastrup Airport. It now was almost one o'clock on Friday morning.

The young SS lieutenant found it difficult to keep his eyes away from Lili Lund. She sat on the far side of the seat and stared into the opaque night as though she were alone in the world, but what it was she had was there and the lieutenant to whom she had not spoken a word since they left Dagmar House was aware of it as almost palpable and no farther away than the tips of his fingers. It was not the perfume and not the body hidden under a bulky fur coat and not the face of which he had had but a single glimpse. But it was all of these and something else and he had never been stirred by a woman so sweepingly and so quickly.

He stook out the slim black cigarette case with the death's head insignia and for the third time offered her a cigarette. To his pleasant surprise, she accepted. He held the matching black lighter under the cigarette and saw her face again. It was a face to see.

Lighting a cigarette for himself with rising exhilaration, the lieutenant said, "I do not believe we were introduced. May I present myself, Fraulein? I am Obersturmführer Curt Noske."

Her only reaction was the brief brightening of the tip of her cigarette.

"Are you comfortable?" Lieutenant Noske said.

"Thank you."

In the darkness he closed his eyes for a moment at the sound of her voice. He had known exactly how it would sound and it did. "It will not be very long now," he said. He said it as a prelude to saying he was sorry it would not be longer, but he could not manage that after all.

He contented himself with smelling the perfume and being conscious of her nearness and imagining some magical time in the future when they would meet again. It was, she would tell him in some dimly lighted place, holding the champagne glass gracefully in her hand, it was only the circumstances of her leaving Denmark that caused her to act in the way she did. And he would reply that he had instinctively understood that, and that he had by a marvelous coincidence just been promoted to *Hauptsturmführer* and had been unhappy

344

because there was no one to celebrate with, and she would reach out and touch his hand lightly and say that was not true now, was it?

He was projecting his mind dreamily to what would happen next, and after that, when he became aware the car was slowing to a stop.

"What is it?" he called to the SS man driving.

Lili, looking through the window at nothing, was certain she could tell him.

"I do not know, sir," the driver replied. "There appears to be some kind of accident." He strained his eyes through the windshield. "I believe I see some Danish police."

"Find out what has happened," Lieutenant Noske ordered. "Tell them a Luftwaffe aircraft is being held waiting for us."

This was unexpected luck, he thought, as the driver got out of the car. It might be more than an accident. Perhaps a bridge was out, saboteurs. He was terribly aware of the woman sitting next to him.

"Do you have a cigarette, Lieutenant?" Lili asked.

He whipped out the case again and saw that her hands were shaking slightly as she took a cigarette. "There is nothing to be concerned about, Fraulein," he said with assurance. Then he took courage. "It would not disappoint me if we were delayed."

He turned his head as he heard a rapping on the window on his side. He saw a tall captain of the Danish police. He cranked down the window and leaned out. He started to ask what the trouble was but he got out only the first two words. A garrotte was slung around his neck and twisted expertly, and Lieutenant Noske, dead, was shoved back into the car.

Lili, who knew everything as she had known everything all her life, smoked Lieutenant Noske's cigarette calmly, and when the door on her side was opened she accepted the hand extended to her and got out of the car without protest. It would be stupid to protest. She was sure when it happened to Arne Johansen, he took it that way, that he said balls to the whole bloody mess. And it took him more than four hours to make them understand that, and it took them more than four hours to bring one boy to peace.

28.

A LITTLE LESS than twelve hours later, shortly after noon on Friday, the eighth day of October of that year, Kate Hansen held her hands clasped tightly around her bursting belly and braced her feet against the seat of the jolting taxi.

One more bump, she thought, one more rut—if that little monster hits one more hole, I'm going to fly open. No, not you, little monster, she explained, patting her belly tenderly, that little monster at the wheel. "Driver!" she said. "For the love of God!"

Mikkel Steffen Olsen, with his Hitler mustache and his face of a frustrated clown, turned and grinned. Since the time he had taken the family of Rabbi Rasmussen to the railroad station in Copenhagen, he had, for some reason beyond him, become the favorite taxi-driver for Police Captain Erik Melchior and he knew that this was special cargo, very special.

"It's fantastic," he said. "Would you like a drink now?"

"No, I would not like a drink now," Kate Hansen said. "Is this some kind of game?"

Mikkel Steffen Olsen asked out of the side of his mouth, "Game? Game, did you say?" She ought to have a drink, he thought, special cargo or no, she must be losing her mind, her condition without doubt, talking about games at a time like this. "What kind of game?" he asked patiently.

"Every pothole? Do you have to hit every one? Or is it just a matter of pride?"

Very funny, he thought, very, very funny, sometimes

346

Police Captain Erik Melchior gave him a pain in the ass. "I'm sorry," he said. "I'm doing the best I can, lady."

"Of course," she said.

"You're sure you wouldn't like a drink?"

"No, thank you."

Mikkel Steffen Olsen swerved the taxi violently to avoid a rupture in the pavement and the sleeping Niels Rider toppled forward and Kate Hansen grabbed him and pushed him back. Niels muttered something, opened his eyes, smiled, closed his eyes and began again to snore gently.

The road from Copenhagen to the island of Moen for a large part followed the main highway south to Gedser and the ferries to Germany. Kate Hansen held her belly with one hand, knowing if she let go for a moment, a single moment, it would happen, and with her other hand kept Niels from falling over, and she watched the steady, unbroken stream of German military vehicles moving north, and she wondered what in God's name she was doing there.

She knew, of course. Or she knew what she heard. Or what she remembered she heard, or thought she remembered. It was all so mixed up and made such little sense and it happened so quickly after that that she didn't know now what she remembered or only dreamed.

"A pregnant woman," Poul Klampmann had said. "Peter needs a pregnant woman."

That was for openers. That was what had greeted her on the telephone. Like a hole in the head, she had thought. "Of course," she said, going along. "Where do you suppose he might find one?"

"I had one all lined up," Poul Klampmann explained. "But Mother Nature beat me to the draw."

"Please?"

"A six-pound boy. Kate, I'm stuck. I've called all around, but they're all too early or too late. There's only you."

It had gone on like that for a few more minutes and then she had asked, "Did Peter tell you to get me?"

"He told me definitely not to get you," Poul said. "But I'm stuck."

Perhaps that was what had decided her. In any case, without clearly knowing what was going on, she was whisked off to the clinic in the Carlsberg breweries and she was transferred to a taxi with a funny-looking little Hitler at the wheel, and Niels, the boy who had come wounded to her house that day and then was dragged off by the Gestapo, was carried unconscious into the cab and placed next to her, and they started off.

"Don't ask me," Poul Klampmann had said, although she was too bewildered to ask anything. "But you're on your way to the hospital. That's all you have to remember."

"What about him?" she did ask, nodding toward Niels.

"Your husband," Poul shouted as the taxi pulled away. "Up all night with you. Exhausted."

He waved, and the taxi moved into the stream of traffic and passed through Copenhagen, and then took the road south to Koge and beyond.

The taxi hit another rut and Niels grunted and she gentled her belly, thinking, if this keeps up much longer I'll have to stick up my thumb to keep the little bastard in; thinking, what a hell of a way to be spending the last few days of pregnancy—except it had been the last few days for the last few days and for the last few days before that.

She listened to the clatter of the German vehicles of war, some of them obviously quite new, and she looked at the endless faces of the German soldiers, some of them new, too, and she wondered who, who on God's earth, was ever going to stop them? What were they all doing, Peter and Poul and the little doctor who committed suicide—or was he shot dead before he went out the window? they never were sure —Moller, that was his name, and the boy who was killed yesterday, they had to bring down the entire building but they brought it down, that's the way they were, and Niels, next to her, half dead. What were they doing? What kind of child's play against these trucks and half-tracks and weapons' carriers that were chewing up an inoffensive Danish road, the way they were chewing up the world?

Whatever it was, she knew, she knew in her foolish woman's way, her foolish, pregnant woman's way, that they were all living their lives as they had never lived them before and never would again. On both sides. Nothing would ever equal these times. And those who survived were making memories and would live off the memories in the time to come, and in the end the memories would become selective, it was impossible to remember pain, only humor and excitement and fun, and that was what made it always happen all over again, not to the same men perhaps, they might become too old, but to their sons, to whom they passed the memories that would get more and more filled with special life as the years and years passed.

Moen, Poul Klampmann had told the funny little driver, whose brows had shot up so high they got lost under the brim of his cap. There was to be a big transport from Moen that night, Poul had told her, and that was where Peter Hansen was and that was where she was going despite Peter Hansen, who had said definitely not her, going with a baby in her belly and a wounded boy who might or might not be alive when they reached there, if they reached there, if the gray uniforms and the green uniforms and the black uniforms let them reach there. Or the ones who didn't wear uniforms, who wore black suits and black hats, like black widow spiders the deadliest of them all.

Moen. She remembered Moen. She remembered the chalk cliffs, the only cliffs of any kind in all of Denmark, owned by some baron—where else but in Denmark could one man own the only cliffs in the land? She remembered the cliffs at night, rearing whitely from the dark sea, resting against a tangled forest of pine and beech, harkening back to another time when Denmark was a land of Vikings, who made sounds in the world that caused men to quaver.

She remembered spending a weekend with Peter Hansen at an inn near Moen before they were married, in the winter when there were no tourists cluttering the forest paths, when the pebbled beaches were empty, when the bleakness and fog and isolation were all they wanted, filling the world, the whole world, with themselves.

Would it ever be that way again? she wondered, watching

the enemy pouring north like poison, would it ever again be that the limits of everything, of passion and tension and agony and release could be supplied by her, by her body, by herself? Or was that gone now? Was the capacity for feeling so enlarged by the acts of sabotage and the killings and the escapes and the loss of those who did not escape and the deliverance of the wanted and the Jews, was it all so big now that she could never again quite fill it? Would it always be less in some way for Peter Hansen than it was?

She lit a cigarette. The wind heightened and the sun was obscured by sudden slate clouds, and in a few moments it was another place, a different place, a strange place. She had to remember, she told herself. She had a Viking in her belly, she had to remember that, and that, she realized, was as it should be because the Viking to come had a kind of Viking for a father, and she wondered why she had never thought of that before.

The first car of a new convoy shot past, a Mercedes in military dress, two proud officers in the tonneau, and behind them a fresh demonstration of the inexhaustible, ineluctable power of the Third Reich.

They reached a narrow part of the road. A German corporal waved them on, glancing at them without interest.

"Are you all right?" Olsen asked.

"Never better," she said. "Not in my whole life."

"Sure you don't want a little snaps?"

"Might pickle the baby. But thank you."

"Peter Hansen, you swine, you're not going to do this to me!" Niels announced in a clear and loud voice.

Olsen almost ditched the car. Kate whirled.

"It's all right," she said. "He's just talking in his sleep."

But at that moment Niels opened his eyes and sat upright.

"You're not going to do it, Hansen," he said. "You're not going to hand me one of those free trips to Sweden."

The car began to wobble again. "I have a needleful of sleep, lady," Olsen said. "As soon as I get a chance, I'll give it to him."

"Hansen," Niels shouted. "Where the hell are you?"

Where the hell indeed was he, she thought, looking closely at Niels' face, seeing the open eyes were not seeing anything. She gripped his wrist and he tore it away.

"Fuck you, Peter Hansen," Niels said. Mikkel Steffen Olsen's ears turned scarlet.

"Now," Kate Hansen said. "Pull over and give it to him now."

"Peter Hansen!" Niels bellowed. "You're dealing with a dedicated man!"

"Now," Kate Hansen said.

"Oh, Jesus," Olsen said.

She felt the car slowing again and then Olsen pulled off onto the shoulder and she looked through the windshield and saw a large military lorry and next to it, and even more frightening, the familiar black Volkswagen.

"You're a bastard, Peter Hansen," Niels said.

"For God's sake, shut him up," Olsen said.

"You can take Sweden and shove it up your ass," Niels said.

"Lady!" Olsen implored.

She took his hand and held it tightly. "Niels," she said. "Quiet, Niels."

"As the British say," Niels said.

"Lady, lady." Olsen was almost weeping.

"Niels, listen to me," Kate begged. "Germans, Niels. Germans."

"Fuck you, Peter Hansen," Niels said. "Or did I say that?"

"Niels," Kate said. "Listen. Gestapo, Gestapo, Gestapo."

He turned his head and looked at her for the first time. He squinted as though trying to see into the sun.

"Gestapo, Gestapo," she whispered in incantation.

She saw the eyes pull themselves into focus and she believed he heard and saw, but then they went away again and by now the black suits and black hats were approaching and, without glancing into the rear of the taxi, the Gestapomen indicated the driver was to get out.

Kate stole a quick look at Niels. He was staring ahead,

351

puzzled, biting on his upper lip. She took his hand. He didn't seem to notice it.

Still showing no interest in the passengers, the two Germans began a search of the front of the car. They picked up odd pieces of paper, a street map of Copenhagen, a map of Sealand, a form showing the trips the driver had made, some rags covered with soot, some rags covered with grease, a screwdriver, a wrench, a magazine with pictures of girls, an almost full bottle of aquavit. After careful examination, each of these was tossed into the road. The bottle of snaps was set down carefully.

The two Germans, one of whom was dark and ordinary, the other the German of cartoons, red-faced and with no neck, finished their search simultaneously, as though it was a kind of act, a vaudeville turn that had to end at exactly the same moment.

Kate Hansen dug her nails into Niels' wrist as the Gestapomen now moved toward the rear of the car, making the two steps they each took appear somehow like a march.

The man on her side was the fat man whose head rested on his shoulders like a balloon and, as he stuck his head into the open door, she bulged her belly out still farther and she knew now what Peter Hansen, the Viking, had in mind, she knew it with a magnificent flash of pregnant woman's brilliant intelligence, and the fat face broke into a grin that looked as though it would never stop, certainly not at the ears, maybe not at Berlin, and the little piglet eyes beamed with as much pride as if he had himself deposited into that perfect Aryan woman the perfect Aryan baby that must be there.

He said something in German Kate could not understand to the man on the other side and he took off his hat instantly and bowed, and his grin, if not so broad, was less so only because the frame was smaller.

"A baby," the fat man chortled in Danish. "A baby."

He reached across Kate Hansen, no mean feat, and grabbed Niels Rider's hand and pumped it violently, his eyes almost weeping in happiness. He backed away religiously in

352

the presence of Motherhood and closed the door carefully. Both Germans then scooped up everything they had taken out of the front of the car, including the bottle, and put them back.

The fat man stood back and waved his hand. "Hurry," he said in Danish. "And good luck!"

"Hurry it is," Olsen said heartily as the Gestapoman on his side almost shoved him back into his seat.

The taxi lurched forward. The Gestapomen waved. Kate stuck out her arm and waved back. They passed the block and were again on the open highway.

"Where," Niels Rider asked, "am I?"

Mikkel Steffen Olsen pulled over to the side of the road again and inserted a needle into Niels Rider's arm, so quickly and deftly he had almost finished injecting the drug before Niels Rider knew what was happening. Niels tried to pull his arm away but it was too late.

"What a thing to do," Niels said sadly, "to a dedicated man." He put his head on Kate's shoulder and went back to sleep.

Presently they crossed the new bridge to Moen and she moved him away gently and rested his head on the seat, "Mr. Olsen?"

"Yes, lady?"

"Did you mention snaps?"

"Ha!" He picked up the bottle and thrust it at her.

"Skoal," she said. She put the bottle to her lips and drank deeply. That Hansen. He had it all figured out, she thought as the fiery, soothing, bracing, calming, cooling, warming liquid went down. He had it all worked out and he could have written the slop, the action and words. What hadn't she known about him and how long had they been married?

She leaned forward and returned the bottle to Olsen, who asked if she minded and she said no, she didn't mind, she didn't mind anything. He tilted the bottle. She folded her arms serenely over her belly and felt the protest.

"Nonsense," she said.

There was the feeling now of island, of separation, and the

strong air of the sea, and they passed a desolate moor and on it she saw silhouetted the flat, round rocks, stretching across the wild land in pairs, one on top of the other. They marked, Hansen had told her that last time, the graves of ancient Vikings and below the rocks, he had told her, they still drank and wenched and fought and relived older fights. She thought of them and of Hansen and of the other Vikings who still strode the land, and she said to the rocks, you wouldn't be ashamed of them, you wouldn't be ashamed at all, and she felt the fire and the pride in her blood.

It was more than the rocks and it was more than the snaps. It was both of those, of course, but it was beyond them. She had discovered the headiest feeling of all. She had outwitted the enemy. She had faced them in their darkness and she had outwitted them. And it was more than even that. It was now that she shared that with him.

PART V.

1.

THEY CAME to Moen. They came from all directions. They came from many places. They came from hospitals. They came from hotels. They came from farmhouses. They came from the cottages of fishermen. They came from outbuildings on the estate of the baron who owned the cliffs and from the outbuildings on the land of the baron who owned Liselund. They came from a home maintained by the State for the declining days of unmarried Danish noblewomen who had been registered there by their parents when they were young as insurance against lonely old age.

They had been kept in these places for nights and days, hidden against the enemy, hidden and fed and treated for ills, and now they were brought to Moen, in taxis and ambulances, in trucks and farmers' carts, brought on the roads and the dirt lanes to the forest of pine and beech and bracken that grew untamed and matted on rolling land behind the chalk cliffs.

They found waiting for them in the darkening woods, almost lost, wraithlike in the wisps and tendrils of fog that rose wetly and silently from the afternoon sea, students from colleges, from as far as Copenhagen, and boys and girls posted a few feet apart in human linkage to guide them down the twisting, treacherous steps that led to the beach more than four hundred feet below.

With their children, their suitcases, their paper bags, in bitterness and gratitude, in hope and despair, they made their way down the steep, slippery notches cut out of the earth and bulwarked by wooden risers soaked and greasy in the damp autumn air.

357

Overhead, German patrol planes passed back and forth, low and noisy in the stillness of the exodus. The people looked up from the forest and steps and beach, and to many it seemed they could see the men in the aircraft and it seemed impossible the men in the aircraft could not see them.

When they climbed down the final uncertain step onto the beach and looked back and up, they saw a terrifying sight. The chalk cliffs of Moen had been used for some time by the Germans as a target against which to test their new missiles. Normally the rockets exploded on contact, but for some reason one had not and now was stuck into the side of the cliff, midway between the beach and the summit.

To the hundred and fifty Jews who were gathering on the beach at Moen on the afternoon and early evening of Yom Kippur, the Day of Atonement for that year of 1943, there seemed, as the shadows gathered and the fog thickened, to be a face, a chalky white face on the side of the cliff, two eyes made of dark pockets of lichen, a nose made of an outcrop of rock, a mouth that was a smear of gorse, and, sticking into the mouth, a big cigar, the whole a fat, Nazi, Gestapo face, looking down upon them jeeringly, daring them to try to escape.

2.

GENERALOBERST EUGEN VON KOBE finished the last of the mountain of fresh prawns, and with a slab of rich country bread wiped up the last of the sauce that was as exquisite as the fat chef had promised it would be. He sat back, loosening his collar as the waiter poured another beer, and watched with anticipatory eyes as the maître d'hôtel wheeled in a table bearing a huge silver casserole.

358

General von Kobe was tired from a long, tedious day of inspecting coastal defenses. But there were compensations. He had been assured the hotel in Nykoebing set one of the best tables in southern Sealand, war or no war, and thus far he agreed. Most heartily.

The dining room was almost empty in the late afternoon. Generaloberst von Kobe found quiet and peace after a clamorous day. The snaps, brought by the owner of the hotel from the cellar where it had been mellowing for just such an occasion, was absolute nectar.

The hotel owner, because of certain other persons in the hotel, was nervous and flustered at having for a guest the Nazi military commandant of all Denmark. His trepidations caused him to find a couple of bottles of wine that had in some mysterious manner remained unnoticed in the same cellar for long years.

General von Kobe inspected the wine, considered, consulted his taste buds, found they had already been directed on a definite course by the snaps and beer, rejected the wine and opted for more beer.

He observed the hotel owner carrying away the wine with excruciating care, so not to disturb its somnolent serenity, and had second thoughts. He instructed the owner to put the two bottles, together with any others of comparable eminence, into a suitable hamper and then into his car. He proposed, he said graciously, to provide himself with the means to recall the excellence of the hotel at future, leaner meals.

Now the cover of the casserole was removed. The cart was wheeled closer. The Prussian general tossed off another snaps and peered into the huge dish held open before him. It was, the maître d'hôtel repeated, a unique dish of Old Denmark, an indescribable mixture of pork and veal and sausage and vegetables brewed with herbs and spices of choice and proportions privy only to the chef.

It was while the general was savoring the perfume that rose moodily from the casserole that his aide-de-camp, a slender, tenor-voiced lieutenant colonel named Kramer, marched into the room, clicked his heels, said, "Herr Generaloberst!"

Von Kobe had had Lieutenant Colonel Kramer as aide for only three months, but he had already developed an excruciating sensitivity to the delicate nuances of Lieutenant Colonel Kramer's voice. The present voice, he decided, was the voice of trouble; not truly serious trouble but trouble of a special nature, and Generaloberst von Kobe would bet a drink of snaps he knew what the trouble was.

If only by some miracle, by snapping his fingers, by ignoring the man, by making a wish, he could cause Lieutenant Colonel Kramer to vanish. Too much to hope for. Some things were beyond the power even of Prussian generals.

"What is it, Kramer?" he asked in a discouraging voice, knowing it would not in the least discourage.

"Herr Generaloberst . . ." Kramer started.

"You have already said that," von Kobe said. He looked at the unique dish of Old Denmark and then at the maître d'hôtel. That gentleman looked unhappy and General von Kobe wondered whether it was because he was afraid the masterpiece would get cold or because he was afraid of what Lieutenant Colonel Kramer was going to report.

"I have just received information of the greatest importance," Kramer said.

"Now let me guess what it could be," von Kobe said. "The Allies have invaded the continent. Hermann Göring has lost forty pounds. You have been promoted to full colonel. No, that is impossible. I would have to recommend that."

"Herr Generaloberst," Kramer continued, undaunted. "It has come to my attention that this hotel is being used to give shelter to Jews and at this very moment they are being smuggled away."

Von Kobe, again smelling the honor of Old Denmark, raised his eyes slightly and looked again at the maître d'hôtel. That gentleman's face was without expression. Von Kobe moved his eyes four degrees west and fixed them on the hotel owner. His face was stone as well.

"What is your command, Herr Generaloberst?" Kramer asked.

Von Kobe straightened in his chair. "My command is for the maître d'hôtel to serve my dinner before it gets cold."

The maître d'hôtel broke into a smile and acted instantly. The hotel owner maintained his inscrutability. So it was only the food with the maître d'hôtel but the other with the hotel owner, the general reflected.

"But about the Jews," Kramer persisted. "What will you do about them?"

"Nothing," von Kobe said. He saw a flutter cross the face of the hotel owner.

"Herr Generaloberst?"

"Nothing, Kramer," von Kobe said dangerously.

"But the order, Herr Generaloberst, the order from the Führer."

"Nothing!" von Kobe roared. He pounded his fist on the table. The beer glass toppled over. Waiters sprang to the table and mopped up the beer. The general kept smashing his fist on the table. "Nothing! Nothing! Nothing!"

The maître d'hôtel held the filled plate in his hands. The hotel owner folded his arms.

"But Herr Generaloberst," the unfortunate Kramer said.

"Get out of here!" The roar turned into a bellow.

Lieutenant Colonel Manfred Kramer, sensing he was not entirely pleasing his commanding officer, backed slowly away, his lips still moving from habit but no sound coming out.

Von Kobe watched a new cloth being laid, a new beer poured, a new snaps glass filled. He drank down the snaps in a single swallow to wipe away the irritation of Lieutenant Colonel Kramer and he looked down at the plate that was set before him.

"This had better be good." The bellow turned into a growl.

The maître d'hôtel stood next to the hotel owner and both watched the Prussian general take his first taste of the glory and memory of Old Denmark. The general looked up and nodded slowly and with reverence. The hotel owner departed after a small bow, deciding to put the good wine in the general's hamper after all.

3.

IN ANOTHER PART of the hotel, as they were leaving by a side entrance outside which a produce truck was waiting, Rabbi Rasmussen and his family, Mendel Cohen and his family and nine other Jews heard the German shouting coming from the dining room.

Mendel Cohen turned white and began to shake. Rasmussen put his arm around his shoulder and walked with him to the truck.

A few minutes later, the hotel owner ran out of the side entrance to tell them everything was all right. But by then the truck had left for Moen.

In the truck, Mendel Cohen clasped his hands and stared. Rasmussen watched him somberly, knowing what Cohen was hearing and what he was thinking, and he wished God had provided him with words to be used at a time like this.

4.

PETER HANSEN and Anders Jessen arrived at the chalk cliffs in the pickup truck a little after four o'clock, trailed by Captain Erik Melchior in his police car.

Anders unlocked the tailgate of the truck and helped Nina Lange down. Major Helmut Boldt, his hands in cuffs, dropped lightly to the ground after her. The third person to climb down was Dr. Emil Hurwitz.

Anders peered into the interior of the pickup. "What about her, Mr. Hansen?"

"Yes, Mr. Hansen, I've been asking myself the same question," Boldt said.

Anders stared angrily at Boldt and then turned to Hansen. Hansen looked into the truck. Lili Lund sat at the far end, leaning against the partition. Her hands and feet were bound; her eyes were open, unblinking, the yielded eyes of a trapped animal with no hope; her face was distorted by the gag in her mouth.

Hansen turned away. "Leave her here for the time being."

Anders closed the tailgate and locked it. Hansen told one of the resistance youths to watch the truck and then followed the others down to the beach.

Anders moved ahead with Hurwitz, Nina Lange and the German officer. Hansen walked slower, Melchior at his side.

"You ask yourself why," Melchior said. "All these years as a policeman, the people I've seen, the things they've done. I always ask myself why. Why? This girl, this Lili. Why?" He shook his head. "It's a sickness, and what we're going to do, what we have to do, what kind of cure is that?"

"The whole world is a bloody sickness," Hansen said. "That's why we're here. Smuggling Danes out of Denmark because an insane Austrian ruling Germany doesn't want them here. You can't get much sicker than that."

"Why?" Melchior shook his head again. "Why?"

"At the moment all I'm concerned with is the immediate how."

Melchior stole a glance at Hansen. He saw what was in his face and he looked ahead again. They passed one of the school boys posted on the steps. The boy raised a cheerful finger to the tip of his cap.

Hansen paused for a moment and looked at the boy; he

was no more than seventeen. Hansen continued on. "It will be all right, Erik," he said after a moment. "You'll see, it will be all right."

The refugees were gathered in small groups on the beach, dark patches against the pebbles and sand and the chalk cliffs. From old habits, from memories, some of the children, finding themselves on a sandy beach, began to play, to make castles, moats, ponds and complicated canals.

As Hansen and the others stepped onto the beach, they saw one group of Jews, including Rabbi Rasmussen, peering up through the strands of fog at the rocket jutting from the cliff.

"Yes," Hansen said. "I'd been told about that. My God, it looks vicious."

"It is," Boldt said.

"What is it, Mr. Hansen?" Rasmussen asked.

"German guided missile."

"The London Special," Boldt said. "The Führer's dream. The rabbit out of the hat." He backed away for a better look. "How he is counting on that! And he may be right. He often is."

The Jews looked curiously at Boldt.

"I knew we'd been testing them somewhere around here," Boldt said. He raised his hands to shield his eyes. "I've never known one not to detonate on contact."

The Jews saw the manacles.

Boldt lowered his hands. "The English are going to see quite a few of those." He said it in the tones of a professional soldier, without inflection, without regret, without pride.

"I think the English would like very much to see this one," Melchior said. He walked around, to see the rocket from all sides. "Peter, we ought to get some construction men down here and have them try to rig up something to lower that."

"Get some demolition men first," Boldt said. "And defuse it. It's no part of our bargain, Hansen, but I'll tell you this, and for free. That little devil has the most sensitive fuse we have been able to devise. Which means it is probably as

364

sensitive as any that exist. It would astonish you how many men were killed during its development. Breathe on it, it explodes. Look at it crossly, it explodes. Talk to it, it talks back. Nastily." He could not prevent a smile from creeping on his mouth as the refugees instinctively began moving away. Now the note of pride entered his voice. "There is nothing in the world like it. It's the Führer's big play. And he could win with it, Hansen, he could win."

A Luftwaffe plane droned overhead. The aircraft appeared grayly in the misty shrouds and then vanished.

"One of them may see it," Mendel Cohen said suddenly.

"Yes," Hansen conceded.

"They would report it. Then they would come here. To investigate. Troops. The Gestapo."

"There is that risk," Hansen said. "But I hope to have you on your way long before that."

Cohen nodded and then he had another thought. He started to shake again. "They may have already reported it," he said, looking around, up the steps, as though the Germans were already there.

"They may have," Hansen said. "But I doubt it."

"Why?" Cohen asked. "Why do you doubt it?"

"Because I have to," Hansen said.

Boldt, gazing at the rocket, murmured, "I doubt it as well."

Mendel Cohen moved a little closer to Boldt. "Who are you? Why do you have those irons on your wrists?"

"I am an officer in the German army," Boldt said.

Cohen recoiled. "A German? A German officer? Here?"

"Put up with me, friend," Boldt said. "I will try to be as generous with you."

"Boldt, about the rocket," Melchior said, staring up. "Why do you think it hasn't already been spotted by one of your planes?"

"I will give you the benefit of my personal knowledge, Captain," Boldt said. "And again for free." He turned his eyes to the missile. "Any German pilot who saw that would simply destroy it. By firing at it." He looked at Melchior. "It would blow up with the God damnedest most marvelous bang."

"Why are we standing here?" Cohen demanded. "Right under it?"

"Why indeed," Boldt agreed.

Some of the refugees collected their belongings and their children and moved farther down the beach. Mendel Cohen started to go, looked at Rasmussen, hesitated, and then took his daughter's hand and left. His wife followed them silently.

"But it might not be necessary to shoot at the rocket," Boldt said in a manner so arid it was almost pedantic, the manner of a bored lecturer in a military school. "Sound waves could do it so easily. Sound waves from the planes. Even our talking here."

"That's enough, Boldt," Melchior said.

"Try to keep that policeman's voice to a whisper, Captain," Boldt admonished. "Once I saw an avalanche started by one man shouting to another."

A few more of the refugees moved away.

"Shut up, Boldt," Melchior said harshly. "What the hell are you trying to do here, start a riot? Don't you know what these people have been through?"

"Excuse me, Captain," Boldt said. "I was under the impression you asked the question in the first place."

"You've answered it," Melchior said. "Now shut up."

Boldt looked at Melchior curiously. "I suppose in time one gets used to it. But it is really a novelty, to be given orders by a Jew."

"I'm sure it must be," Melchior said. "But when one turns traitor, one must expect almost anything."

"One does not have to turn traitor for that, Captain," Boldt said. "One just has to grow up."

"All right, all right," Hansen said. "Christ, I'm getting to sound like a bloody policeman myself." To the Jews who were still close, he said, "Please try not to worry. If you feel uncomfortable under that thing up there, then move away, but don't go too far. We'll have to be able to move you fast when the boat gets here."

"There are so many of us," Rasmussen said.

"We have a very large fishing boat," Hansen said. "Large enough for everybody. It will come round as soon as it gets dark."

Boldt, casting a trained eye on the water, said, "I would guess the drop-off is very gradual and that water remains shallow for some distance. Do we all swim out to this very large fishing boat?"

"No, Major, we do not," Melchior said. "We just happen to have a dory tucked away for that purpose."

"The boys will row everybody out," Hansen said. "Good exercise for them."

"Those boys," Rasmussen said in a low voice. "Those boys and those girls."

"Yes," Hansen said. "Aren't they?"

Hansen looked up and down the beach and at the people who were still coming down the steps. He called the rabbi to one side. "Dr. Rasmussen, you can help me. I know how nervous and frightened your people are. Move among them, will you? Try to keep them calm. Everything has been worked out carefully. Tell them that. They'll listen to you."

Rasmussen smiled. "I'll do the best I can, Mr. Hansen. But I cannot promise much."

"But you're a man of God, Dr. Rasmussen," Hansen said. "These people are your flock."

"I'm their rabbi," Rasmussen said. He shrugged. "But it's a little different from being a priest or pastor. Or even a good dentist." He shook his head. "I'm not a leader, Mr. Hansen. I'm not supposed to be. I'm a teacher. That's what the word means."

"But won't they obey you?"

"Obey me? I'm ahead of the game when they sit down for a moment and listen to me." He smiled again. "It's always so hard for a non-Jew to understand. I don't stand between this so-called 'flock' and God, Mr. Hansen. My only job is first to know and then to explain God's Law in the Torah. A Jew is supposed to show a little respect for scholarship—and

367

sometimes he does—but responsibility for his actions? That, Mr. Hansen, is his alone."

Another German patrol plane flew overhead. They craned their necks, but they could not see it.

"Isn't there someone?" Hansen asked. Then he said, "There's Morten Torres. What about him? Can he control them?"

"Mr. Torres? Where?"

Morten Torres was making his way slowly and carefully down the slippery steps. He managed even that with dignity. The head of the Jewish community was dressed faultlessly. His cane was firm in his hand. His homburg set perfectly on his fine, lean head.

"Look at him, Mr. Hansen," Rasmussen said admiringly. "Calm. With style, as always. Look, he might be walking down a stairway in the palace to be presented to the King. He is a brilliant lawyer, Mr. Hansen, and probably would be most persuasive."

Hansen saw that Captain Melchior, who had moved over to listen, was grinning. "Who among you has authority?" Hansen asked the rabbi. "Isn't there someone?" He looked irritably at Melchior. "What the hell are you smirking about?"

"Yes," Rasmussen said. "We have an Authority and, as it happens, sunset on this day begins the time when we ask Him to forgive us our sins. It is possible that because of this singular coincidence my people may feel a little more respectful toward me. But I doubt it, and if so, not much." He smiled, a sudden, warm, open smile. "You can see, Mr. Hansen, that we are a thorny people and why we have so many enemies. I have often thought how much simpler my life would have been if I had been born to be a good Catholic priest, preferably Irish."

"Yes," Hansen said. "I suppose so." He looked at Melchior. "Well, I've always got you. Whoever else people won't obey, they'll always obey a cop. Circulate, Erik. Make them understand it's not the end of the world." He turned back to the rabbi. "Excuse me, Dr. Rasmussen, but with all due respects, I need an authority a little closer to hand."

Melchior touched his fingers to his cap in a most mocking salute, bowed courteously to Torres, started on his rounds.

Torres watched him pass and then paused in front of Hansen. "I hardly recognized you out of costume, Mr. Hansen." He nodded curtly to Rasmussen and then looked around. "So we are in the final act of our little drama."

Dr. Hurwitz shook his head. "First the chief rabbi, and now the head of the Jewish community. Peter, this is a VIP."

Torres leaned on his cane. It sank into the sand. He jerked it out angrily. "Mr. Hansen, I can understand these people wanting to flee their country. That is their decision and their privilege." He glanced incuriously at Boldt. "But I request that you return me to Copenhagen."

"We've been all through that, Mr. Torres," Hansen said.

"I don't care what we've been through," Torres said, again looking at Boldt, who came closer. "I do not want to leave Denmark."

"I'm afraid you have no choice, Mr. Torres," Hansen said.

"No more than you would have with us, old man," Boldt said cheerfully. "You understand that."

"Who are you?" Torres asked.

"German swine," Anders Jessen said. "He bought his life by betraying his country."

"I consider my life that valuable," Boldt said to Torres. "Don't you?"

"That's no concern of yours," Anders said heatedly.

"On the contrary," Boldt said. "Everything here is everybody's concern." He studied Torres. "These people are risking their lives to save you. Why aren't you grateful?"

"I have no talent for gratitude," Torres said.

"That's obvious, old man. But why?"

"My name is Morten Torres. Mr. Morten Torres."

"A curious name for a Jew."

"Nevertheless it has been my family's name for more than five hundred years."

"A Jewish policeman," Boldt said. "Now a Jew with lineage." He looked at Hansen with amusement. "You maintain an odd country here."

"Shut your damned mouth, you swine!" Anders said.

"You are very young," Boldt said after a moment. "Very young and undoubtedly very brave." He held up his manacled hands. "Is this what makes you so brave?"

Anders lunged at him and was stopped by Hansen's arm. "It's getting dark, Anders," Hansen said quietly. "Better have a look at the dory. The boat will be here soon."

For a moment Anders pressed against the arm, which held like an iron bar. Then he nodded and left.

"You're a charmer, Boldt," Hansen said.

"He's a young fool!" Boldt's voice was harsh. Something of the German crept into the Danish words. Nina Lange moved a few paces nearer to him and looked up at his face.

"He is young and still has ideals," Torres said bitterly. "And he has the strength of a man who has put them away like toys."

"Very pretty, old man," Boldt said. He looked at Nina and then turned his face to the sea.

"Don't make demands, Boldt," Hansen said.

"Go to hell!" Boldt said, feeling Nina's eyes still on him. "You couldn't go back on your word if your life depended on it."

"I haven't," Hansen said. "But I might try to make an exception in your case."

"Not you, Hansen," Boldt said, his mouth tightening. He wanted to tell Nina to stop looking at him, to stop listening. "Not you," he repeated. "You are afflicted with integrity."

Hansen held himself very still. "It's your world still, Boldt," he said. "Your world and your words and your rules. Still. But it will end, and when it ends and we get rid of the last of you we'll have to give Denmark a bath."

Boldt lifted his head slightly and went white around the lips. He raised his shoulders and walked away. Nina Lange watched him for a moment and then followed slowly after him.

Anders Jessen ran up. "Mr. Hansen," he said, breathing hard. "You'd better come."

"What is it?"

"The rowboat."

Major Helmut Boldt walked away from the water toward the cliff, wondering why he had said all the wrong things, how did he get trapped that way, why he went on, it was a triggering, and with her listening and her eyes on him. He couldn't stop. He started and then he couldn't stop, and he could hear himself and know he sounded just what he was and he wondered why but he could not stop.

He found a portion of the cliff that sloped to a low mound, and he sat down and laid his bound hands in his lap, and he saw her coming to him slowly, tentatively, and he said nothing now because he was afraid to say anything. He didn't trust himself or his words. It was a confusion. He had felt many things in a crowded life, but he had never felt so confused before. He lifted his hands and rested his head tiredly on them.

She sat down silently next to him. He did nothing. He was afraid to take his hands away from his head. He was content to know she had followed him and wanted to be near him, and he did not want to try to put anything else into the words and foul it up, and he felt if he reached to her, however lightly, in whatever way, she would run, like a frightened animal.

Morten Torres found a place to sit down. He glanced at Boldt with contempt and then folded his hands over the handle of his cane and looked at the darkening water. The fog was growing denser in the gathering dusk. Gulls wheeled and squawked in the dying sky.

Presently Boldt said, "Old man."

Torres shifted slightly and ignored him.

"Old man, tell me. Why is it that you do not want to leave Denmark?" Boldt asked.

"That is my affair," Torres said.

"Tell me," Boldt said. "To pass the time."

"It would be pleasant," Torres nodded, his eyes still on the water rippling on the beach, "to sit on a beach at Moen

371

waiting to be carted away from my own country like a bag of dirty laundry and explain my feelings to a German."

"You could do just that, old man," Boldt said. "In years you are quite an old man but there must be something in you that is still quite young."

"I'm tired," Torres said. "I'm tired and I'm as old as you think and this is not the happiest moment of my life. If there is anything of decency left in you, please, just let me be."

"He wants to talk," Nina Lange said to Torres. Both men turned and looked at her. She was leaning forward, her eyes somber. "He wants to talk, Mr. Torres. Something is happening to him, too, Mr. Torres, and he is asking you to speak to him."

She fell back and began to tremble as though the few words had drained her. Dr. Hurwitz walked over to her.

"Mrs. Lange, I've told you before, I'm a doctor. I'm a doctor of medicine. Is there anything I can do for you?"

She nodded. "Yes, Doctor. I would like to be with my husband and sons. Could you do that for me, please?"

"Stop!" Boldt commanded savagely.

Hurwitz shrank back at the sound, the German sound. But then in the failing light he saw something else. Something that had been absent entered Nina Lange's face and remained there briefly and then vanished.

Torres saw something, too, and as a man who had dealt for many years in courtrooms with hundreds, thousands of witnesses, he understood what he was seeing and it angered him and bewildered him.

Boldt looked at Nina Lange and at Hurwitz and then at Torres. He saw the old man's hands grip the cane handle, so that even in the dwindling light he could see the whiteness of the knuckles, and he saw the thin face and the jaw muscles hard. "Are you containing yourself, old man?" Boldt asked. "Would you like to kill me? With your stick, perhaps?"

"Why would you like to kill him, Mr. Torres?" Nina Lange asked. "Can't you see we're all together? Can't you see we've all lost our way?"

Torres looked at Boldt. "No, I would not like to kill you," he said.

372

"Not even that?" Boldt asked. "Why not, old man? You should be delighted with just the thought."

Torres lowered his head wearily. "It would do me harm to do so," he said in a subdued voice. "And it might do you good, and I have no desire to do you good. Living is something that has to be learned and dying is no way to learn it."

He gazed at the sea. Boldt looked at the thin, ascetic profile, the arched hawk nose, the slender, fragile fingers curled round the grip of the walking stick, like wax crayons half melted by the sun.

"You see, your worst time is yet to come," Torres went on in a voice so low Boldt had to lean over to hear it in the bleak screams of the gulls and the dull sucking of water and the distant grind of an airplane. "You will discover all your values are false, that everything you have been taught to believe is false. And at that moment you will kill yourself unless God is generous enough to permit you to go insane. Or perhaps by some undeserved miracle, you will discover a secret strength to make yourself over and start your life again. But you are a little old for that. Birth pains are for infants, weak enough and close enough to God to bear them." He was silent. He said at last, "When your moment of judgment comes, I would like to be there."

"To have a good laugh?" Boldt asked harshly.

"To console a madman. Or to welcome back a human being."

"Mr. Torres," Boldt whispered. "Tell me why you do not want to leave Denmark. You know what would happen to you if you remained."

Morten Torres stared at the sea, and as the light seeped away he was enveloped with the knowledge that this was the evening of the Day of Atonement, this was the evening of Yom Kippur, this was the evening of Kol Nidre. He wrapped the knowledge around him like a shawl.

"Tell me, Mr. Torres." Boldt's voice was barren. "It is important to me."

"Should that stir me?"

Boldt stared at him and then he closed his eyes and nodded

373

heavily. Nina Lange's glowing eyes searched the details of his face.

Boldt clasped his hands. "Then tell me something else, Mr. Torres. Even if you do not want to leave Denmark, why are you so hateful toward those who are trying to save your life?"

Torres remained silent, for so long Boldt abandoned hope for an answer, and he knew he could not ask again. Then the old man turned slowly and contemplated the German.

"It is something that is perhaps beyond your grasp," he said sadly. "They are doing more than saving my life. They are giving me freedom."

"I understand that," Boldt said.

"But what you do not understand is that freedom is the privilege to act as I please," Torres said.

"Even toward those who risk death to give it to you?"

Torres raised his gaunt face. "Especially toward them."

5.

As THE LAST of the sun slipped away, Peter Hansen and Erik Melchior hunkered down and examined the dory in its hiding place behind a clump of gorse. On the side of the rowboat, neatly drilled by machine-gun bullets, was a swastika.

6.

As the sun gave way, the darkness leaped out from the
beach as a living thing into the sea. The gulls were stilled.
The fog was enmeshed in a new night wind and was driven
back over the water and the water sprang clear and tormented the shore. A star blinked and then another, and then
a third, and the rabbi spoke in the open, empty night.

*"Our God and God of our fathers, as evening casts its
shadows over the earth, ushering in the most solemn day of
the year, we join with our fellow Jews throughout the world
in prayer and meditation."*

From all parts of the beach the people gathered, black
ghosts against the dying gleam of the chalk wall. The men
wore skull caps or hats or caps, and those who had no other
covering spread kerchiefs over their heads. Sons stood with
their fathers as the quiet, penetrating voice repeated the
ancient words of the Yom Kippur prayer. The women stood
behind the men, holding, carrying, cradling small children. A
young woman stood shyly apart from the others, giving her
baby milk from her breast, listening to the words.

The faces were snuffed out like candles from Rabbi Rasmussen's sight in the closing of the night, first the faces of
the women, and then the faces of the men, and finally every
face, even those closest to him. They were different faces and
there were different things on the faces, he thought, as they
dimmed and faded and finally disappeared, but one thing was
on all of them: peace. Where they were and the danger they
were in and where they were going and whether they would
get there was not of the chief importance now. Now was the

time of the Word. Was there ever in all history a people who so revered the Word?

"We put aside all petty thoughts and vain desires," he said to those whom he could no longer see. *"What is our life and of what avail our strength? What is our wealth and to what purpose our power?"*

Boldt gripped his manacled hands around his knees and leaned forward and listened. Nina Lange touched him timidly. When he looked at her, she pointed toward the rocket.

"Will it really explode?" she asked.

"That is what it was made to do."

"By talking?" She pointed toward the sound of Rasmussen's voice. "Like that?"

He took her hand between his hands and pressed it. "No," he said.

"Were you lying?"

He breathed out hard. "I suppose so. Exaggerating."

"Why?"

Because there are so many of them and I am one, he wanted to say. "It's my nature," he said.

A German patrol plane shattered the quiet.

He gripped her hand more tightly. "There is nothing to worry about," he said. "You must believe me."

She nodded. "I believe you."

When the aircraft was gone, Rabbi Rasmussen said, *"We lift our eyes unto Thee, O Lord, and yearn for Thy light and inspiration. . . ."*

He paused and lifted his head and looked towards the sea. From a distance he heard the muffled sound of a boat.

7.

THE BARON looked exactly as a baron should, particularly a
baron with Viking blood. He was large, too large to be
considered portly. His hair was tawny. His face was ruddy.
His eyes were deep and blue and clear. In another time he
would have worn boots and spurs and held a sword with
grace. Now he wore a wine-colored velvet smoking jacket
and carried a massive cigar.

"I am supposed to know nothing of this," he said, looking
at Melchior and then at Hansen and then at Melchior again.
He surveyed Melchior's police uniform. "You know, you
might give me a bad name."

"The people have been given shelter in your buildings,"
Hansen said.

"I am officially ignorant of that," the baron said.

"They have eaten from your table. They have been fed
and cared for by your servants," Hansen said.

The baron sighed. "There is so much that goes on round
here of which I am never informed." He looked again at
Melchior. "I suppose we could consider this an official police
requisition."

"If that will salve your conscience," Melchior said.

The baron shrugged. "One doesn't need much conscience
to justify a barn door. Why, in God's name, a barn door?"

"I've explained that," Hansen said. "And we don't have
all that time."

"You explained the Germans shot up your rowboat. Made
a swastika design." The baron chuckled in a rich baritone.
"You know, Mr. Hansen, I would never have credited them

with that much humor." He frowned. "How can you consider going on with this?"

"It's too late to change plans now," Hansen said. "If you
would just lend us your barn door to use for a raft. It's not
much, but there's no time."

"Why not just take another boat?" the baron inquired,
drawing on the magnificent cigar.

"Another boat?" Hansen asked.

"Another boat?" Melchior echoed.

The baron removed the cigar and looked from one to the
other. "My goodness, you sound like a music-hall act."

He led them from his house to the barn and closed the
barn door behind him. He struck a match and lit a kerosene
lamp and then, with the gesture of a genie, pointed to a small
rowboat hanging from a stud on the wall. He stood back,
puffing on the corpulent cigar, contemplating the door
thoughtfully, as Hansen and Melchior lowered the boat. He
put out the lamp and slid open the door.

"Such an innocent door," he murmured.

"Thank you, Baron," Hansen said.

"Preciseness, gentlemen," the baron said, shutting the
door. "When you want a rowboat, don't go around asking
for a barn door."

"No," said Hansen in a small voice.

Hansen and Melchior carried the boat down the dirt path
leading from the baron's estate to the clifftop. As they reached
the steps, Anders Jessen rushed up to them. He looked at the
rowboat and grinned.

"The fishing boat is here, Mr. Hansen," he said.

"Get the boys together," Hansen said. "As many as you
can round up."

Anders pointed to the boat. "Can I help you with that?"

"No, just collect a lot of backs, broad backs. We'll have to
make God's own number of trips with this."

Anders nodded and ran off. With Hansen in the lead, the
two men made their way cautiously down the greasy
steps.

"Why am I always landed with the rear?" Melchior asked.

378

"It's your face," Hansen said. He slipped, almost pulling Melchior down with him. He grabbed at the rickety wooden railing.

"What's the matter with my face?" Melchior wanted to know.

"Too Danish," Hansen said.

"For a Jew?"

"For a cop."

They moved down carefully again, feeling their way, step by step, struggling to keep their balance and footing against the unwieldy, awkward little dory. They stepped onto the beach at last, paused for a moment to catch their breath, and then started with the boat for the water.

As they passed the people listening to the voice of the rabbi, Hansen asked, "Shouldn't you be there?"

"I am," Melchior said.

They set the boat in the water. Hansen ran over to the other boat with its Nazi calling card and removed the oars and oar-locks. He returned and set the oar-locks in place.

"Peter," Melchior said, "this damned thing leaks."

Hansen examined the baron's boat more closely, feeling with his fingers. The wood had dried and shrunk from disuse and was shipping water.

"It won't hold more than two or three at a time," Melchior said.

"Then let's get started with the first three," Hansen said.

He looked up to see Anders and a dozen or more of the college boys hurrying toward them. He went to the woman who had nursed her baby, took the baby from her arms, brought them both to the boat. He picked up a small girl and carried her to the boat and helped her mother in after her. One of the college boys took the oars and a moment later the tiny craft moved toward the dim bulk of the fishing boat.

Melchior joined the Yom Kippur services. Hansen knelt and stared at the sea. He jammed his pipe into his mouth and clamped down on it. He looked at his watch. He waited. Then he heard the dipping of the oars and a moment later saw the rowboat emerging from the darkness. He looked at his watch again.

"All right?" he asked the boy. "Is everything all right?"

"Everything is fine, Mr. Hansen," the boy said. "A few more trips and this boat won't be giving you much trouble. The wood is swelling."

"Good," Hansen said. "Good."

Four persons were put into the boat and another boy took his place at the oars. "What was his time, Mr. Hansen?" the second boy asked.

"Time?"

"You were looking at your watch."

"Oh, that. Six minutes."

"Even? Six minutes even?"

"No. Thirty seconds or so."

"Hell, I can beat that."

"Ten crowns," the first boy said.

"You have a bet."

The second boy made the trip some fifteen seconds faster than the first boy, but the bet was called off because it was agreed Hansen had not attempted to time the first boy exactly and, anyway, the boat was leaking worse then. Now the boys quickly organized a pool, pledged ten crowns each, appointed an official timer, winner take all.

The shuttle proceeded smoothly. Bit by bit, the rabbi's congregation was nibbled away. A little more than an hour later, almost half the people had been transported safely from the beach to the fishing boat.

The fastest time was holding at five minutes and forty seconds.

8.

IN THE PALE reflection from the stars, through the vapors of the sea night, Rabbi Rasmussen saw his wife and three youngest children being taken to the rowboat. Lotte turned and looked back at her husband, a look—nothing more at this time of her duty and this time of his. Without pausing in his words to the worshippers who remained, the rabbi glanced at Jorgen standing at his side. The boy shook his head vehemently and moved closer to his father. Rasmussen peered into the darkness, over the heads of those in front of him, trying to follow Lotte and the children with his eyes.

"On this Kol Nidre night," he said in the stillness, *"sanctified by sacred memories, united with the generations of the past, recalling the piety and devotion of our ancestors, we stand in Thy presence stripped of all pretense and revealed in all our weakness."*

Lotte and the children now were dim shadows among other dim shadows.

"Oh Thou Who seest all," the rabbi said, *"Thou knowest how frail and fragile we are."*

It was at that moment the beam of light leaped in from the sea and a voice cut through the glare. The words were in German but they were not unfamiliar and everyone on shore understood. "Halt!" the voice commanded through a bullhorn. "Halt! Do not move!"

The single shaft of light now was joined by other lights and the order was repeated and a woman screamed and then the people flushed like wild birds startled by a hunter. They ran back on the beach, back toward the cliff with its unexploded missile, back toward the steps and paths leading up the cliff.

Rabbi Rasmussen and Jorgen pushed their way forward to a rowboat, and then there was a new sound from the sea, several new sounds, all of them blending into the familiar rattle of death. The shallow water forced the deep-bellied German patrol boat to remain too far off shore for accurate shooting and many of the bullets fell harmlessly into the water or spent themselves futilely on the sand.

Hansen and some of the boys got Lotte Rasmussen and her children out of the rowboat and hurried them away from the water. Rasmussen and Jorgen joined them, and all of them ran to the cliff. A bullet caught one of the college boys in the side. Hansen threw him over his shoulder. Before he started for the cliffs, he looked out toward the fishing vessel. He gave a prayer of thanks when he saw the boat, hugging the shore, slip around a point of land and disappear in the direction of Liselund.

Now the beams of the patrol boat stopped sweeping and held their terrain of light in sequence so that a broad part of the beach was illuminated in a blinding brilliance. The machine guns maintained their fire and the sand erupted in tiny volcanoes.

By now most of the refugees had gained the safety of the cliffs and were out of range of the bullets. Melchior ran to the foot of the steps with a child under each arm. He passed the children on and then waded into the log-jam of panic-stricken people funneling into the stairway.

Anders Jessen, running along the beach, saw it was almost clear. The wounded had been helped or had pulled themselves out of the zone of fire. The dead lay in ungainly, shapeless masses as they had fallen, looking in the cold glare of the light like piles of vegetation, like seaweed washed up on the shore.

Anders saw a movement in one of the dark, dead heaps, and he heard a child cry, "Mama! Mama!" He ran over and found a boy of eleven, blood trickling down his leg, violently shaking a woman.

382

"Mama!" the child screamed.

Anders saw the woman was dead. Her face and body were marked by a slanting line of bullets. He tried to pick up the child. The boy clung hysterically to the dead woman. Anders tore him away and started for the cliffs.

"Give him to me," a voice ordered.

Anders kept running.

"Give him to me!" It was a voice that possessed curious command. He saw Boldt running at his side, his manacled hands extended. With Boldt was Nina Lange, pulling along a little girl. Anders passed his wounded boy to the German and then turned back to the beach for a final look.

He squinted at the dazzling light and saw the beach was now quite clear, and he started for the steps and stopped and turned and looked again. He saw someone standing erect, facing the sea, still, her arms at her sides, facing the sea and the lights and the bullets. He ran to her and, when he got closer, he shouted her name.

She stood there unheeding, although by now she had heard, and then she started walking into the sea. The water lapped at her feet and the firing seemed to increase in intensity and anger as the Germans saw their last target, and the water and sand spurted around her. The water was at her ankles when Anders brought her down. He closed his arm around her waist and half carrying her, half dragging, he made his way to the cliff and shoved her behind a pile of fallen stone.

He went over her swiftly to see if she was wounded. He found blood and his heart tightened, and he saw it was his own blood from a crease on his arm.

"Ellen," he said, stroking the hair away from her face. There was another noisy discharge. He pulled her down, sheltering her, although his mind told him the bullets could not now reach them.

"Ellen," he said again.

She was limp. Her eyes were open and her breathing was easy and she was not trembling. It had been a simple decision, he realized with horror, to stand there and be killed, and there was no reaction, for there was nothing to react from.

The lights turned off, one by one, and there was a distant, hollow sound of guttural German and the engines of the patrol boat revved up, and in a little while Anders raised his head and the sea was empty of everything but itself.

"Is that blood?" she asked.

He turned to her swiftly. "It's nothing."

"Whose?"

"Mine. It's not important."

"You should do something about it."

He seized on that as something and he lifted her and held her against him. She remained limp. She neither gave nor took, neither resisted nor surrendered.

"Ellen, Ellen," he whispered, kissing her hair, her neck, her cheek.

She giggled. "You have your little field-mattress again." He stood up and took her hand and helped her to her feet and led her to the steps.

9.

THE REFUGEES struggled up to the top of the cliff. Panting, gasping, crazed with fear, they lurched into the safety of the forest.

Working on the wounded with Dr. Emil Hurwitz near the pickup truck, Hansen looked up to see Captain Melchior arriving with the last of the people from the beach. He watched them disappear into the trees.

"Scattering like quail," Melchior said, breathing hard. "We'll have hell's own time collecting them again. And that patrol boat will send a signal. This place will be crawling with Gestapo."

Mendel Cohen nodded. "I told you," he said in a dead voice, "I told you."

"What's the damage down there?" Hansen asked the police officer.

"I counted five dead. There may be more. What about them?" He gestured at the wounded.

"Eight or nine. Nobody serious," Hansen said.

"What now?"

Mendel Cohen tugged at Melchior's uniform sleeve. "Nothing now. There's nothing now. We sit and wait for the Gestapo."

"Less of that," Melchior said. It was the voice of the law.

Rabbi Rasmussen, kneeling at the side of the wounded man, looked up. "There's no need for that kind of talk, Mr. Cohen," he said quietly.

"We can't escape them," Mendel Cohen said as though he was speaking to retarded children. "It's no use."

"I said less of it!" Melchior said.

Mendel Cohen shook his head wearily. "You're fools. You won't listen to me. It's no use at all." He limped off with his wife and daughter.

"Mr. Cohen!" Rasmussen called out.

Mendel Cohen waved his hand hopelessly and continued on.

"Peter?" Melchior said.

"I'm trying to think," Hansen said. "Klintholme. It's the closest harbor."

"Too close," Melchior said instantly.

"I'm hoping they'll think that, too."

"No good," Melchior said. "It's just a few kilometers from here. If they come here, they'll search there, too."

"These people can't stay here," Hansen said. "I can't get enough cars quickly enough to get them away. I'll just have to play it the Germans won't believe we'd dare to try again from a place that close by."

"Peter, don't be a damned fool!"

"I'll have to manage another boat," Hansen said as though Melchior had not spoken.

"Damn it to hell!" Melchior said furiously.

"Who do I know at Klintholme?" Hansen said to himself.

Melchior stopped what he was going to say and looked at Hansen searchingly. "Can you do that, Peter?"

"Yes."

"You're sure?"

"Yes."

"Do you believe that?"

"God damn it, yes!"

Melchior grinned. "God damn it, yes!" he said. He gripped Hansen's arm. "I believe it, Peter. I believe it because you say it. Isn't that something?"

"It's an improvement," Hansen said. A child cried out as Hurwitz applied antiseptics to its wound. "The bastards," Hansen said. "The pricks. Oh, Christ, Erik, I'm going to fuck them. I'm going to fuck them royally."

"As the British say." Then he said, "That little son of a bitch."

"Yes," Hansen said. "Wasn't he?"

Both men looked at the pickup truck inside which Lili Lund was being held captive.

Hansen shook his head. "I don't know, Erik. I'm trying to be smart. I'm trying to be smarter than they are and they have a long head start. I don't know whether I'm being smart about Klintholme, but I'll tell you one thing, Erik, I am smarter than I was a week ago. I believed it. Checking on her father. I couldn't work that out. And it cost. Because I was stupid, it cost. And Arne Johansen had to pick up the chit, and now she's going to have to pick it up again just as though it never was paid."

"Before you start wiping your eyes, Peter, remember Arne Johansen wasn't even the first," Melchior said harshly. "There were four others in Norway before him."

"I should have known that," Hansen said.

"How could you know that?"

"I don't know."

"How?"

"I don't know! But I should have. Christ Almighty, in some way I should have. Then maybe we'd still be stuck with our living legend instead of a dead hero."

Melchior looked at the pickup again. "Have you checked on her?"

Hansen shook his head. "There's nowhere she can go."

One of the college girls rushed out of the wood. "Mr. Hansen!" she said. Even in the night, her face showed white.

"What is it?" Hansen asked.

She tried to talk but instead turned her head and vomited. Hansen gripped her arm. "What is it!"

She again tried to talk and then to point, but she could not stop the vomiting. Finally she gasped, "Come. . . ." She caught her breath and broke away for the woods.

Hansen and Melchior followed her. Just inside the shelter of the trees, she stopped and pointed and then turned her head away again, and her body began to shake.

"Good Lord," Hansen said.

Lying on the ground were Mendel Cohen, his frail wife, and their daughter. The throats of all three were slashed. Their blood made a common pool on the matted forest floor.

"Emil," Hansen said.

Hurwitz hurried over. He glanced down and then knelt and looked at the three of them. "They're dead, except Cohen." He took a straight razor out of Cohen's hand. "If he could be taken to a hospital, they might be able to save him."

"For what?" Melchior demanded. "He's better off dead."

Hurwitz stood up slowly. "He's a human being. And you're a policeman, Captain Melchior, not Almighty God."

After a moment Melchior said, "There's a police clinic in Stege. Somebody help me get him into my car. Peter, I'll see you in Klintholme."

Hansen watched Mendel Cohen being carried away and then, to some of the students who had drifted up, he said, "Bury the other two. Be sure you cover the blood well. We don't want any of their dogs sniffing them out. Then take the others to Klintholme."

When the wife and daughter of Mendel Cohen were buried in the earth of Moen, the boys and girls set out to find the Jews who had fled into the woods. They could not turn on their flashlights and often in the dark they passed near people who held their breath and their silence, not knowing who it was who was searching. Even when the boys and girls whispered who they were, there were those who did not trust them.

10.

DRIVING BACK from the clinic to Stege, Police Captain Erik Melchior considered the case of Mendel Cohen, tailor; Mendel Cohen, smallish, inoffensive, who until then in his life had used a sharp instrument only to cut cloth.

All his adult life, Captain Melchior was plagued with the whys, the whys of everything that had crossed his official life, and he wondered now what it had taken to bring Mendel Cohen to the point where he was able to cut the throats of his wife and child. His own throat? After the first two, that must have been easy.

Was Mendel Cohen a coward, or had he managed for himself the highest kind of courage? Whom had he killed first? Had his wife watched him murder their daughter? Or had he killed the mother first, knowing she could not allow the other? Had it been something Mendel Cohen had discussed with his wife or was it something instantly born and as quickly done?

And what had misguided his hand that minute fraction so that the final incision was not the fatal one?

388

For the purgatory of Mendel Cohen was that he would live. If he were lucky, he would go mad. But there would be that moment before the madness set in when he would know what he had done and what he had failed in doing. And that moment, Melchior thought, must then contain a distillation of all the remorse there was in this world.

He lit a cigarette and then in the rear-vision mirror noticed two small black-out lights behind him. He was still on a traveled road and it did not concern him. When he turned off the paved road onto a dirt road, the lights continued behind him and now he thought he might have a follower.

He drove for another minute or two and then stopped the car and got out and lifted the hood and bent over the motor. The other car stopped a few yards behind him. Three men stepped out and when he saw the uniforms he was very glad he was in an official car and that he was wearing a respectable uniform of his own.

One of the men walked toward him rapidly, followed by the other two. Melchior straightened and touched his cap in salute.

"Glad you happened along," he said. "My engine's conked out."

"I am Sturmbannführer Wolfgang Becker," the man in the lead said.

"Yes, we've met," Melchior said.

Becker peered at him. "I remember, Captain." Then he said, "You just brought a man to the hospital in Stege?"

"Yes."

"A Jew?" Becker asked, jamming his thumbs into his belt.

"Was he?" Melchior asked.

"Did you know that?"

"He was in no condition to inform me."

"Do not be insolent," Becker said.

"I am not, Major. The man was unconscious."

"Where did you find him?"

"Lying near the road."

"Was he alone?"

"Yes."

"We received a radio from one of our patrol boats,"

Becker said. "A large number of Jews were seen on one of the beaches under the cliffs of Moen. Do you know anything about that?"

"No, I'm afraid not."

"Where were you bound?"

"Back to where I found the man. To see if I could learn what it was all about."

"Forget that," Becker said. "You can be of service to me."

"Of course, Major. Would you like me to take you to the Moen beach?"

Becker shook his head. "They won't be there now," he said. "But there is a small fishing village nearby. Klintholme, I believe it is called."

Oh, Peter Hansen, Melchior thought, you're playing with pros. "Yes, there is, Major."

"You will take us there."

"Of course, Major. Just let me have another look at this damned car. No maintenance these days, no maintenance at all." He stuck his head under the hood again and tried to work it out. Not now, he told himself. There must be a fourth one behind the wheel of the car.

"Never mind that," Becker said impatiently. "You will ride with me."

Melchior unwrapped his long body from the fender. He slammed down the hood and followed Becker and the two other men to the Gestapo car. For the first time, he found value in the German compulsion to march. Under the protective noise of the hammering heels, he unsnapped his pistol holster.

"You know, Major, Klintholme and Moen are almost next door to each other," Melchior observed conversationally. "I should think they'd pick a place farther away."

Becker turned to him with a blinding smile. "Would you? That is how we are different. If I were in charge of that transport of Jews, I would say to myself, the Germans are basically stupid fools and they would never in a million years guess we would try again so close to Moen. That is what I would say to myself and that is why I want to have a little look at Klintholme."

Peter Hansen, Melchior thought wistfully, what are you going to do without me?

They reached the black Mercedes. One of the Gestapomen sprang forward and opened the rear door. Becker turned to the Danish police officer.

"What is your name?" Becker asked. "You never said."

"Melchior, Major. Police Captain Erik Melchior, Jew."

Melchior shot Becker through the heart, thinking, before he turned the gun on the others, that he had that one at least, and he shot the second man, and then the third, and by that time the man behind the wheel had out his own pistol as Melchior had known he would, to get three of them clean took luck, the fourth would have been a miracle and there aren't many miracles around these days, Peter, and Melchior felt the ache, a blow first and then the ache, and he squeezed the trigger again and, as he fell, the ache now taking over all of him, he saw the three of them were down and the fourth was slumped over the wheel with a hole in his face.

Melchior tried to press his hand on the ache but it was too large now and the words came to him unbidden, *"Shema Yisroel, Adonai elohenu, Adonai echod,"* and he just had time to say them again in the language that had been his privilege and his family's privilege for more than two hundred years, *"Hoer Israel, Herren vor God, Herren er en."*

11.

CAPTAIN ROLF KRAG drank heavily from the snaps bottle, wiped his lips with the back of his hairy hand, clattered the hand as big as a ham on the table, shaking the kerosene lamp, streaking the chimney with soot, and shouted, "I don't want blood money!"

"How much?" Peter Hansen asked.

"I don't want blood money, taking these poor people to Sweden!"

Hansen stretched his legs under the wooden kitchen table. "How much?"

Captain Krag emptied another quarter of the bottle. He rolled the bottle neck between his fingers and looked up at Hansen shrewdly from under his rocky brows. "Five thousand crowns," he said.

"For the lot?" Hansen asked. "That's decent of you, Krag."

"Five thousand," Krag said. "Per head."

Hansen nodded, unsurprised. "Too much."

Krag leaned across the table. "Don't tell me too much, Hansen," he said. "I know the spot you're in. The Sound is stinking with the German swine. You won't get another boat from here to Copenhagen."

"Too much," Hansen said.

Krag banged the bottle on the table. "Don't keep telling me 'too much.' You know the risk."

"I've got almost seventy people out there," Hansen said.

Krag smiled winningly. "I've got the only boat in Klintholme big enough to take them."

"You're a bastard, Krag," Hansen said. "You're a money-grabbing, thieving, heartless bastard."

"I'll take them all!" Krag shouted, raising his arms. "Pile them in like sardines! At five thousand each."

"God damn you," Hansen said. "We're dealing with people here."

Krag's hand crashed down again on the suffering table. "Don't tell me what we're dealing with!" he roared. "I know what we're dealing with! We're dealing with my boat and my life! You're not going out there. I am! I can get caught going over. I can get caught coming back. I can be sunk out there or shot or be left in jail to rot, what's left of me after the Gestapo swine get through. Don't you sit on your God damned Copenhagen ass and tell me what I'm dealing with!"

He shoved the bottle into his mouth so hard Hansen thought he might crack his teeth. He watched the thick neck throb as the snaps went down.

"Stop that drinking," Hansen said. "You'll be too drunk to take the boat across. And I am going with you."

Krag removed the bottle from his mouth and looked at Hansen for a long time. "You'd better talk out of the other side of your mouth, Mr. Hansen. I can take my boat over to Sweden drunk or sober, I can take it over with my eyes shut, I can take it over with my eyes shut, drunk and my hands tied behind my back. Don't tell me how to run my boat."

He lifted the bottle to his lips and poured down the snaps until the bottle was empty. He wiped the trickle from his chin and set the bottle carefully, tenderly, on the table. "Four thousand."

"One."

"Peter Hansen, you're a swine, you're a blood-sucking Copenhagen swine, asking an honest fisherman to risk his neck for that kind of small change—three thousand, and that's rock bottom."

"Fifteen hundred, and that's the top."

Krag shook his head pitifully and somehow gave the impression his eyes were filling with tears. "Swine, Peter Hansen, Copenhagen swine, beating down a poor, simple fisherman who's going to save the lives of Jews he's never set eyes on." He thrust out his hand. "Fifteen hundred. Done!"

Hansen took out a packet of money and laid it on the table.

Krag's eyes glinted. "You knew," he roared. "You knew you'd beat me down!" He picked up the money and threw it down again. "You had it all counted out!"

"Get going," Hansen said. He backed away from the table.

Krag shoved a big, calloused, horny-nailed forefinger under Hansen's nose. "You're the one's been holding me up. I've been ready to go ever since you stuck your ugly Copenhagen head into my door. Now let's get those damned Jews aboard my boat and then get the hell away from here."

He stood up, sending the table sliding half a dozen feet

across the room. He grabbed his pea-jacket from a hook, clapped a fisherman's cap on his head, started for the door, remembered something, ran over to a corner cabinet, took out a bottle of snaps, shoved the bottle into his pocket.

"What the devil are you waiting for?" he shouted at Hansen.

12.

KRAG LEANED over the side of his boat. "This is Captain Noah Krag speaking," he said. "Welcome to my Ark."

The villagers stood at the wharf at Klintholme and watched the Jewish refugees climb into the fishing boat.

"Welcome back to Denmark," the villagers said softly.

"Climb down the hatch," Krag bellowed. "Make yourself comfortable. When you travel with Krag you travel first class."

The younger men went down the hold first and then reached up for the children, the women and the older people.

Anders Jessen helped Ellen over the side of the boat. She moved as though in sleep. He lowered her into the hold and then went back onto the jetty.

"Welcome back," the villagers said. Some of the women were wiping their eyes. "Welcome back to Denmark."

Krag waved his bottle. "Down the hatch, friends, down the hatch!" He took a deep slug.

Anders walked over to Hansen, who was looking at his watch. "He'll wake the dead," Anders said.

"The water's too shallow for a patrol boat," Hansen said.

394

"They could hear him in the middle of the Sound."

Hansen shrugged. "He's the captain and it's his way." Then he said, "Anders."

The boy looked at him.

"I've got something for you to do on this trip."

"I know."

"The girl in the pickup," Hansen said. He looked at his watch again.

"Yes," Anders said.

"You know all about Arne Johansen, don't you?"

"Yes."

"Keep remembering that," Hansen said.

Anders looked at him angrily. "I don't need that, Mr. Hansen."

"Perhaps I do," Hansen said.

Anders Jessen's gentle eyes gazed at him through the long, curling lashes. "One thing, Mr. Hansen," he said. "Is that why Ellen is here?"

Hansen nodded.

"To watch? To see? For me to know that?"

Hansen nodded.

"You know what she's been through, Mr. Hansen?"

"Yes."

Anders held him for another moment and then he turned abruptly and walked toward the pickup. Hansen stared after him. He breathed deeply. He saw that Emil Hurwitz was standing next to him.

"He has a good face," the doctor said.

"Yes."

"He seems unsuited for this kind of work."

"He's an artist. He makes ceramics."

"An artist." Hurwitz removed his glasses and let them drop to the end of the ribbon.

"I have to destroy him, Emil," Hansen said.

"Yes, I can see why that would be necessary."

"I've lost Arne Johansen. I'm losing Niels Rider. My number ones. My weapons. Together or alone, it was always done. Whatever it was. This boy hasn't reached that point. He still thinks. He still feels. Maybe he always will. Maybe I won't be able to do it."

He watched the people, the people climbing aboard the boat and the people standing on the jetty.

"Welcome back," the villagers said. "Welcome back to Denmark."

"I need a new Orange and a new Blaze, Emil, and he's for starters."

"Yes."

"I have to take him apart and reconstruct him," Hansen said tonelessly. "Like a piece of crockery. Like a piece of his own clay. I only hope to God that if he lives until this is all over he'll be able to undo what I've done to him."

Emil Hurwitz looked at Hansen and saw something pass behind his eyes, something so naked, so personal, he turned his head. He saw Anders walking past, leading Lili Lund.

She was still gagged and her hands were bound behind her back. She walked quietly. She offered no resistance. As she approached Hansen, she raised her head slightly and her beautiful eyes fell upon him. Then she passed on, past Major Boldt and Nina Lange, past Rabbi Rasmussen and his family, past Morten Torres, past the villagers on the wharf who grew silent when they saw her.

Captain Krag, looking down from the bridge, saw Anders lift the girl aboard. "A half-way ticket!" Krag shouted. "I won't charge you for that one, Hansen!"

"All right, Emil," Hansen said. "Your go."

"Peter . . ."

"Don't hold up the boat, Emil."

Hurwitz sighed. "Good-bye, Peter."

"I'm going along," Hansen said.

Hurwitz looked at him in surprise.

"I have to do it to myself," Hansen said.

"Welcome back," the villagers said as the last of the Jews went aboard. "Welcome back to Denmark."

13.

ANOTHER FISHERMAN from the village helped Krag spread a tarpaulin over the hatchway.

"Makes it cozier for all of you down there!" Krag shouted into the dark hold. "And there'll be ice on top of it. Proper refrigeration. Traveling with Krag is traveling first class!"

Just before the last of the canvas was drawn into place, Krag tossed a tallow candle to Emil Hurwitz who was nearest the opening.

"When the hatch is closed, you can light that," the captain said. "And if you feel the boat slowing down, douse it! If the Germans stick their dirty faces into the hatchway, I want them to see melting ice and darkness and not a God damned thing else!"

The tarp was stretched tight and Krag, with the help of the other fisherman, covered it with chopped ice. They secured the hatch cover and the fisherman climbed back to the jetty. Krag started the engine. The fisherman untied the lines and cast off.

"Hansen!" Krag bellowed. "If you're coming, climb aboard! Or maybe you've had second thoughts!" He laughed uproariously.

Hansen looked up the single road leading into Klintholme. He shook his head and started for the boat. He collared one of the students.

"There'll be a taxi arriving here with a wounded man," he said. "Get him inside one of the houses. And when Captain Melchior shows up, tell him I said to stick him away somewhere and get him a doctor."

"Yes, sir," the boy said.

"The rest of you clear out of here."

Hansen swung himself aboard the boat. He looked up the road again. Then he climbed to the bridge.

"Are you ready, Mr. Hansen?" Krag asked politely.

"I'm ready."

"You don't get seasick, do you, Mr. Hansen?"

"I don't know, Captain. We'll just have to find out."

Krag moved up the throttle and the boat eased away from the wharf. Hansen took another look up the road and then he said, "Hold it, Krag."

"Hold it?" Krag demanded. "Hold it for what?"

"Get back to the dock."

"You're not making sense!"

"It might mean another fifteen hundred," Hansen said, straining his eyes at the pair of dim lights approaching on the road.

"You're making sense," Krag said.

Krag threw the engine into reverse and returned to the dock. Hansen dropped down from the bridge and climbed back on the wharf. He ran to the car and saw it was a taxi and he opened the back door.

"Good God," he said.

"Hello, Peter," Kate said.

"Good God." He stood there, stunned.

"You said that, Peter."

"Good evening, Mr. Hansen," Mikkel Steffen Olsen said. "Well, here we are, safe and sound."

"What are you doing here?" Hansen asked his wife.

"I'm a dedicated woman."

"Where's Mary?"

"She got herself unpregnant. A boy. Six pounds. Bouncing, I think they called it."

He looked closer at his wife, at Niels sleeping at her side, at his wife again. "But you?"

She patted her belly. "I thought it might help. The long ride and the bumpy roads," she said. "And all."

"It didn't."

"It did." She craned her neck and looked at the boat. "Where are they?"

"Below deck."

"How many?"

"About seventy."

"Including Emil?"

"Including Emil."

Hansen beckoned to a couple of the college boys. They got Niels carefully out of the car. He opened his eyes and muttered something uncomplimentary and closed them again. They carried him gently to the boat.

"You're a horrid, selfish bastard, Peter," Kate said. "You never told me. You never said how exciting this could be."

He looked at her again. "You're pootled," he said.

"Dedicated," she said. "The word is 'dedicated.'"

"She only had one or two, Mr. Hansen," Olsen said gallantly. "She needed it after the Germans stopped us."

"Germans," Hansen said.

"Do you have a patent on Germans, Peter?" Kate said. Her eyes crinkled. "Now I've got something to tell you, Peter," she said.

"She was very good, Mr. Hansen," Olsen said.

"Magnificent," she said. "I'll tell you all about it on the way home." She looked at him. Then she said, "I won't tell you all about it on the way home."

"Be careful with her," Hansen said to Olsen.

"Don't worry, Mr. Hansen," Olsen said. "I know every hospital between here and Copenhagen. Part of my trade."

"I've got to go," Hansen said to Kate.

"Don't say it that way, Peter," she said. "You don't have to say it that way any more. Just lean over and give me a kiss if you can manage it."

He stuck his head into the car and kissed her on the lips. Her eyes remained open. They were very clear.

"Hansen!" Krag shouted.

He straightened and started for the boat.

"Peter," she said.

He turned and looked at her again.

399

"You were wrong, Peter," she said. "It did help. It helped a great deal."

Hansen ran to the boat and climbed aboard. He looked toward the taxi. "Take care of her, Emil," he said.

Dr. Emil Hurwitz stepped out of the shadows. "You saw," he said.

"You're a little old for scurrying, Emil," Hansen said, his eyes still on the taxi.

"It was the boy, Peter, the wounded boy," Hurwitz said, trotting along the wharf to keep up with the boat. "He needed a little extra room."

"Take care of her," Hansen said.

"Naturally." Dr. Hurwitz set the pince-nez into place and peered up at the moving boat. "Naturally, Peter."

"Welcome back to Denmark," the villagers said for the last time, although they knew by now no one aboard the fishing boat could hear them.

Presently the boat was gone and Hurwitz walked to the taxi and got in. Mikkel Steffen Olsen started back for Copenhagen.

Kate Hansen offered Hurwitz a cigarette and, when he refused, took one for herself. He lit it for her.

"You're liable to end up the last Jew in Denmark," Kate said.

Hurwitz removed his glasses and leaned back against the seat. "A sad thought. But under the circumstances, a lovely one."

400

PART VI.

"Very old fish," Hansen said.

"The older the better, Mr. Hansen. And for our purposes tonight, especially so."

"Do you think we'll have visitors?" Hansen asked, feeling the snaps warming him, smelling the brisk air, beginning to feel good.

Krag had another drink before he replied. He wiped his mouth. "Who gives a shit? I put it to you openly, Hansen, who in God's green world gives a shit?"

"I do."

Krag snorted. "You? You're a Copenhagen gentleman, Mr. Hansen. Your appearance would never fool me. But don't worry, they'll never, never notice."

"I'm glad to hear that," Hansen said.

Krag waved a reassuring hand. "If they come aboard, they'll never notice. And do you know why? I'll tell you. They're stupid." He waved the bottle for emphasis. "All Germans are stupid."

"Is that a fact?" Hansen asked, reaching out and taking the bottle from Krag, who watched him, grinning like a triumphant devil.

"They're all stupid, Mr. Hansen," Krag went on. "They're the stupidest people in the world. And do you know why?"

"Why?" Hansen asked, finding himself wiping his mouth with the back of his hand exactly like his mentor.

Krag jabbed a finger like a belaying-pin into Hansen's chest. "They all think alike. But that's not the worst of it. No. The worst of it, Mr. Copenhagen Hansen, is they don't know how to laugh."

Hansen, in the act of returning the bottle, had more mature thoughts and had another drink instead.

"They know how to cry," Krag said. "And they know how to sound like barking dogs. But they don't know how to laugh. Not for fun." He jerked the bottle out of Hansen's hand. "And if you put it to Krag, anybody who doesn't know how to laugh is stupid."

He finished the last of the snaps and tossed the bottle into the Sound. He looked around, startled. "In God's own name, what's that?"

Hansen cocked his head. From inside the hold came the sound of singing, a faint, single voice in mournful song.

"What is that, Mr. Hansen?" Krag asked again.

"A prayer, I think."

"Prayer? Sounds more like a belly-ache."

"That's what it must be, a prayer. This is the holiest night of their year."

"That caterwauling? You mean that?" Krag listened for a moment. "Well, they have something to pray for tonight, haven't they?"

"Maybe I'd better put a stop to it," Hansen said, rising, "if we can hear it up here."

Krag pushed him down. "Time enough for that."

The captain dived into the locker again and this time emerged with a full bottle of snaps which he did not fling at Hansen. He opened it, listening to the somber sound from the hold, drank and then lowered the bottle slowly.

"Time enough for that," he said again. "It's kind of pretty, and if it makes them feel any better, what the hell, let them pray." He held the bottle out to Hansen. "Besides, it might do some good."

2.

THE HOLD CREAKED and stank of slime and bilge-water and fish long gone. The belly of the boat, packed with refugees, rolled and wallowed and the air was old and stale and reused from one person to the other.

In the small light of the candle, Jorgen Rasmussen sang

Kol Nidre. Rabbi Rasmussen stood next to him, his strong face, now beginning to stubble with beard, silent and grave.

The weak, wavering light reached out only to those closest to them. The rest of the crowded hold was in darkness. The people, those who could be seen and those who could not, forgot the smell and the heat and the place and listened raptly in this most sacred moment of this most sacred time.

"*Kol nidre ve-esoray vacharomay v'konomay v'chinuyay v'kinusay. . . .*"

Jorgen's voice was low and true and sweet, and spread like a balm.

3.

It was, Lili Lund knew, her wrists chafed by the cord that bound them, her mouth aching from the gag, it was a dirge for her. She did not know the words or the meaning, but the sound was there, the sound of death, the sad sound of death, and she wondered how it would happen and in what manner and she knew it must happen before long, before Sweden— sooner, before Swedish water.

It made sense, she thought, longing now only for a cigarette, nothing else. It made its own kind of sense. She had done and she must pay. Simple justice. Only the thing they never knew, the thing nobody ever knew, not even Arne, was that she had paid, she had paid in advance, she had paid all her life, and it might be argued that she had earned a little credit.

It didn't really matter. She thought of Arne and the way they had been together in the end, and she knew it would never be that way again so maybe it didn't matter what was going to happen to her, how it was going to happen—suddenly shivering although the hold was like an oven now and as airless—maybe it didn't matter because there was nothing left anyway.

Only there was. She knew. You always forget, no matter how good or bad, you always forget, and if she had been permitted she would have forgotten because nobody goes on remembering forever.

Arne, she thought, listening to the low lament, the threnody for her death, Arne, I would have forgotten you, I would have forgotten everything about us because you don't remember forever, you only think you remember and all you're doing is thinking back and that's something else entirely, that isn't remembering, you can't remember with your mind, only with your body, and your body forgets.

Your body forgets, Arne, and that's the only true memory, what the body remembers, for so long as the body remembers it, and I would have forgotten you and the next man would have begun to wipe it away and after a while it would have all been wiped away, all the things we had and all the things we did and all the things we promised each other we would one day do, all of that would have been wiped away.

4.

"... Miyom kippur zeh ad yom kippur habo olenu l'tovoh. . . ."

Except for the sound of the boy's voice and the full, muffled beating of the engine, the hold was in silence.

Listening to the prayer as he had every year on this night

408

for far more than half a century, it passed again through the mind of Morten Torres how much purer it would have been if he had not been abducted from the synagogue, if he had been allowed to go along with the others caught in the Nazi trap. There was a purging there in the synagogue, a reckoning with the old God of the Jews, the God he understood.

And what had to come to them afterward he understood, too. A concentration camp was an honest shame.

When Jorgen finished, the silence in the hold was more than an absence of sound. It was manifest; it had life, presence. It was where Kol Nidre had been.

The words, the old, known sound lingered, and as Torres sat there in the damp smell he became slowly aware of the degree of his transgression. His thin, tired fingers clung to the handle of the walking stick as though it was a handle keeping him there and he prayed, God forgive me the false pride, I am thankful, Oh Lord, that You saw fit to take me from the hand of my enemies, forgive me for denying Thy decision.

But, he thought stubbornly, if I had the choice I would be with them.

Major Boldt touched his arm. "What was that all about, Mr. Torres?" he asked.

Torres, removed in his own thoughts, did not reply.

"I asked you a question, Mr. Torres," Boldt said.

Torres turned to the German. He could just discern the outlines of Boldt's face. "I beg your pardon," he said with distaste.

"What was the boy singing?"

"Why do you ask?"

"For the simplest of reasons, Mr. Torres. I would like to know."

"So you could have a good Nazi laugh?"

"What was that boy singing, Mr. Torres?" Nina Lange asked. "I would like to know."

"It was a prayer, Mrs. Lange," Torres said presently. "It is called Kol Nidre."

"What does it ask of God?" Nina Lange asked.

"It is a very old prayer," Torres said. "It is a plea to absolve us of our vows to God."

"That is asking a packet," Boldt said.

"During the year vows are made. They cannot be fulfilled," Torres said, conscious of the German. "It is said the prayer comes from the time when Jews were forced to deny God in order to escape persecution. There were lands where the Jews were required to make vows to accept another faith and Kol Nidre brought relief to their tormented consciences." He turned his head away to end the discussion.

"But why do you have to ask, Mr. Torres?" Boldt asked. "If He is God, He ought to know why you did it and what is really in your heart."

"He knows," Torres said with difficulty. "But He must also know we have the grace to ask."

"Grace? It sounds more like begging."

"It is no disgrace, Major, to beg of God."

"I am sure," the German said. "But I still say He ought to know. And if He is God, whatever you do you do because He causes you to do it, so if you have what you call the grace to pray, then it is only because you are granted this grace, as opposed to others who are not."

Torres now looked at him intently. "You should have been a lawyer, Major," he said.

"I have often thought that, Mr. Torres," Boldt said easily. "I always thought I had that kind of incisive mind. What is your business?"

"Lawyer," Torres said.

Boldt laughed. He hastened to say, "That was no Nazi laugh, Mr. Torres. And to keep the records straight, as you lawyer fellows are fond of saying, I never was a member of the Nazi Party."

"Of course not," Torres said. "And one day it will turn out that nobody was."

Boldt gave a low, short chuckle. "I wish I could see your face now, Mr. Torres. I would like to remember it." After a moment he said, "Well, no matter, I suppose it does not hurt to pray. Just so long as you remember the rules of the game."

"What rules, Major? And what game?"

"The private arrangement each of us has with God."

"Do you believe in God?"

"We all do, don't we, one way or another?"

"I don't know."

"I don't know either, Mr. Torres. I see things and I think, no. I see other things and I think, yes. And the rest of the time I don't know and I don't care. But you believe, Mr. Torres?"

"Yes, I believe," Torres said, and now for some reason beyond him he did not mind saying it to the German. "I believe in the God of the Old Testament. A stern God. A just God. A God that punishes and rewards. A God Who requires certain courtesies paid Him. That's why the Kol Nidre. Certainly He can look into our hearts and we should be able to say it without saying it. But it must be said. God has His dignity, too."

5.

ON THE BRIDGE Hansen suddenly raised his head and looked at Krag. The captain chuckled.

"I was waiting to see how long it would take for you to pick that up," he said. "I heard it at least three minutes ago. But then I have the ears of a weasel. The eyes of a hawk and the ears of a weasel."

"Never mind the menagerie, Krag. What is that?"

"That, Mr. Hansen, is a trawler," Krag said with elaborate politeness. "Another fishing boat just like this fishing boat."

Hansen grunted and took his pipe and pouch out of his

pocket. "As a point of interest, Krag," he said, stuffing the pipe, "how can you tell?"

Krag grinned his grin. "They all have a voice, Hansen, and they all have a message, and I can hear the voice and understand the message." He looked at the sky and at the water and breathed in deeply and peacefully. "It all depends where you live, Hansen, and the place I live is on the sea."

Hansen grunted again and, sheltering the match from the freshening wind, lit his pipe. He noticed Krag looking at him earnestly. "Anything on your mind, Krag?" he asked.

Krag drank some of the snaps. He rested the bottle on his knee, his eyes still fixed on Hansen. "That girl," he said at last. "The half-way ticket."

"What about her?" Hansen asked.

"You going to do it? Yourself?"

"No," Hansen said.

"Didn't think so," Krag said. He took another drink. "It's none of my business, but what did she do?"

"As you said," Hansen said, puffing on the pipe, "it's none of your business."

Krag leaned forward, his eyes glittering angrily now. "Maybe not, Mr. Hansen, maybe not. But I'll tell you something. You're stalling. You're stalling because your balls are soft as mush. And I'll tell you something else, Mr. Hansen. There's a line running down the Sound. You wouldn't see it with your fancy Copenhagen eyes but it's as plain to me as though it's painted down the middle of a road. And on the other side of that line is Sweden." He jabbed Hansen with the bottle, but gently so as not to spill anything. "You stall much longer, Hansen, and the girl has slipped through your fingers and has won herself a safe port, along with all the other poor benighted bastards down below." He looked at Hansen derisively and then broke into a roar of laughter as a new thought struck him. "And in that case, Mr. Hansen, just to make it worse, I'll have to charge you another full fare!"

He laughed so hard his eyes teared. He wiped away the tears and had another drink. Hansen pulled on his pipe and watched him morosely.

412

6.

Now THE SOUND was getting choppier and in the hold some of the people were getting sick. There was no place to go to be sick. They were sick on themselves and their neighbors. The smell of vomit joined the other smells and the sound of spewing mixed with the throbbing of the engine.

The sound of Kol Nidre lingered in Ellen Oppenheim's ears, linking itself to all the times before, to the sound of her father's unmusical voice suddenly filled with music given him, lent him, for that time and that time alone. Where was he now? Where were her father and her mother on this Kol Nidre night?

She looked at Anders Jessen, at the fine, delicate profile silhouetted against the yellow candle, at the long, curling lashes that always embarrassed him, and she turned away in confusion. She had thought it was all gone, gone and dead and buried forever in a cemetery at Gilleleje.

She looked at him again, wondering at her feelings, at the golden glow around his head, at the gentle face, and she remembered a bench in the square and the pigeons perching on her shoulders and wrist and lap, and a young boy who took clay in his hands and made beauty, and how she had always thought how young he was, no matter his age, how young he was.

"How did you manage it, Anders?" she asked. They were the first words she had spoken since the beach at Moen.

He turned to her swiftly in surprise.

"How did you manage to be here?" she asked. "Was it to take care of me?" When he did not reply, she said, "You wouldn't admit that, would you?"

He wet his lips. "Ellen," he said.

She put her finger on his mouth. "You don't have to say it," she said. Her eyes moved across his face as though rediscovering something almost forgotten. Then she smiled, a shy, hesitant smile, and she said in faint echo of her old teasing manner, "Since you've become so important, you've got strong and silent, just like a hero in a film."

"Ellen," he said in a low voice, "listen to me."

There was a sound of footsteps on the deck above and she felt his hand tighten. The people in the hold became still. The hatch cover was raised.

"Anders." It was Hansen's voice.

Anders nodded slowly before answering. "Yes, Mr. Hansen."

"Better bring her up."

"Yes, Mr. Hansen," Anders said again.

Ellen smiled slowly again. "Well, it's another girl, is it?"

He closed his eyes.

"Who is she? Why do you have to take her on deck?"

Major Boldt shifted closer. "Tell her, Anders."

"Well, what is it?" Ellen asked. "I'll try not to be jealous."

Anders raised his face and even in the dimness she saw such pain she felt a chill run through her. "What is it, Anders?" she whispered.

"Tell her, Anders," Boldt said. "Tell all of them."

Anders looked at Ellen in torment and then lowered his head. "She's a spy," he said almost inaudibly.

"Who is a spy?" Ellen asked, feeling herself slipping back into confusion. She shook her head, trying to comprehend, or trying not to comprehend what she was already beginning to know.

"Over there," Boldt offered. "And you had better look quickly."

Ellen gazed at Lili Lund, at the gag, at the hands bound behind her back, at the dulled eyes that looked back directly at her.

"Ellen," Anders said in a strangled voice. "She betrayed Arne Johansen." His fingers tightened again. "Others. She was judged. Sentenced."

414

"Judged? Sentenced? Judged and sentenced by whom?" Boldt asked.

Ellen felt ice rising in her. "And what is it you have to do?" she asked Anders, knowing, thinking she knew, hoping she was wrong.

"Execution," Boldt said. "Or murder. Depending on what side of the fence you are sitting."

Ellen looked at Lili again and then turned slowly to Anders. His head was still lowered and his hands now were clenched. She felt herself slipping, slipping, and she asked, clutching, "Anders, in the name of God, what is he talking about?"

"I doubt whether God has anything to do with this," Boldt said judiciously. "But that also depends on the side of the fence."

"You have said enough," Morten Torres said.

"It is the celebrated half-way ticket to Sweden, Ellen." Boldt said. "And what Anders has to do is to take this woman, who is quite young and very beautiful, he has to take her up on the deck, strangle her and then throw her body into the Sound."

Ellen closed her eyes and shook her head.

"Boldt," Torres said.

Boldt gazed at Anders. "And from the look of him, Ellen, he has never done this before. This may be considered a kind of initiation. After he kills this woman, he will be a full-fledged member of the gang."

"No," Ellen said. "I don't believe it."

Boldt reached out and pulled the gag from Lili's mouth. "Tell them," he counseled. "Tell them it is true."

"Arne is dead!" Anders said. "She betrayed him."

"And so she must die," Boldt said.

"She betrayed him," Anders said again, looking at the faces that were closing in on him.

"Before you choke her to death, Anders, just explain one thing." Boldt leaned closer to the boy. "Why is it right for you and wrong for us?"

"It's different," Anders said.

"You kill your enemies. We kill ours."

"It's different. It has to be different."

"Yes, it is different," Boldt said evenly. "The Third Reich is a government. That is the difference. Whether you like it or not, Germany is a government, a sovereign State. And you? All of you? What are you but a pack of self-appointed hoodlums? Who gave you the right to pass sentence on anyone?" Boldt peered at the faces around him, grouped, intent, half seen, like faces in a Flemish painting. "Speak, Mr. Torres, you are the law. Speak, Rabbi, you interpret the law of God." He gave a short, hard laugh and looked at Anders. "Grow up, boy," he said quietly. "Say you have to do what has to be done and then do it and be done with it. That is the way the world is, boy, and our mistake is that we are always stupid enough to come out and admit it."

Anders covered his head with his hands. "It can't be the same," he said. "Nothing would mean anything."

Boldt laughed again. "Do you still look for meaning, you poor fool? The only meaning is to win."

"Why are you speaking like that?" Nina Lange asked.

He turned to her. "They have to understand," he said harshly. "They all have to understand. Whatever becomes necessary is done."

"Anders!" Hansen called down the hatch. "We don't have all night. Bring her up!"

"Yes, Mr. Hansen." Anders said.

"Whatever it is," Boldt said, "it will be done."

Anders brought himself slowly to his feet in the wallowing craft and moved toward Lili.

"No," Ellen said. "Anders, no."

"What do you know about betrayal?" Nina Lange asked. "What do you know about death?"

"Anders," Ellen said very softly, "you cannot."

Anders took another step toward Lili and another. Rabbi Rasmussen moved in front of him. "She is right," the rabbi said. "You cannot."

Boldt chuckled merrily. "It was the rabbi," he said. "I wondered who it would be, the rabbi, or the law, or love. And the Old Testament religion won the day. All right, Rabbi, tell him—tell him what he must not do."

416

"Please, Dr. Rasmussen," Anders said. "Please, you must not try to stop me."

"Of course not," Boldt said. "He has received his orders, and even in that imitation army they obey."

"Please, Dr. Rasmussen," Anders said. "Please, step out of the way."

"No, Rabbi," Lili Lund said suddenly. "Don't let him."

"You betrayed Arne Johansen!" Anders said tightly.

"There was a reason." She cowered behind the rabbi. "Rabbi, there was a reason."

"You cannot do this, Anders," Rasmussen said. "Then the German would be right. You would be the same as they are."

"Well," Boldt said. "You surprise me, Rabbi. I always thought you believed in the eye for the eye and the tooth for the tooth."

"Step out of the way, Dr. Rasmussen," Anders begged. "You're only making it worse."

"For whom?" Boldt asked.

"She has to die!" Anders said, looking at the rabbi, at Torres, at the others.

"It's the fashion now," Nina Lange said.

"She has to die," Anders repeated in whispers. "It isn't punishment. It isn't that. It's to stop it from happening."

"Anders!" Hansen called down savagely. "Do I have to go down there myself?"

"God forgive me, Rabbi," Anders said.

He pushed Rasmussen aside and Torres and the next man and he reached Lili Lund. He bent to pick her up. She twisted out of his grasp, crawled away on her knees, got to her feet, lurched toward Ellen, stumbled and fell, crawled to Ellen's feet.

"It becomes comical," Boldt said. "It is unfair to death."

"Don't let him," Lili panted, looking up at Ellen, straining at the cord that bound her hands. "There was a reason."

Anders tried to force his way to her. People closed in front of him, blocking him, and he felt Rasmussen's hand tighten around his wrist. He jerked his arm. The rabbi's grip was like a vise.

Lili gasped for air. "Please don't let him," she said. "There was a reason."

She saw the tears fill Ellen's eyes, and when Ellen put her hand on Lili's cheek she rubbed against it, like a lost, bewildered cat.

"Please, please, don't let him," Lili said. Then she stopped abruptly and her face changed and she struggled to her feet.

Anders twisted his head to see what she had seen. "No," he said quickly. "You've given enough."

"Niels," Lili said, and it was another voice. She lifted her head. "This is correct."

It was, she thought, and the pleading had been an insult, to Arne and to herself and in a way to the whole world, the whole fucking world. As the British and Arne Johansen and Lili Lund said.

It was Niels' small gun and it made a small noise and a small entry. She was still trying to speak to Niels Rider, to tell him again it was quite correct, when she fell, the blood starting down her face from between her eyes. She fell against Ellen and Ellen caught her and sank with her to the floor. Ellen moved her head from side to side slowly, no longer able to weep, the numbness coming over her again, holding death in her arms.

Pacing the deck, Hansen heard the shot. He ran to the hatch and dropped into the hold. He pushed his way through the transfixed people to where Ellen sat cradling Lili against her breast. He looked at the bullet hole and then raised his eyes and saw Niels and the gun in his hand and then Anders. He picked up Lili's body and slung it over his shoulder and went back to the hatch.

He looked up and saw Krag's outstretched arms. He handed the body to Krag and climbed back on the deck. He took the body and started for the side of the boat. Krag kicked a length of chain towards him.

"Bodies float, you Tivoli seaman," he said.

Hansen put Lili down on the deck and tied the chain

418

around her long legs. He picked her up and dropped her into the Sound. He leaned against the side of the boat. Lili's coat billowed with air and the body floated and then was swallowed.

"Here," Krag said.

Hansen took the bottle. When he handed it back, Krag asked, "Is your Copenhagen belly okay?"

Hansen nodded.

"Good," Krag said. "Tell your friends to be quiet and then close the hatch. We're going to have company."

7.

HANSEN PEERED into the night. He still could just barely make out the sound of the distant engine. "How can you be sure?"

"I cannot be fooled," Krag said.

"I know, the eyes of the hawk and the ears of the weasel. Or was it the other way round?" Hansen bent his ear to the sound.

"Don't go too far, Hansen," Krag said. "Or when the Gestapo comes aboard, I turn you over. For impersonating a fisherman." Krag swallowed some snaps. "Hansen, rub your hands on the deck."

Hansen looked at him. "What did you say?"

"Hansen, you're dressed like a fisherman and you smell like a fisherman and you might even look like a fisherman to these stupid Germans. But your hands say the only fishing you ever did was on a Sunday outing."

Hansen held up his hands. He looked at Krag again. Then he rubbed his hands on the deck and on the side of the boat.

"I read a book once about the revolution in Russia," Krag

said comfortably. "They used to look at the men's hands to find out if they were really workers. The Germans are not as smart as the Russians, of course, but why take chances? Maybe one of the Gestapomen read that same book once."

The engine of the other craft suddenly was loud and close. Hansen looked toward the sound. Krag laughed and held out the snaps bottle.

"Here, Hansen, take on a little Dutch courage." He watched Hansen drink deeply. "Are you scared?"

"Yes," Hansen said.

"Good. Then you're a man of feeling. Krag is a man of feeling."

"Are you scared, too?" Hansen asked.

"No. But only because they're Germans."

They both looked up as a voice boomed through the night, "Hallo, there!"

"Hello," Krag said. "Just like he's a friend." He raised his own voice. "Hallo!"

Hansen felt the knotting again. It was becoming an old pal.

"Stand by to be boarded!" the voice said.

"Stand by to be boarded," Krag repeated. "What the hell does he think I am, a battleship?" He took another drink. "The swine. The damned, filthy swine. My God, I hate German swine."

The patrol boat appeared on their starboard as though it had passed though an invisible curtain. It made Hansen clutch the side of the bridge and compress his lips. One moment there was nothing and the next the formidable little vessel was there.

The German craft slipped close to the fishing vessel and Krag and the German skipper from experience adjusted their speeds so that the three Gestapomen could transfer from one to the other.

The leading Gestapoman carried a powerful torch. He turned the light on Hansen's face and then against Krag.

"Put down that damned light!" Krag roared, shielding his eyes. "What the hell are you trying to do, blind me?"

The German lowered the light and played it on the deck. In the darkness, Hansen could just make out he was a man of middle size with a small face that seemed overwhelmed by the military cap. He wore the rank of *Obersturmführer*.

"What are you doing here?" the Gestapo officer asked Krag.

"What am I doing? What the hell do you think I'm doing?" Krag asked with monumental contempt. "I'm trying to fish, that's what I'm doing, and anybody but stupid German swine could see that!"

Hansen looked swiftly at the German lieutenant. The Gestapo were quick to shoot, no matter where or when or whom. But the officer made no move and when he spoke it was in the same unangry voice.

"Have you Jews aboard?"

"Jews?" Somehow Captain Krag managed to inject into that short, one-syllabled word astonishment, incredulity and the suggestion the German was an idiot.

My God, Hansen thought, and wasting his life fishing.

"Jews," the officer repeated.

Krag held out his arms expansively. "Look around. Look anywhere you like. Only do it fast. Half of what I catch ends up feeding German bellies and if you make me miss the run I'll report you. So move! Hansen!"

Hansen looked at him. "Yes?"

"Hansen, open the hatch so these idiots can see what we have in the hold. Go on, go on," he said to the Germans, "I haven't got the whole night!"

Hansen slid back the hatch and the Gestapo lieutenant poked into it with the torch. Nothing was to be seen but the black tarpaulin and the melting ice.

"Are you satisfied?" Krag shouted. "Or would you like to climb down and have a closer look?" He laughed loudly. "You'll stink of fish for a week but that wouldn't bother me at all."

Again Hansen cast a quick glance at the officer.

"No," the lieutenant said, "I think all is quite in order."

"Then get the hell off my boat and let me get about my

business," Krag said. "Fish don't wait for anybody, not even the bloody, damned Gestapo."

The lieutenant signed to the other two Gestapomen and they returned to their own boat.

Hansen closed the hatch and sat on it, feeling very, very tired, and then he heard another voice say, "Just a moment, please." He looked toward the voice because it was not unfamiliar to him.

"Give me the torch, Muller," the voice said.

Hansen stood up slowly. He watched Colonel Buhle swing his leg over the side of the patrol boat and step carefully onto the deck of the fishing vessel. He walked over to Hansen and looked at him without raising the torch. He looked at the closed hatch and at Hansen again and then he walked the length of the fishing boat, as though measuring its size. When he returned, Krag was standing next to Hansen.

"Now what's this?" Krag blustered. "Are we going to go through all this damned nonsense again?"

Buhle glanced briefly at Krag, dismissed him. "The comedy is at an end, Captain. Get back to the bridge."

Krag raised an arm and opened his mouth for protest.

"Do as he tells you," Hansen said quietly.

Krag hunched his massive shoulders and went back to the bridge. He picked up his snaps bottle and looked dourly at the German boat.

Buhle sat down on the hatch cover. He flicked off the big flashlight. The night went very black. "How many?"

"About seventy," Hansen said.

"And you."

"And me."

Buhle stared out at the sea. "You are going the whole distance, Mr. Hansen. Look at you. You could almost be believed."

"What are you going to do, Colonel?"

"The whole distance," Buhle said again. "All of you, the whole distance. Max Greiner. Georg Siebert. The Langes. The Johansen boy. Even General von Kobe in a very dangerous way. All of you, in your own ways, the whole distance. You are keyed in to something."

422

"What are you going to do about these people, Colonel?"

Buhle raised his eyes. "What is my whole distance, Mr. Hansen?"

The German officer stood up and walked slowly forward on the pitching deck. After a moment Hansen followed him. Buhle rested his arms on the port gunnel and looked again at the dark, churning water. "The Danes, I can understand. I think I understand. You were pushed and you could not be pushed any more. But the Germans." He paused. "Max Greiner. He was my friend. You know that he killed himself."

"Yes," Hansen said.

"How did you know that? It was given out that he was shot accidentally."

"All right, Colonel," Hansen said.

Buhle gazed at him for a moment and then his eyes went back to the water. "All right," he said. "I think about him, Mr. Hansen. He was afraid of something. What was he so afraid of? He had nothing to prove. To no one. All he had to do was to go on doing what he was doing."

"Apparently he could not go on doing what he was doing."

"He could not, Mr. Hansen. That is why he stopped doing it. But why did he have to stop that way? What was he afraid of?"

"You know what he was afraid of, Colonel," Hansen said.

"I would have protected him. No matter how foolish he had been, in some way I would have protected him."

"I didn't mean you."

"Himself? Is that what you mean? He was afraid of himself?"

"But that's not the answer either, Colonel," Hansen said. "What was it in himself that he was afraid of? That's closer, isn't it?"

Buhle turned and faced him. "Do you know, Mr. Hansen?"

"I'm not sure. I think so."

"Could you make me understand?"

"I don't know."

423

"Because of your lack or mine?"

"I don't know that, either."

The sea splashed against the bow. The spume swept up and brushed their faces. Buhle turned away and looked down at the black water.

"What are you going to do, Colonel?" Hansen asked again.

Buhle raised himself slightly. "I do not know what I am going to do, Mr. Hansen," he said very slowly. "I am trying to understand what I must do. And you do not help me, Mr. Hansen."

Hansen breathed out hard. He wanted words, more than at any time in his life he wanted words, and he had none.

"Why did Georg Siebert risk his career, his life, to notify the Jews?" Buhle asked.

Hansen's eyes narrowed.

Buhle, reading his thoughts, smiled faintly and shook his head. "You do not have to admit anything to me, Mr. Hansen. I am not attempting to trap you or Siebert. But I know the warning came from him."

Hansen said nothing.

Buhle made a slight movement with his hand. "Do not worry. I will not inform them in Berlin. Let them do their own work." He shrugged. "I can tell you, it will get them nowhere."

"Them?" Hansen asked.

"It is funny, is it not? But is it right?"

"Right?" Hansen repeated. "Since when have you concerned yourself with that, Colonel?"

Buhle turned to him slowly. The spray had wet his cheeks and had covered his lips so he seemed to be sweating. His eyes were flat. He asked in a still voice, "Is this how you are trying to save your Jews, Mr. Hansen?"

"What do you want me to say?" Hansen asked. "Is all this amusing you, Colonel? Playing cat and mouse? Knowing there are seventy souls under your feet and you can act God?"

"You paid me one hundred thousand Danish crowns for

424

one soul, Mr. Hansen. What do you offer me now? Seventy
times one hundred thousand?" Buhle stood erect and looked
at Hansen scornfully. "Or are you going to haggle with me
that not even a precious Jew is worth as much as a Danish
saboteur?"

He turned abruptly and walked rapidly toward the patrol
boat. Hansen stared after him helplessly, knowing he had
blown it.

Buhle paused at the hatch and looked down at it. Hansen
went to him.

"All of you, going the whole distance," the German said
in a low, wondering voice. "What is it that you know?"

"If I knew, Colonel, I would tell you."

"Not good enough!" the German said raspingly. "What is
it that you know?"

Hansen filled his lungs and breathed out hard. "I wish I
could pull it out of a hat, Colonel. I wish I could say something. But I don't know. Every day I realize how little I
know. I keep stumbling and falling on my face just trying to
learn."

"Learn against us?"

"That. Everything."

There was the faint sound of a baby crying below. Both
men looked down at the closed hatch.

"Perhaps we might learn something together, Mr. Hansen," Buhle said.

Hansen shook his head. "I doubt that, Colonel. I want you
to get the hell off this boat and let us go on. But I doubt
that."

"Even afterwards?"

"After you've lost the war and you come crawling around
begging to be forgiven?"

Presently Buhle said, "It must be gratifying, Mr. Hansen,
to know that one day you will be in a position to dispense such
largesse." He was silent for a moment, his eyes on the hatch,
and then he said quietly, "You seem to be my problem, Mr.
Hansen. You know something and I must find out what it is.
Perhaps if I do, then you will know, too."

He crossed the deck and swung back into the patrol boat. He gave an order and the German vessel increased speed and turned sharply away and in a few moments was gone in the night.

Hansen shivered with the cold. He walked slowly to the bridge.

8.

THE HOLD was in darkness. The smell of vomit and urine turned sour in the dead air. The people were thrown against each other as the boat yawed and wallowed in the open water.

Again there was the heavy tramping of feet on the deck above. Again the hatch was opened.

"Now hear this! This is the captain speaking!" Krag roared at his wit. "Come up! Come up and smell the free air of Sweden!"

9.

IN THE BRIGHTENING LIGHT, the land appeared before them, first just as a slightly darker line in the darkness, and then slowly a land, a land with a shore and docks and buildings and small hills behind them. It was in the early morning an empty, quiet land, with freshness on it.

"Sweden!" Krag shouted. "A good place if you happen to like Swedes!"

He swung the wheel back and forth so that the boat began to dance a jig in the water. The people clutched the sides of the boat and thought he was mad. Then someone started to laugh and the laughter swept through them with the bright air and the breeze and the people fell into each other's arms and kissed and discovered for the first time who they were— kin, friends, who had without knowledge of each other traveled in darkness, met in darkness, shipped in darkness, and who now looked at each other for the first time in the light.

Hansen, seeking Niels Rider, picked his way through the laughing, crying refugees. He paused for a moment where Rabbi Rasmussen, surrounded by a small group of men, was speaking the words of one of the first prayers for the Day of Atonement.

"Blessed are Thou, Oh Lord our God, King of the universe, Who opens for us the gates of mercy. . . ."

Hansen instinctively reached up to remove his cap and then he remembered the Jews did it the other way. Rasmussen caught his eye. The rabbi's voice was stern, as befitted the utterance of the solemn prayer, but there was on his face, ennobled by the words, an expression of such infinite gratitude that Hansen found himself blinking before he moved on.

He found Niels stretched out near the bow. Niels opened his eyes as Hansen knelt alongside him.

"Hello, boss," Niels said. His long face was white and drawn.

"Hello, Niels."

"Am I all right?" Niels asked.

"Yes."

"Am I going to live?"

"I'm afraid so."

Niels nodded. He closed his eyes for a moment and then

427

opened them. "Are you angry with me? For down below?"

"No," Hansen said.

"The little bastard," Neils said. He shifted slightly and winced with the pain. "Did he die all right?"

"Yes."

"Hard?"

"Very hard."

"Not alone."

"No, not alone."

Niels nodded. He closed his eyes again and was silent for so long Hansen moved to get up. Then Niels said, "Mr. Hansen, it was right that I killed her."

"Yes," Hansen said. "I suppose it was."

10.

CAPTAIN KRAG steered his boat toward the jetty. It was clear now, a bright, shining, clean morning, and now the people were appearing on land, walking from the little houses toward the pier.

"Hey, Swedes!" Krag roared from the bridge. "This is Captain Noah Krag arriving in his Ark! Two of every kind, just as it says in the Good Book!"

The pier filled more and more with Swedes as Krag brought the boat to land. He swung the boat around, aimed for an open place at the dock, came in at the wrong angle, smashed into the pilings, bounced away, shouting with laughter.

"We'll try again!" he called out.

He hit the jetty again and then again, not hard, laughing each time, drinking the snaps, and presently the people on the boat and the people on the pier were laughing with him, and then he swung the boat round for the last time and berthed it with such ease, such style, such indifference, the people broke into cheers. Hansen looked at him and shook his head.

Men on the pier hastened to make the lines fast and the Jews started off the boat. Holding the neck of the snaps bottle, Krag leaned against the bridge and watched benevolently. "Well, Hansen?"

"Well, Krag?"

"In the navy they say, 'well done.' "

"Then there's no need for me to say it."

"Hansen, you're a swine." Krag held out the bottle. "But have a drink."

"Save it," Hansen said. "For the trip home."

He climbed down from the bridge and went ashore. He saw a Swedish policeman approaching and the fear that sprang into the eyes of the refugees. Hansen walked up to the policeman. Rasmussen joined him.

The policeman touched the visor of his cap. "The superintendent of police sends word that he is a very busy man and does not have time to question any of you," the policeman said.

Hansen smiled. Rasmussen looked at him questioningly.

"It's his way, Dr. Rasmussen, of telling us we won't be bothered by the police." To the policeman Hansen said, "I will need your help. I have a wounded man here who must be taken to a hospital. And I have a German army officer who is placing himself in the custody of the Swedish authorities."

"We will take care of the wounded man first," the policeman said.

Now Rasmussen saw that many Swedish women were walking up to the Jews, carrying small trays with small cakes. The Swedish women smiled broadly and offered the cakes to the Jews. The children looked at their parents. Smiling, polite, but firm, the Jews refused.

"Those women don't know it's a fast day for Jews," Hansen said. "I'll explain it to them. They'll be terribly hurt."

"Wait," Rasmussen said.

429

They walked to where the Swedish women stood bewildered.

"The seven kinds of cake," Hansen said. "The tradition."

Rasmussen picked up one of the cakes. The Jews became silent. He turned to them. With a great effort of will that he hoped did not show, he took a bite of the cake and made himself swallow it. The Jews cried out in joy. As their rabbi had done, now they did, and as the cakes, all seven kinds, vanished, mostly down the mouths of the children, the faces of the Swedish women were wreathed in smiles.

Now more Swedes appeared, men and women, and they picked up the children and the bags and the packages and the valises and led the refugees to their village.

Rasmussen saw Anders Jessen walk over to Ellen, who was standing apart from the others, facing the sea. He saw Anders speak to the girl. She made no response and after a few moments Anders walked away.

The rabbi went to the girl. "You didn't take any cake, Ellen," he said.

"No, Rabbi."

"Here, take some of this." He held out what was left of his cake.

"No thank you, Rabbi."

He looked at her intently. "As a rabbi, I tell you that in this emergency this ritual law may be broken. It won't be a sin, Ellen."

"I'm not worried about sinning, Rabbi."

"You should be."

She turned away. "He would have done it, Rabbi," she said dully. "If the other one had not done it first, he would have done it."

"Yes," Rasmussen said. "An old-fashioned word. 'Duty.' "

Her lovely large eyes were lifeless. "Then the German was right, Rabbi. We are all the same. Even you said it."

Rasmussen shrugged and pursed his lips. "Perhaps I was wrong. Obedience is like a bomb, Ellen. It can be used by either side. The question we have to decide is who is in the right, the Nazis or our countrymen who have saved our lives."

430

The rabbi looked around and saw his wife and children. He went to them and picked up the last-born and took his wife's hand and joined the other Jews being received by Sweden.

With Nina Lange remaining at his side, Major Boldt sauntered over to Morten Torres. The lawyer had seen the dread that had swept through the refugees at the appearance of the Swedish policeman. Now he was watching as others disembarked.

"Well, Mr. Torres," Boldt said. "It appears you have won."

The old man held more tightly to his stick. "You are quite wrong, Major Boldt. It is you who have won."

Boldt looked puzzled. "I am afraid I do not understand, Mr. Torres. You are all free."

"Free of what?" Torres watched the last of the people climb ashore. "You made us run. Everywhere. You turned us into animals cowering in a stinking bilge. Whatever it is that makes a man is gone from us now and you have taken it."

"It does not appear to have been taken from you, Mr. Torres," Boldt said with a slight smile. "You are as unreconstructed as ever."

"Everything is gone from me. That is why it does not show." Torres watched the people moving toward the village. "It may come back, to the children, please God. It may even come back to some of us. But whether it comes back or not it was taken." He was silent. Then he said, "Someday, Jews who now are children or who are not yet born will read about these days in books and they will ask, how did it happen, how did we let it happen, why were we so submissive? And what answer, Major Boldt, will we be able to give them?"

Boldt gazed at the thin, taut face. "People forget, Mr. Torres. It is the reason for everything." He looked up to see Hansen and the Swedish policeman walking toward them. "I will agree with you on one thing, Mr. Torres. Perhaps you do not have to feel so grateful to the Danes, after all. Perhaps it should be the other way round. I think they have been lost from the day we entered their land and I think the Jews have

431

shown them the way to find themselves." He nodded to the policeman. "The question I ask myself, Mr. Torres, is who will do that for us?"

Boldt turned his face to Nina Lange. She glanced at him and then averted her eyes. Boldt squared his shoulders and started off with the policeman.

There was a sudden, strange sound. Morten Torres was chuckling.

Boldt turned in astonishment. "What is so amusing, Mr. Torres?"

Torres shook his head slowly. "How odd it will be. A Jew visiting a German in a prison camp."

A curious expression passed over Boldt's face. "Bring cigarettes," he said. "It is the correct thing."

He looked again at Nina Lange and then continued on with the policeman.

Nina Lange watched him go and then she started running after him. He turned to have a final glimpse of her. She stopped. They gazed at each other across a dozen yards. She lowered her head and walked back. Boldt watched her and, when the policeman touched his arm, he went toward the village.

Ellen stood motionless for a long while with her eyes on the water and then she turned toward the boat. She saw Hansen and Anders untying the lines. "Anders," she said.

He looked up. He dropped the line and went to her.

"You're going back," she said.

"Yes."

"Yes," she repeated.

"Ellen," he said. "I'm sorry."

"No."

"That you had to see. That it had to happen that way. But you must know that I would have done it."

"Yes."

"You must understand, Ellen," he said quietly. "That's all we have, to believe. To believe in what we are doing. You must understand that."

432

"Yes, Anders."

"If you can see it that way after a while, wait for me."

"If I cannot?"

"Then," he said, "there is nothing."

"Jessen!" Krag shouted. "You're holding up the Krag Line."

He started for the boat.

In a voice so low he almost did not hear her, she said, "Anders."

He turned.

"Forgive me," she said.

"There is nothing to forgive."

"You don't know. I was going to Germany."

He walked back to her slowly. "Germany?"

She turned to the water and folded her arms. "During the night. I decided it. I was going to get there somehow and find out where Mama and Papa were and go to them. But I won't do that, Anders. I'll stay here and I'll wait and I'll give you your child."

He gripped her. "You know? You know so soon?"

"Anders!" Hansen called out. "I'd like to let you stay. But I'm afraid I need you."

"You said we have to believe in something," she said. "I haven't got anything else."

Anders held her until her arms hurt and then he ran back to the boat and climbed aboard.

She watched the boat back out into the small harbor and then swing around and head for the open Sound. She watched, a cold October sun on her back, until she could no longer see the boat, and then she turned and walked to the village.

PART VII.

1.

POLICE CAPTAIN Erik Melchior was buried during a wintry rain in the graveyard of the Lutheran church in Klintholme.

The service was performed by Pastor Lars Duul, who journeyed from Randers for the purpose. The church was filled with the villagers. The ceremony was brief. The eulogy was omitted.

As the coffin was lowered into the ground, Peter Hansen said to his wife, "One day we can bury him where he should be. Until then, I don't suppose he'll mind waiting here."

As they left, the village women were placing flowers around the newly turned earth, welcoming Erik Melchior back to Denmark.

2.

DRIVING TO COPENHAGEN, Peter and Kate Hansen stared silently at the drenched countryside. Kate shifted and rubbed her belly.

437

"How do you feel?" he asked.

"About what?" she asked. "About Erik or me?"

"I know how you feel about Erik."

"I feel the same about me. Rotten."

They rode in the rain along the rolling hills of Moen. They passed the long line of Viking burial stones striding across the Viking land in the Viking weather of rain and wind, and they looked at each other with the same thought.

He reached over and took her hand. "The way they move around down there, he's close enough."

Author's note

THE HISTORICAL FACTS of this book are largely true. The names of the people—except for people in history—have, of course, been changed and in some instances, such as Peter Hansen, several persons have been combined into one.

To gather this information, I interviewed close to fifty persons in Denmark, all of whom were involved to one degree or another in the Danish underground. Fortunately for me, they were very young during those days and are still around, patiently agreeable to being interrogated by someone who wants to find out how it was. Only one condition was imposed upon me, and this by every man and woman I spoke to, without exception: the names of my informants must not be used, not even in acknowledgment.

The reason? A peculiar and another facet of Danish character. No one wanted to seem to be trying to claim for himself credit for what everybody did, and for what every one of them, almost everyone in Denmark, in fact, considered, and still considers, not an act of heroism but simply something any human being would have done.

So here, not mentioning names, as promised, my thanks.

Now, just to point up the historical background:

After Dr. Werner Best sent his famous telegram to Hitler, the warning of the planned action against the Jews on the Jewish New Year was given to the Danes by an official of the German Consulate in Copenhagen, Georg Ferdinand

Duckwitz, who became the first ambassador from West Germany to Denmark after the war.

A total of 8,007 Jews, including 686 half-Jews, were smuggled out of Denmark to Sweden, most of them during those first two weeks of October, 1943. Another 460 Jews who were not alerted or who disbelieved the alarm were rounded up and sent to the Theresienstadt concentration camp.

During the absence of the Jews, the Danish Ministry of Social Justice took care of their homes, apartments and businesses. The Torahs were kept in safety. Neighbors watched over Jewish pets, tended Jewish gardens. There was scarcely any stealing or looting of any kind.

Because of insistent Danish pressure on the Nazi authorities, 400 Jews survived Theresienstadt and returned to their homeland after the war with those who had taken refuge in Sweden. Most of those who died were elderly and quite probably would have died in the passage of that time in the natural course of events.

Thus, virtually the entire community of Danish Jews was saved, as well as the foreign Jews who had fled to Denmark from Nazi persecution elsewhere in Europe.

This dreadful Danish quality of human decency apparently was insidious.

In a lecture about the rescue of the Danish Jews delivered on the occasion of the meeting of the Board of Directors of the Claims' Conference in Copenhagen on March 25, 1962, Mrs. L. Yahil, from Israel, stated that the head of the Gestapo in Copenhagen, a man previously associated with Auschwitz, had

> tried in vain to prevent the action against the Jews and, not succeeding, he sabotaged it as much as he could—and that was quite a lot. In speaking with Danes on this subject, most of them state it would not have been possible to carry through the rescue work had the Germans not to a certain degree looked the other way.

In an article titled "Why There Was a Resistance," published in the *Berlingske Tidende*, in Copenhagen, on May 2, 1965, Mr. Kai Johansen, Deputy Under-Secretary of State for Press and Information, and an active member of the underground during the occupation, wrote:

> *The action of the Danish Jews had a totally different effect to what the Nazis had foreseen. Up until then the various parts of the Resistance Movement—the military Intelligence, parachutists, arms groups, saboteurs and the illegal press—had each worked by themselves without any real coordination. On those October nights along the Danish coast and in the organization of transports to the ports and from there to Sweden—all this created a certain amount of coordination.*
>
> *This action against the Danish Jews was a decisive factor in the awakening of the majority of the Danish people to the realization of what they might expect if the Nazis won the war.*
>
> *The organized resistance period began. Random actions were replaced by coordination and systemization.*
>
> *From the Autumn of 1943 Denmark was, if not formally, then nevertheless in reality, in the ranks of the Allied nations.*

After delivering the Jews, the underground, having learned its trade, continued its activities. One of the chief targets was the rail line down Jutland. A German division being transferred from Norway to fight in what came to be known as the Battle of the Bulge was stalled in Jutland until after the battle was decided. In the opinion of some military experts, that division might have made the difference.

Upon liberating Denmark from the Nazis, British Field Marshal Montgomery commented that the Danish resistance was in all Europe "second to none."

E. A.